HARD SPELL

"A cool mix of cop show and creature feature. Gustainis had me at 'meth-addicted goblins'."
Marcus Pelegrimas, author of the Skinners *series*

"A magical mystery tour of a murder case rife with supernatural suspects. Sit down for an enchanted evening of otherworldly entertainment!"
Laura Resnick, author of Unsympathetic Magic *&* Vamparazzi

"The cops act like real cops, the vampires act like real vampires, and the monsters aren't messing about. The plot twists and turns like a twisty turny thing, and moves like a weasel on speed. The real things feel real, and the supernatural things feel like they might be. The prose is a joy to read, and the whole thing was more fun than is probably legal."
Simon R Green, author of A Walk on the Nightside

"Punchy dialogue, a fun alternate history, explosive action, and a hero whose monsters haunt him even beyond the job... Gustainis has given us a fantastic supernatural cop story that just dares you to put it down!"
Chris Marie Green, author of the Vampire Babylon *and* Bloodlands *books*

"A winning mix of urban fantasy and hard-boiled detective fiction."
Jennifer Estep, author of the Elemental Assassin *series*

JUSTIN GUSTAINIS

Hard Spell

An Occult Crimes Unit Investigation

ANGRY ROBOT

ANGRY ROBOT

A member of the Osprey Group
Midland House, West Way
Botley, Oxford
OX2 0PH
UK

www.angryrobotbooks.com
High stakes

An Angry Robot paperback original 2011
1

A catalogue record for this book is available
from the British Library.

ISBN 978-0-85766-114-2
EBook ISBN 978-0-85766-116-6

Set in Meridien by THL Design.

Printed in the UK by CPI Mackays, Chatham, ME5 8TD.

To Karen,
white witch and resurrectionist,
who brought me back to life

"Science cannot deal with the supernatural."
Michael Clough

"For we wrestle not against flesh and blood, but against principalities, against powers, against the rulers of the darkness of this world…"
Ephesians 6:12

"Death is when the monsters get you."
Stephen King

This is the city – Scranton, Pennsylvania.

It used to be a coal town, back in the days when anthracite was king. That was a long time ago – the last of the mines played out in the 1950s. But people here are tough, and they learned to adapt. Today, Scranton's got a healthy economy based on light industry, tourism, and retail. They've cleaned out a lot of the culm banks left by the mines, too.

It's a good place to live and eraise a family – apart from vampires, werewolves, ghouls, wizards, and the occasional demon.

Scranton's got a "live and let unlive" relationship with the supernatural, just like everyplace else. But when a vamp puts the bite on an unwilling victim, or some witch casts the wrong kind of spell, that's when they call me.

My name's Markowski. I carry a badge.

Also a crucifix, some wooden stakes, a big vial of holy water, and a 9 mm Beretta loaded with silver bullets.

I was never a Boy Scout, but "Be Prepared" is still a

good motto to live by. Especially if you plan to keep on living.

America's been coming to terms with what law enforcement calls the "supernatural element" for more than fifty years now. It hasn't always been a real smooth adjustment.

It was World War II that did it. I sometimes wonder if FDR would have been in such a hurry to send the GIs off to fight if he knew what some of them were going to bring back home – and I'm not talking about the clap or war brides, either.

But I guess he would've done it anyway, FDR. Somebody had to stop Hitler and those other bastards. But I bet the troops coming home would have got a much closer look, if anybody in authority suspected that some of them were... changed.

The experts figure that there were always a few supernaturals (or "supes," as most of us call them) in America. All those legends had to come from *someplace*. But the creatures were usually real careful to keep their heads down.

The supes in Europe mostly decided just to stay there, and leave the New World to the humans. Until pretty recently, getting to North America involved a long sea voyage. It would have been pretty hard for a supe to keep hidden for all that time, and getting found out probably meant a quick trip over the side. Unless he did a Dracula and killed everybody aboard. Vamps'll do that – they're vicious bastards, most of them. But that solution presented problems of its own – like who was going to run the boat come sunrise.

Anyway, most supes figured America wasn't exactly their land of opportunity. The early colonies had been founded by the Puritans, a bunch of tight-ass religious fanatics who'd left England because they decided the place wasn't righteous enough for them. And what guys like Cotton Mather had in mind for supes became pretty clear during the Salem witch trials, which took place after the European ones had died out. So supes generally stayed away for a long time.

Some of them probably got to North America in 1918, following what they used to call the Great War. But the U.S. was only in that one for the last eighteen months or so, and we didn't send nearly as many guys over as we would next time out. Still, I bet if you took a close look at the more than half a million U.S. deaths attributed to the flu epidemic of 1918, you'd find quite a few that were supe-related.

Then came World War II. Millions of Americans got put into uniform and sent over to Europe. There, some of them were bitten by vampires and lived to carry their curse back home. Others were victims of werewolf attacks. And a bunch more made the acquaintance of various witches, wizards, sorcerers, necromancers, and other practitioners of the black arts.

A few years later, easy access to air travel made it possible for European supes to migrate westward without any problems. Quite a few of them did. There wasn't much left of Europe by then, anyway.

The revival of interest in monster movies after the war didn't happen by chance. It reflected a country that was starting to get used to what was *really* going bump in the night. Movies like *I Married a Zombie* weren't always fiction, if you know what I mean.

The 1940s also brought McCarthyism. Tail Gunner Joe started out by going after domestic Communists, but the political witch hunt soon turned into a real one when he widened his net to ensnare members of the supernatural community (who the right-wingers referred to as "Supies"). I guess we've all seen the footage of those hearings, with McCarthy browbeating the witnesses: "Are you now, or have you ever been, a member of a coven?" It didn't come out until long afterward that Roy Cohn, the Committee's top inquisitor, was actually a closet werewolf.

McCarthy wasn't necessarily wrong. Some supes really *are* dangerous, take it from me. He just didn't know when to stop. He started out trying to unmask vamps in the State Department, and more power to him (he was smart: subpoenaed everybody who worked the night shift). But then McCarthy's early success made him arrogant. He figured it was his duty to take down every supe in America, along with those humans who supported them (he called them "Supesymps," for Supe Sympathizers, except when they were known as Fellow Flyers). A lot of innocent weres, witches, and trolls were caught up in McCarthy's inquisition before the public finally had enough and stopped backing him.

The civil rights movement didn't openly include many supes, at first. But then Martin Luther King, Jr, gave his famous "I Have a Dream" speech at the Lincoln Memorial. He said that he looked forward to the day when "black men and white men, Jews and Gentiles, Protestants and Catholics, naturals and supernaturals" would live together in harmony.

There was a rumor going around that J. Edgar Hoover had a tape of King "entertaining" a vampire, but I don't believe that. No human as good as Dr King was would mess around with vamps. Probably. But nobody's ever explained why the bullet that killed him was made of solid silver.

It was Lyndon Johnson who really sealed the deal on supe equality. Riding high on the wave of public sentiment that followed JFK's assassination, he pushed through Congress a whole bunch of civil rights bills. One of them gave supernaturals the same rights and responsibilities as all other citizens.

It didn't exactly hurt his credibility when Johnson revealed that one of his daughters, Luci Bird, had willingly succumbed to a vampire and planned to marry him. That nighttime White House wedding was quite an event, I hear – even if some in the media did start referring to the bride as "Luci Bat." Far as I'm concerned, there are worse things she could have been called.

You can find supes everyplace now, but they're not evenly distributed. There's lots in the big cities, of course. A big population means more potential "blood donors" if you're a vamp, a bigger client base if you're a witch or wizard for hire, and more to eat if you're a ghoul. It's true that some, like the werewolves, used to settle in mostly rural areas – simpler to hide, I guess, and farm animals are easier prey than people. But even that's changed now.

Scranton's got about seventy-five thousand people, which puts it about midway between New York City and Hicksville. But there's an awful lot of supes here, relative to the population. Nobody understood why that was, until 1966. That was when a couple of profs from the local university figured out that a whole bunch of ley lines intersect in the Wyoming Valley. Several of them come together right here in Scranton.

It's not known for sure where ley lines came from – there's four or five major theories, and every one makes my head hurt. But all the experts agree they exist.

They're a powerful source of magical energy, ley lines. The more lines intersecting, the stronger the energy. Passon and Warner, the professors, proved that there are four points in and around Scranton where at least ten different ley lines come together. That's kind of a big deal, in magical terms. Or so they say.

I hope those two profs got tenure, or whatever they call it. They helped answer a lot of questions.

The intersecting ley lines are like a magnet for supes, which explains why we've got so many. They were drawn here over the years, even if they didn't realize why. Weres, vamps, ghouls, witches, trolls, you name it. We've got 'em all in Scranton. Lucky us.

The Occult and Supernatural Crimes Investigation Unit, which everybody calls the "Supe Squad," is located in the basement of police HQ. There's no windows down there, but none of us mind. You never know what might get out through a window when you're not looking. Or what might get in.

I pull the night shift, which is the busiest time for our kind of work. I've racked up enough seniority to get whatever shift I want, but I work the graveyard (yeah, I know) because I like the action.

The boss is Lieutenant McGuire. They say his wife was grabbed by a gang of werewolves years ago, and that McGuire tracked them down, all by himself. When he left the house where they'd been hiding, there wasn't a creature alive inside, including McGuire's wife, who was found with a silver bullet in her brain.

McGuire always claimed it was a stray shot that killed her. But there are stories about that – rumors, really. Stories that one of the weres had already bitten her, that she was infected with lycanthropy. Some of the stories say that she begged him to do it.

It might be true. McGuire's an okay guy and a good boss, but he's got a darkness about him that has nothing to do with the fact that he doesn't see much sunlight.

Despite whatever may have happened in the past, McGuire's no vigilante. He plays by the rules.

But may Almighty God help any supe who breaks them.

It's not against the law to be a supernatural creature, or to engage in most kinds of occult rituals and practices. But there are laws concerning all that stuff. The bottom line for supes is the same one that applies to humans: you can't hurt anybody.

Unless they give consent, and you'd be surprised how many do. But there are rules about that, too.

I never understood why somebody would open a liquor store. Sure, it's a business, just like anything else; buy stuff and sell it for a profit. And I'm not one of those church ladies who think nobody should sell booze. Somebody's going to, as long as the stuff is legal. And Prohibition proved just how stupid it was to make it *illegal*.

My problem's not moral, it's practical. A liquor store is a small, cash-intensive business. It doesn't have many employees, and it has to stay open late because most people do their drinking in the evening. Can you say *big fat target*?

There's a reason why you never hear jokes about somebody knocking over a hardware store.

In Pennsylvania, the sale of hard booze and wine is handled by the LCB, the Liquor Control Board. All these places with the bottles in the window and "Wine & Spirits" over the door are really state-run liquor stores. The only difference is where the profits go – it doesn't make the places any less tempting to some lowlife with a drug habit and a gun.

Even if the lowlife in question isn't human.

My partner and I had been out trying to turn up witnesses to a bad case of fairy-bashing when we got the radio call directing us to the State Store on Mulberry. Even if I didn't know where the place was, it wouldn't have been hard to spot once we got within a couple of blocks. The multiple sets of flashing red lights guided us in, just like beacons at the entrance to Hell.

As we got closer, Big Paul said from the seat next to me, "Jeez, they really called out the cavalry. Must be four, five units here."

Paul di Napoli had been my partner for just over four years. Despite being too fond of his wife's pasta, he still moved around pretty good when he needed to, and he passed the department's physical fitness test every year. The last time had been close, but Big Paul still managed to make the grade. The fact that his cousin Angie is head of the Officer Fitness Board probably didn't hurt, either.

"Gotta be a supe inside," I said. "All this firepower already here, they wouldn't need us, otherwise." I parked the car as close as I could to the scene, and began rummaging through the gear we keep in a locked box between the front seats. Without looking up I asked, "You see SWAT anyplace?"

The Sacred Weapons and Tactics unit was usually called in to deal with any violent (or potentially violent) confrontations with members of the supe community.

They're trained in negotiation. They also know what to do if negotiation fails, and they do it real well.

"Nah," Paul said, "but I ain't surprised. Didn't you hear about the hostage situation goin' down on the South Side?"

"Uh-uh." I stowed several small objects in the pockets of my sport coat.

"Couple of guys from Patrol was talkin' about it just before we left the House tonight. I guess some wizard wannabe had a fight with his old lady, and things got out of hand."

"Doesn't sound like SWAT's kind of problem." I put a vial containing fresh crushed garlic in my shirt pocket. I could either repel a vampire or season some kielbasa, depending on how things worked out.

"I hear the dude's barricaded inside his apartment – and somehow he got his hands on a charged wand."

"Shit. They'll be out there a while, then."

"Most likely. Looks like it's up to us, bro. Whatever *it* is."

"Yeah, well, 'twas ever fucking thus." I closed the lid on the case, but didn't lock it. I might have to get it open again, in a hurry.

I put my ID folder in my breast pocket, so that the badge would hang over the front. "Let's go join the party."

We ducked under the yellow crime scene tape and headed toward the nearest prowl car. A uniform named Flaherty noticed us first, and came over, a frown on his thin face. "Jeez, what took you guys so long?"

"We stopped to get our hair done," I told him. "Who's the ROS?"

He gave me a look, then pointed with his chin. "Matthews. Over there."

I was glad that the Ranking Officer on Scene was Matthews. He was smart and steady and didn't have anything to prove.

Matthews was on his radio as we came up on him. He saw us, and I heard him say, "Never mind – they're here," and sign off.

We all shook hands, then I asked him, "So, how bad is it?"

"Couple tried to take down the liquor store. A squad car arrived before they could get out, and they decided not to give it up. They've got hostages."

"Goblins?" I heard Big Paul mutter. "What the fuck?"

Goblins are nasty little bastards, but they usually give people a wide berth. You find them near garbage dumps and junkyards, mostly. They don't tend to come into densely populated human areas.

"Near as I can figure," Matthews said, "they braced the clerk with those homemade knives they use, and told him to empty the register. The clerk might've thought it was a joke. Anyway, I guess he told them to fuck off, and so they cut him. I dunno know how bad."

"I bet he gave up the money after that," I said. "So, why are the gobs still in there?"

"Customer in the back of the store, some woman looking over the expensive wine they've got back there. When she saw what was going down, she called 666 on her cell. That's how we know what happened. There was a black-and-white a couple of blocks over. They got here pretty quick."

"And the gobs refused to come out with their claws up," Paul said.

"You got it," Matthews said. "They'd found the woman by then, so she and the clerk are both hostages."

"What I don't get is why goblins are doing shit like this," I said. "It's not their style."

"I dunno." Matthews shrugged. "The first uniforms on the scene say the gobs were acting real twitchy, even for them. Hysterical, even."

Big Paul and I looked at each other. "Meth," I said, and he nodded.

Surprise and anger chased each other across Matthews' face. "Did you say *meth*? Are you fuckin' serious?"

"Do I look like I'm kidding around?" I said. "There's been rumors the last couple of months that some of the local goblins have figured how to cook meth. Story goes, some big drugstore dumped a bunch of expired OTC drugs, including a whole shitload of cold medicine."

"We checked it out," Paul said. "Since it's not prescription meds, the drugstores don't gotta keep track of it. The ones that are part of a chain, they send the expired stuff back to some central warehouse, and those guys dispose of it like any other trash – at a dump or landfill."

"We called the company HQs of a couple of the big drugstore chains that have stores in town," I said. "They told us they'd be happy to discuss their waste disposal practices with me – right after I showed them a court order."

"Which we can't get, because the corporate HQs are outside our jurisdiction," Paul growled.

"Goblins on meth." Matthews shook his head. "Just what we fuckin' need."

"Maybe we oughta put this bitch session on hold 'til later," Paul said. "There's hostages, remember?"

"Yeah, you're right," I told him. I looked over at the liquor store, the flashing red lights bouncing off its windows like something at one of those rave clubs. "Guess we're gonna need CIs." I gestured with my head toward where we'd left the car. "You wanna...?"

"Sure." Big Paul lumbered off in the direction we'd come from. Then he stopped, and turned back.

"Vests, too?" he asked.

I shrugged. Goblins weren't shooters, everybody knew that. "I don't want one," I told him. "But if you're feeling wussy, be my guest."

Paul grinned at me. "Yeah, and fuck you, too." Then he pivoted and went back to the car.

Matthews looked at me. "CIs? What the hell d'you need a confidential informant for? We *know* where the little green bastards are."

"Yeah, we do. That's why he's getting some special cartridges out of our vehicle. They're tipped with cold iron. Different kind of CI."

Nobody knows why cold iron works against the creatures of *faerie* – goblins, trolls, dwarves, and all the rest. Might just as well ask why silver kills a werewolf, or why vamps can't stand sunlight. Some philosopher has probably spent years trying to figure it all out. But as Paul and I approached that liquor store, I was just glad that my Beretta held a fresh clip of 9mm CI slugs.

The weapon was holstered, for now. No point in spooking already jazzed-up goblins. My last combat pistol test showed that I could bring it up to firing position in 1.3 seconds and hit what I was aiming at 92 percent of the time. I figured that would be good enough.

There wasn't much danger of getting shot, anyway. Goblins don't use guns, and if this pair was breaking with tradition, they'd have busted some caps by now. Goblins aren't famous for their patience, even without meth.

The whole front of the liquor store was glass. As we approached, I thought I saw a flash of green from just above the check-out counter. They knew we were here, all right.

I pushed the heavy door open slowly, Paul right behind me. A long gray counter ran along the wall to the left, and we walked slowly toward it, our footsteps loud in the stillness. I stopped about twenty feet away. Big Paul would take up position about fifteen feet back and a little to my right, as always. If I went down, he'd be in a good position to nail the bastard responsible.

"I'm Detective Sergeant Stanley Markowski," I said, as calmly as if I was meeting someone at work. "This is Detective Paul di Napoli." Keep everything cool, that was the idea. The fact that my pulse was pounding in my ears like a crazed conga drummer didn't matter. "Whaddaya say we try to work this out? There's no need for anybody to get hurt."

The clerk had already been hurt, I knew that. But I decided not to mess up my pitch with inconvenient facts.

Goblin voices always remind me of fingernails being scraped across a blackboard. The one coming from behind the counter was no exception. *What you want?* it screeched.

"I want to talk."

No talk – want car. Get car or we cut humans.

Most goblins don't speak English real well, and the only phrase of Goblin that I know translates as "Your mother mates with trolls under every bridge in town."

"Don't cut humans," I said. "Talk instead. Talk better."

Talk no good. Want car, go away far. No prison.

"Why come here? Why rob?" Talking to gobs always made me sound like some nitwit in an old Tarzan movie. Can't be helped, though. Simple words and syntax are all they understand – in human language, or their own. Goblins aren't real bright.

"*Money. Lots of money at liquor place.*"

I caught movement out of the corner of my eye as something shifted in the parking lot outside. I hoped the uniforms out there weren't getting ready to try something stupid. Matthews had promised me that no breach would be attempted until Paul and I got out of there. His word was good, but if some higher-up arrived on scene and overruled him....

A full breach almost always results in casualties. Sometimes those include people caught in the middle.

"Why money?" I asked. "Goblin not need money."

Living near dumps, goblins usually forage for what they need. Sometimes they barter with other goblin tribes for stuff they can't find on their own.

"*For powder. For powder, need money much. Want powder. Need money.*"

Just as I'd figured. Meth-head goblins, Jesus.

"If I give powder, let humans go free?"

"*You get powder? Shit talk. Cop got no powder.*"

"Cops find lotsa drugs. Take during arrest, for evidence. You want powder, or no?"

I heard some whispering going on behind the counter. Behind me, Paul muttered, "I hope you know that the fuck you're doin'."

"*We get powder, let one human go. Then give car. Need car.*"

"I give powder, you let both humans go."

"One *human*. One!"

Hysteria was rising in the voice, making it even uglier than before. "Okay, one human," I said. "I go get powder now. Back soon."

"*Get quick, or we cut.*"

As we hurried back to the police lines, Paul said, "I ain't gonna ask if you're fucking nuts, cause I already know the answer to that one. You're gonna try something tricky, right?"

"I hope so," I told him. "Whether it'll work depends on if she's on duty tonight, or Dispatch can find her."

"Her who?"

"Rachel Proctor."

Big Paul stopped walking and looked at me. "The department witch," he said.

"That's the one."

The black-and-white unit pulled up to the command post thirty-six long minutes later. A uniform I didn't know got out of the passenger side. Looking in Matthews' direction he said, "Sir, I got a package for Sergeant Markowski."

"That's me." I went over, and he handed me a thick white envelope. "Thanks," I said, and before he had even turned away, I was slitting it open. Inside was a sealed, sandwich-size baggie containing three or four ounces of crystalline white powder. There was also a note from Rachel Proctor, the department's consulting white witch. "*No guarantees, but it ought to work. Good luck.*" She hadn't added "*You'll need it.*" She didn't have to.

Two minutes later, Big Paul and I were back inside the liquor store. I was about twenty feet away from the counter when one of the screechy voices yelled, "*Stop! No more close! We cut!*"

"I have powder," I said, as calmly as I could. "Have meth. Here. See?" I held up the baggie and let it dangle. One of the goblins stuck his head up for an instant, then disappeared again.

A few seconds later I heard, *"Throw powder. Throw here!"* The need in that voice was almost palpable.

"One human first," I said. "You made promise. I bring powder, one human let go."

"Throw bag here, or cut humans! Cut bad!"

"You cut humans, no powder. And no car."

More muttered conferring. Then a man crawled out from behind the counter on his hands and knees. He was in his undershirt. Somebody had used one sleeve of a blue-striped outer shirt to bandage his upper left arm. The fabric was soaked with blood, and dripping.

"It's all right," I told him. "Stand up, and walk toward us. It's gonna be okay."

The guy stood, but it wasn't easy for him. I guess he was stiff from sitting all that time, or he might've been woozy from blood loss, or both. Early fifties, probably. Tall, skinny, and scared half to death.

I kept my eye on the counter as Paul led the clerk to the door. The uniforms would get him into an ambulance.

"Drug now!" The goblin voice was a scream. *"Drug now, or cut woman. Cut tits off! Now!"*

"Here!" I said and tossed the baggie underhand. It cleared the counter and disappeared behind it. I felt my guts, already tight, clench a little harder. This was going to be the tricky part.

More mutterings and stirrings from behind the counter. Then I heard sniffing sounds, the kind you make when sucking in air deliberately. There's different ways to ingest meth. It seemed these gobs were snorters.

There was a clock on the wall above the counter. I watched it for two long minutes before calling "Goblins! Goblins, hear me?"

A new sound answered me. It was wordless but had a rising inflection, like somebody asking a question in his sleep.

"Goblins, you let woman go free. Let human go. Let go *now*."

Thirty-two more seconds crawled across the face of that clock. Then there was a stir behind the counter. A woman stood up slowly, using the counter as leverage. She was a fortyish brunette who had probably known too many Twinkies in her time. "Don't shoot!" she yelled, and threw her hands in the air. "Don't shoot!"

"Nobody's going to shoot you, ma'am. You can put your hands down. Just walk over to me. Easiest thing in the world. Take all the time you want. Just walk over here."

She nervously looked down and to her right. When nobody tried to stop her, she shuffled out from behind the counter and walked unsteadily toward us, her eyes still wide with terror.

Paul put his big arm around the woman's shoulders and led her toward the door. I still kept my eyes on the counter, although the hard part was over now.

I heard the door open behind me, and Big Paul's voice saying, "Come on, move it. Get her out of here."

Then I heard the door close and familiar footsteps coming back.

"All clear," Paul's voice rumbled.

We could have killed both of them, the goblins. Fired through the counter until our guns were empty and the little green bastards were dead or dying. No one in authority would've said "boo" about it.

But we didn't have to do it that way, so we didn't. Killing is never my first choice when taking down a suspect. Well, hardly ever. And if Rachel's spell had worked the way it was supposed to, nobody should have to die.

"Goblins!" I called. "Stand up! Stand up now!"

And it worked. Instead of being told "Blow it out your ass" in Goblin, I saw two furry green heads appear over the counter top. Two sets of black eyes peered at us blearily.

"Goblins! Drop knives. Drop knives. Now! Do it now!"

After a long pause, I heard the metallic clang of something hitting the floor. Then again. The knot in my guts loosened a little.

"Goblins! Come here! Come to me!"

Without even looking at each other, the two creatures slowly came around the counter. I've seen goblins before, and these two looked typical. Four feet tall, more or less. Green fur over black skin. The misshapen heads were standard, but their confused, vague expressions were probably due to Rachel's magic, not goblin genetics.

As they shuffled toward us, I reached slowly for the handcuffs on my belt. An amalgam of cold iron and silver, with a binding spell added for good measure, they would hold the greenies secure until they could be put into a special cell. The county jail's got accommodations for all creatures great and small, human and inhuman.

I cuffed one goblin's paws behind his back, while Paul did the other one. As I went through the near-automatic movements, I thought about the conversation I'd had with Rachel Proctor, once Dispatch had connected me to her phone.

"I need something that looks like meth, smells like it, hell, tastes like it," I told her. "But instead of getting buzzed, I want them made compliant and cooperative."

"So you can tell them what to do."

"Exactly. It's my best chance of getting the hostages out unharmed. The gobs, too, for that matter."

"Why not a simple knockout potion? Aren't you being a little too clever, Sergeant?"

"Can you guarantee instant unconsciousness for both of them, at exactly the same time?"

"Of course I can't," Rachel said impatiently. "No potion works instantaneously, and there's no guarantee they'd both use it at the same – oh, I see."

"Right. If they felt themselves being drugged unconscious, they might have enough time to knife the hostages. They would, too."

"Quite possibly. They're mean little buggers, most of them," she confirmed.

"I don't want them realizing they've been drugged until I start telling them what to do – not even then, if possible."

"And you need this immediately, of course."

"I need it before two strung-out goblins lose patience and start cutting up a couple of innocent humans. How long you figure I ought to wait?"

"Bastard," she said, but without heat.

"That's between Mom and Pop, and they're not here."

A sigh came over the line. "All right, send a police car over to my place, but tell them to wait outside. I'll bring it out as soon as it's ready, assuming I can make it work. Maybe twenty minutes, start to finish."

"When can you start?"

"As soon as I stop talking to you," Rachel said, and hung up.

As Big Paul and I led the unresisting goblins toward the door, I thought about what I could do to show my appreciation for Rachel's efforts. I was wondering if witches liked flowers when I heard the insane screech behind me, followed instantly by Paul's voice shouting, "Fuck!"

I whirled to see a goblin – the undrugged, uncompliant third goblin that nobody had known about – rushing at Paul. It held a knife with a foot-long blade in one green, furry paw.

I'd seen Paul's scores on the yearly firearms qualification, including "Draw and Fire." He was slower than me, by three-tenths of a second. But he still had plenty of time to draw down on the meth-crazed goblin.

I had my own weapon out now, but Paul's bulk blocked my shot. No problem. I knew he could double-tap that little green fucker without my help, and I'm sure Big Paul knew it, too. Right up until the instant that his weapon jammed.

I heard the click from Paul's Colt Commander, and knew instantly what had happened. And Paul froze. He should have dropped to the floor and given me a clear shot. That's standard procedure. Christ, they even teach it at the police academy. Instead, he just stood there, pulling the trigger on his useless weapon over and over, as if hoping that it would finally fire.

Paul's goblin prisoner was between us, and I wasted a precious couple of seconds shoving him out of the way. I reached for Paul's shoulder with my free hand, intending to push him aside so I could get a clear shot of my own. But by then it was far too late.

I felt the impact as the goblin's blade slammed into Paul's chest, unprotected by the body armor I'd said we didn't need. I heard his grunt of pain and surprise, saw the spray of blood from the wound – the bright red arterial blood that continued to spurt as Paul fell to his knees, giving me at last a clear view of the goblin that had knifed him, its face made even uglier by the rage and drug-induced madness stamped on it, then made uglier still by the impact of my bullet between its crazed black eyes.

The head shot was an instant kill, I knew that. There was no reason for me to empty the other seven rounds of cold-iron-tipped 9 mm into the green, misshapen body as it lay sprawled on the floor. No reason at all.

I tried to stop Paul's bleeding with pressure, and pretty soon I had a lot of uniformed help. But Paul still died before they could get him into an ambulance. They said later that the goblin's blade had severed one of the arteries leading to his heart. He'd bled to death internally in under a minute.

Nobody could have known there was a third goblin hiding in back, they said. Big Paul should've remembered to keep his weapon clean, they said. It was nobody's fault, they said. Everybody, from the chief on down, seemed to accept that.

Everybody but me.

Skip ahead about seven weeks.

I arrived for my shift a few minutes before 9pm, nodded to my partner, and sat down at my desk to check the messages and email that had come in during the day.

The Supernatural Crimes squad room is a cramped rectangle, with the detectives' desks set flush against the walls at the long sides. The shorter end at the front has McGuire's office and a door leading to the small reception area. The other end's got a door that leads to interrogation cells, a tiny lounge with coffee and vending machines, and the locker room.

Two of the other detective teams were already there. Pearce and McLane had the pair of desks opposite mine. McLane had bad acne as a kid, and has the pockmarks on his face to prove it. He had one of those four-dollar lattes in front of him as he paged through today's *Scranton Times-Tribune*. I noticed that the front page was all about some corrupt politician; the *real* news story will be if they find one in the Wyoming Valley who *isn't* corrupt.

Pearce, who's built like a fireplug, had a pair of earphones in, his big, square head bobbing to whatever the iPod was cranking out, although I'd bet it was the Dixie Chicks. Pearce used to fight in Golden Gloves, and his nose has been broken so many times he's become a mouth breather.

Further down on my side of the room, Sefchik and Aquilina sat at their abutting desks, arguing quietly about something. That didn't mean much – they always argued. But they've stayed partners for going on three years. Sefchik had the blond-and-blue looks of a choirboy, offset by the mouth of a Marine DI. As usual, he had a bottle of Diet Pepsi on his desk, and his partner drank from it as often as he did. You gotta like somebody pretty well to swap spit with them like that. Maybe Sefchik would have felt differently if Aquilina was a guy.

Carmela Aquilina was one of the unit's two female detectives. Cops being cops, she had to put up with a fair amount of shit when she first joined the squad. There's only one locker room for everybody, and guys were always trying to catch a glimpse of Carmela in the shower. She got so sick of it that she started walking around the locker room naked all the time, locking eyes with anybody she caught staring. We're so used to it now, nobody really looks anymore. Maybe that's what she had in mind to begin with.

I was barely halfway through my email when the lieutenant appeared at the door of his office and called out a couple of names, one of them mine. There was a report of something weird going down, and my partner and I had caught it.

My new partner was Karl Renfer, a tall, gangly kid, all elbows and knees. Far as I'm concerned, a "kid" is anyone younger than I am, and Karl's just past thirty. He'd been with the Supe Squad about six months. I remember when he'd been a basketball standout at Abington High. After graduation, he joined the army, and they made him an MP. He says that's when he realized he wanted to be a cop.

Karl'd had a pretty good record in uniform, and ordinarily I'd be okay about him riding with me. I've gotta have a partner, and it might as well be him. But there was already a cloud over him in the unit.

When he first transferred in, Karl had been paired up with Marty O'Brian, who's about eighteen months away from his pension. Not one of my favorite cops, O'Brian. It's not that he's extremely lazy, or stupid, or mean, or careless about regs. He's just a little bit of all those things, so I don't have a lot of use for him. But he's been on the job a long time, and that earns him some degree of respect. I guess.

One night, O'Brian and Renfer had been sent to check out a cemetery at the edge of town, where a voodoo *houngan* had been spotted trying to raise zombies. Following procedure, they'd split up, with O'Brian approaching through the front gate and Karl finding another entrance at the side, or maybe the back.

At least, that's the way it was supposed to go down.

There was a *houngan* at work, all right. He'd already raised four zombies by the time O'Brian arrived on the scene. Instead of giving it up, the old man sent his newly created shamblers after O'Brian, who was forced to kill (or re-kill) all of them. In the process, a stray bullet found its way into the *houngan's* head, as well.

That's the way O'Brian tells it.

Karl Renfer didn't arrive until after the shooting was over. He said all the other cemetery gates were locked. He'd checked every one, and then tried to climb over the fence. But the church had been worried about vandals, so the fence was high and difficult. Karl wasn't able to get in until he found a trash barrel that he could up-end and use to boost himself over the top. He got to where O'Brian and the action was as soon as he could.

That's what Karl claimed, anyway.

O'Brian said Karl was yellow, that he'd been cowering somewhere while O'Brian heroically risked his life against the zombies and their evil master.

There'd been no way to prove or disprove either story. The only possible witnesses were dead, either for the first or second time. After a Review Board hearing, Karl was cleared and sent back on the job. But O'Brian refused to work with him anymore, and, like I said, he's got a lot of seniority.

So the new guy needed a partner. And for my sins, they gave him to me.

O'Brian's an asshole, and maybe this was just more of his self-promoting bullshit. But "maybe" isn't good enough in this job. You have to be able to trust your partner all the way, every time. If there's any doubt about that, then the partnership isn't going to work.

Every time we went out on a call, that doubt rode with us like a third passenger.

I was thinking about Big Paul again as Karl brought our unmarked car to a stop in front of the address we'd been given, just off North Keyser Avenue. The expression on his face when Paul realized he wasn't going to make it...

Then I pushed all that stuff out of my mind and focused on the job. Wool-gathering's for sheep, and sooner or later, sheep get slaughtered.

The place looked like an abandoned warehouse. That figured. I sometimes think companies build these things and leave them deserted just so bad guys will have someplace to hang out.

There'd been a report that some Satanists were holding sacrifices in there, although nobody'd caught them at it yet. But this was the first night of the full moon, and if there was any coven activity going on, tonight was a good time for it.

We've got freedom of religion in this country. You can worship Jesus, Jehovah, Allah, Vishnu, Satan, or Brad Pitt, for all the law cares. But killing dogs, cats, goats, or whatever – that comes under the animal cruelty laws, although some Santería practitioners are fighting it in the courts.

Normally, dogs and cats would be a job for Animal Control, or maybe the SPCA. But every serious Satanist cult I ever heard of eventually moved up to sacrificing what they call "the goat without horns" – a human being.

Unless somebody stopped them first.

I turned to Karl. "Stay here. I'll call you on the radio if I find anything interesting."

Karl gave me a look I was already getting tired of, and said, "When are you gonna stop treating me like a fucking rookie?"

"I'm treating you like my partner," I told him, "who happens to be the junior partner on this team and is supposed to do what he's told. And I'm telling you to wait here."

I got out, and just before slamming the door shut I snapped, "And stay awake!"

I was pissed off, but I couldn't have said at who. Maybe both of us.

I made a careful circle of the warehouse. All I learned was that the loading dock was in back and there was a normal-sized door on the north side. I approached the door and carefully tried the handle. It was unlocked.

I wasn't sure whether I was happy about that or not.

Inside, it was darker than the boots of the High Sheriff of Hell. I thought I could hear voices chanting, but they weren't close.

I took out my flashlight, and held it well away from my body before flicking it on. If the light was going to draw hostile attention, I didn't want any of it hitting me. But nobody shot, or shouted, or seemed to give much of a shit that I was there at all.

I wasn't sure whether I was happy about that, either.

The flashlight beam showed me that this part of the warehouse was divided into rooms by sheets of cheap plywood. There were a couple of hallways at right angles to each other. I followed the one where the chanting seemed loudest.

After rounding a couple of corners, I saw a door with light under it – the faint, flickering light you get from candles.

That door was unlocked, too. These people were either really stupid or really cocky. I turned the knob and pushed the door open slowly, praying the hinges wouldn't squeak.

I soon learned it wouldn't have mattered if the door was wired to start playing "The Star-Spangled Banner", in stereo. The people inside were so intent on what they were doing, they didn't even notice me. At first.

I slipped inside the room and quickly counted the house. It looked like thirteen of them. Well, that figured. They were all dressed in those hooded gray robes that were probably the height of fashion in the fourteenth century.

The cultists were standing in a rough semicircle, their backs to me. As I crept closer, I got a better view of what they were all staring at. That's when I realized it wasn't a case for Animal Control any longer.

This coven had already moved beyond goats and chickens. They had gone all the way to the big time.

The scrawny blonde teenager they had on the floor, tied spread-eagled and gagged, was dressed like a street-walker. No surprise there.

Prostitution is the only job that requires a woman to go someplace private with a complete stranger. That makes working girls easy prey for guys who have more on their minds than a quick blowjob. Psychos have known that ever since Jack the Ripper, if not before.

It looked like they had just finished cutting her throat.

Her blood was flowing slowly across the wooden floor in the direction of the pentagram that somebody had drawn there in yellow chalk. It didn't take Sherlock Holmes to figure out what they had in mind.

These morons were trying to conjure a demon.

Despite what you see in the movies, a summoning isn't all that easy to do. Hellspawn don't much like to be bothered by humans, who they regard with contempt. And most of the grimoires that you find are either completely worthless or they've got just enough accurate information to get you killed. Or worse.

Conjuring a demon is like that proverb about grabbing a tiger by the tail – the slightest mistake, and you're lunch. I wondered if these fools would succeed in calling something from the netherworld. If they did, they might soon wish they'd failed.

I had just decided to sneak back out and radio Karl to call for backup when the stream of the girl's blood reached the pentagram. As soon as it did, the air in the center began to shimmer and sparkle. The conjuration had worked, after all.

Something from Hell was on its way.

I drew my weapon and stepped forward. Summoning a demon is a crime all by itself, and there was no way to tell whether these clowns had constructed their pentagram properly. If they hadn't, we could soon have a demon loose in my city, and I was *not* going to let that happen.

"Police officer!" I yelled. "Stop the chanting and put your hands in the air! *Do it!*"

Most of them whirled to face me, eyes wide with shock. But some were so mesmerized by the pentagram, they couldn't tear their eyes from it.

The cultists who had turned my way were starting to put their hands up when I realized that I had miscounted. There were actually twelve of them gathered around the pentagram. I figured that out when Number Thirteen jumped me from behind.

The thirteenth guy had been out of the room – maybe in the john, puking over the sight of blood, I don't know. But he picked a bad moment to come back.

Lucky for me, the bastard didn't have a weapon. Instead, he jumped on my back, threw a forearm around my throat, and tried to grab my gun with his other hand.

Most of the others had turned back to stare in awe at what had just appeared inside the pentagram. I only had time for a quick glance, but I saw that it was a class-four demon, which is about all you'd expect from Amateur Night. Not a heavyweight like Lucifuge Rofocale or Baal, thank heaven, but still enough to cause plenty of trouble if it got loose.

Two of the cultists started toward me, I guess with the idea of giving their buddy on my back some help. I tried to bring my gun to bear on them, but Number Thirteen's hand on my wrist kept pulling it away.

Since I couldn't shoot them, I decided to do the next best thing.

I'd seen a guy do this in a bar fight, years ago. It had impressed me so much that I tried it myself in the gym a couple of times, where it didn't work real well. But I didn't have a lot of options.

I took two running steps, tucked my head down, and went into the beginning of a forward somersault. It wasn't the full deal, not with Number Thirteen clinging to me like a tumor. But it took us right into the two approaching cultists like a huge bowling ball, knocking them sprawling, and ended up with Number Thirteen going down hard on his back with me on top of him. He let go of me then – he was too busy trying to remember how to breathe.

I scrambled to my feet, sensed movement behind me, and turned just in time to catch another cultist's fist square in the face. The guy was no Muhammad Ali, but the punch was enough to knock me off balance. I went down, more pissed off than hurt, and immediately started to get up again.

Then something far stronger than a human hand grabbed my ankle, and in a heartbeat I knew that my leg had breached the pentagram.

The demon had me.

Most people can think pretty fast when they have to. Even me. In a flash I considered my options, and none of them looked very good. I still had my gun, but shooting a demon is a waste of time, even with silver bullets. And Arnie Schwarzenegger in his prime couldn't have broken the grip that thing had on my leg.

I was just thinking that my best option was to put the pistol in my mouth and pull the trigger when Karl Renfer appeared behind one of the smaller cultists, grabbed him at the neck and crotch with those big hands of his, and heaved.

"Here's dinner, Hellfuck!" Karl yelled, as he threw the struggling man right at the demon's ugly, misshapen head.

The kid was stronger than he looked.

Class-four demons aren't very smart. If this one had been brighter, it would have hung on to me with one clawed hand and grabbed the airborne cultist with the other one. Kind of like dinner plus dessert.

Instead, the stupid thing let go of me to grab its new prey, and I rolled away from that pentagram faster than a scalded cat on speed.

I got to my feet just in time to see the demon bite the cultist's head off and swallow it whole.

I waved my gun at the rest of the coven. "Freeze, motherfuckers! Hands in the air – you're all under arrest!" One of them made a dash for the door, but only got a few steps before Karl shot his leg out from under him. It didn't take long for us to get the rest face down on the floor, fingers interlaced behind their necks.

I looked at Karl. "You call for backup?" I asked. My voice was a little unsteady.

He shook his head. "Wasn't time, once I saw what was going down in here."

"Okay, I'll do it now."

I took out my radio, got the station, and told them what we were dealing with. The dispatcher promised to send help immediately. "Be sure to tell 'em to bring an exorcist," I told her. "We got something that needs to be sent back to Gehenna."

As I clicked the radio off, I looked toward the pentagram. The demon was still devouring what was left of the unlucky cultist. Demons are real messy eaters.

Karl saw where I was looking. "Ate the outfit, too," he said. "Must be the extra fiber."

It wasn't all that funny, and definitely a 10 on the Insensitivity Scale, but I laughed. And laughed. It was all I could do to stop it from turning into tears. Coming that close to being eaten alive can shake you up some.

Even a tough guy like me.

So the crime scene people took our statements, the department exorcist sent the snarling and screeching demon back home, and the poor hooker's body was carted off to the morgue. The cultists were on their way to the county jail. They'd be arraigned in the morning.

Only a few of the robed idiots had actually seen Karl

throw one of their buds to the demon. God only knows what kind of story they'd be telling. But if it came down to it, Karl and I would be more credible in front of a jury than a couple of cultists facing murder and summoning charges.

A medic said my ankle was badly bruised, but nothing was broken. He taped it up tight and told me to take ibuprofen for the pain.

As Karl and I headed back to the car, I said, "That was quick thinking in there, earlier. Pretty good job of power lifting, too. I guess I owe you one."

There was enough light for me to see his grin. "Okay, so you're buying breakfast, even though it's my turn."

"Deal," I told him. "But you're driving, since I'm injured, and all."

As Karl started the car I said, "You know, those guys in the robes might have been onto something. I sometimes think that Satanism is the perfect religion."

He looked at me like I'd just grown a second head.

"No, really," I told him. "Way I figure it, if you're a Satanist, and you fuck up – well, you go to heaven. Right?"

Karl laughed a lot longer and harder than the feeble joke was worth. Then he turned on the lights and drove us out of there.

The kid was going to work out okay.

For Karl and me, the rest of the shift was paperwork: arrest reports, a Supernatural Incident Report, all that stuff. And since Karl had fired his weapon, he had to talk to the Internal Affairs people, who surprised everybody by quickly agreeing that it was a righteous shoot.

We were able to knock off about 6:00, just as the sun was coming up over the city. Karl said, "See ya," and headed off to his car, but I stood at the top of the steps for a minute, watching the sunrise. I know that Scranton's not a big deal like New York or San Francisco. But I still like the way the skyline looks at dawn.

It's not a big town. And the way most people figure these things, it's not a great town, either. But it's my town. And protecting it from the forces of darkness is my job.

The shit hit the fan three months later, and none of us even knew it – at first. On the night in question (as we say in court) I came on shift at the usual time. I barely had the chance to sit down at my desk when McGuire was at his office door. "Markowski, Renfer!" he barked. "You got one."

We'd caught a homicide. The stiff, according to McGuire, was in a house on Linden Street. The address was near the campus of the University of Scranton, which I attended for three years before running out of both money and ambition.

"We know anything about the perp?" I asked. "Vamp, werewolf, or..."

McGuire shook his head. "Or none of the above. It isn't clear the killer was a supe."

I let my raised eyebrows ask the next question. McGuire got it immediately.

"It's our case," he said, "because although the perp might not have been a supe, the victim *was*."

I heard Karl mutter under his breath, "Well, fuck me to Jesus with a strap-on dildo."

I couldn't have put it better, myself.

The house on Linden Street was typical for that neighborhood – a mid-size Victorian with a front yard the size of a postage stamp. The uniforms had secured the scene, but forensics hadn't shown up yet. There's a joke around the station house that if forensics ever arrives on time, it's a sign of the Apocalypse.

I think the forensics guys started that one themselves, to stop detectives from bitching.

Inside, I hung back a little and let Karl ask one of the uniformed cops, "So, what do we got here?" He just loves saying that at crime scenes. What the hell, we were all young once.

One of the uniforms, a stocky guy named Conroy who I knew slightly, led us down a dim hallway toward a room where lights burned brightly. Halfway there, the smell told me this was going to be a bad one.

What crept up my nostrils was a mixture of blood and shit and sweat and fear, and if you don't think fear has an odor, just ask any cop. Overlaying all of that was something a lot like roast pork, which is what burned human flesh smells like.

I don't eat roast pork anymore. I haven't since my second year on the job, when I arrived at a crime scene shortly after a guy had doused his sleeping wife with gasoline and set her ablaze.

From the warning my nose had given me, I wasn't surprised by what was waiting for us in that room, which the owner of the house probably called his study. I saw Karl's face twist when he saw the corpse, but I wasn't worried about him. He'd been a uniform himself for six years before joining the Supe Squad. Like any cop, he'd seen plenty of the ugliness the world has to offer. Although maybe nothing quite so ugly as this.

The vic was a male Caucasian, early fifties. He was tied, with heavy fishing line, to a sturdy-looking wooden chair that probably belonged behind the ornately carved desk over near the window. Shelves on every wall were filled with old-looking books, but the man in the chair wouldn't be consulting them any more. It's pretty hard to read once your eyes have been burned out.

The man was naked, so it wasn't difficult to see everything else that had been done to him – cuts, bruises, and burns covered the body from scalp to shins. I stepped forward for a closer look, making sure to breath through my mouth as I did.

The tissue damage around the burns suggested a very hot flame, the kind you get from a blowtorch. I glanced around the room, but didn't see anything that would produce that kind of heat. Maybe the perp took it with him. On the floor not far from the chair was a wide strip of duct tape, about six inches long, all wrinkled and bloody.

Karl started to say something, stopped, cleared his throat, and tried again. "How'd you know the guy was a supe?" he asked Conroy. "He's no vamp, that's for sure, and a were would probably have transformed and got free. That ain't silver holding him to the chair."

Before Conroy could answer, I said, "Look here." Taking a pen from my pocket, I leaned over the vic's left hand. I slipped the pen under his fingers, what was left of them, and gently lifted the hand up. Despite the blood smear, the tattoo of a pentagram was clearly visible on his palm. I'd seen the edge of it from where I was standing.

"Wizard," Karl said.

"There's something else you guys oughta see," Conroy said. "It's in the next room."

We followed him through a connecting door into what was clearly the wizard's bedroom. The ceiling light was burning, along with a two-bulb floor lamp.

I asked Conroy, "Were these lights already on?"

"Yeah, that's why I decided to take a look," he said. "Everything's *exactly* the way I found it." He sounded defensive, and I wondered why.

The four-poster bed was shoved over against a wall, fresh drag marks clearly visible on the polished hardwood. Where the bed had been standing was a hole in the floor, maybe a foot square. The matching pieces of wood used to conceal it had been pried up and tossed aside.

Inside the hole was a safe with its heavy door open. I looked inside and saw cash, lots of it, although there was plenty of room left. The bills were divided into stacks bound with rubber bands.

Now I knew what had gotten up Conroy's ass: he was afraid we might accuse him of helping himself to some of the dead guy's money.

I straightened up and looked at Karl. "Whoever it was, he didn't come here for money," I said. "The bills haven't been messed with at all." The last part was for Conroy's benefit, although it was also true.

"Unless maybe he *was* after the money," Karl said, "but got scared off by somebody before he could grab it."

I shook my head. "Anybody who's hard-core enough to do all that–" I pointed with my chin toward the study "he's not gonna be stopped by a surprise visitor."

"Yeah, maybe you're right." Karl turned to Conroy. "We got a name on the vic?"

Conroy checked his notebook. "Kulick, George Lived alone."

"Who called it in?" I asked him.

"There's a housekeeper, Alma Lutinski, comes in once a week. Has her own key. She found the stiff, went all hysterical, and started screaming her lungs out. The neighbors heard her and called 911."

"We'll need to talk to her," Karl said. "Where is she?"

"She really lost her shit, so they took her to Mercy Hospital. The docs'll probably give her a shot, get her calmed down a little."

"I doubt she got a look at the perp," I said. "Otherwise, he would've iced her, too. But we'll find out what she has to say for herself, later. Maybe she knows what the late Mr Kulick's been up to lately. And with who."

There were voices coming from the hallway now. "Sounds like forensics is here," I said. "Finally."

"Wanna start canvassing the neighborhood?" Karl asked.

"Might as well," I said. "Shit, we might even find a witness. That happens every three or four years."

I looked at Conroy. "Make sure the forensics guys pay close attention to that safe, okay? I'd like to know what else was in there besides money."

We went back out through the study, careful not to trip over the forensics techs, who were crawling all over the place like ants on a candy bar. "Guess whatever was in that steel box was real important to somebody, haina?" Karl said.

"Two somebodies."

"Two?" Karl's brow wrinkled. "The perp, for sure..."

"Kulick was the other one." I looked once more at the savaged piece of meat that had once been a human being. "Otherwise, he would have given it up long before all that was done to him."

Our canvass of the neighborhood turned up precisely zip. Richie Masalava, the M.E.'s guy at the crime scene, guesstimated that Kulick had been cold about twenty-four hours, but nobody we talked to remembered seeing or hearing anything unusual the day before.

When Karl and I got to the hospital, the tranquilizers had worn off enough so that Alma Lutinski was more or less coherent. She said she had been George Kulick's housekeeper for about two and a half years.

"I dust, I vacuum, I sweep and mop up. That's all." Her voice sounded husky, like the kind you get with heavy smokers, but I couldn't smell any tobacco on her. I wondered if Alma had screamed herself hoarse inside George Kulick's house.

"Once in a while he leaves a note," she said. "'Dust the venetian blinds,' so I dust them. 'Clean the shower,' two-three times, maybe. He leaves a check on the kitchen table, every week. Never bounces. Not like some."

"You never saw him when you came over to do your cleaning?" Karl asked Alma.

"A few times, he's there. But then he goes into that room, his 'study' and closes the door. It's like I'm there by myself. I like that, nobody bothers me."

"But didn't you have to get into the study to dust?" I said.

"Oh, no." Alma shook her head. "Never the study. 'Stay out,' he says. 'Don't worry about the dust, the dirt,' he says. Why should I argue – I need more work to do?"

Karl gave her his special smile then, the one he once claimed could charm the knickers off a nun. "Bet you went in at least once, though, didn't you? Looked around a little, maybe checked out his desk, all that crazy stuff he had in there. Weren't you curious? Just a little?"

The look she gave him reminded me of a nun, all right, but not the kind who'll slip her knickers off for you. Her expression was right out of Sister Yolanda's playbook, and I was glad for Karl's sake that there wasn't a big wooden ruler handy.

"You little snot," Alma said venomously. "You think I snoop? Look around? You think I steal, maybe, too, huh? He says stay out, I stay out. I'm a good Catholic woman, you German bastard."

Karl and I backed away slowly, the way you do from a Doberman that's slipped its chain. Once we were safely outside, Karl said, "I think maybe she took a dislike to me. He shook his head. "'German bastard.' Talk about old country."

"Maybe you should have tried for her knickers, instead," I said.

Things were quiet among the supe community the next few nights – nothing that the other detectives couldn't handle, anyway. Karl and I spent the time going through George Kulick's personal effects. We were looking for names of friends, associates, relatives, even enemies – anybody who could tell us what Kulick kept in that safe besides money.

We came up empty on all counts. The only letters we found were professional correspondence, like the letter from a magical supply house, saying that the shipment of powdered bat wings he'd ordered would be delayed. Stuff like that. If he had an address book, we didn't find it. No diary, of course. My luck never runs that good. No answering machine for somebody to leave a juicy message or two.

Phone records revealed no incoming calls for the last four months, and only two outgoing. Both of those were made to the local Domino's Pizza place.

Kulick didn't even have a home computer. Guess he did his communicating in ways that Bill Gates had never heard of – although there were news stories that Microsoft was getting ready to release a new product line called Spell Software.

I checked with my contacts in the magical community, but nobody knew George Kulick – or would admit to it, anyway. And no relative ever claimed the body, so it was buried in some land that the city owns in a local cemetery just for that purpose. In the old days, I guess it would have been called the potter's field.

Driving home at the end of the third fruitless night, I found myself wishing that the forensics guys would pull off one of those miracles that you see on TV every week – the kind where they find some microscopic bit of evidence that would give us the perp's name, address, phone number, and astrological sign.

Because what we had right now was shit.

After two more nights of no leads, no evidence, no witnesses and no dice, McGuire was talking about putting this one in the Pending Cases file, the place where unsolved crimes go to die.

I could see his point. The other detectives in the unit were overworked, picking up the slack we'd left to work Kulick's murder. Things were getting busy again – the supes don't stay quiet for long. But the idea of just letting this one go made my whole face hurt. Nobody should have to die the way George Kulick did. Nobody. Except maybe the bastard who'd killed him.

Near the end of our shift on the fifth night, I closed another cardboard box full of Kulick's stuff and said to Karl, "I guess if we're going to clear this one, we're going to have to go to the source."

He turned and stared at me.

"There's only two people who know for sure who whacked Kulick, right?" I said. "The perp and the victim."

Karl shrugged. "Yeah, so?"

"It's pretty clear that the perp hasn't left us anything to go on," I said. "So I guess it's time to ask the vic."

"But the vic is fucking..." Karl's voice trailed off as his eyes narrowed. "Stan, you're not gonna–"

"Yeah, I'm gonna. I don't see what other choice we have, if we're going to find this motherfucker."

"Necromancy's against the law, for Chrissake!"

"Not if it's conducted as police business, by a duly licensed practitioner of magic. And I know just where to find one."

Rachel Proctor was barely five feet tall, and built lean. She had auburn hair, smart-looking gray eyes and a beautiful smile. The smile put in an appearance when I first walked into her office, but once I'd started talking, it was gone, baby, gone.

She was looking at me as if I'd just suggested that we have three-way sex with a goat some night. A real old, smelly goat.

"Necromancy's against the law, Stan. You of all people ought to know that."

"And you of all people ought to know that it's legal with a court order, Rachel."

"And what do you think your chances are of getting *that*?"

I pulled the court order out of my inside jacket pocket and laid it gently on her antique oak desk. "Pretty good, I'd say."

She looked at the folded document for a few seconds, then at me for a few more, then she reached out one of her small, delicate hands to pick it up. She unfolded the order and scanned it quickly. "Judge Olszewski. I should have known."

Rachel tossed the paper back on her desk. "Your *paisan*."

"We prefer *homie*," I said.

"I suppose you two hang out together at meetings of, what is it? – the Polish Falcons?"

I shrugged. "Man's gotta do something with his free time, and Mom always told me to stay out of pool halls."

She managed to combine amazement and annoyance in one slow shake of her head.

"So," I said. "Can you do it?"

"A better question is *will* I do it?" She leaned back in her chair, a huge leather thing that made her look like a kid playing on the good furniture. "Explain to me, slowly and carefully, why you want me to do this, and what you're hoping to accomplish by it."

So I laid it out for her. I started by describing what had been done to George Kulick, in as much detail as I could without sounding like some kind of freak sadist who was getting off on it. To her credit, Rachel was looking a little queasy when I was done.

She swallowed a couple of times, then said, "And you've exhausted all of the usual means of getting information about this... atrocity."

"Every damn one," I told her. "Witnesses: none. Forensics: none. Associates: none. Friends and family: none. Enemies: none."

"Well, one, anyway," she said grimly.

"Depends on how you define your terms," I said. "Whoever tortured Kulick wanted the location and combination of that safe. Once he got that, I expect he put Kulick out of his misery pretty quick. I don't think it was personal."

"I doubt that it made much difference to Mr Kulick," she said, and made a disgusted face.

"What do you say we ask him and find out?"

She sighed, then there was silence in the room for a while. I'd made my pitch. The rest was up to her. Nobody could order her to perform a necromancy – it was her call.

Rachel was studying her right thumbnail as if it was the most fascinating thing in the world. Without looking up she asked, "Where was he buried?"

"In one of the city-owned plots at the public grave-yard."

"Well, that's something," she said. "No hassles with the Church to worry about. And it's not hallowed ground. When did interment take place?"

"Day before yesterday. But he died a week ago. They kept him on ice at the morgue for a while, in case somebody claimed the body. When nobody did, they planted him."

"And in life he was a wizard, you say."

"Yeah," I said. "He had the mark on him – and about a gazillion books on magic in his library. Why – does it matter?"

"Indeed, it does. It means his spirit will be harder to control, once it's raised. I'll have to take extra precautions."

"So you *will* do it." I didn't bother keeping the relief out of my voice.

"Against my better judgment, yes, I will," Rachel said, sounding tired. "And I suppose you need this done im-mediately, if not sooner?"

I shrugged. "Afraid so. The longer we wait, the greater the perp's chances of getting away with it. And a guy who'd do Kulick like that, you gotta figure he won't be squeamish about torturing somebody else to get what he wants."

She gave me a look that said she knew I was trying to manipulate her emotionally, and she didn't like it.

But she didn't tell me that I was wrong.

"As you're aware, Stan, I'm a practitioner of white magic. But what you're asking for here is gray magic."

I knew that one. "Black magic, performed for the purpose of good."

"Exactly right. Normally, necromancy is one of the blackest of the black arts." She sighed deeply. "I'll need to get permission before I can proceed."

I tapped the court order that lay on her desk. "We've already got this. What more do you need?"

The thin smile she gave me didn't look much like the one I'd received walking in. "The kind of permission I need comes from a court you've never heard of, Stan. But it is one that I dare not disobey. I'll let you know, one way or the other, as soon as I find out."

I stood up and slid the court order back in my pocket. "When do you plan to put in the request, or whatever it is you have to do?"

"A few seconds after I see that door close behind you. So, get."

I got.

The next day, I was getting ready for work when "Tubular Bells," the theme from *The Exorcist*, started playing in my shirt pocket. I touched an icon and brought the phone to my ear. "Markowski."

Rachel Proctor's voice said, "Tomorrow night, at midnight. I'll need a day to prepare. Pick me up at my house about 9:00." She paused a moment. "You're going to be there, you know."

"I wouldn't miss it for the world," I said. I might even have been telling the truth.

The next night, I brought the car to a stop in front of Rachel's house at 8:59. A few moments later, she was tapping at the passenger-side window.

"Pop your trunk."

I pulled the lever. She disappeared from view, and then I felt the springs shift a little as something heavy was placed in the trunk. The lid slammed shut, and then Rachel was slipping into the passenger seat next to me.

She looked terrible.

Even in the light from the street lamps, I could see circles under her eyes that she hadn't bothered to hide with makeup. The skin of her face seemed looser, somehow, like someone recovering from a bad accident.

"What're you *staring* at?" she snapped. I was stammering an apology when she laid a gentle hand on my arm. "Sorry, Stan. I know I look a fright – almost like one of the stereotypes of my profession."

"Are you sick? Maybe we can–"

"No, I'm not sick, in the usual sense of the term. I haven't slept, that's part of it. I last ate something... this morning, I think, but I forget what it was. I've been working pretty much nonstop since you left me yesterday. Necromancy takes a lot of preparation, and we're not exactly blessed with time, are we? A lot of the work involves setting up protections for the necromancer." She paused, then added, "That would be me."

"Protections against the corpse? I thought–"

"We won't be raising his corpse, Stan. You've been seeing too many movies. What we're going to resurrect, if this works, is his spirit – and that is infinitely more dangerous."

"How come?"

"Protecting myself from a physical body is a piece of cake, comparatively – there are a hundred spells that could do it. But guarding against a pure spirit is harder, because of all the different ways it can manifest. And the fact that he was a wizard makes it even trickier."

"Why should it? Dead is dead, no? Except when it's undead."

"I wish it were that simple. A dead man is a dead man, Stanley. But a dead wizard is... well, a dead wizard."

Rachel turned to face forward. "Come on, let's get this circus on the road, before I come to my senses."

After a while, the silence in the car started to get uncomfortable. For me, anyway. "Proctor," I said. "That name has... associations for me. Something to do with the Salem witch trials, maybe?"

"Very astute. I'm a descendant of John Proctor, who was hanged as a witch after being denounced by his housekeeper."

"Your family history of witchcraft goes back a long ways, then." I said.

"That it does – on both sides. My mother, whose maiden name was Brown, was a direct descendant of the Mathers – Increase, and his son, Cotton."

"Mathers – like in *Leave it to Beaver*?"

From the corner of my eye, I saw a glimmer of a smile.

"I've always thought that ought to be the title of a porn flick. Or maybe it was, and I missed it."

"I didn't know witches liked porn."

"Don't generalize from one example, Stan. And don't play dumb, either. You know who the Mathers were."

"The guys behind the witch trials."

"That's an oversimplification, but – yeah."

"Sounds like an interesting family."

"It was that, all right. Proctors on one side, Mathers on the other – and me in the middle."

"You mean they used to–"

"Let's not talk any more, Stan. It's distracting me."

"Distracting? From what?"

"Praying."

Grave 24-C looked like all the other plots in this corner of the city cemetery, apart from the freshly turned earth on top. There'd be no headstone, of course. Anybody willing to spring for a marker to put on George Kulick's grave would probably have paid for a proper funeral in the bargain, and he'd likely have buried the guy in a better class of graveyard, too.

I helped Rachel Proctor set up for the ritual of necromancy, which was supposed to reach its climax at midnight. My help had mostly consisted of performing vital tasks such as "hold this" or "bring that."

As she laid out her materials, Rachel said, "I'm going to follow the Sepulchre Path of necromancy. It's the easiest, but it should allow us to get the information you need. If I do it right, it will temporarily grant me the power of Insight, which is the ability to see what the deceased saw in the last moments of his life."

"Could be pretty ugly, considering how he died," I said. "Can't you just call up his ghost and ask him who the killer was? I've heard of that being done."

"Yes, it can be done." She carefully opened a packet containing a dark blue powder and poured some into a bowl. "But probably not by me. That would require the Ash Path, which is far more difficult. You'd need a real adept to have a chance of pulling that one off. And when it comes to this stuff, an adept I ain't."

A little later I asked, "How many, uh, necromantic rituals have you been involved in, so far?"

Without looking up from what she was doing, she said, "Including tonight?"

"Sure."

"One."

"Oh."

She had made three concentric circles on the ground near Kulick's grave. The outer ring, I could see, was made of salt. The two inner circles were laid down using powders that I didn't recognize. The one making up the middle circle was red. The innermost circle was in white. "This is where you'll stand when it starts," Rachel had said. "Whatever happens, do *not* leave the inner circle until I have given the spirit leave to depart and I explicitly tell you it's safe. Always assuming I'm able to summon his spirit in the first place."

"What's so special about the inner circle?" I asked.

"The white circle is the strongest, kind of like the innermost ring of a rampart," she said. "It is your place of refuge, and mine, too, if things get hairy. Kind of like a shark cage when Jaws is in town."

I didn't remind her how relying on the shark cage had worked out in the movie, let alone the book.

"Why don't you just stay in the white circle the whole time, if it's safest?"

"Because I need access to the altar, which cannot itself be within the circle. Did you bring a personal object of Kulick's, as I asked you – something he had a lot of physical contact with?"

I produced a silver Montblanc pen. "Here. This was found on his desk blotter. Looks like he used it quite a bit."

"Good. Then we can begin."

Just outside the outer ring, Rachel had set up the small portable altar we'd brought with us. On it burned three candles – red, white, and black. They sat at the points of a triangle drawn on the altar; the lines were red at the sides, but black across the bottom. She had also placed there several other objects, including bowls, small bottles, and a variety of instruments – some of which I recognized, others whose function I could only guess.

I was glad it wasn't windy, otherwise those candle flames wouldn't have lasted long. Then it occurred to me to wonder whether Rachel had anything to do with that.

Using a long handmade match that she sparked into life with a thumbnail, she lit two sticks of incense, placing each one in a container at opposite ends of the altar. It didn't take long for the smoke to make my eyes water.

"What the hell is that?" I asked.

"One is wormwood, the other is horehound," she said. "And I'd be careful about using the 'h' word right now – you never know what it might summon by accident. In fact, it would be better if you didn't talk at all, Stan."

I've been told to "shut up" before, but never so politely.

Facing the altar, Rachel stood with her hands spread wide. Then she began what I later learned is known as a "Quarter Call":

Spirits of Air,
We call to you.
The Breath of life
the Knowledge of life,
the Wind of life,
it blows from thee to me,
be with us now.

Then she turned forty-five degrees to her left, and continued:

Spirits of Fire,
We call to you.
The Heat of life,
the Will of life,
the Fire of life,
it burns from thee to me,
be with us now.

She made another quarter turn. She was facing me now, but I don't think she even saw me.

Spirits of Fire,
We call to you.
The Heat of life,
the Will of life,
the Fire of life,
it burns from thee to me,
be with us now.

Another turn, and she chanted:

Spirits of Earth,
We call to you.
The Flesh of life,
the Strength of life,
the Earth of life,
it moves from thee to us,
be with us now.

Then she faced the altar again.

I call upon Hecate,
goddess of the crossroads.
Bless my work, and my endeavors.
Protect and keep me safe from harm.
From every place that harm is wrought.
From every evil that walks.

Protect me, wise one, guard me now.
O great Hecate, I beseech thee:
Watch over me this night
that I might do this work
both faithfully and well.
In thanks for your protection
I make this offering now.

There was a small wooden box on the altar. Rachel raised the lid and quickly reached in. Her hand came out holding something that moved in her grasp.

I looked closer. She was holding a brown-and-white mouse, its tail twitching like a hooked worm. I wondered whether she'd trapped it herself or bought it at a local pet store. Either way, things weren't looking too good for Mr Mouse right about now.

Black magic requires a sacrifice – a blood sacrifice. It has its roots in the ancient religions, and their gods always required blood. In the case of some, like the Aztecs, the blood had to be human.

I guessed the mouse was the smallest offering that Rachel thought would allow the ritual to work. Or maybe it was the biggest thing she could bring herself to kill.

She closed the box again, and held the mouse down on its lid with her lift hand. With her right, she picked up a knife with an ornately carved handle.

"*Spiritus!*" she said loudly, held the knife up to shoulder height, then lowered it. She did this twice more. Then, with the mouse still pinned against the top of the wooden box, she cut off its head with one quick, economical movement. I expect the little guy was dead before he even knew he was dying.

I noticed that a breeze had sprung up, but the candle flames didn't flicker. The smoke from the incense rose straight up, as if the air was perfectly still. Maybe over there, it was.

Rachel seemed to hesitate before beginning the next part of the ritual, but when she spoke, her voice was clear and strong.

Colpriziana,
offina alta nestra
fuaro menut,
I name George Harmon
the dead which I seek.
Spirit of George Harmon
you may now approach this gate
and answer truly to my calling.
Berald, Beroald, Balbin,
Gab, Gabor, Agaba!
Arise, I charge and call thee!

She repeated this twice more, a little louder each time. The smoke from the incense sticks had thickened and come together into one mass that grew as I watched. According to the laws of physics, what I was seeing was impossible. But I had a feeling that the laws of physics didn't count for much right now.

Using a sharp stick of polished wood that I knew was her wand, Rachel made a big X in the air above the altar. A few moments later, she repeated the movement. Then a third time.

I don't know how long it was – a minute, maybe two – before I noticed that an outline was appearing in the gathered smoke. An outline in the form of a man.

Rachel must have seen it about the same time I did, because she started chanting, over and over: "*Allay fortission fortissio allynsen roa!*"

I don't know how many times she repeated that

phrase before she decided it was enough. But when she stopped, the quiet was almost oppressive. It wasn't just the absence of sound. The silence was like a force, pressing against my eardrums. The outline of the man in the smoke was clear and distinct, like a silhouette you'd see through the blinds of a lighted room at night.

Then Rachel spoke, her voice only a little louder than normal. "I bid you welcome, spirit of George Kulick. I charge and bind thee now, to answer what I ask of thee, to harm none present, and to depart when thou hast been dismissed. I do this in the terrible names of Baal, of Beelzebub, and of Asmodeus."

I once asked a warlock why spells contain all those "thee"s and "thou"s, and other stuff that nobody says anymore.

"When it comes to theory, no one is more conservative or fundamentalist as a magician," he'd told me. "It would make Southern Baptists look wild, by comparison. Lots of the spells in use today were first translated into English in the fifteenth and sixteenth centuries, when people *did* talk like that. The belief is, if a spell works, you don't mess with it, even to update the language. You'd never know what effect even the smallest change would have – until it was too late."

Rachel took some powder from a jar and sprinkled a generous amount into one of the bowls. It immediately burst into flame, even though the bowl was nowhere near the candles, or any other heat source. "Speak to me now, George Kulick. Give to me the sight of thy death, and of he who did bring it upon thee. Let me see as thou hast seen, know as thou hast known, and learn as thou didst learn. Grant unto me the Insight into thy departure from this life, George Kulick, that I might take vengeance against thy tormentor."

Things began happening very fast, then. The candles on the altar went out, all in the same instant. The incense stopped burning as if it had been doused with water. The small cloud of smoke that had borne the outline of a man dissipated into nothing.

Then Rachel Proctor collapsed to the ground. A few seconds later, she started writhing and screaming – screaming like one of the damned.

I stood outside Room 8 of Mercy Hospital's Intensive Care Unit and looked through the window at the still form on the bed. Rachel lay there, mercifully quiet, surrounded by machines that hummed and beeped as they kept track of every biological process of her body.

"At least she doesn't seem to be in pain now," I said to Charlie Mulderig, who's been a doctor at Mercy for as long as I can remember.

"No, she's not," Charlie said softly. "It wasn't easy. She's under very heavy sedation. For a while, I was afraid we were going to anesthetize her."

"You mean, like in surgery?"

"Exactly like in surgery. The pain centers of her brain were going crazy. And, apart from the humanitarian concerns, there was a real danger that she'd have a stroke if it continued."

"Jesus."

"Problem is," Charlie continued, "you can't keep someone under surgical anesthesia indefinitely without a substantial risk of brain damage. Fortunately, we found a combination of painkillers that worked, at least for the time being."

"What the fuck was causing it, Charlie? Far as I could tell before the EMTs got there, there wasn't a mark on her."

"There isn't a mark, in the sense you mean it. No evidence of trauma, anywhere on her body. And we found no evidence of anything internal that might have caused it, like a ruptured appendix or a kidney stone."

"It must have been the magic, then." I ran down for him what Rachel had been doing just before her collapse.

Charlie shook his head. "When it comes to magic, you're talking to the wrong guy. I don't pretend to understand that stuff. In fact, according to everything I learned in med school, magic ought to be impossible."

"Except that it isn't."

"No, I've seen too much evidence to the contrary."

"Yeah, me, too."

"I can imagine," he said. "Oh, yeah, that reminds me: I did find out something that may be of interest to you. As she was finally going under, Ms Proctor stopped screaming and started muttering intelligible words. Well, more or less intelligible."

Charlie produced a folded sheet of paper from a pocket of his white doctor coat. "One of the nurses wrote some of it down, after they'd got her stabilized."

He unfolded the sheet and peered at it over the top of his glasses. "Apparently, she was saying something like *I'll never tell you, you sick fuck. You'll never get the book, never.* I gather it went on like that for a while, repeating the same stuff, over and over."

He refolded the paper and handed it to me. "Here, for whatever use it is. I wonder who she thought she was talking to?"

After a few seconds I said, in a voice that I barely kept from breaking, "She was talking to whoever tortured and killed George Kulick."

• • • •

"The necromancy worked too fuckin' well," I told Karl the next night. "Not only did she raise the spirit of the late George Kulick, but he was able to get inside her head, somehow. That's gotta be what happened."

"I thought you said she'd set up protections against that stuff," Karl said.

"That's what she told me. But she'd never done one of these rituals before. Maybe she messed up somehow. If she did, it's my fault. I'm the stupid sonovabitch who pressured her into it."

"Or maybe Kulick was just stronger than she expected. The dude was a wizard, after all."

"Could be either one, could be both," I said. "She was trying to plug into Kulick's last moments, and it looks like she succeeded, big time. All of a sudden, she was right where Kulick had been, at the end."

"And Kulick was being tortured. Which means that Rachel–"

"Was going through the same thing – at a nerve level, anyway. Not so much as a bruise on her, but she still felt all the stuff that had been done to Kulick. I didn't think even magic could do that."

"Why not?" Karl said. "They do it with hypnosis."

I looked at him. "What the hell are you talking about?"

"My cousin Cheryl's a therapist. You know, like a shrink. I guess she uses hypnotism in her job. Helping people recover memories, stuff like that. She told me once that when she was in school, they had 'em watch movies of some of the experiments in hypnosis. From like thirty years ago. Stuff that you couldn't get away with today. One guy in this film was put into a real deep trance, right? Then the hypnotist told him he was on fire."

"Bet I can guess what happened then," I said.

"Fuckin' A. Cheryl said the guy was on the floor, screaming like he was being burned alive."

"Just like Rachel, who thought she was being tortured to death."

"Cheryl said it took days to get that guy's screams out of her head."

"I've got a feeling," I said, "that it's gonna take me a hell of a lot longer than that."

"It's Charlie Mulderig, Stan. I'm calling about Rachel Proctor."

"Hey, Charlie. How is she?"

There was a brief silence, then: "She's gone, Stan."

I felt an icy fist reach into my stomach, grab my guts, and twist them.

"Stan? Are you there? Stan?"

"Yeah, Charlie, I'm here." I cleared my throat, then did it again. "What happened? Heart failure?"

"No, Stan, I'm sorry for... Rachel isn't dead, as far as I know. She's just – *gone*. Missing. Her bed in the ICU is empty."

The icy fist loosened its grip, but only a little. "Did she regain consciousness, Charlie?"

"Not according to the nurses, and they were checking on her every hour or so. And if something had gone bad at any time – irregular heartbeat, sudden drop in blood pressure, something like that, the alarms built into the monitors would have gone off at the nurses' station. Those were still functioning, by the way. We checked."

"Could some nurse have missed something? Maybe forgot one of the hourly checks?"

"No way, no how. The ICU nurses are the best in the

hospital, Stan. They do not fuck up, and that would constitute a *major* fuck-up."

I closed my eyes and tried to make my miserable excuse for a brain work. "You've got surveillance cameras over there, Charlie. I've seen 'em."

"Yeah, we do, and I know what you're thinking. There's one trained on the hallway right outside the ICU. Our security guy is reviewing the disc now."

"There's no other way out of there, except for the windows, is there? And the ICU's on the fifth floor."

"Exactly. However she left, conscious or not, on a gurney, in a wheelchair, or walking, she had to go along that corridor. We'll find her – well, find her image, anyway."

"Give me a call when you do."

I put down the phone and sat at my desk, staring at nothing. I was thinking about magic – and about disappearing acts.

I didn't hear back from Charlie until the next night. He called right after I came on shift.

"So, how did she leave the ICU, Charlie? Was it under her own power, or was she taken?"

There was a long pause before Charlie said, "We'd like to discuss that with you face-to-face, Stan. Can you drop by Mercy sometime tonight?"

"Who's *we*?"

"The head of security. And me."

"All right, Charlie, I'll come over now, if the boss doesn't need me. But give me the short version now – how did she get out of there?"

"There actually isn't a short version, Stan. That's why we'd like to discuss this with you in person."

Arguing with him was just going to waste time I could

better spend driving to Mercy Hospital. "I'll be there in twenty minutes," I said. I asked Karl to stay at the squad and call me if anything urgent came in. Then I got moving.

The head of security at Mercy was an ex-cop named Sam Rostock. He'd let himself go to seed after leaving the force, to the point where his belly now hung over the belt of his Wal-Mart grade slacks – but I guess muscle tone isn't too important when your toughest job is getting people to leave the hospital after visiting hours are over.

I sat down after the introductions – which were unnecessary, but Charlie didn't know that. I was looking at Rostock but speaking to Charlie when I said, "So what was so important that you couldn't tell me about it over the phone?"

"I checked the video feed from the camera that's aimed at that hallway," Rostock said. "The one outside the ICU. Checked it twice, for the period when what's-her-name, Proctor, was brought in until an hour after she was declared missing."

I expected more, but Rostock stopped talking and just sat there, looking at me. It was impossible to read his face – he'd been a cop, after all.

"There's nothing, Stan," Charlie said finally. "No indication that she left the ICU, either under her own power or with assistance. Nothing."

"I don't suppose that a body was wheeled out of there, in a body bag or under a sheet, maybe," I said. "Or somebody in a wheelchair who'd suffered bad facial burns and was heavily bandaged – anything like that?"

"Of course I checked stuff like that – you think I'm *stupid*?" Rostock said. "And it wasn't hard to do, because not one patient, living or dead, was taken out of the ICU during that period. Not *one*."

I ran my hand through what was left of my hair a couple of times. "What about visitors? Did you check to see whether one more visitor left there than went in?"

"My God, I never would have thought of that," Charlie said, softly.

"Well, I did," Rostock said, but without the defensiveness in his voice. "Same time period – an hour before she was admitted, in case somebody was already in there, visiting in another room, to an hour after she was found gone. Every damn visitor that went in there is accounted for. And this is spring, so nobody's wearing hats or scarves that could hide their face. The ones who came in, went out. And only them."

"Except for the nurses and doctors," I said.

"Not bad," Rostock said, as if he meant it, "but I thought of them, too. Every doctor, nurse, and med tech working here is somebody I've met personally. I make a point of that. Plus, each one has a photo on file with Human Resources, the same picture that's on their ID badge. And with the computer system we have, I was able to do close-ups on the faces of everybody who passed through that door, in either direction. Nothing suspicious. Nothing even close."

The three of us sat there for a while. "Okay, then," I said, finally. "Let me summarize the facts, such as they are." I ticked them off on my fingers as I went along.

"One, Rachel Proctor was brought into the ICU, from the ER, at 4:18am two days ago. Two, Rachel Proctor did not leave the ICU through its only door, and getting away through the fifth-floor window is only gonna work if you're a bird. And three, Rachel Proctor is undeniably gone."

I looked at each of them. "Accurate?"

Their silence said it all.

"So, what happened was impossible, except that it did," I went on. "And there's only one thing that makes the impossible happen, these days – and that's magic."

"Why would Rachel use magic to make herself disappear?" Karl asked me. "If she wanted to leave the hospital, all she had to say was, *Okay, I'm all better – release me*."

"Yeah, it makes no sense. Unless she wanted to disappear from sight for a while, you know, hide from somebody. Or something."

"Hide from who?"

"Maybe from me. Can't blame her for that – I'm the asshole who got her into this mess, whatever it is."

"Don't start with that again, all right? The chick's all grown up, and everything. She knew what she was getting involved in – probably better than you did. And nobody held a gun to her head that I know of. Or a wand."

"I know, but – *what did you say?*"

Karl looked at me. "Just that nobody forced her to–"

"No, about a wand."

He shrugged. "I said *wand* cause it seemed more, like, appropriate for a witch, that's all. What's the big deal?"

"I don't know how big a deal it is," I told him. "But you just reminded me that Rachel's not the only one in this case who can work magic."

Karl frowned. "What are you talking about, man? Who else in this mess can...?" He let his voice trail off and his eyes went wide.

"Exactly," I said. "George fucking Kulick, that's who."

I started to explain to Karl the idea that had just occurred to me – but then the old man came to see us, and
that changed everything.

Louise the Tease, our PA, came back to tell us that we
had a visitor. We call her that (not to her face) because
her size 8 body is usually crammed into a size 6 dress,
but she refuses to date cops – something about not wanting to take her work home with her. Louise said that
someone up front was asking for whoever was working
the Kulick murder.

Karl and I looked at each other, then did a quick game of
paper-rock-scissors. His paper wrapped my rock, so I stood
up and headed for the small reception area. On the way, I
had a brief fantasy that George Kulick's killer had walked
in to confess, and we'd be able to close this case out tonight.

Yeah, and a goblin will be the next pope.

Whoever had the steel in his spine to do all those
things to Kulick wasn't going to get all mushy and re-
morseful about it now. I just hoped that whoever *had*
come in wasn't going to be a waste of time.

It turned out to be an old guy, thin and pale, but not
frail looking. His iron gray hair was combed straight back
to form a widow's peak. The gray suit had probably been
new during the Kennedy administration, and the white
button-down shirt underneath it had been washed so
often that it was closer to beige. He wore it buttoned to
the neck, with no tie.

"I'm Detective Sergeant Markowski," I said. "I understand you have some information about a case we're
investigating."

The old guy got to his feet smoothly. He had none
of the shakiness about him that you'd expect from

somebody who looked to be in his seventies. That got me wondering.

"My name is Ernst Vollman," he said, his voice firm and clear. "If you refer to the murder of George Kulick, yes, I thought some conversation on the subject might be mutually beneficial."

Mutually beneficial wasn't exactly what I had in mind, but I let it slide. Instead, as Vollman came closer, I put out my hand to shake.

I don't usually do that with civilians – whether they're suspects, witnesses, or informants. I like to maintain a certain distance with the public, but this time I made an exception. It seemed like he might have hesitated for a moment, but then Vollman took my hand and shook it briefly.

I noticed two things about that handshake. One was a sense of strength you wouldn't expect in an old guy. He didn't go all macho on me and try to squeeze, none of that bullshit. But suddenly I was aware that if he put his mind to it, he could break every bone in my hand without raising a sweat.

The other thing was, his hand was cold. I know that old folks sometimes have circulation problems in their extremities, but this went way beyond that. This guy was *cold*.

That's when I knew for sure.

I gestured toward the squad room and followed Vollman toward the door, working hard to keep my face blank. Ernst Vollman represented something that Karl and I didn't have five minutes ago: a lead. So I was going to be very nice to this old man, for the time being. Even if he was a fucking vampire.

I told Vollman to sit in the visitor's chair next to my desk, and then Karl rolled his own chair over, placing it so that our visitor couldn't look at both of us at once. It's an old cop trick designed to keep suspects off balance.

The old man didn't seem fazed by the seating arrangements. When I introduced Karl, Vollman looked at him for a long moment, as if planning to draw him from memory later. Or maybe have him for lunch. Then he turned his attention back to me.

"I have been away from the city for several days," he said, "and only learned of Mr Kulick's tragic death upon my return last night."

"Return from where?" Karl asked.

"Oh, a number of places," Vollman said. "I travel a great deal, you see. To visit friends, relatives, old acquaintances. Sometimes they ask me for advice, or a favor, or to settle some small dispute."

"So this isn't your job, then – travelling around," Karl said.

"Not at all. I am long since retired. But I like to occupy my time usefully, when I can."

"Where did you retire from, Mr Vollman?" I thought I'd join the conversation.

Vollman made a small gesture. "I have done a great many things to support myself, over the years. Mostly, I have been self-employed."

"Self-employed doing *what*?" Karl asked him. He was starting to get impatient with the old man's bullshit, and I didn't blame him.

"Consulting, mostly. Some investments. Occasionally, import-export." Vollman's smile was as thin as the rest of him. He knew he was ducking our questions, and he knew we knew it, too. He also knew we couldn't do shit about it. For the moment, anyway.

I decided to cut through the crap and see if there was

anything underneath it. "What do you know about George Kulick's murder, Mr Vollman?"

"I do not know who killed him, if that is what you are asking. But I believe I know something almost as important."

Vollman paused, probably for effect. "I am fairly certain I know *why* he was killed."

There was a silence that lasted several seconds before I broke it. "If you're waiting for someone to feed you the next line, I'll do the honors: why was Kulick killed?"

Vollman gave me another one of those little smiles. "I do have rather a tendency toward the dramatic, don't I? Please accept my apologies." He made the smile disappear. "I believe Mr Kulick was murdered because he was the possessor, in effect the guardian, of a certain object. An object of great value."

Karl leaned forward, frowning. "The killer left something like forty grand behind. Even if what he came for was worth more than that, why not take the cash, too?" It was a question the two of us had been scratching our heads over ever since we saw what was in Kulick's safe. Who walks away from forty thousand bucks?

Vollman gave Karl the kind of look that village idiots must get really tired of. "The answer, I would think, is obvious, Detective. Kulick's killer had no interest in money." He shook his head a couple of times. "There is more than one measure of value, my young friend."

"The object, as you call it, must've had something to do with magic, then, since Kulick was a wizard," I said to Vollman.

"Yes, that is quite true."

"So, what's it to you?"

The wrinkles around Vollman's eyes compressed a little. "I do not understand your meaning, Sergeant."

"I mean, since when is the business of wizards of any interest to a vampire?"

Vollman sat slowly back in his chair and looked at me.

I've got good peripheral vision, and from the corner of my eye I could see Karl's hand move slowly toward the top drawer of his desk, and the crucifix he kept there. He needn't have bothered. Any vamp who wanted to cause trouble wouldn't pick a police station, especially the Supe Squad, to do it.

Probably.

Still, I was suddenly aware of the weight of the Beretta on my right hip, with its standard load of eight silver bullets that had been blessed by the Bishop of Scranton. Part of me wished the old vamp would give me an excuse to use it.

"The handshake, yes?" Vollman said to me, after a moment. "It was the handshake that revealed my... true nature... to you. I wondered at your reason, since you do not, forgive me, Detective Sergeant, strike me as the friendly type."

Friendly? I wanted to say. *Hey, I'm one of the friendliest guys around – except to the bloodsucking undead.*

"How I know doesn't matter, Mr Vollman," I told him. "I asked you a question: why do you care about George Kulick and what happened to him?"

Another long look. I was about to tell Vollman that I was getting tired of his theatrics when he said, "The reason I am interested in the fate of that particular wizard..." He turned his left hand over, palm up, to reveal an old, faded, but unmistakable tattoo of a pentagram. "...is because I am a wizard myself."

• • • •

Karl and I looked at each other for several seconds before we returned our attention to Vollman.

"I've never met anyone with your particular... combination of attributes before," I said.

"Nor have I, and I have lived far longer than either of you gentlemen. However, there is nothing, in theory, to prevent someone from living in both worlds, should he choose to. Mind you, in my case the choice was not made freely."

"How do you mean?" Karl asked.

Vollman shrugged his thin shoulders. "It is a long story, but, in brief, I was already an accomplished wizard when I was attacked and... transformed... by a vampire. That was in the year 1512."

I noticed that Karl was frowning. "I don't get it," he said. "Somebody who can work magic should have been able to handle a vampire without too much trouble."

"Magic is not something that can be invoked at a moment's notice," Vollman told him. "Had I been given the time to prepare a defensive spell, I would surely have prevailed. But I had no inkling that a vampire was in the vicinity, and so was caught unawares."

"Which also explains how Kulick was subdued by whoever tortured him," I said. "He didn't have a spell, or whatever, ready to use against his attacker."

"Very likely," Vollman said, nodding. "Unlike a gun or a knife, magic cannot usually be brought to bear at a moment's notice. Although, given time for preparation, it can be a very potent weapon, indeed."

"You said Kulick was taking care of some valuable object," I said. "I assume that's what was ripped off from his safe by whoever killed him. Care to tell us what it was?"

Vollman looked at his hands for a long moment. "I suppose I must, since it is of vital importance that it be

recovered. George Kulick was entrusted with a copy of
the *Opus Mago-Cabbilisticum et Theosophicum*, written by
Georg von Welling around 1735 – although parts of it
are older. Far older."

"Don't think I know that one," I said. "But I've got a
feeling that it isn't this month's selection from the Book
of the Month Club."

"The work is not well known, even among the
cognoscenti," Vollman said. "The *Opus Mago*, as it is usually called, is quite rare. Only four copies are believed
still in existence. It is – and I beg your indulgence of the
cliché – a book of forbidden knowledge."

"I get it," Karl said. "Like the *Necronomicon*."

Vollman looked at him. "The *Necronomicon* is a myth,
a product of the fevered brain of that writer Lovecraft,"
he said scornfully.

Karl shrugged. "Some people say different."

"And some people," Vollman said, "once said the Earth
is flat. Indeed, I knew several such individuals personally." He made a shooing away gesture with one hand.
"But whether this *Necronomicon* exists is irrelevant. The
Opus Mago, I assure you, is all too real."

"What's in it that makes the book forbidden?" I asked him.

"Spells, of course, along with descriptions of rituals,
conjurations, directions for the making of certain imple-
ments and ingredients. Also, illustrations of certain...
symbols."

"So far, that sounds like a description of something that
every practitioner has on his bookshelf," I said. "Or hers."

Vollman nodded slowly. "In a general sense, perhaps.
But the particular rituals and spells contained in the *Opus
Mago* are used for the invocation and control of only the
darkest powers. It is said that portions of the book were

dictated by Satan himself, but that is probably a myth."
He stopped, and stared at his hands for a moment. "Yes,
a myth, almost certainly. In any case, this material is
something no workaday wizard or witch would have access to. Nor is it anything they would wish to acquire."

"You talking about calling up demons?" Karl asked.
"Hell, we ran into one of them a couple, two, three months
ago. No big deal."

I wouldn't call almost having my head chewed off "no
big deal", but I knew what Karl meant. Any number of
wizards already had the knowledge necessary to conjure
demons. Fortunately, most of them were smart enough
not to do it.

"No, the power of the *Opus Mago* goes far beyond that,"
Vollman said. "It is a great and terrible book. I have not
looked within it myself, mind you. But I was present
when it was given to Kulick for safekeeping."

"Why?" I asked him.

Vollman frowned. "*Why*? What do you mean?"

"The way you put that suggests that you didn't give
the book to Kulick, but you observed the transfer take
place. Why were you there, if you weren't the guy handing over the book?"

Vollman gave one of those little gestures that you associate with Mafia dons in the movies. It combined
modesty and arrogance in exactly the right proportions.
"There is, in this area, a loose confederation of those who
are what you call 'supernaturals.' I have the honor to be
its leader."

Karl and I looked at each other for a second, then
turned toward Vollman.

"So it's you," Karl said.

Vollman gave us raised eyebrows.

"We'd heard that someone took over after Martin Thackery got staked," I told him. "But none of the supes we know would give us a name. You're the new *boyar*, the Man."

"As good a term as any, I suppose," Vollman said, nodding.

"Well then, Mr *Man*," Karl said, "why don't you tell us who you think killed George Kulick, before my partner and me are too old to do anything about it?" Sometimes I really like that kid.

But I didn't much like what Vollman told us next. "I have absolutely no idea," he said.

So much for our hopes of clearing this case quickly. There was silence while Karl and I digested the bad news, then I said to Vollman, "But you must have some idea about the *kind* of person who did it."

"I might," Vollman said. "But then I expect you have already reached some conclusions of your own."

My chair creaked as I leaned forward. "Whoever did Kulick that way has got a strong stomach and good nerves," I said. "He didn't lose control, like they sometimes do. He just kept doing stuff to Kulick until the poor bastard broke and told him where the safe was. Gave up the combination, too. He must've, since the safe wasn't punched, peeled, or blown."

"Kulick was tough, you gotta give him that," Karl said. "He took a hell of a lot of punishment before he finally gave it up."

"He had sworn an oath," Vollman said stiffly. "He was chosen to safeguard the book because he was the kind of man who takes such oaths seriously."

"Don't be too hard on him," I said. "He suffered for that oath, in ways you can't even imagine."

Vollman gave me a bleak look. "Do not underestimate what my imagination is capable of, Sergeant." He gave a long sigh. "But you are right. Kulick's memory will be honored for what he did – or tried to do."

"Still, the average criminal, no matter how motivated, hasn't got the gumption to carry out that kind of systematic torture," I said. "This is somebody with a real vicious streak. And then there's the business with the money."

"The money that was left in the safe, you mean," Vollman said.

"Right. Even if all he wanted was the book, the killer could have taken the money, anyway. If he had, we'd be assuming a simple robbery as the motive, and the Major Crimes guys would be investigating it. Which means the perp is either dumb, or arrogant beyond belief – doesn't give a shit what we know, or think."

"The individual who committed these acts is certainly not stupid, Sergeant," Vollman said. "But unbridled arrogance is not only possible – it is virtually certain in this instance. Making use of the spells contained in the *Opus Mago* would be similar to what a friend of mine once said about studying the work of the philosopher Hegel: one must be highly intelligent in order to do such, and profoundly stupid to wish to."

Karl started to say something, but he was interrupted by a commotion from the reception area. I stood up, went to the door of the squad room, and looked out.

Four people, three men and a woman, were standing at the P.A.'s desk, all of them screaming at Louise the Tease. From what I could gather, one of their tribe had been busted earlier in the evening, and they'd all come down to demand his release, on the grounds that he was king of the gypsies. It's the same crap they usually pull when one of their own gets picked up. Everybody's the king of the gypsies, unless it's a woman who's been arrested. She gets to be queen.

Louise the Tease is known not to take no shit from nobody, but she was outnumbered, and nobody can kick up a fuss like a Gypsy. I was about to head over there and give her a hand when I realized that Vollman was standing just over my right shoulder. "Permit me," he said quietly.

I moved aside, and he stood in the doorway, where I'd been. I expected him to go into Reception and approach the P.A.'s desk, but he stood where he was.

"*Chavaia!*"

The gypsies must have understood the word, because they all turned toward Vollman, looking both startled and annoyed. Then they saw who it was, and the annoyance vanished like a coin in a conjuring trick. Both their voices and expressions became very still.

"*Dinili, te maren, denash! Te khalion tai te shingerdjon che gada par brajo ents chai plamendi!*"

Vollman didn't yell, but it didn't look like they had any trouble hearing him. "*Te lolirav phuv mure ratesa. Arctu viriumca ba treno al qua pashasha. Mucav!*"

Without another word, the four gypsies turned and left the room. They didn't quite run.

Vollman nodded once, then turned and returned to his seat. I followed.

Karl stared at the old man. "What the hell did you say to them?"

Vollman produced the thin smile again. "I merely suggested they stop bothering the young lady and take their concerns elsewhere. Without delay."

"I notice they didn't give you an argument," I said.

Vollman shrugged. "For some of these people, I am, as you say, the Man."

"So, what kind of person would want this book, the *Opus Mago*, bad enough to torture and kill for it?" I asked Vollman. "We're talking about a wizard or witch for starters, right?"

"Almost certainly," he said. "No one else would have any hope of being able to make use of it."

"You said something about 'arrogant' before," I added.

"Indeed, yes," Vollman said. "As I told you, the *Opus Mago* contains spells and rituals for invoking the darkest of dark powers. It is considered a book of forbidden knowledge, and closely guarded, for that reason."

"So where's the arrogance come in?" Karl asked.

"In the belief that anyone, regardless of training or experience, can hope to control such powers once they have been summoned," Vollman said.

"You're saying nobody could do it," Karl said.

Vollman shook his head slowly. "I will not say that, not with certainty. But I think it highly unlikely that such control, even if it were achieved, could be maintained for long."

"Maybe we ought to stop pussyfooting around this with terms like 'dark powers' and all that," I said. "You're not talking about just conjuring up some demon, are you?"

"No," Vollman said. "As your partner reminded us earlier, that has become almost a mundane practice in these times."

"What then?" I was afraid that I already knew the answer.

And I was right, I did. "Something very, very bad," Vollman said. "There are a variety of spells, invocations, and rituals contained within the *Opus Mago*. Each, it is believed, permits access to a spiritual entity of immense power and great malevolence. One, supposedly, contains the means for calling up Quetzalcoatl, the Aztec snake god, which has grown immensely powerful from the all blood sacrifices made to it over centuries."

"But all that human sacrifice stuff ended hundreds of years ago, once the Spaniards took over," I said.

Vollman looked at me and shrugged. "If you choose to believe so."

"What else?" Karl asked. "There's got to be more than that."

"Indeed there is, Detective," Vollman told him. "For example, there are those who say the book describes a ritual for awakening one or more of the Great Old Ones, those creatures that supposedly existed before man, and which still await the day when they may supplant him."

"Now I know you're yanking our chains," I said. "That stuff's right out of Lovecraft, and you already said he made it all up."

Vollman shook his head. "No, Sergeant, I only said that Lovecraft made up the *Necronomicon*. The veracity of his other material is… open to dispute, shall we say. Some maintain that he discovered things that man was not meant to know, and it was that knowledge which eventually drove him mad."

"You keep saying things like 'there are those who say,' and 'it is believed,'" I said. "So, you haven't looked at the book yourself."

"No, I have not, nor did I ever wish to," Vollman said. "But I have, over the years, talked to several people who did." He gave me the thin smile again. "They were the ones who survived the experience, with their sanity intact, of course."

"So, all right," Karl said. "This *Opus Mago* is a recipe book for cooking up different kinds of Truly Bad Shit. And it's been stolen by somebody who plans to whip up a big, smelly batch of it."

"Inelegantly put, Detective," Vollman said with a nod, "but an admirably succinct summary, nonetheless."

"Big question is," I said, "how are we going to know when he makes the attempt?"

Vollman's thin face, which would never be used to illustrate "cheerful" in the dictionary, became even more solemn. "You will know, Sergeant," he said. "Have no concerns on that account. You will know."

The first of the murders occurred four nights later, and we almost missed it.

The case could easily have been written off as a routine homicide. It would have been, too, if Hugh Scanlon hadn't given me a call.

Turned out, it was the right thing to do. This homicide was anything but routine.

A lot of "regular" detectives don't like the Supe Squad very much – I think they take that "when you look into the abyss, the abyss also looks into you" stuff too seriously. But Scanlon's all right. I knew him from when we were both in Homicide. I eventually moved on to Supernatural Crimes for reasons of my own, but Scanlon kept working murders, and he's a Detective First now.

The crime scene was the alley behind *Tim Riley's Bar and Grill*, and by the time Karl and I showed up, the routine was well under way. Nudging some rubbernecking civilians aside, I lifted the yellow crime scene tape so

Karl could duck under it. Then I followed him down the alley, the smell of rotting garbage strong enough to gag a sewer rat.

We made our way through the usual collection of the M.E.'s people, forensics techs, uniformed cops, and Homicide dicks, all of them busy or trying to look that way. Mostly they ignored us, apart from one or two hostile glances. But eventually Scanlon spotted us and came over.

"Vic's a white male, around thirty, throat cut, bled out where we found him," he said. Scanlon's never been known to use two words when he can get by with one.

"So why call us?" I asked him. "Sounds like a bar fight that moved out here, then went bad."

"I thought so, too," Scanlon said. "Then I saw something. Come on."

He led us over to where some forensics guy was taking photos of the body, his strobe flashing in the semi-darkness.

"You about done?" Scanlon asked him.

The guy looked up and realized he wasn't being asked a question. "Yeah, sure, all finished," he said, and backed off.

Scanlon produced a pencil flashlight and clicked it on. The beam lingered for a moment on the throat wound that looked like a sardonic grin, then moved up to the victim's face. The dead guy had a thick head of brown hair, and some of it was combed down over his forehead. With his free hand, encased in a latex glove, Scanlon lifted the hair away so that we could see the victim's forehead clearly, and then I understood why we'd been called.

Three symbols I'd never seen before were carved into the victim's forehead – one over the left temple, another over the right one, and a third square in the middle.

The man in the alley wasn't just a murder victim.

He was a sacrifice.

Inside the bar, Karl made the rounds of the customers while I had a word with the bartender, a pretty brunette in her mid-twenties whose nametag read "Andrea." She wore black pants on her slim hips, and a matching shirt, the cuffs folded back a couple of turns to leave her forearms bare.

I described the vic for her and asked if she remembered serving him.

"Yeah, sure. He was the double Scotch and water. Sat over there" – Andrea gestured to the right with her chin – "third stool from the end."

"Notice anything unusual about him?"

She glanced back toward the spot where the vic had been sitting, as if it helped her remember. "Well, he wasn't exactly killing that Scotch. When I figured out he wasn't coming back, I cleared the space. Glass was still full – he hadn't touched a drop."

Why would somebody come into a bar, order booze, then not have any? Unless he came to do something besides drink.

"He didn't stiff you, did he?"

"Hell, no. He paid when I served him, just like he was supposed to. It's either that or run a tab, but I'm only supposed to run tabs for regulars." Andrea leaned closer and lowered her voice a little. "Listen, um, the guy paid with a twenty, and left his change on the bar. I didn't touch it until I was taking the glass away. By then, I figured he was either absentminded, or a hell of a good tipper. What should I, you know...?"

"Might as well treat it like a tip and keep it," I said. "Let the guy's last act on earth be something good, even if he didn't intend it that way."

"I like the way you think," she said. "Thanks."

She straightened up, restoring the distance between us.

"Do you remember him talking to anybody?" I asked her.

"Uh-uh. He sat by himself, and I didn't see anybody come over. Only time I heard him talk was when he ordered the Scotch." She frowned. "Wait – his phone went off, once. I remember, cause the ringtone was this old Blue Oyster Cult song that I like."

"'Don't Fear the Reaper'?"

"Yeah, that's it. How'd you know?"

"Lucky guess," I said. "So he got a phone call. Did you hear any of the conversation?"

"Nah, I had customers further down. Anyway, I don't eavesdrop. I just went down his way cause I needed some ice." I saw her eyes narrow.

"What?"

"Nothing, I guess. But it wasn't long after the call that I noticed his chair was empty. At first, I just figured he went to the john."

I glanced down and saw that the inside of her right arm was covered with thin scars running in all directions. I looked up before Andrea caught me staring.

So she was a cutter. She fit the profile – it's almost always young women who feel the need to wound themselves in that particular way, over and over. Some of them do it so they can stop feeling whatever's gnawing at them. Others do it in the hope of feeling something, anything at all.

I thanked her for the information and got up from the bar stool. Mentioning the scars wasn't going to do anything except embarrass Andrea. I wanted to think that she'd gotten help someplace and put it all behind her, but I knew better. A couple of those cuts were as fresh as yesterday's tears.

We've all got our demons. And most of them can't be exorcised with a razor blade – even for a little while.

Karl and I walked back to our car, which we'd had to park half a block away. The bars were closed now, and the streets had grown quiet. Some tendrils of fog from the Lackawanna River were wrapping themselves around the trees and lamp posts.

"Since I came up with zip from the customers, that phone call of yours is about the only lead we've got, unless forensics finds something," Karl said.

"The CSI guys? Hell, they'll probably crack the case tomorrow. Don't you watch TV?"

"Well, just in case they don't, I hope one of the phone companies will tell us who called the vic tonight."

"That would be nice," I said. "Not as good as the perp confessing on the front page of the *Times-Tribune* tomorrow, but still not bad."

"Is your buddy gonna send us a copy of the autopsy report?"

"Yeah, along with the crime scene pictures, for all the good they'll do."

"It was no bar fight, that's for sure," Karl said. "Hell, I knew that, soon as I got a look at the vic's wound."

"How do you mean?"

"Guy's throat was sliced, haina?" Karl said.

"Yeah, so?"

"So in any kind of a fight, guy uses a knife, you're gonna have stab wounds as the COD. Maybe some defensive cuts around the hands and arms, but the real damage comes from punctures." Karl kicked an empty soda can and sent it clanging into the gutter. "This was no fight, this was pre-fucking-meditated murder."

"Could've been a mugging," I said. "Guy comes up behind the vic, knife to his throat, says, 'Give it up, motherfucker.' The vic struggles, maybe gets in a good kick backward or something. Then the perp panics, bears down too hard with the blade, the vic tries to pull away, and it's good night, sweet prince."

"Yeah. But," Karl said.

"'But' is right. We've got that artwork carved into his forehead."

"You ever come across anything like those–" Karl stopped talking suddenly, and a moment later I realized why.

Somebody was leaning against our car.

The man was just a lean silhouette, until he turned his head a little and let the streetlight's glare fall on his face.

It was Vollman.

"You were summoned tonight to the scene of a crime," Vollman said. "A murder, in fact."

"How the hell did you know that?" Karl asked him.

Vollman gave one of his narrow smiles. "I have my resources," he said. "Perhaps, in this instance, something as mundane as a scanner that picks up police radio broadcasts."

"You seem to know why we're here, Vollman," I said. "But that doesn't explain why *you* are."

"I assume the murder had one or more... *occult*... elements, or you gentlemen would not have been called to view the aftermath," Vollman said.

"Yeah. So?" I took a long breath, made myself a little calmer. Vollman was a fucking bloodsucker, but for the moment, we needed him. The minute we didn't...

"May I ask what those elements were?" He was a polite leech, I'll give him that.

I took another one of those long breaths, then looked at Karl, who shrugged, "Why not?"

"The victim had some esoteric symbols carved into his forehead," I said. "Three of them. Could be occult-related, although they don't fit in with any system of magic that I ever heard of."

Even in the half-light, with the fog getting thicker, I could see something cross Vollman's lean face. I wondered what it was. After a long pause he asked, "Can you describe them?"

"I can do better than that," I said, reaching for my notebook. "I drew them."

I showed Vollman my version of the marks from the victim's brow. He looked at them as if he was trying to burn the images into his memory.

"These drawings are accurate?" he asked.

"Pretty close," I said. "I should have photos to check them against in a day or two, if it matters. There wasn't enough light to use my phone camera."

"You recognize them?" Karl asked.

"Not precisely, no," Vollman said, without taking his eyes off the paper. "They are very old in origin, I think. Sumerian, or possibly Babylonian. I have some books that I can consult."

"And if you find something, you're going to let us know, right? Since we've been so open with you about this case and everything," I said.

"Of course," Vollman said. "But in the meantime, Sergeant, may I offer a suggestion?"

As if I could fucking stop you. "What?"

"Ask whoever conducts the autopsy to look closely at the throat wound, with special attention to any trace elements that may be found there. It is very important,

I think, to know exactly what was used to inflict the fatal cut."

"What was *used*?" Karl said. "Shit, that oughta be obvious. It was a knife, and a damn sharp one, too. Or a straight razor, maybe."

Vollman nodded. "I expect you are correct, Detective. But a crucial point is the material that the blade was made of."

"Why's that so important?" I asked him.

"The answer to that depends on what you find out," Vollman said with another one of his toothless smiles. Didn't want to display his fangs, I guess.

The smile didn't last long. "I will be, as you say, in touch."

Vollman took a couple of steps back, the fog and darkness making his form indistinct.

"I need you to do better than–" I began, then stopped. "Vollman? Vollman!"

He was gone, the stagy old bastard.

Karl summarized my feelings very well. "Fucking vamps," he said.

The autopsy report only took twenty-four hours or so, which was almost as big a miracle as the one that followed "Lazarus, come forth!" It informed us that the victim died of "exsanguination following a single deep, narrow laceration that severed carotid artery, windpipe, and jugular vein, with aspirated blood as a contributing factor."

In other words, somebody cut the guy's throat, and he bled out and died, inhaling some of his own blood in the process. Big surprise.

The tissue analysis of the wound area took another couple of days. Would've been longer, but the Homicide guys had put pressure on the lab. Good thing, too, or we might have had to wait a week or more for the results. Nobody rushes stuff for the Supe Squad.

Homicide was treating this as their case. For the time being, we were letting them think it was. But we still got copies of all the paperwork. Scanlon saw to that.

"Silver?" Lieutenant McGuire stared at the top sheet of the lab report I'd just dropped on his desk. "They're sure?"

"Sure as the lab is likely to be," I said. In the chair beside me, I heard Karl give a quiet snort of laughter. He was probably thinking about some of the notable fuck-ups the lab had made in the past.

"I could have a sample sent to the FBI in Washington," I said, with a straight face. "They've got better facilities, as they're always reminding us."

"Sure," McGuire said. "And the results might even come back before I collect my pension. But I doubt it."

He was right. When it comes to requests from local law enforcement, the FBI lab could make a glacier look speedy.

"You didn't get to the good part yet," I told McGuire. "Keep reading."

He gave me a look, then returned to the lab report. McGuire's a fast reader, and I wondered how long it would take him to get to the punch line.

One Mississippi, two Mississippi, three Mississippi, four–

"A *vamp*? The vic's a fucking *vampire*?"

I was about to say something stupid like "Yeah, where do we send the medal?" when Karl piped up with, "Must be, boss. It's pretty hard to fuck that up, once you know what to look for. There's, I think, nine different tests they can do."

We both looked at him. He shrugged and said, "I read a lot, okay?"

McGuire sat back in his chair, frowning. "Why would somebody use a silver-coated knife to off a vampire? There's plenty of easier ways to do it."

"Beats the shit out of me," I said. "But Vollman thought we might find something interesting in the wound. That's why I requested the tissue analysis."

"Who's Vollman?" McGuire asked. "Oh, right – your informant, I remember now. Maybe you better ask Mr Vollman why he thought the laceration would have unusual material in it."

"I'd love to," I told him. "But I don't know how to contact the bloodsucker."

McGuire raised his eyebrows at that, then lowered them in a first-class glare that included both Karl and me.

"The old bastard wouldn't give us his contact information," Karl said. "Said he'd get in touch with us, instead."

McGuire shook his head in disgust. "Then you two clowns had damn well better hope–"

"Excuse me, Lieutenant?" Louise the Tease had appeared in McGuire's door. "I'm sorry to interrupt, but there's a man here to see the detectives." Louise looked at me. "It's the one who was here before – Vollman."

I thought that kind of timing only happens on TV, but maybe Karl and I were having a change in our luck. And about time, too.

We excused ourselves and got out of his office before the lieutenant could finish cutting each of us a brand new asshole.

"Silver," Vollman said thoughtfully, after I'd told him about the lab report. "I thought it might be some such."

"And you thought that *why*, exactly?" I asked.

"Has the knife itself been found?" Vollman asked, instead of answering my question.

"Not so far," Karl told him. "Homicide had uniforms searching a five-block radius. They checked all the usual places where somebody would dump something – sewer grates, dumpsters, trash cans, like that. *Nada*."

"Look," I said. "We both know you don't need a silver-plated knife to kill a vampire, although it seems to do the job pretty well. So the silver must have some other purpose."

"A ritualistic purpose. Gotta be," Karl said.

"And you knew it," I said. "That's why you told us to check for foreign substances in the wound. I want to know what you know about this, Vollman."

The vampire/wizard looked at his hands for a long moment. They had long, thin fingers and the skin was free of the brown spots you associate with old folks. Guess vamps don't have liver problems. And for them, sun damage is never an issue – except when it's terminal.

"I know little," he said finally. "But I suspect much, and fear even more."

I slammed my open hand down on my desk. "Why don't you cut out the cryptic bullshit and tell us something straight out, just for a change?"

Vollman raised his head and looked at me. He didn't seem to change expression, but I was suddenly very aware that I was sitting opposite a five hundred year-old monster who's probably killed more people than I've had meals.

But I've faced down creatures as scary as Vollman before. I didn't blink or look away. I wasn't afraid of him – or so I told myself.

The old man held my gaze, then nodded, as if he had just confirmed something. "Very well, Sergeant. But what I know does not, regrettably, amount to a great deal."

Vollman settled himself in his chair before going on. "The symbols you showed me were, in fact, from the language of ancient Sumeria. They do not constitute a word, but rather seem to form the first three letters of the name of an ancient god."

"What god?" Karl asked him.

Vollman looked uneasy for the first time since I had met him. "I would prefer not to say the name aloud. This is a powerful and quite malevolent deity. It probably makes no difference whether its name is spoken, but I have learned something of prudence in my long life."

I knew what he meant. There are some names it's better not to say out loud, if you don't have to. Speaking of the devil doesn't necessarily make him appear – but it *might*.

"All right," I said. "Would you be willing to write it down for us, instead?"

"Yes," he said. "That I am prepared to do."

I found a pad in one of my desk drawers and handed it to Vollman, along with a pen. After a moment's hesitation, he wrote something on the pad and passed it back to me.

He had written the word "Sakosh."

It meant nothing to me. I showed the pad to Karl, who glanced at the name, looked back at me, and shrugged. He'd never heard of it, either.

I tossed the pad on my desk. "So, somebody killed a vampire last night with a silver blade, then carved the name of some old Sumerian god on the guy's forehead.

What's this got to do with the *Opus Mago* and George Kulick?"

"Perhaps nothing," Vollman said. "But I hold very little faith in coincidence."

"Me, too," I said. "So?"

"So, the man in the alley was clearly a sacrifice, yes?"

"Fair assumption," I said.

"A sacrifice is used in magic to give power to a spell or incantation."

"Right."

"Most magical rituals that involve sacrifice call for the death of an animal. The sacrifice of a human being is used only in the blackest of the black arts, when some great evil is being contemplated."

"Agreed."

Vollman looked at Karl, then back at me. "Then ask yourselves this question, which has been haunting me for the last several nights: how monstrous must a spell be that requires the sacrifice of a vampire?"

There was a silence that Vollman finally broke by saying, "And remember the *Opus Mago* is a forbidden book precisely *because* it contains spells to be used for invoking the most potent of the dark forces, which are precisely the kind of powers that would require such an... extreme... sacrifice."

"So your theory," Karl said, "is that whoever stole the *Opus Mago* plans to carry out one of those blacker-than-black rituals, and that the guy who got his throat cut is supposed to kick-start the process."

Vollman nodded. "That is the conclusion that I have reached, based on the available information."

Karl's chair creaked as he leaned forward. "So how do we find the guy who's doing this shit?"

"If I knew that…" Vollman shrugged instead of finishing the sentence.

"If you knew that, you wouldn't need us," I said. "That's the most honest thing you've ever said to us, even if you didn't really say it."

Vollman didn't respond to my dig. Instead, he asked politely, "Have your police colleagues produced any useful leads in the case of George Kulick?"

"Not a damn thing," I said. "No witnesses, no murder weapon, and the forensics stuff is pretty much useless."

"They found some stray hairs on the corpse," Karl said, "but whether they come from the perp or from the vic's girlfriend, or his mother, or whoever, we don't know. And a DNA match won't work until they have a suspect to match it to."

"I was just remembering something you said the other day," I told Vollman. "Whoever would mess around with the *Opus Mago* would have to be a wizard of 'supreme arrogance,' or something like that. I had the impression that you believe most practitioners of the Art wouldn't be caught dead with that book, so to speak."

"You are correct," Vollman said. "Even *I* have not read it – apart from a quick perusal, to verify its authenticity."

"You wouldn't read it," Karl said. "Okay, who *would*?"

Vollman raised his hands a few inches before dropping them back in his lap. "I have no idea."

"But among the local supes you're the man," Karl said. "You told us so yourself. So you ought to know which of the practitioners would have the stones to try a spell from this book."

"I ought to know, yes, and I do," Vollman said. "The answer to your question is, 'no one.'"

"None of the local wizards, witches, sorcerers, or

wannabees would give it a try? You're sure?" Karl was like a terrier with a rat. He gets that way sometimes.

"Quite certain. The person in this area with the greatest chance of surviving such an attempt is, frankly, myself. And I would not venture such insanity."

"So it's an outsider," I said. "Somebody who came here for the express purpose of stealing the *Opus Mago* and making use of it."

Vollman thought about that for a while, or pretended to. Finally, he said, "You must be correct, Sergeant. I can think of no other explanation."

"Why here?" Karl asked. "Why Scranton?"

"Remember, there are only four copies of the *Opus Mago* known to remain in existence, Detective," Vollman said. "Kulick was the guardian of one of them. There were only so many places the thief could strike."

"Where are the other three?" I asked him.

Vollman counted them off slowly on his fingers as he spoke. "One is in London," he said, "in a secure vault at the British Museum. Another is in Cologne, Germany. The third is held in Johannesburg, South Africa. And the fourth is – *was* – here."

"Are the other three copies still where they're supposed to be?" I was wondering whether Scranton was the thief's first stop, or his last.

"I have made inquiries within the last few days," Vollman said. "Yes, all three are still in place." He held up a hand, palm toward me, for a moment. "And if I may anticipate your next question, no attempts have been made to steal the other copies."

"So, whoever it was wanted the book, he picked Scranton as the best place to rip it off," Karl said. "Maybe because he heard the *Opus Mago* was guarded by just one guy and a dinky little floor safe."

Vollman stirred in his chair a little, as if the accusation in Karl's voice had made him uncomfortable.

"He came here for the book, then stuck around," Karl went on. "Why would he do that?"

"Perhaps he is in a hurry," Vollman said. "He wants to waste no time in putting one of the spells into practice."

"It would be good if we knew what the spell was," I said to Karl. "Might give us a better idea of what we're dealing with."

I turned to Vollman. "We know about the silver knife, and about the name of–" I stopped, and tapped the pad on my desk, where he had written the ancient god's name. "–this guy here. Is that enough to go on, for somebody to look in one of the other copies and work backwards?"

Vollman sat there for a while, frowning. Then he said, "I can ask. You understand, I have no authority over those people. But if I explain what is at stake here, it may be that one of the other caretakers can be persuaded to search through his copy of the *Opus Mago*. Perhaps, given what we know, he can determine the exact nature of the spell that is being undertaken by this lunatic, whoever he may be."

"Or 'she,'" Karl said.

Vollman dipped his head in acknowledgment. "Or she."

"If you can do that right away, it would be a very good thing," I said. "And in the meantime, Detective Renfer and I will talk to some of our contacts in the supernatural community."

Vollman looked at me. "To what end?"

"To see if there's a new wizard in town."

• • • •

In Scranton, there's no shortage of what my mom used to call beer gardens. There are straight bars and supe bars. That doesn't mean a supe can't walk into any joint in town for a beer (or a Bloody Mary – with or without real blood), assuming he's of age and has the money to pay for it. Discrimination's against the law. Anyway, no bartender's going to refuse to serve somebody who might come back during the next full moon and tear his throat out.

But most supes prefer the company of their own, and the biggest supe bar in town is *Renfield's* on Wyoming Avenue. I'd been there plenty of times before.

The place was busy when Karl and I walked in a little after 3am. Supe bars usually stay open all night and close at dawn, for obvious reasons.

You'd think we might get a hostile reception in a place like that, but you'd be wrong. Cops on the Supe Squad spend as much time investigating crimes committed *against* supes as we do on crimes with a supe perpetrator, and the supe community knows that. If a cop is fair in his dealings with them, the supes remember.

And if he's not fair, they remember that, too.

I try to be fair, even when dealing with vamps. You can't let your personal views get in the way of your work – it's not professional. And I'm always professional. Well, almost always.

We got nods of welcome from a couple of ogres sitting in a corner, and a quiet wave from a werewolf we knew. The rest of the customers ignored us, or pretended to.

Elvira was tending bar, like she usually does on weeknights. That's not her real name, of course. But she's tricked out like that vamp wannabe who got famous hosting bad horror movies on TV. Why an attractive human would want to look like a vamp is beyond me, but I guess a girl's gotta make a living. Like the original, our Elvira's got boobs big enough to look good in the low-slung dress that's part of the get-up, and I bet that cleavage of hers is good for a lot of tips.

When she slinked over, I ordered a ginger ale for myself and a seltzer for Karl. That thing about no booze on the job may be a cliché, but it's also a rule.

Besides, if I was going to drink, I wouldn't do it in a supe bar, despite my good relations with most of the locals. There's always the chance that I'd get careless and have one too many.

A circus animal trainer may get along pretty well with the lions, tigers, and leopards in his act, but he'd be a fool to turn his back on them.

Elvira was back within a minute. She placed our drinks in front of us, and I dropped a twenty on the bar. As she reached for it, I placed my hand on top of hers. Nothing painful – I just wanted to get her attention.

She looked at me through all the mascara and eyeliner that surrounded her baby blues. "What?"

"Seen any new faces, the last week or so?"

She wrinkled her forehead in thought. "Gosh, no, I don't think so. You guys lookin' for somebody in particular?"

I nodded. "A practitioner, gender unknown. New in town, and a real heavy hitter."

"I haven't heard about anybody like that, Stan," Elvira said. "Honest."

"Put the word out, will you?" I said. "Quiet, no drama. But make it clear that if anybody can give me a line on this new spellcaster, I'd owe them a heck of a big favor."

Yeah, I really said "heck". I'm no Boy Scout, but it's not smart to say words like "hell" in a supe bar. You never know what might be listening.

Elvira promised to let her customers know that I was in the market for information, and I told her to keep the change from my twenty.

I turned around and leaned my back against the bar. It was the signal that I was open for business, if anybody had any. I've found it's better to let supes approach me, rather than the other way around. Some of them spook easy, you might say.

Off to my left, Karl was deep in conversation with the LeFay sisters, a couple of young witches from up the line in Dickson City. He could have been asking about our wizard, or trying to set up a threesome for later. Either way, it didn't look like he was having much luck.

A few minutes later, I realized that Barney Ghougle had slipped onto the stool to my right. I hadn't seen him approach, but then nobody beats a ghoul for sneaky.

Everybody calls him Barney Ghougle, even him. His real name is something unpronounceable, except by another ghoul. Barney looks kind of like Peter Lorre used to, back when he was a young actor making films in Germany – like *M*, where Lorre played a degenerate child murderer. The resemblance ends there, though. I'm sure Barney would never hurt a kid.

Which doesn't necessarily mean he wouldn't eat one, if it was already dead.

I nodded in his direction. "Hey, Barney."

"Sergeant," he said in that raspy voice of his. "And how are you this fine evening?"

Even from several feet away, his halitosis made my nose wrinkle. Ghouls have the absolute worst breath in the world.

"I'm a little frustrated, to tell you the truth," I said.

"Indeed?" He took a sip of what looked like a double bourbon on the rocks. "Perhaps I might be able to assist you in some way, if I knew the cause of your distress."

Barney talks like that because he's a mortician, and I guess somber formality helps when you're dealing with the grieving. I hear that his funeral home is pretty successful, but I'd never do business with him. I like my relatives to be buried with all their parts intact.

"Maybe you *can* help," I said. "I'm trying to get a line on a practitioner."

He nodded sympathetically. "There are so many," he said. "And yet I would have thought you knew them all. The local ones, at least."

"That's just it," I told him. "This one might not be local. He, or maybe she, could be new in town, say within the last week or two. Somebody who's major league, or thinks he is. The kind who takes on the really hard spells."

"I see." Barney sucked an ice cube out of his drink and chewed on it noisily for a few seconds. "I have not had the honor of meeting such an individual myself, sad to say."

I turned and looked at him. "Sounds like there might be a 'but' lurking in there someplace."

"How well you know me," he said with a tiny smile. "I was, in fact, about to say that I may have heard something about a new arrival to our fair city, a visitor who would seem to fit your description."

He didn't say anything else. The silence between us dragged on for a while.

"All right," I said with a sigh. "What do you need?"

Barney took another sip of his drink before answering. "My brother," he said, not looking at me.

"Algernon? Don't tell me he's been busted again."

The little ghoul nodded glumly.

"Same thing?" I asked. "Indecent exposure?"

Another nod. "It is really most embarrassing," he said.

I knew he meant it. Among ghouls, eating the flesh of the recently dead was no big deal, but having a relative who likes to wave his weenie around in front of the living is a scandal. Especially if he keeps getting caught.

"Who filed the complaint?" I asked. "Do you know?"

He nodded slowly. "Some woman in Nay Aug Park. I gather she was on a bench, tossing peanuts to the squirrels, when Algernon approached her and asked if she'd like to see some real..." He let his voice fade out, with a despairing gesture.

"I'll find out who she is," I told him. "See if maybe I can persuade her to change her mind about pressing charges. You may have to part with a few bucks to make her happy."

"Which I would do, gladly," Barney said. "Thank you."

"You're welcome. Now, about that spellcaster..."

"Yes, of course." He gestured with his chin toward a table in one corner of the room. "It was there, in fact, that I learned what I am about to tell you. A week ago it was, or a little longer. While waiting for a friend to join me, I noticed that two of our local wizards were conversing at a nearby table. I'm afraid I may have eavesdropped."

I didn't doubt it for a minute. Most ghouls are incredible busybodies. That's why they make such good sources for information.

"And what did you hear?" I asked.

"One was saying that he had recently encountered a man downtown, bumped into him quite literally. Someone whom he had known years ago and who has since achieved quite a formidable reputation for the use of black magic. But when greeted, the man apparently said something along the lines of 'You must be mistaken,' and walked away, quite brusquely."

"Mistaken identity, maybe," I said. "It happens, you know."

"Truly it does," Barney said. "But the one recounting this tale said he was absolutely certain that the fellow was the one he'd known, especially after he'd heard the man speak. Apparently he has a rather distinct Irish accent."

"A name," I said. "Please tell me that you got a name for this guy."

"In point of fact, I did," Barney said. "Whether it's a first name or last I can't say, but the practitioner I over-heard referred to him as *Sligo*."

The morning sun was bright, but inside this windowless place natural light never entered. It was probably too embarrassed. The cheap fluorescents in the ceiling gave off a sickly blue-white glow that made the people – Homicide dicks, forensics techs, uniforms, the rest of them – look like overflow from a zombie convention.

I pushed aside a couple of inflatable love dolls that were hanging from the ceiling and leaned over the counter to take a look at the guy who was lying on the floor. He stared back at me, the way corpses usually do. If I'm lucky, that's all they do.

In life he'd apparently been in his early twenties, with longish blond hair and a bad complexion. There was blood on the garish Hawaiian shirt that was unbuttoned to his navel, and more of it pooled under the body.

"Name's Peter Willbrand," one of the uniforms said to me. "Worked the counter last night, was supposed to've closed up at ten. The day guy found him when he opened up this morning, a little before nine."

I'd been home for about three hours, and asleep for two, when the phone rang with the news that had brought me here to Fantasy Land, a depressing little shithole around the corner from the city bus station. Adult Books and Videos, the sign on the door said. Marital Aids, it said below that. Further down, Individual Viewing Booths, was followed by Supe-Friendly.

Taped to the counter was a small poster that somebody had made on a PC, advertising what was playing in the jerk-off booths this week. In addition to the usual stuff, I noticed *Ogre Gangbang 3*, *Werewolves Gone Wild*, and something called *The VILF Next Door*. Guess that's what the sign outside meant by "Supe-Friendly."

The coroner's guy on the scene was Homer Jordan, who went to Penn State on a football scholarship and still has the linebacker's shoulders to prove it. "So, how long's the *corpus* been *delicti*?" I asked him.

"At least three hours, no more than eight. I might have a better idea after I post him."

"Or not," I said.

"Or not," he said with a little smile. Figuring precise time of death is a bitch for pathologists, always has been. But cops keep asking.

"How about COD?" I asked.

"Gunshot wound to the heart. That's officially preliminary, but, hell, Stan, you know what a bullet wound looks like, same as I do. That's what killed him."

Fantasy Land had a string of small bells tied just above the door on the inside, probably so none of the pervs could sneak out without paying for their copies of *Kiss My Whip Magazine*. I heard the jangling and turned to see

Karl come in, looking about as grumpy as I felt. Guess the thing with the LeFay sisters hadn't worked out.

Or maybe it had, and that's why he was so pissed to be up early.

Karl took his time walking over, sourly taking in the racks of magazines and paperbacks, the Blu-Ray discs and DVDs, and the glass cases displaying every kind of vibrator, dildo, and butt plug known to man – or woman. As he got closer, I saw him looking at the poster for this week's porn videos. "What's a VILF?"

"Means *Vampire I'd Like to Fang*," I said.

"I didn't think places like this existed anymore," Karl said. "What with all the Internet porn, online sex shops, stuff like that."

"Not everybody's as good at finding smut on the Web as you are," I said. I batted the foot of an inflated love doll and set it swinging gently. "Besides," I said, "what Internet site is gonna be able to provide a guy with one of these honeys? On short notice, I mean."

"Yeah, and speaking of short notice, what the fuck are we doing here, anyway?"

I pointed to my left. "Over there," I said.

Karl bent over the counter, looked at Peter Willbrand's corpse for a few seconds, then came back. "Okay, that's why Homicide's here," he said. "But why us?"

"Good question. I was wondering, myself." I looked over at Homer, who didn't bother to conceal the fact that he'd been listening. "You know anything about that?" I asked.

"I've got no idea who called you guys, but I think I know where the impulse must've come from. Here, check this out."

Homer eased behind the counter, careful not to step in the blood pool. He produced a pair of tweezers, bent over the dead guy, and carefully pulled back the collar of his gaudy shirt.

There were three symbols carved into the corpse's nearly hairless chest.

I didn't recognize them, but the alphabet looked like something I'd seen before.

Karl and I looked at each other for a couple of seconds, then I pulled out my notepad and started carefully copying the stuff down.

When I was done, I turned to Homer. "You've got photos of this, right?"

"Course I do," he said. "I assume you want copies?"

"You assume right, Homes." Homer likes it when I call him that – makes him feel like he's hanging with the cool kids.

Homer watched as I put the notepad away, then asked, "What's that stuff on his chest say? Do you know?"

"Uh-uh," I said, shaking my head. "But I'm pretty sure I know what it means."

"Well, what?"

"Trouble."

Homer grinned with delight. "Damn, I love that kind of talk."

"I know you do," I told him. "But do me a favor, will you? Peel back the vic's upper lip for a second."

He gave me a strange look, but didn't ask any questions. Pulling out the tweezers again, he bent over the corpse, got a grip on the thin flap of flesh below the victim's nose, and lifted it up.

All three of us stared at what Homer had uncovered, but Karl was the first one to speak. "Sonofabitch. Fangs."

By the time I finally got home from the crime scene, I was able to grab only three more hours of sleep. Then it was time to get up again, shower, eat, feed Quincey (my hamster, who's named after a hero of mine), and head back to the squad for the start of my regular shift.

My email messages included one from Homer, who'd managed to do the autopsy on our vic right away. Must have been a slow day at the morgue.

Stan:

You owe me lunch, man (and not at Mickey Dee's, either) – I was planning to play golf this afternoon, not cut up a dead vamp for the Supe Squad.

Okay: to the surprise of nobody, Mr Willbrand's death was caused by a single gunshot, bullet penetrating the left ventricle of the heart and lodging therein. Death was instantaneous, or near enough as makes no difference. I got the round out, more or less intact. It's a .38, but here's the weird thing: sucker looks like it's made of charcoal. That's right, something you'd use in your BBQ grill, except a lot smaller. I've sent it to the lab, and you'll get a chemical analysis from them, eventually. But I'll bet my next paycheck that I'm right.

I've heard of silver bullets – and I bet you know more about that stuff than I would. But charcoal? What the fuck is up with that?

Love & kisses,

Homer

By the time I was finished, Karl was reading over my shoulder. "He asks a pretty good question there, near the end."

"Sure does." I clicked the mouse a couple of times to add a copy of Homer's message to the case file. "Silver bullets, sure. Even gold, a couple of times. Wasn't there a guy in some old James Bond movie that was known for using gold bullets?"

"Francisco 'Pistols' Scaramanga," Karl said immediately. "*The Man with the Golden Gun*, 1974. Christopher Lee played him. Based on the last of the Bond novels that Ian Fleming wrote, before those other hacks started doing them. Movie was okay, but the book kind of sucked. Fleming was just going through the motions by then, rehashed a lot of stuff he'd done already. He died soon after."

Karl is the biggest James Bond nut I've ever met, or even heard of. He's got the books, the DVDs, soundtrack albums, movie posters, and even – as he once admitted, after swearing me to secrecy – the complete set of 007 action figures.

I'd only asked the James Bond question to postpone dealing with the fact that we probably had some kind of nut/wizard/serial killer operating in town, using each murder as an ingredient in some kind of elaborate spell to accomplish a goal that I couldn't even imagine.

I was about to say as much when my email pinged, announcing a new message. I checked the address, to see whether it was worth reading.

The message had come from *Vollmanex@aol.com*.

Son of a bitch.

I understand there has been another killing that seems relevant to our matter of mutual concern. Is my information correct?
Vollman.

"Wonder how he knew we'd be here?" Karl asked.

"The old bastard seems to know everything – except how we're gonna clear this case," I said.

I clicked "Reply," typed "You bet it is," and sent it.

Less than a minute later I was reading, *Do you have AOL Instant Messenger, or something similar? If so, what is your screen name?*

"Why do I feel weird about doing IM with a vampire?" I said out loud. "I mean, what would Dracula say about this shit?"

"Probably, 'I vant to haf a chaaat vith you... in real time,'" Karl said, doing a pretty fair Bela Lugosi.

I sent Vollman my AOL identification. After a few seconds, the computer made that annoying *zziiiing* sound, and a chat window opened.

Inside the window was "**VollWiz**: *Are we connected?*"

The rest of the conversation (if you can call it that) went like this:

Supecop1: *Yes, I'm here.*

VollWiz: *Does this latest murder bear similarities to the first one?*

Supecop1: *Some. There was cryptic stuff carved into the victim's chest.*

VollWiz: *The same as last time?*

Supecop1: *No, different symbols. Looks like the same alphabet, though.*

Vollwiz: *Can you send me a copy?*

Supecop1: *My keyboard doesn't have the symbols. I doubt they make a keyboard that does.*

About half a minute went by. Then:

Vollwiz: *Do you have a text scanner available?*

I knew what Vollman was getting at, and it annoyed me that I hadn't thought of it myself.

I pulled my notebook out and found the page where I'd copied the message found on Willbrand's corpse. Handing it to Karl, I said, "Do me a favor and run the scanner over this, will you? Put it on a thumb drive for me."

"Right," he said, took the notebook, and headed out of the room. I turned back to the keyboard and typed:

Supecop1: *I should be sending that to you shortly.*

VollWiz: *Very well. Now, as to cause of death: I have heard it was a gunshot. Can you confirm that?*

Supecop1: *Where do you get your information, anyway?*

Vollwiz: *Please, Sergeant – let us not waste each other's time.*

I stared at the screen while trying hard to keep control of myself. I didn't have to take shit like that from some bloodsucker, even if he was also a wizard.

By the same token, telling Vollman to go fuck himself wasn't going to get these cases cleared.

It would sure be fun, though.

I took in a deep breath, and let it out slow.

Supecop1: *Yeah, he died of a gunshot wound. If you know that, I guess you know he was one of you... people.*

Vollwiz: *If you mean he was undead, yes, I was aware of that. May I assume that the bullet that killed him was silver?*

Supecop1: *No, you may not. Lab report says the slug was made of charcoal. It's like he was trying to barbecue the guy from inside. You ever hear of that?*

Vollwiz: *In fact, I believe I have.*

Supecop1: *I thought I was pretty well up on the ways to kill a vampire.*

At the last second, I'd added "ire" to that last word. Some vamps don't like being called vamps.

Vollwiz: *I'm sure you are, Sergeant. And this method of murder is not inconsistent with the knowledge you possess. Consider: what IS charcoal, anyway?*

I figured out what he was getting at in about three seconds, then spent another ten feeling stupid.

Supecop1: *Charcoal's super-compressed wood, isn't it? Wood – as in wooden stakes.*

Vollwiz: *Exactly. It is an uncommon method to kill one of my kind, but effective. As you have seen yourself.*

Supecop1: *Yeah, I guess I have.*

Vollwiz: *Have there been any other developments in the case?*

Supecop1: *Yeah. I may have a name for the perp. I guess you could call that a new development.*

It's hard to be sarcastic online. Unfortunately.

Vollwiz: *Indeed? That is most interesting. Congratulations.*

Supecop1: *Don't pop any corks just yet. There's no way to know for sure whether it's our guy, but I like him for it. From what I hear, he's: 1. a wizard. 2. new in town. 3. acting secretive – pretending to be somebody else, etc.*

Vollwiz: *I agree, he sounds like a promising candidate. What is his name?*

Supecop1: *Calls himself Sligo.*

No response. I watched the empty screen for a while, then typed:

Supecop1: *You still there?*

Still no answer. I was starting to wonder whether the connection had been broken, when this appeared:

Vollwiz: *Are you absolutely certain?*

Supecop1: *Certain that's the guy? Hell, no. Certain that's what my informant told me? Yeah, I'm sure, since I don't have wax in my ears, or anything.*

Karl appeared over my shoulder, holding a thumb drive. I attached it to the computer, downloaded the file, then sent it to Vollman's email address as an attachment.

Supecop1: *I just sent the file with the symbols I copied from our latest vic. It's pretty accurate, I think.*

I waited. Nothing, for maybe two minutes, then this appeared:

VollWiz: *I will be in touch with you later.*

Then the chat connection was broken.

"Motherfucker," I heard Karl mutter from behind me.

"Yeah, I know," I said. "But at least he's given us a way

to find out where he hangs his cloak, and that's something we've been wanting to know."

I looked up the customer service number for AOL and called them. It took the better part of an hour to find a supervisor with the authority to look up a customer's mailing address, and to convince her that I had the authority to ask for it.

Finally, I heard her say, "Very well, Sergeant. What is the email address you have?"

"It's V-o-l-l-m-a-n-e-x at aol.com."

I heard her keyboard clacking in the background. Then silence. Then more clacking, followed by another stretch of silence.

"I'm sorry, Sergeant," the supervisor said, "but we have no account listed under that address."

"Has it been cancelled recently? Say, within the last hour or so?"

"No, sir. We have never had an account under that name. It simply doesn't exist."

I hung up the phone and said to Karl, "Fuck Vollman and the hearse he rode in on. I'm getting tired of that old bastard and the way he keeps jerking us around. It's time we started acting like goddamn detectives, for a change."

"Sounds good to me," Karl said. "You got any particular kind of detecting in mind?"

"Yeah, I do. Sligo, or whoever the perp is, has offed two guys so far, right? Why those two? Were they picked at random, or–"

"Or is there a common factor?" Karl said. "Some pattern he's following."

"Exactly. Why don't you get on that, see if you can find anything about the vics that stands out."

"Okay. What are you gonna be doing?"

"See if I can find out more about this forbidden book," I told him. "Vollman said there were only four copies in existence. Let's see if he was right."

Karl went over to his own desk, and I turned back to my computer and brought up Google. I typed in *Opus* and *Mago* and clicked "Search."

A few seconds later I was looking at the first hundred of my 28,343 hits. A lot of them involved classical music, although several seemed to refer to some penguin in a comic strip.

Realizing where I went wrong, I went back to the search screen. This time, I put quotation marks around *Opus Mago* so the search engine would read it as a phrase.

Eight hits. That was more like it.

Seven of the references were duds. Five of them lumped the *Opus Mago* in with fictional works like the *Necronomicon*, the *Lemegeton* of Solomon, and the *Grimorium Verum*. Shows what they know. Two other hits brought me to bogus black magic sites, constructed by obvious wannabees who'd probably run screaming for their mothers if they ever got close to the real thing. It didn't take me long to figure out that these morons didn't know the *Opus Mago* from the *Kama Sutra*.

The one hit left was a news item saying that a professor at Georgetown University had translated some fragments of the *Opus Mago*, which the article said was one of the oldest and most obscure works in the black arts. Dr Benjamin Prescott was described as "one of the foremost authorities on the ancient grimoires." Then I read that Prescott had refused to allow his translation to be published. Anywhere. Ever.

• • • •

Georgetown University, I found out, is a big place – especially if you're trying to find your way around by using their website. I finally learned that Professor Prescott's office was located in the Department of Theosophy, and even persuaded a campus operator to connect me to his direct line.

That's where my luck ran out. I'd been hoping against hope that I'd find Prescott working late in his office, but all I got was an answering machine.

I left a message saying who I was, but not what I wanted. I asked him to call me back the next night, anytime after 9:00. Then I got his email address from the campus directory, and sent him the same message that way.

The professor could read the email at any time – whenever he felt like checking his account. And if he was one of those people who didn't do that regularly, he'd probably get my phone message tomorrow. Assuming he wasn't off on a research trip to Transylvania, or someplace.

The rest of the evening was typical of a night shift for the Supe Squad, if you'd want to call anything we deal with "typical."

A ghost was haunting one of the girls' dorms at Marywood University. Marywood's coed now, but it used to bill itself as the Largest Catholic Women's College in America. Some guys at the U (a Jesuit school that used to be all-male, back in the day) used to say "Mary would if Mary could, but Mary goes to Marywood."

I hear that Marywood girls are a little different, these days.

A haunting isn't necessarily a big deal, but the pesky spirit was hanging around the bathrooms and ogling the young lovelies as they stepped out of the shower. Some

of the girls were terrified; others were downright offended, since the ghost liked to make comments about
their attributes. Not all of his observations were kindly.

Turned out the spook was the spirit of an old guy
who'd been a janitor at the school for years. He'd come
back to live out some of his fantasies.

We sent for an exorcist. Several Jesuits at the U are
qualified and on call. Father Martino compelled the old
guy's ghost to depart the premises, and imposed a geas
on him against returning. Before he was expelled, I suggested he start haunting one of the city's strip clubs,
where nobody would much care how much skin he
looked at. He seemed to think that was an idea with
some merit.

Then we got a call that a female vamp was using Influence
on some of the customers at *Susie B's*, our local lesbian bar.
A lot of vampires have powers of fascination. That "Look
into my eyes" stuff you see on TV is real, although it's exaggerated – like everything else on TV. Despite what you
hear, Influence can't take away somebody's free will – but
a proficient vamp can weaken it quite a bit. And sometimes, that's all they need.

Karl and I dropped in at the bar and talked to the
owner, Barbara Ann, who'd called in the complaint. She
wasted no time pointing out the bloodsucker among her
clientele. "She's the one at the corner table sitting by herself – but she won't be alone for long," Barbara Ann said.

We went to have a word with the young lady (who
was probably neither very young nor much of a lady),
ignoring the hostile glances from some of the other customers. Men aren't popular in *Susie B's*, and cops even
less so.

The vamp said her name was Lucretia. It might even have been true – she had an old-country Italian look about her: midnight black hair, with eyes to match, pale skin, and red, red lips. Nice tits, too – for a vamp.

I was surprised that she found it necessary to use Influence in order to get laid – here, or anyplace else. Of course, she was probably in the habit of using her beautiful mouth for more than cunnilingus. Most ladies who'll happily spend a few hours trading orgasms with another woman will draw the line when it comes to giving up a few pints of the red stuff.

Karl and I took turns explaining to Lucretia that the law prohibits the use of Influence to secure consent for any kind of transaction, whether sexual, commercial, or vampiric.

"I really don't know what you're talking about, officers," she said, all wide-eyed innocence. "I wouldn't do a thing like that. *Now I think you should both leave.*" Her words seemed to echo inside my head, and Lucretia looked right at me as she said them, those coal black eyes burning into mine irresistibly...

She must have been pretty old. Her Influence was strong. I actually felt my feet begin to move under my chair, before my will reasserted itself and made them stop. If I'd had any doubts that Miss Lucretia been using her power improperly, they'd just been staked, but good.

I smiled at her and shook my head. "Nice try, Vampirella, but no sale."

Our police training includes the use of deep hypnosis to make us pretty much immune to that kind of stuff, and we get boosters twice a year.

Then, mostly to see what would happen, I said, "You know, I don't think Vollman would approve of you taking advantage of people this way. It doesn't exactly reflect well on your kind, does it?"

Her heart-breaker's face grew very still. "You know Mr Vollman?" Lucretia asked, in a tight, quiet voice she hadn't used before.

"Sure," Karl said, with a shrug. He'd picked up on what I was doing. "We do favors for him sometimes – and vice versa."

"You don't want us to ask him for a favor that has your name on it, do you, honey?" I said gently.

Lucretia shook her head stiffly. In a quick rush of words she said, "No, I'm sorry, I won't do it anymore, I have to go now, g'night."

She stood up and quickly walked out of the place, without once glancing back in our direction.

"Guess Vollman wasn't shitting us," Karl said, as he watched the beautiful vamp's departure. Maybe he was checking her ass for clues.

"Nope," I said, and pushed my chair back. "Looks like he really is The Man."

I'd been on duty less than half an hour the next night when my desk phone rang.

"Supernatural Crimes. Sergeant Markowski."

"Yes, Sergeant. This is Dr Benjamin Prescott from Georgetown University. I believe you've been trying to get in touch with me."

So the professor wasn't one of those Hey-call-me-Ben types. Well, he had lots of company.

"Yes, sir, I have. Thanks for getting back to me."

"Quite all right. So, what can I do for the Scranton Police Department? I assume this has something to do with my visit. I hope there isn't a security issue that's arisen."

There was a wheeze in Prescott's voice, as if he suffered from asthma. Maybe he was just a heavy smoker.

"Visit?" I said. "Sorry, I don't get what you mean."

There was a pause, then he said, "I'm speaking at the University of Scranton the day after tomorrow. It's part of the Thomas Aquinas lecture series that most of the Jesuit colleges participate in." Another pause. "I gather all this is news to you?"

"Yes, sir, it is. But I'm glad to hear you're going to be in town. It'll be easier than trying to do this over the phone."

"Easier to do *what*, Sergeant?" He was starting to sound impatient.

"To ask you some questions about the *Opus Mago*."

The silence that followed had me wondering if we'd lost the connection. Then Prescott said, "Okay, cut the bullshit. Who are you, really?"

"I'm who I said I was, Professor."

"Really? Seems to me that anybody can answer the phone by saying 'Supernatural Crimes.' I bet you've been doing it all day, haven't you, waiting for me to call."

"Professor, I–"

"What are you, a reporter? I don't talk to you people, not about that subject. Why can't you get that through your thick skulls and stop *bothering* me?"

I sighed, loud enough so that he could hear it on the line. "Professor Prescott, I left my direct number on your answering machine because I figured it would be easier than making you work your way through the system. But, okay, I tell you what: let's hang up, and you get the number for the Scranton Police Department from Directory Assistance, or the city's web page. I could give it to you myself, but you'd probably think it was a trick. So, get the number, call it, then tell the switchboard you want Supernatural Crimes. That'll get you this office, and our P.A.'ll transfer your call to me when you give her my name. Think that'll ease your mind?"

More silence. Finally, Prescott said, "I suppose that won't be necessary. But I hope you understand that I have to be careful about discussing certain aspects of my work."

"I understand completely, sir. The *Opus Mago* is a pretty scary book, from what I hear. That's why I wanted to talk to you about it."

"I assume your interest isn't... academic?"

"No, it's not. We've had three murders that appear to be tied to the book in some way. And I'm afraid we might be due for more if I don't figure out what's going on."

"On what basis did you conclude that the homicides you refer to have anything to do with... the book we're talking about?"

He doesn't want to say the name out loud. Interesting.

"The first victim had a copy of the *Opus Mago* in his possession. He was tortured to make him tell where the book was hidden, then killed after he gave it up."

"My God." The wheezing in Prescott's voice was worse now.

"The other two victims are apparently part of some kind of sacrifice connected to a spell from the book," I said. "At least, that's the theory we're working from right now."

"And how on earth did you reach that unlikely conclusion, Sergeant?"

"Each victim had occult symbols carved on their bodies, symbols that aren't part of any recognized system of magic. I've been told that the symbols may have been taken from the *Opus Mago*."

"Told? By whom?"

"A local guy who's acting as a... consultant on this case. His name's Vollman, Ernst Vollman."

There was no long pause this time. The name was barely out of my mouth before Prescott said, "I'm afraid I can't help you."

"Professor, listen, if there's–"

"I really doubt there's any real assistance I could offer," he said. "I've only translated fragments of the book in question, and I can't see how my *very* limited knowledge on the subject could be of any use to you. It would just be a waste of your time – and mine."

"Professor Prescott, I–"

"I'm sorry, Sergeant. Goodbye."

A second later, I was listening to a dial tone.

I hung up and said several nasty things about Prescott under my breath. Once that was out of my system, I grabbed my Rolodex and looked up the phone number of a guy I know who's a professor at the U.

If he didn't know the time and place of Prescott's guest lecture, he'd sure as hell know how to find out.

I was hoping to hear from Vollman before my shift was over. Instead, I got a call from Lacey Brennan.

Lacey works the Supe Squad over in Wilkes-Barre, which is twelve miles away and the biggest city in the Wyoming Valley, after us. We've done a little business over the years when a case crossed jurisdictional lines – like the time when a werewolf serial killer was going around tearing up people in both her county and mine.

Lacey's a good cop. A fine-looking woman, too, but I wasn't hot for her or anything.

Besides, she was married.

The first thing I heard when I picked up the phone was, "Hey, Stan, how many vamps does it take to change a light bulb?"

"I'm fine, Lace, thanks for asking," I said. I'm used to her supe jokes by now, although they never seem to get any better. "I don't know, how many?"

"Trick question – they can't do it. Because when it comes to changing light bulbs, vampires suck."

"That one's a hoot, it really is. I'm cracking up, but deep inside, where it doesn't show." If I ever actually laughed at one of her jokes, I think Lacey'd be offended. "So, to what do I owe the pleasure?" I asked.

"I hear you've got murder vics turning up with weird shit engraved on the bodies."

"Where'd you hear that?" There's no reason to hide stuff like that from Lacey, but in this job caution becomes a habit after a while.

"Ah, you know how the rumor mill is. Cops gossip worse than old ladies at a bake sale."

"Well, you heard right. Two corpses, so far. We're still working on what the symbols mean."

"Anything unusual about the CODs?"

"Cause of death for the first one was a slit throat. The second guy was shot."

"That doesn't exactly sound out of the ordinary, Stan," Lacey said.

"No, but get this: the knife was apparently coated with silver, and the bullet we dug out of the other vic seems to be made of pure charcoal. Oh, and there's one thing I forgot to mention: both victims were vamps."

"Holy fuck," she said softly. I never figured out whether Lacey swears because she wants to be considered one of the boys, or if she's just a natural guttermouth.

"My feelings exactly," I said.

"What about the perp – you got any leads that aren't totally worth shit?"

"Bits and pieces, but nothing solid yet. Why?"

"Because it looks like your perp's broadening his range. I'm pretty sure last night the motherfucker did one over here."

I got authorization from the lieutenant to put in some overtime the next day in the cause of inter-departmental cooperation. The chief always loves to hear about stuff like that. When my shift was over, I headed home to grab a few hours' sleep. After lunch, I'd head down the line to Wilkes-Barre, to see whether Lacey Brennan had turned up the third victim of our serial killer.

It had been a long couple of days, and I was planning to hit the sack as soon as I got home. I would have, too, except for what was waiting on my front steps.

My headlights illuminated her for a second as I made the slow turn into the driveway, a young woman with dark hair who looked like early twenties, wearing blue jeans and a long-sleeved sweatshirt. As the lights passed over, her eyes reflected back a red glow.

Far as I know, there's only one creature with eyes that show red in response to light. Not cat or deer or raccoon or fox – nothing in the natural world.

Vampire.

But even without the red reflection, I'd have known what she was.

I parked in the right half of the two-car garage. It had come with the house – a big, weathered Cape that had been just about the right size when my family and I had lived there. But I live alone now, and the place has more space than I need. A lot more. I've thought about selling, but I've lived there a long time, and I'm used to the house and its ghosts.

The front porch has three concrete steps leading up to it, and the vampire was sitting on the bottom one. I eased myself down next to her.

We sat there in silence for a while, until she asked, "Aren't you going to invite me in?"

"I... you know I can't do that."

Her shoulders twitched in what I assumed was a shrug. "Just checking."

We sat there some more, letting the silence grow between us. Then she said, "Damn, I wish I still smoked. It would give me something to do at times like this."

"Guess there's no reason why you can't take it up again, if you want to."

She made a sound that in a human might have been laughter. "Yeah, lung cancer isn't much of an issue any more, is it?" She shook her head gently. "No, no more tobacco for me. There's only one thing that I crave now."

There was nothing for me to say about that. The quiet settled back down over us, like a shroud. Finally, I said, "So, to what do I owe the–"

"Pleasure? Is that what it is?"

"Sure. You know I'm always glad to see you."

"And yet you won't invite me inside."

I decided to let that go. We'd covered this ground before, and it led exactly nowhere.

After a while, she said, "There's somebody new in town, killing vampires."

I didn't bother to ask how she knew. "Yeah, two so far. That we know of. And maybe one in Wilkes-Barre. I'm checking that out tomorrow – later today, I mean."

Her voice was bitter when she said, "Have you given him a medal yet?"

"I do my fucking job!" I snapped. "I'm a professional. If somebody's committing murders, he's breaking the law. And when I find him, and I *will* find him, he's going down. Period."

She nodded slowly. In a normal tone she said, "Yeah, that's what I told them."

"Told who?"

"Some people I know. There's been a lot of talk in the local community–"

"You mean the vamp, uh, vampire community."

"That's the only one I hang with, these days. Some of them are saying that you're giving this guy, the killer, a free pass because he's hunting vamps. Your feelings about us aren't exactly a secret."

"Listen, I just *told* you–"

"I know you did." She placed her hand on my wrist for a moment, and I made myself not pull away. But her touch was cold, so cold. "And I said the same thing, myself."

"Thanks for the endorsement," I said. "And you're telling me about this because..."

"Because some of them are saying they should deal with this themselves. Find the killer themselves. And dispense justice themselves."

"That would be about the worst thing they could do, for a whole bunch of reasons. *Vigilante* is just another word for *murderer*, as far as the law's concerned."

"I know." It must be hard to sigh when you don't need to breathe, but she managed it. "I said that, too."

"And did they listen?"

"I think so. For now. But if these murders continue, with no arrest, people are going to start paying attention to the hotheads."

"I don't think Vollman would like that too much."

She didn't react to the name the way the vamp in *Susie B's* had, but I'm pretty sure I saw her back straighten a little.

"You know Mr Vollman?"

"He's helping us with the case. And, far as I know, *he* doesn't think I'm slacking off."

"I'll be sure to pass that along."

I noticed her shoulders were shaking slightly. "What?"

"You and Mr Vollman – working together. You must *love* that!" She sounded genuinely amused. I guess it was kind of funny, at that.

"Well, since you know so much already, you might as well know this: I don't think the killer's a Van Helsing."

"Really? What, then?"

"Some kind of wizard, looks like. He's got his hands on a copy of something called the *Opus Mago*, which is supposed to be the Holy Grail of grimoires."

"I think I sense an oxymoron in there someplace."

"You know what I mean."

"Yeah, I do. So this book is supposed to be high-octane evil."

"Exactly. And it looks like the two dead vamps, uh, vampires are the first couple of ingredients for some kind of spell he's working."

"Holy fuck."

"I think I sense some kind of oxymoron in there."

"Yeah, and fuck you, too," she said, but without any heat behind it. "Must be one hell of a conjuring he's got going – and that's *not* a fucking oxymoron."

"No," I said, as a ball of ice formed in my stomach – the same one that showed up every time I thought about what this wizard might have in mind. "No, it's not."

"Two dead, so far – and vampires, at that."

"Two, maybe three. I'll know that later today, probably."

"Maybe three." She nodded slowly. "What do you figure his magic number is, so to speak?"

"That's something Vollman is trying to find out," I said. "I hope he does it pretty damn soon."

I checked my watch. "Not to rush you, or anything, but the sun'll be up in–"

"Seventeen minutes. Plenty of time."

But she stood up anyway, stretching a little.

"Where are you crashing these days? Someplace close by?"

She turned to look at me. "I'll tell you that," she said, "the first time you invite me inside."

I nodded, letting nothing of what I was feeling show on my face. Or so I hoped.

I stood up, too. I wanted to put my arms around her and hold her close, just for a couple of seconds. Instead, I just nodded and said, "'Night, Christine."

"Goodnight, Daddy."

And she was gone.

Driving through downtown Wilkes-Barre, you'd never know the place had been practically underwater for several days, back in 1972. That's when Hurricane Agnes passed through the Wyoming Valley. Worst storm we've ever seen, and it sent the Susquehanna River over its banks and into the city. I was just a kid then, and Scranton wasn't affected by the flood, but I remember the TV and newspaper pictures of the huge mess it made.

One of the grisliest forms of damage occurred when the flood reached the local cemeteries. It washed some of the dead out of their graves and then deposited them all over town, once the water receded. Corpses, some long dead and others more recent, were found on people's lawns, in the middle of streets, just everywhere.

I understand the local ghoul community still talks about those days among themselves. They refer to it as the Great Smorgasbord.

Thinking about stuff like that helped keep my mind off the fact that we might have a third murder in this spell cycle, or whatever it was, with no real leads and no way to know how many more deaths had to occur before the shit really hit the fan. We didn't even know what form the shit would take.

But it was going to be some seriously bad shit, I was pretty sure of that.

The taxpayers of Wilkes-Barre must be pretty generous, because their police department is located in a nice new building that always made me a little envious whenever I visited – not that I'd ever admit that to Lacey. Anyway, there's a downside to working there. It *is* in Wilkes-Barre.

Even if I hadn't been in the building before, I wouldn't need to ask where to find Lacey. Along with the rest of her unit, she was in the basement. The Supe Squad is *always* in the basement.

Their P.A. was a young black woman named Sandra Gaffney, who was getting her PhD in Criminal Justice from Penn State. She took this gig to support herself while writing her dissertation. You can tell right off she's not a typical civil servant – not only is she intelligent, she's actually pleasant most of the time.

"Hey, Sandy," I said. "How's it going?"

She looked up from her computer and gave me a smile. "Hey yourself, Sergeant. You drop by to see how some *real* police work is done?"

"You got it," I said. "Detective Brennan said she'd give me some pointers. She's expecting me."

"I'll give her a buzz."

Sarah picked up her phone, punched in three numbers, and muttered something I couldn't hear into the receiver. I noticed that next to her computer she kept a small stuffed toy bear with a dirty face, who looked like he'd seen better days.

Hanging up the phone, Sandra said to me, "She'll be right out."

"Thanks. How's the research going?"

"Pretty good. This place gives me more data every damn day."

Detective Lacey Brennan came around the corner. A little taller than average. Blonde hair, worn short. Blue eyes. Killer body – not that I ever paid much attention.

"Guy walks into a bar," she said. "Orders a cocktail, sips it for a while. But it turns out that he's a werewolf, and while he's sitting there drinking, the full moon comes out. So the guy transforms, right? Fur, fangs, the whole nine yards. Then he trots over to the window and sits there, on the floor, howling at the moon. Well, there's a couple of tourists from East Podunk sitting a few stools away. They take all this in, you know, then one of them turns to the bartender and says, 'Fuck – we'll have what he's having!'"

Behind Lacey, Sandy just shook her head. I looked at Lacey, kept my face impassive, and asked, "Yeah? Then what happened?"

She gave me a knuckle punch on the arm. Being a real he-man, I didn't show how much it hurt.

"Come on," Lacey said. "The file's on my desk."

I followed her into the squad room, which looked in most ways like every other detectives' bull pen I've ever seen, except with fresh paint and newer carpeting.

Of course Supe Squads tend to have some features you don't find in, say, a Homicide unit. I passed a wall rack containing several sizes and varieties of wooden stakes, and next to that was a glass-fronted case full of magically charged amulets. A poster on the opposite wall listed the six known defenses against ogre attack. Then there was a big bulletin board full of wanted posters showing renegade vamps, bail-jumping werewolves, a child-killing troll, and one I recognized from our own squad room: an artist's rendering of a wimpy-looking dwarf with a severe widow's peak. His name was Keyser something-or-other, and he was supposed to be the kingpin of a shadowy gang of fairy-dust smugglers. Some crooked supes call him the devil incarnate, but others say he doesn't even exist.

Lacey's area was at the back of the room. Sitting at a desk near hers, scowling at a computer printout, was her partner. Johnny Cedric lost an eye a few years back, during a raid on an illegal coven that had gone very wrong. Could've taken a disability pension and moved to Florida, but he chose to stay on the job. I kind of admired that, even if he was always bragging about how the sinister-looking eye patch got him laid a lot.

"Hey, look what the bat dragged in," Cedric said.

"How's it going, Cyclops?" Cops aren't known for their sensitivity.

"Not bad," he said. "Still trackin' it down and tryin' it out. You over here about our dead guy?"

I nodded. "The M.O. sounds like a couple of corpses we've had turn up in our neck of the woods."

"Oh, yeah, Lace was telling me about those. How recent?"

"Both in the last week, and we're pretty sure they're related to a torture-murder we had the week before."

"Christ. I hope the bastard hasn't relocated here permanently. Not that I'd blame him, of course. Anyplace is better than Scranton, even if you're a serial killer." He squinted at me with his good eye. "You guys got anything?"

"Not a lot," I told him. "One name that's come up is a wizard named Sligo. Supposed to be a big deal black magic practitioner. Ever hear of him?"

Cedric thought a moment before shaking his head. "Uh-uh, doesn't jingle. He's not in the database?"

"Not under that name, anyway. He's supposed to be from Ireland, so I sent a query to Interpol. Haven't heard back yet."

"You wanna finish up the incident reports, Johnny?" Lacey said. "I'll entertain our visitor." Then she turned to me. "Come on, pull up a chair. I'll show you what I've got."

I was sure the double entendre was unintentional. Well, pretty sure.

I grabbed an empty chair and dragged it over next to Lacey's desk, as she pulled a file folder from one of the drawers, placed it on the blotter, and flipped it open. When she did, I noticed that the ring finger of her left hand was missing the wedding band she'd worn as long as I've known her.

Trained detectives notice stuff like that. And sometimes, we're even smart enough to keep our mouths shut about it.

The file contained the usual paperwork you find in any police report, and a set of crime scene photos. The pictures showed a young-looking guy lying on a concrete floor, surrounded by a pool of blood. Something long and thin was wrapped around his neck, looked like a ligature of some kind. In the background, I could see metal bookshelves full of thick bound volumes.

"Where'd you find him?" I asked.

"Basement of the Osterhout Free Library," Lacey said.

I looked at her. "The killer comes in, offs somebody in a *library*, and still gets away clean? I would've thought they'd get him for violating the noise policy, if nothing else."

"The basement doesn't see a lot of use these days, apparently," she said. "What's down there is mostly bound collections of old magazines. With all the stuff that's available online these days, why bother? Although I've always had a warm spot for the place in my heart, or maybe lower."

"Why's that?"

"I gave my first blowjob down there – to my high school boyfriend, when I was fifteen."

I decided that was someplace I didn't want to go. "So who's the vic?"

She checked the paperwork. "Ronald Casimir, twenty-five. Graduate student at Wilkes University."

"That might explain what he was doing in the library basement," I said. "Research of some kind, maybe." Or he could have been in the market for a good blowjob. I looked closer at a couple of the photos. "Is that a garrote?"

"Bingo – you got it in one. Haven't seen one of those used around here before."

"You sure this isn't some Mafia thing? They use wire sometimes, don't they?"

"Not any more," Lacey said. "I talked to a guy I know, works the State Police Organized Crime Task Force. He said the wise guys mostly stopped using garrotes back in the Fifties, once reliable silencers were available. Tradition usually gives way before technology, except maybe in Scranton. And besides, there's this."

She flipped through the photos and pulled one out of the pile. It was a close-up of a man's naked abdomen.

Three esoteric symbols had been carved in the corpse's flesh.

"That look like Guido's work to you?" Lacey asked.

After a long moment, I replied, "No, but it looks a lot like the kind of stuff I've been seeing on corpses in Scranton, recently."

I pulled out my notepad and began to copy down the symbols that were in the photograph.

"What's it say?" Lacey asked. "Do you know?"

"No, I don't," I told her. "But tomorrow night I've got a shot at talking to a guy who might just be able to tell me."

"And you'll let me know anything you find out, of course," she said. "*And* send copies of the two case files of yours."

"Sure, no problem. In the meantime, there's something you can do for me."

Lacey gave me a wicked grin. "What, right here in the squad room? In front of all the guys?"

"That's not what I meant," I said, and hoped that I wasn't blushing. "See if your lab guys can find out what material that garrote was made of."

"Okay, I can do that," she said. "You think it matters?"

"It might," I told her. "It might matter a hell of a lot."

I thanked Lacey for the heads-up, and got out of there before she noticed the bulge that had developed in the front of my pants. God only knows what she'd have said about *that*.

According to my buddy Ned, who taught something called Communications at the U, the guest lecture by esteemed Georgetown scholar Benjamin Prescott, PhD, was scheduled for 8 o'clock, at the Houlihan-McLean Center. A reception would follow.

It took some work, convincing McGuire to let Karl and me attend this thing on company time. But I told him that Prescott was our best chance for getting a translation of the runes, sigils, or whatever they were that were being left on the corpses. Hell, he might even know what ritual they were part of.

As for what we were going to do with that information – well, I'd worry about that when we got it. Or, rather, *if* we got it.

The program they gave us at the door said Prescott's talk was called "The Devil Made Me Do It: Demonic Possession as a Defense in European Witch Trials, 1530-1605."

Ned once explained to me that academic papers usually have a colon in the title, because so many of them are written by assholes.

Before things started, I spotted a couple of witches I knew in the audience. They looked just like anybody else – which is the trouble with a lot of supes, if you ask me.

I wondered if the witches viewed this lecture kind of like "old home week."

The university's president, a tall, skinny Jesuit named

Monroe, made some introductory remarks. He surprised me by being both witty and brief.

Then Prescott came to the podium.

I saw right away where the wheezing in the guy's voice came from – and it wasn't asthma or smoking. Benjamin Prescott must have weighed over four hundred pounds. Put that much pressure on your lungs and ribcage, and breathing problems are almost guaranteed.

That's not to say that Prescott was a slob. His brown hair was carefully cut and brushed straight back. The gray suit he was wearing didn't exactly make him look slim, but it fit his bulk well, and the material looked expensive. I can't afford pricey clothing, but I still torture myself with an issue of *GQ* every once in a while.

A guy that size, you'd expect him to sound like James Earl Jones. But Prescott's voice, as I knew from the phone, was closer to a tenor. I listened to it for the next forty-seven minutes.

I can't say that I paid real close attention to the lecture. The guy wasn't bad – at least he seemed to be talking to us, rather than just reading his damn paper. But I wasn't too interested in what witches and demons were doing back in the seventeenth century. The ones running around today give me enough problems.

After Prescott finished his presentation, he took questions from the audience for about twenty minutes. The ones coming from students were usually polite and to the point. But you could always tell when professors were called on: they usually preceded the question with a mini-lecture designed to show off how much they already knew about the subject. And their questions seemed designed to trip Prescott up, although they didn't succeed, far as I could tell.

I thought about sticking my hand up to ask something like "Professor, what's your opinion of the power of the spells contained in the *Opus Mago*?" But he'd probably just shut me down and move on to the next question. My cousin Tim used to be a stand-up comic. He once told me, "Never take on the guy who controls the microphone. You'll always lose."

Better I should talk to Prescott one-on-one, in a situation he couldn't control. I hoped the reception would give me the chance I wanted.

It did. Sort of.

The post-lecture gathering was held in a big room with hardwood floors and lots of paintings on the walls depicting big deal Jesuits of the past. Karl and I stood in a corner at first, munching some pretty good hors d'ouevres while we watched people coming up to pay homage to the great man. Finally, the traffic in Prescott's direction slowed down.

"Come on," I said to Karl. "It's our turn to welcome our guest to the big city. Try not to look like a thug for the next five minutes."

"Five whole minutes? Gonna be hard."

We made our way over to Prescott, who was standing next to a table on which somebody had put a big bowl of iced shrimp. The professor was scarfing them down, one after another, as if seafood was going to be illegal tomorrow. I stopped in front of him, put a suck-up smile on my face, and stuck my hand out. "Professor, I just wanted to say how much I enjoyed your talk tonight." I was hoping he wouldn't recognize my voice from the phone.

Apparently, he didn't. Prescott squeezed my hand for

about a second before dropping it. "Thank you," he said with a little smile. "I'm pleased you enjoyed it, Mr…"

I was tempted, for Karl's sake, to say "Bond – James Bond," but common sense prevailed.

"My colleague and I," I said, gesturing at Karl, "were so impressed by the depth of your knowledge that we wondered if you could give us your opinion on something we've been working on." Ned had helped me work out some stuff I could say to impersonate a guy with too much education.

Prescott's smile went out like a candle in a hurricane. "Well, I hardly think this is the appropriate place for me to read any–"

"Oh, this isn't a paper, or anything like that," I said. "Just a few images that we'd been puzzling over. Can't make head or tail of them, to tell you the truth, and we figured that if *anyone* could help us out, it was you."

The smile I had plastered on was starting to make my face hurt.

Prescott grabbed another shrimp out of the bowl. "Well, if we can do this quickly, I suppose it might be–"

"Hey, that's terrific," I said, and pulled from my pocket a sheet of paper where I had copied the three sets of symbols we'd found on the murder victims.

Prescott popped the shrimp into his mouth and took the paper from me. I signaled Karl with my eyes, and he took a slow step to the side, blocking Prescott from a quick exit in case he tried to walk away once he realized we'd conned him.

Prescott's eyes narrowed as he stared at the symbols on the paper. After a few seconds, I said quietly, "Those were found carved into the bodies of three recent murder victims. Rumor has it they were taken from a spell that's part of the *Opus Mago*. You remember the *Opus Mago*, don't you, Professor?"

His eyes wide open now, Prescott looked up from the paper and stared at me in shock and anger. He drew in breath to speak, but I'll never know what he intended to say.

Prescott's mouth was open, but instead of angry words, what came out were a series of hoarse grunts. His fleshy face began to turn a deep shade of red.

"Christ, he's choking on the shrimp!" I said to Karl. "Your arms are longer – quick, Heimlich him!"

Karl immediately slipped behind Prescott and threw his arms around the big man's midsection, clasping his hands together in front. He gave the quick, hard squeeze that was supposed to constrict Prescott's diaphragm with enough pressure to send the shrimp back out of his windpipe.

Nothing happened. Other guests were starting to converge on us now, asking urgent questions that I paid no attention to. I whipped out my badge and held it up. "Police officer, get back!" I yelled. "Somebody call 911!"

Karl shifted his grip a couple of inches and tried again. Still nothing.

Prescott's color had gone from red to purple.

Karl moved his hands again, took a deep breath, and squeezed hard.

Nothing came out. Prescott's knees were starting to sag now. There was no way Karl could keep him on his feet and work the Heimlich maneuver at the same time, so I moved in, directly in front of Prescott, so close that our chests were touching. I grabbed a handful of his belt on each side and braced my elbows against my hips, trying to hold up what was quickly becoming four hundred-some pounds of dead weight.

"Go on!" I grunted. "Do it! Quick!"

Karl adjusted his grip once more and I heard him grunt as he gave another desperate squeeze.

And a piece of half-chewed shrimp popped out of Prescott's gaping mouth and hit me right in the face.

A moment later, it was followed by the remains of his dinner.

Must have been a hell of a big meal. Spicy, too.

Back at the squad, I took a long, hot shower, then put on the set of spare clothes I keep in my locker for times like this.

I figured that some of the smell of Prescott's vomit must be still clinging to me, the way Lieutenant McGuire's nose kept wrinkling while Karl and I told him about our little adventure in academia.

Or maybe he just thought it was our story that stank.

"So, I assume after the professor stopped choking to death, he was in no mood to answer any of your questions," McGuire said sourly.

"We never got the chance to find out," I told him. "He could breathe okay, but couldn't stand up or speak. Somebody called 911, and the EMTs showed up and took him to Mercy Hospital."

"But he turned out to be okay, right?" The way McGuire said it, there was only one correct answer to that question.

Too bad we couldn't give it to him.

"Actually, uh, no," Karl said. "The docs think maybe he had a stroke."

McGuire gave Karl a look that would've raised welts on some people. "A stroke."

"They're not sure if it was brought on by the choking, or if something else caused it," I said.

McGuire gave me some of the same look, and it's a wonder I didn't start bleeding right there.

"So, I assume Professor Prescott is planning to sue the city over what you two morons did?" he said, finally.

I took a deep breath and let it out. "We don't know," I said.

McGuire blinked. "What – they wouldn't let you in to see him?"

"No, we got into his room at the ICU for a couple of minutes," I said.

"So what's he got to say for himself?" McGuire asked.

"Not a lot," Karl said. "See, he's, uh, kind of in a, well–"

"A coma," I said. "Prescott's in a coma."

McGuire didn't say anything to that. He sat back in his chair and closed his eyes. Using the first two fingers of each hand, he began to rub his eyelids, very gently.

"There's one thing more, boss," I said.

"Of course there is," McGuire said dully, still massaging his eyeballs. "Who could possibly think that I've suffered enough already? What is it?"

"You're going to be getting a couple of letters," I said. "Probably tomorrow, or the next day."

"I don't suppose those would be your letters of resignation?" McGuire said. Without waiting for an answer he went on, "No, of course not, how silly of me. My luck never runs that good." He rubbed his eyes some more. "What letters?"

"One's from the president of the U," Karl said. "Father, uh..."

"Monroe," I finished for him. "Father Monroe. And the other one's from the mayor."

McGuire still didn't take his hands away from his face. "The mayor was there," he said. "Of course, he would be.

He likes that intellectual stuff, or pretends to. I assume these are letters of complaint, maybe even demands for your badges?"

"No, sir, not exactly," I said. "They're letters of commendation."

That got McGuire's eyes open. "*Commendation?*"

"For Karl's and my, uh–"

"Heroic efforts, they said," Karl said.

"Right," I went on. "Our heroic efforts in saving the life of an honored guest of the University and the city, who, uh, tragically forgot to chew his food before swallowing it, and nearly died as a result. The mayor mentioned some kind of award, too. He said he'll call you tomorrow."

McGuire looked at me, then at Karl. For a couple of seconds, I wasn't sure if he was going to kiss us right on the lips, or draw his weapon and shoot us.

Finally, he said, "Get out of my office. And light an extra candle the next time you're in church, you stupid, lucky bastards, because somebody up there sure as shit likes you, for reasons that beat the shit out of me. Now get out."

We got.

The rest of our shift was spent at our desks, for which Karl and I were thankful. We'd both had enough excitement for one night.

It wasn't until we'd signed out and headed for home that one of us almost died.

Like everybody else in the precinct, we parked in the lot behind the building. It's surrounded by chain-link fence that's topped with razor wire, and there are surveillance cameras trained on it from a couple of different angles. A friendly wizard put a protective spell on it for good measure. Quite a few people (and some others who aren't, strictly speaking, people) don't care for cops. Our personal cars might make a tempting target for some slimeball out for a little cheap revenge.

Karl and I each grunted "See ya later" and headed off to our cars. I drive a Toyota Lycan. It's old, a little beat up, and rusted in spots, but it still runs fine – kind of like me, give or take the rust.

Getting behind the wheel of your car doesn't require much concentration, and I was thinking about the twists and turns of this case as I slid into the driver's seat. A small portion of my brain processed what I was seeing – magazines, fast-food wrappers, statue on the dashboard, an empty soda bottle–

I don't keep a statue on my dashboard.

My eyes were moving toward the strange object before my mind could scream out a warning. That's what I get for not staying alert.

The statue was four inches high and made from some kind of gray stone. It depicted a woman wearing a robe, the kind they wore in that cable series about Rome. The finely detailed face was beautiful, but above that the hair was thick and ropy. After a moment, I realized it was supposed to be a bunch of snakes laying atop the woman's head, in place of hair. Then those stone reptiles started coiling and writhing and I knew what I was dealing with – but by then, it was too late. Far too late. I swear the evil little thing smiled at me, as I felt my whole body start to stiffen and harden.

I had locked eyes with a Gorgon statue, modeled after the creature of Greek myth that could turn anybody who looked at her into stone. Charged with the proper spell, the statuette could duplicate the powers of the original, at short range. And I knew that whoever had cast the spell on this little charmer had done it right, because I was *turning into stone* – and there wasn't a goddamn thing I could do about it.

The transformation hurt like a bastard, as my bones, muscles, and blood all began to take on the qualities of solid rock. But the pain in my body was nothing – I knew, with sick horror, that I was well on my way to becoming something that was going to be useful only in a public park. Or maybe as a lawn ornament.

Then the windshield exploded.

I couldn't move, or even blink, so I was powerless to avoid the shower of safety glass that filled the car for an instant after the window's detonation. What was left of my brain was still processing the sensory overload when Karl Renfer's second bullet blew that Gorgon statue into a million harmless little pieces.

With the ensorcelled object destroyed, the spell was broken. I could feel myself returning to flesh and blood and bone. That hurt some, too, but I wouldn't have traded the feeling for anything this side of Angelina Jolie.

Karl stuck his head through the opening that had once contained my windshield. "Jeez, Stan, are you okay?"

To my great joy, I managed a small nod.

"Sorry I took so long," Karl said. "I was parked over the other side of the lot. Turns out, somebody left me one of these little prizes, too."

I commanded my arm to move, and it did – a little slowly, a little stiffly, but it moved, allowing me to start brushing pieces of glass out of my hair.

"I saw my statue through the rear window of my car,"

Karl said. "I knew it didn't belong there, but it took me a couple seconds to figure out what the fuckin' thing was. Then I figured I'd better haul ass over here and see if you'd got one, too."

"One of the better ideas you've had lately," I said. My voice was husky and my lips felt numb, but I could talk. "Thanks for the rescue mission, kid," I said. "Perseus couldn't have done a better job himself."

"He used a sword, haina?" Karl asked. "Saw the reflection in his shield, then just closed his eyes, and swung."

"Something like that," I said. "Well, I'm glad you kept yours open. That was some damn fine shooting, Mr..." I let my voice trail off. The kid deserved it.

Karl grinned like a kid on Christmas morning. He was still holding his gun, so he brought the arm across his body, cupping the elbow with his other hand so that the pistol was pointing in the air. In a passable imitation of the young Sean Connery he said, "Renfer. Karl Renfer."

We'd originally been heading home, but Karl and I decided to have breakfast together, instead. I bought.

As we sipped our first cups of coffee in *Jerry's Diner*, breathing in the good breakfast smells of coffee and cholesterol, I noticed that Karl was frowning into his cup.

"What's the matter?" I asked. "Something swimming in your java?"

He looked up, the frown still in place. "No, I'm just trying to figure out who wanted to turn us into lawn ornaments."

I added a big slug of milk to my cup. We'd ordered what Jerry's menu calls Ranger Coffee, a special blend with double the caffeine. I liked the jolt, but poured straight, the stuff was strong enough to dissolve a badge in. "I was assuming the Evil Wizard Sligo," I said. "But I haven't given it much thought, yet. I think some of my brain cells are still a little rocky."

Karl smiled. "That's a good excuse. I'd stick with that one – it oughta be good for years." Then the smile faded. "Yeah, I figured it was Sligo too, at first. But think it through. Why would Evil Wizard Sligo want to off us – or turn us to stone, which is even worse?"

I drank some coffee and ignored the urge to go scale a cliff barehanded. "Standard answer is, we're getting too close to him. He wants to stop us before we get the chance to stop him."

"Yeah, but we ain't got shit. This case is no closer to being cleared then it was when they found Kulick's body."

"We know a lot more than we did then," I said. "We know why Kulick was killed, and we've got a pretty good idea why the vamps are being murdered."

"Yeah, we're pretty sure about the *why*, but we come up nearly empty on the *who*."

I started to speak, but Karl waved a hand to cut me off.

"I know, one of your snitches overheard some dude saying that there's a new wiz named Sligo in town. We've been running with it cause it's all we got, but it's thin, Stan. Not even enough probable cause to get a search warrant, assuming we had someplace to search. Which we sure as hell don't."

"Well, if you got some great idea that we haven't tried yet–"

"That's not what I mean." Karl leaned toward me. "We're doing what we can with this bitch kitty of a case. But right now, we don't have anything worth killing us over. If Sligo, or whoever it is, knows so much, how come the motherfucker don't know *that*?"

Our food came, and I started into my eggs-over-greasy while I thought about what Karl had said.

After a while I put my fork down. "Okay, so maybe Sligo *doesn't* know we've got shit. He knows we're on the case, but thinks we're doing better than we are. Guess he doesn't know us too well."

Karl swallowed a mouthful of French toast before saying, "I dunno, Stan. The Evil Wizard is slick enough to find out who's investigating the murders, and a good enough magician to get in and out of that parking lot without tripping an alarm – hell, he even knows which *cars* we drive. But he hasn't figured out that we're going nowhere with this case?"

"Well, when you put it like that..."

We ate in silence for the next few minutes. Then Karl said, "Look, could be I'm full of shit. Wouldn't be the first time. Maybe Sligo's just paranoid, and decided to take us out as a precaution."

Brave man that he is, he signaled the waitress for more coffee.

"Or maybe," he said, "somebody else besides Sligo wants us dead."

The next night, we hung around the squad room just long enough to check messages and make sure that Rachel Proctor hadn't turned up yet – alive, or dead. After that, it was just like the old song: we were off to see the wizard.

Jonas Trombley made magic, and maybe worse, out of a big old house in Clark Summit, a borough just east of Scranton. When we rolled up a little after 9:30, there was no light showing anywhere. That didn't mean anything;

if the wizard was working tonight, it would most likely be in a room with no windows at all.

I rang the doorbell a couple of times, with no result. So I put my thumb on it and kept it there. Even from the porch, I could hear the buzzing sound the thing was making inside. I was prepared to keep my thumb on that button for an hour, and I was betting that Trombley knew it, too. "So," I said over my shoulder to Karl, "You been watching that documentary series on HBO, *True Blood*?"

A couple of minutes later, Karl was describing a book he'd been reading about some scientists who'd accidentally opened a doorway to Hell. I was about to ask if it was fiction or nonfiction when the big wooden door finally cracked open.

A man's voice said from inside, "Do you realize what I could do to you, without lifting a finger, for disturbing me like this?"

"Nothing, I hope," I said. "If you did, that would be black magic, wouldn't it, Jonas? And that stuff's illegal. Now open the, uh, darn door, so we can get this over with."

I heard the voice mutter something that sounded suspiciously like "asshole," but the door opened wider. There was enough light from the street for me to make out a human shape inside. Then it waved one hand, and at once the house was ablaze with light.

Once we were inside, Jonas Trombley said, "Close the door."

I was tempted to say, "Why don't you show off some more, and close it yourself?" But the visit had already started on a negative note. No point in growing that into a symphony.

"In here," Trombley said, and motioned us into what turned out to be a living room furnished in what I think of as Thrift Shop Modern. Whatever money Jonas Trombley was making off the practice of magic, he wasn't spending it on an interior decorator.

Once we were seated, he looked at Karl, then at me and said, "So?"

I didn't answer right off, which is an old cop trick. Sometimes, if you don't tell them what you want right away, citizens will fill the silence with some interesting information. I took those few seconds to study Jonas Trombley, who I hadn't seen in three years.

He didn't seem to have aged any, which could be the result of magic or just good genes. Blond, slim, and fit-looking, he looked to be in his late twenties, although I knew he was thirty-four. He wore a zippered velour shirt in what I guess is called royal blue above a pair of designer jeans that were no tighter then the skin on your average grape. The sandals he wore displayed what I was sure was a professional pedicure.

I didn't know, or care, if Trombley liked girls, boys, or both – but whatever his preference was, I would have bet that he got more ass than a rooster, even without the magic.

Once I realized that he wasn't going to blurt out anything useful, I said, "Made any Gorgon statuettes lately, Jonas?"

He tilted his head a little and looked at me, not answering right off. Maybe Trombley wanted to give me a little of my own silent treatment, but most likely he was taking a few seconds to think. I'd always figured there was a lot going on behind those hazel eyes of his – maybe too much.

A smile made a cameo appearance on his lean face before he said, "Those nasty little things require black magic, detective – which, as you pointed out a moment ago, is illegal."

"Can we take that as a *no*?" Karl asked.

Trombley turned to him and raised one eyebrow, a trick I've never been able to manage. "You may."

"Well, somebody's been making them – two, to be exact," I said. "And I'm thinking that he – or she – probably did it for hire. Would you know anything about that?"

More silence. I could almost hear the wheels turning in Trombley's brain as he weighed how much to tell me, and what it might be worth to him – as well as the cost, if I caught him holding out on me.

"Do you know any ecdysiasts, Sergeant?" he asked. "Professionally, that is." He sat back in his chair. "I meant your profession, of course – not theirs."

If he was planning to make me feel stupid for not knowing what an ecdysiast is, he was wasting his time. "Yeah, I've met a few strippers," I said. "Some human, some not."

"Do any of those, um, *ladies* ever turn tricks on the side?"

"They don't tell me about it, if they do. Anyway, I'm not the Vice Squad."

I heard Karl stir impatiently in his chair. But I was willing to wait. There was a point that Trombley was trying to make, and I wanted to find out what it was.

"But some strippers do 'hook' on the side – fair to say?" Trombley asked.

"Yeah," I said with a shrug. "So?"

"I have a couple of... acquaintances in that profession. Not prostitutes, you understand. These ladies only exhibit their bodies, not sell them. But they tell me that there is a certain kind of man who assumes that every stripper is also a 'working girl.' Some of them can be quite obnoxious in their quest for sexual favors."

"Look, buddy, we don't have all night..." Karl began, but Trombley held up the hand again.

"Of course, Detective, and I won't delay you unnecessarily. But I wanted to make the point that people, ignorant people, sometimes make assumptions about what various... professionals will and will not do for money."

I thought I could see where this was going. "You're comparing yourself to a stripper?"

He gave me the smile again. "Only figuratively, of course. Although it's a venerable profession. Almost as old as mine."

"Somebody asked you to make a Gorgon statue," I said.

"Indeed, yes. Two of them, in fact."

"And the fact that we're having this conversation means you turned him down. Or was it her?"

"I did decline, yes. And I was quite insulted by the assumption the man was making. I do not dabble in black magic, nor will I – for any amount of money."

"Because you're such a law-abiding citizen," Karl said, not bothering to hide the sarcasm.

The look Trombley gave Karl this time was definitely of the turn-you-into-a toad variety, but his voice was mild when he said, "That's right, Detective. But more to the point, I am not subject to self-delusion."

"Meaning what?" I asked.

"Meaning I do not assume that I could make a pact with any of the Dark Powers without eventually paying the ultimate price."

"Your life, you mean," Karl said.

"No, Detective. My soul. Unlike some foolish practitioners of the Art, I have never forgotten that when you make a deal with the devil, the notes come due in brimstone. Invariably."

"All right, you didn't take the job," I said. "But somebody did."

Trombley looked at me more closely. "Yes – I should have seen it sooner. You've had a brush with the Reaper recently. Clearly he came in second best." It was hard to tell whether his voice contained relief or regret.

"Well," he went on, "I have no idea who among my fellow practitioners might have accepted that commission. I could give you a list of names, but you're as familiar with the local magic community as I am. Perhaps even more so."

"What about the guy who tried to hire you?" Karl asked. "Did you get a name?"

"He called himself Thomas L. Jones," Trombley said, deadpan. "Do you suppose that could have been an alias?"

"How about a description?" I said.

"White male, mid to late twenties," Trombley said with a shrug. "Well built, average height, brown hair cut conventionally, clean shaven, rather attractive brown eyes." He looked at me. "I realize that probably describes about five thousand of the local residents, but I may be able to narrow the field for you. Excuse me a moment."

He stood up smoothly and left the room for what I assumed was the kitchen, judging by the clinking of glass that soon followed. I had a feeling that the wizard wasn't planning to offer us refreshments. Just as well – I hate to be rude, but I wouldn't eat or drink something this guy gave me if it came with a *nihil obstat* from the pope himself.

Karl and I were exchanging silent "What the fuck?" looks when Trombley came back into the room.

"Here you go," he said, and gently tossed a glass in my direction. I picked it out of the air and saw that it was the kind of squat, wide glass people often serve booze in. I think it used to be called an Old Fashioned glass, after the drink. Maybe it still is.

"When the gentleman called on me, I offered him some hospitality," Trombley said. "I didn't yet know what he wanted, and so treated him like any other potential client." He nodded at the glass in my hands. "After I learned what 'Mr Jones' had in mind, and asked him to leave, I thought I'd best put that glass aside without washing it. It should now have three sets of prints on it, Detective. Mine, which are on file with the application for my magic license, your own, and those of the elusive Mr Jones. Perhaps you'll be able to identify him from those."

As we got to our feet, Karl asked him, "How come you waited until now to share this information with the police?"

Trombley gave us a nonchalant shrug. "Until now, I had no reason to believe he had found someone to indulge his foolishness. As far as I knew, no crime had been committed."

Karl looked at me, and I gave him a shrug of my own. If Trombley wanted to play innocent, there was no way we could prove otherwise. And he *had* provided us with the glass.

As he saw us to the door, Trombley said, "Regardless of how the prints work out, don't bother to return the glass. I'm sure it will make a nice addition to one of your kitchens."

Then we were on the porch, the door closing firmly behind us.

Snotty bastard.

• • • •

We didn't even have to send the prints on Jonas Trombley's glass to the FBI. They rang the cherries in the Scranton PD's own fingerprint files.

"Jamieson Longworth?" I looked at the mug shot on my computer screen, full face and profile. The image seemed vaguely familiar, but I couldn't say from where.

I turned to Karl, sitting next to me. "Who the fuck is he?"

"Let's find out," Karl said. "Keep going."

I clicked a couple of times, and there it was: an arrest report. And it was recent.

"Holy shit," Karl said softly. "He's one of the cultists. From the warehouse."

"And now he wants payback?" I said. "I've busted people who ought to hate me a hell of a lot more than him, and none of *them* tried to get me turned into stone."

"I'm surprised the guy's not still in County, awaiting trial," Karl said. "Assuming what's-his-name, Trombley, wasn't yanking our chains. Because of the hooker, those cultists were all charged with felony murder, haina? They should've been looking at some pretty high bail."

"Let's find out," I said. I clicked my way to the case file and started scrolling.

It didn't take long. "Yeah, old Judge Rakauskas set bail at half a million each, fifty-K cash equivalent," I said. "Either way, that's a lot of green for your average lowlife to come up with."

"And only one of them did." Karl was looking at the screen.

Jamieson Longworth.

"Okay, that puts the bastard on the street," I said. "But it still doesn't explain why he–"

"Wait," Karl said. "Scroll down some more."

"To where?"

"To the name of the guy who ended up as Purina Demon Chow."

I'd heard that, on the advice of their attorneys, the surviving cultists had clammed up tighter than a banker's wallet. They weren't saying anything about anything, including the name of their buddy who Karl had thrown to the demon. They weren't even admitting that there *was* a demon. And any ID the guy had been carrying had been consumed, along with the rest of him.

I sat there frowning at the monitor until Karl said, "Try the M.E. He might have something."

It took a few seconds to find the medical examiner's report. In one of the appendices, it said that forensics had found enough DNA to make an identification of the deceased.

Ronald Longworth, age twenty-one. Same address as the cultist who had made bail.

Jamieson Longworth's brother.

I started to say something, but then my computer made a *ping* and a little tab appeared on the bottom of the screen. It read, "New mail from Vollmanex@aol.com."

I looked at Karl for a second, then clicked open my mailbox. Sometimes when it rains, it pours.

Nobody would ever accuse Vollman of being verbose – not online, anyway.

I have examined, with considerable difficulty, a copy of the Opus Mago. *Only one spell in it calls for the sacrifice of Nosferatu. The one attempting to cast this spell must not succeed. He must be stopped, at any cost.*

The number of Nosferatu sacrifices required for the sacrifice is 5.

• • • •

"Five vamps," Karl said. "Which means two to go."

"You can do subtraction," I said. "That's a good start. We'll have you up to the multiplication tables by next week."

"Yeah, if any of us are still here next week. What do you figure the Big Bad is – the one Vollman says is gonna happen if the spell goes off as planned?"

"The End of the World as We Know It, maybe? I think I've heard that one a few times before. And the World as We Know It is still here."

"Yeah, but maybe that's because the good guys always stopped the bad guys who were gonna cause it," Karl said. "You ever think about that?"

"Right now I'd rather think about how to find Jamieson Longworth, before his tame wizard manages to do us in. We can't save the world if we've been turned into lawn furniture."

I turned back to the computer. "Last known address for both these guys is in Abington Heights."

Karl snorted. "That explains where he got the money to make bail. Dude's got some coin, if he lives up there."

"Maybe." I brought up the Reverse Directory and typed Longworth's address into it. "Then again, the money may belong to Mommy and Daddy. The property's in their name, anyway."

"Well, I guess human sacrifice is one way to rebel against your parents," Karl said. "But it seems kinda extreme, even if they *are* real assholes."

I stood up. "Let's go talk to them," I said, "and find out."

On our way out to the car Karl said, "Maybe we oughta not mention to Mommy and Daddy that I'm the one who fed their other kid to a demon."

"Yeah, that would make kind of a bad first impression, wouldn't it?"

"Bastard deserved it, though."

"Even so."

"Yeah," Karl said. "Even so."

We don't have mansions in Scranton. People with enough money for a mansion would rather live someplace else. But if there were going to be any mansions in town, you'd find them in Abington Heights. That's where the money lives, most of it. Some of the *really* rich have isolated estates up in the hills around Lake Scranton. But there was enough money in Abington Heights to offset a good-sized chunk of the national debt, if you could only get it away from them, and good luck with *that*.

The Longworths had built themselves a three-story mock Tudor that sprawled across a plot of ground about the size of New Zealand. I wondered what issue of *Architectural Digest* they'd seen it in. "Build us one like this," I bet they'd told the contractor, "only bigger." The immense lawn was so immaculately kept that I couldn't imagine kids playing on it. I wondered where the Longworth brothers, growing up, had played ball, and tag, and generally run tear-assing around the way kids are supposed to.

Maybe they hadn't. Maybe that was the problem, or part of it.

The door was answered by a smiling chubby-cheeked housekeeper who said her name was Mrs. Moyle. She was wearing a tasteful version of what my mom used to call a housedress, except this one had probably cost five times as much. At least they hadn't put her in a maid's uniform.

We'd called ahead and were expected. If we weren't exactly welcome, you couldn't tell it by Mrs. Moyle, who showed us into a living room that wasn't nearly as big as Dodger Stadium.

"Would you officers care for some tea, or coffee, or maybe something light to eat?" she asked.

"No, thank you, ma'am," I said. "We're good."

"A cocktail, perhaps?" She touched her fingers to her mouth in embarrassment. "Oh, that's right, you're still on duty, aren't you?"

"Yes, we are, ma'am. If you could just tell Mrs. Longworth we're here?"

"Oh, of course. Please make yourselves comfortable. I'm sure she'll be right out."

Karl and I sat down on a leather couch that was more comfortable than it looked. Mrs. Longworth kept us waiting exactly five minutes – the same length of time I'd spent cooling my heels in a few other rich people's homes. It must be in a manual somewhere, under "Appropriate Waiting Time for Visiting Tradesmen, Police Officers, and Other Representatives of the Working Class."

Emily Longworth wasn't more than five feet tall, but she hadn't let her height, or lack of it, give her an inferiority complex. Her hair was a shade of auburn that nature never thought of but should have, and she wore a simple gray wool dress that was probably worth as much as my pension fund. I assumed the pearls on the single string around her slim neck were genuine.

She looked at our ID folders closely, whether out of disdain or mere curiosity I couldn't tell. After we were all seated, she said with a tight smile, "So, gentlemen, what can I do for you?"

"First of all, ma'am, I'd like to offer my condolences on the death of your son. I know what a terrible thing that must be."

There was no point in tiptoeing around it. If she was going to vent about it, let her. She might be more talkative, afterwards.

The semblance of a smile was gone as Mrs. Longworth asked me, "Indeed, officer? You've experienced the loss of a child, yourself, have you?"

"Yes, ma'am, I have." *In ways you can't even imagine.*

She saw the truth of it in my face, even if she didn't fully understand what I'd meant.

"In that case, thank you for your... condolences." She'd been about to say "sympathy," I was sure of it – I'd seen the "s" start to form in her mouth, but then she'd remembered that one doesn't accept sympathy from social inferiors.

Next to me, Karl was looking at the carpet as if he wanted to memorize the weave. He'd been pretending that throwing that little bastard to the demon had been all in a night's work, but I knew better. It would be a long time before either of us forgot the screams coming from Richard Longworth as that demon had eaten him alive. The fact that it could easily have been me screaming, as Richard Longworth cheered, was some consolation, but only some.

Closing her eyes, Mrs. Longworth shook her head slowly. "It's been like a nightmare, except even in my most frightening dreams I never thought that my son would be set upon by *werewolves...*"

The word seemed to hang, vibrating, in the air. I opened my mouth to speak, then closed it. I'd been about to say, *Werewolves don't do that kind of thing anymore – not outside the movies,* then I remembered that case in Denver last year.

A guy had been arrested for molesting little kids. He'd been doing it for a while, apparently. The victims had kept quiet a long time, for the usual reason: the scumbag had threatened them, their parents, or their pets with terrible deaths if the poor kids talked.

But one of them finally did. When word got out, the dam broke and more victims came forward. One of them was from a supe family.

The pederast had made three major mistakes, the way I look at it. The first was giving into his sick desires instead of either getting serious psychiatric help or cutting his own wrists. The second was molesting the six year-old daughter of a werewolf. His third mistake, the fatal one, was somehow coming up with the money to make bail.

They call them "short eyes" in jail, and pedophiles are often the target of other inmates. Even killers and bank robbers have kids of their own. But this guy would have done better to stay behind bars and take his chances in the shower room.

What you hear about werewolves is true. The wolf part of their nature means that they tend to form tight social groups, similar to the packs you find in the wild. You think Italian families are close? They've got nothing on your average werewolf clan.

I don't think the Denver cops ever figured out exactly how many weres had been in the group that cornered the child molester after he left his bail bondsman's office. But there wasn't any doubt about how he died. He'd been eaten alive – and they figured he'd taken over an hour to die.

But this kind of thing was really uncommon among werewolves these days, and I was about to say so to Mrs. Longworth when Karl asked her, "Is that what the police told you, ma'am? That your son was attacked by... werewolves?"

"The police? I didn't speak to the *police*. There are some things a mother just shouldn't have to *do*. My husband spoke to them. He told me later, because I insisted on knowing."

"Is that also what your other son, Jamieson, says happened?" I asked carefully. "After all, he was there."

"He was *not* there. I wish you police would get that absurd idea out of your heads. Don't you think he would have tried to protect his own brother?"

Then he could have been eaten by the werewolves, too, I thought – *if there'd been any werewolves.*

"Jamieson spent the evening with some friends in Wilkes-Barre, and he had barely crossed the city limits on his way home when the stupid *police* pulled him over on some trumped-up murder charge. As if my son would have anything to do with a prostitute. It's ridiculous, that's all – it's just ridiculous."

Her face twisted, but she stopped herself from breaking into tears. That just wasn't done – at least, not in front of the stupid police.

I gave Mrs. Longworth a few seconds to pull herself together, then said, "Is your son home now, ma'am?" Fat chance of that, since we'd had to call in advance. And there's no way we'd get authorization for a raid on *this* place – not without a dozen witnesses and a signed deposition from the President. But I'd asked anyway, as an entry to some other questions I had.

"No, he's not here," she said. "He hasn't been for days."

"Doesn't he live here with you, ma'am?" Karl asked her.

"Yes, of course he does, but he's got another place somewhere in town, some kind of bachelor pad, if people still say that. I was against it, but his father said a boy needs to have some privacy."

The boy in question was twenty-seven years old.

"Can you give us the address of this 'bachelor pad' of his?" I asked.

"Oh, I have no idea. Somewhere in town – I don't know. He stays overnight, sometimes. I suppose he brings girls there." Mrs. Longworth looked at me. "*Girls*, decent girls, not... prostitutes."

I wondered how the young women who had sucked her son's cock in his 'bachelor pad' got to be considered *decent girls*, but I suppose everything's relative.

"Would your husband know where the place is, ma'am?" Karl asked.

"Perhaps he would, I don't know. You may feel free to ask him – once he gets back from Tokyo. That will be sometime next month, I believe." The tiny smile was back in place now.

"Can you give us a phone number where we can reach him? Or his email address?" I said.

"Oh, I'm sure I have all that somewhere, but I can't lay my hands on it right at the moment. Why don't you leave me your card, and I'll have my secretary locate that information and call you."

I was betting we'd hear from that secretary at about the time they opened a skating rink in Hell, but I took out one of my business cards and handed it to her. She immediately placed it on the nearby coffee table without even looking at it, as if afraid she might catch something.

"Would it be all right if we took a look at the room your son uses when he's here, ma'am?" I asked. "There might be something to help us find him – just so we can ask him a few questions."

"Would it be all right?" She pretended to consider it. "Well, I suppose so." The smile widened. "Just as soon as you show me your warrant, or court order, or whatever it's called. I have my doubts that any judge in the city would sign such an order – everyone but the police, apparently, knows what a fine young man Jamieson is. But in the event that you should obtain one, I'll have to have my attorney present, of course."

Three minutes later, we were being shown out by the housekeeper. Following Karl out the door, I started to say something when I heard Mrs. Moyle's voice behind me.

"Detective?" She held up a folded piece of paper. "I think you dropped this."

It didn't look like anything I'd had in my pockets, and I was about to say so when I noticed the intense way Mrs. Moyle was looking at me. "I'm getting careless," I said, stepping back to the doorway. "Thank you."

Mrs. Moyle didn't speak as she extended the hand holding the paper, but I saw her mouth form words that I'm pretty sure were "I never liked the little prick, anyway." Then she closed the door in my face.

I waited until we were well away from the house before unfolding the slip of paper. In a careful cursive hand was written "157 Spruce St # 304."

We were working a double shift, so it was just twilight when we left the Longworth place. That used to be my favorite time of day, when I was younger. The light gets softer and the world seems to quiet down a little, if only for a few minutes. But now I look at it as nothing more than the calm before the storm, and the storm comes every night.

As we approached the car, I was scanning the street and noticed a lone figure standing on the sidewalk three or four houses down. I tensed, and said, "Karl." to let him know we might have trouble. It would be just like that prick Jamieson Longworth to set up an ambush outside his own house.

Then I heard a woman's voice singing, an achingly clear soprano that sounded familiar. I relaxed. Nothing to worry about – except for the people living in that house.

"It's okay, but give me a minute, will you?" I said to Karl, and walked toward the woman in the gathering gloom. I saw her watching me approach, but her voice never paused in its melody.

If she'd been silent, I might have missed her in the near-darkness. As always, this stunningly beautiful woman was dressed in black – dress, hose, and shoes, with a black knit shawl wrapped around her thin shoulders. Seeing the outfit, along with her pallor, you might mistake her for a Goth, or maybe a vamp wannabe. Until you heard her voice.

She wasn't singing very loud, although I knew she had the ability to rattle windows up and down the street, if she wanted to. We'd had a conversation about it some time back – that, and the screeching. She'd eventually agreed that, tradition notwithstanding, she could carry out her duty without freaking out the whole neighborhood.

I didn't understand the words of her song, although I assumed they were Old Gaelic – very, very old. The simple melody was sad enough to get you crying without even knowing why. It didn't affect me. I'd cried myself out a long time ago.

I knew better than to interrupt her, but after another minute or so, she let her song fade away into silence. That was only temporary; she'd stay here, singing softly, until what she was foretelling had come to pass inside the house.

It was another big, ritzy place, and the people inside probably lived a comfortable life. But no matter how much money you have, or how nice your house is – if you belong to one of several Irish families, sooner or later you'll get a visit from this lady, or one of her sisters.

"Hello, Siobaghn," I said quietly.

"Sergeant," she said with a nod. "Tis a surprise seein' ye about, it not even full dark yet."

"Putting in some overtime," I said with a shrug. A few seconds passed before I said, "Can I ask who...?" I nodded toward the house.

"The clan Kavanagh. The youngest son, Edward, is about to hang himself in his room, over a love affair gone wrong." Her voice wasn't cold, exactly, just matter-of-fact.

If he hadn't done it yet, maybe there was still time. But before I could start toward the house, Siobaghn laid a gentle hand on my arm.

"No, Stanley, no. Tis already too late – else I would not be here. Ye know as much."

She was right, of course. The banshee doesn't bring death – she just foreshadows it, and she's never wrong. There was nothing I could do.

Nobody knows for sure why the banshee manifests for some Irish families and not others, or why it's only the Irish. I doubt Siobaghn herself could tell you. She just does as she is bidden, and she's been doing it for centuries.

I was about to say goodnight to Siobaghn when I heard Karl's voice shouting, "Stan! We got a ten double-zero! Come on!"

Ten double-zero is radio code for "officer down."

I was moving even before he'd finished, pulling the car keys from my pocket as I ran. Behind me, I heard Siobaghn take up her mournful song again.

A few seconds later, I was behind the wheel and reaching over to unlock the passenger door for Karl.

"Where?" I said as I started the engine.

"It's at 1484 Stanton."

I peeled away from the curb and hit the button that would get the siren going and start the headlights flashing red. We were halfway down the block before it occurred to me that the address Karl'd given sounded familiar, and we'd almost reached the first intersection when I realized why.

It was Rachel Proctor's house.

I wasn't surprised by the flashing red lights that greeted us as we drew within sight of 1484 Stanton Street. Ten Double-Zero doesn't just mean "Officer Down" – it also means every available unit within a one-mile radius is expected to haul ass to the scene at once. By the look of it, five or six black-and-white units had done that already.

Karl and I were just a block away when the radio sparked to life again: "All units, all units: be advised that the ten double-zero at 1484 Stanton has been revised to ten double-zero, Code Five. I say again, the call is now ten double-zero, Code Five."

Magic involved.

As if we'd been practicing for weeks, Karl and I said at exactly the same time, "Fuck!"

As we got closer, I saw two ambulances heading away from the scene. One was moving fast, lights flashing and siren screaming.

The other ambulance wasn't using its lights or siren, and was traveling at a normal speed. Whatever that one was carrying to the hospital, there was no hurry to get it there.

The ranking uniform on the scene was a sergeant named Milner. He looked so white, you could've mistaken him for a ghost, especially in the crazy light being thrown by all those squad cars. And this is a cop with fifteen years on the job, maybe more. He'd seen it all – or so you'd think.

Something else I noticed right off was the *silence*. Get a bunch of cops together, even at a crime scene, and they're gonna talk to each other – about the job, the wife, sports, who's screwing whose ex-girlfriend, *something*. But there were eight cops standing around here, and not one of them was saying a word. I could hear the radio calls coming through the lowered windows of their cruisers, but otherwise – nothing.

I had no intention of taking over command of the scene from Milner, even though I was pretty sure I had rank on him. A lieutenant was probably already on the way. Nobody had told me it was a case for Supernatural Crimes anyway, despite that Code Five on the radio.

We walked over to where Milner was standing, looking at nothing. I expected Karl to say "What do we got here?" But he was silent, too. Maybe he had picked up on the vibe, which was more like a wake than a crime scene.

Maybe that's what it really was.

Milner let go of his thousand-yard stare and looked at me. Before I could ask a question he said, "Lady across the street called 911. Said she saw lights in Proctor's place. She knew it was supposed to be sealed, pending investigation. She was thinking burglars, kids, something like that. So Ludwig and Casey got the call to go check it out."

Larry Ludwig, I knew. He'd been on the job a long time, but never took the sergeant's exam. He told me once that he liked the action of being a street cop. Casey's name didn't ring a bell, which meant he was probably a rookie. Scranton PD's not so big that the cops don't get to know each other pretty quick, if only by name and face.

"Looks as if Ludwig sent Casey around back, then went in through the front door," Milner said. "We found him... or what was..." Milner stopped for a second and cleared his throat. "We found him in the living room."

I waited, but he didn't say anything more. Looking toward the house, I said, "Forensics hasn't been here yet."

"No," Milner said. "I called for 'em. They'll take their sweet fuckin' time, like usual." He cleared his throat again. "SWAT was on the way, too, but I cancelled it, after we went through the place. There's nobody in there. Nobody... alive, anyway. That Proctor cunt is long gone."

I looked at him. "Rachel Proctor's the suspect?" I wasn't sure yet what she was suspected *of*, but for something to get to a cop like Milner's experience, it had to be real bad. "Was there a witness?"

"Nah, not that we know about. But it's her house, ain't it? And she's a fuckin' witch, ain't she?" He pointed toward the house as if he was aiming a gun. "What went down in there wasn't done by no fuckin' Girl Scouts."

Arguing with Milner about what Rachel Proctor was capable of was going to be a waste of time. Anyway, in her current state, I wasn't sure *what* Rachel was capable of.

"Guess we better check it out," I said. "Okay if we open the front door?"

"Yeah, I guess," he said. "Just don't go inside and fuck up the crime scene."

That's something every police trainee learns the first week at the academy, but I wasn't giving Milner the fight he was spoiling for. Let him take his feelings out on somebody else. His wife was in for a rough few hours, I figured. I hoped Milner wasn't a hitter.

"Let's go," I said to Karl, and we followed a narrow, meandering sidewalk to the front door of Rachel Proctor's house.

Three creaky wooden steps led up to the front door, which was painted white, with a light blue trim. Part of the doorframe near the knob was splintered and broken. Somebody had kicked the door in – either Officer Ludwig, or whoever came before him.

Using the back of my hand, I pushed against the door. After a moment's resistance, it came free of the frame and swung wide.

The thick, coppery scent of blood hit me in the face as soon as the door opened. Nothing else in the world smells like that. Once you've had it in your nose, it can stay a long time – maybe your whole life.

All the lights were on in the living room, which made it easy to see what had got Milner acting like he'd had a personal glimpse into Hell. It was hard to imagine Hell as bring much worse.

The walls were giant abstract murals done by an insane artist who had a thing for red. And you could add the ceiling to the exhibit. Display the whole thing in the *Night Gallery*.

And it wasn't just blood, either. Sticking to the walls, the ceiling, the furniture were globs of flesh that I figured had once been bodily organs. I saw what looked like a kidney wrapped around the leg of the coffee table, and flattened against one wall was a fist-sized ball of flesh that might once have been a human heart.

Next to me I heard Karl mutter, "Dear sweet merciful Jesus." I couldn't have put it better, myself.

The room looked like a World War II bunker that somebody had thrown a grenade into, except for one thing: the furniture.

Apart from being covered in gore and guts, Rachel Proctor's living room furniture was intact and in place. All the window glass was still there, too. Whatever kind of explosion had caused the human damage, it had left the surroundings untouched.

How was that possible? There's only one answer, and it's the same one that had occurred to Milner, and probably to the other cops out there, too: magic. The blackest of black magic.

Which left Rachel off the list of suspects, as far as I was concerned. Rachel didn't practice black magic – I was sure of it.

But indications were that Rachel wasn't exactly traveling alone these days. And, judging by the books and gear we'd found in his house, George Kulick had known a few things about black magic. Enough to do this? I was hoping for the chance to ask him about it, and soon.

"Seen enough?" I asked Karl quietly.

"More than enough," he answered, his voice hoarse.

We walked back to where Milner was standing. "I assume that what we saw in there was... came from Ludwig," I said.

Milner nodded. "It was like he just... exploded from inside. They took what was left of him to the morgue. There's enough to bury, I guess." He looked at me. "Ludwig was a good cop, put in a lot of years. He didn't deserve to go out like that." Milner said it like he was expecting an argument from me, but I didn't give him one.

"What about his partner, what's-his-name, Casey?" Karl asked.

"We found him in back, on the ground, screaming. Know why?"

Karl shrugged. "Because he saw what had happened to his partner?"

"No," Milner said, "Casey was screaming because he was covered with spiders – fucking tarantulas, dozens of them."

"I know tarantulas are poisonous," I said, "and they look gross as hell. But their bite's not fatal to humans – probably not even a bunch of bites."

"It wasn't the poison," Milner said. "One of the other guys knows Casey, they're cousins or something. He says Casey had something-phobia. Fear of spiders."

"Arachnophobia," Karl said.

"Yeah, that's it. The cousin said Casey had it bad. Guess somebody else knew that, too, and covered him with the one thing he couldn't stand. He was still screaming once they got those things off him and loaded him into the ambulance."

"Tarantulas aren't native to this part of the world," I said, just to be saying something. "They come from the tropics."

"Yeah, I know," Milner said. "Funny how a whole bunch of them found their way to Casey, huh? Almost like magic." The bitterness could curdle milk.

"I know you like Rachel Proctor for it, but there's something–"

"*Like* her for it? She a fucking witch, and witches use magic, and it was magic that fucked up two cops, decent

guys with families. It don't take fucking Einstein to connect the dots."

"I know, but–"

"But nothing, Markowski. I heard you was tight with
that cunt, but you know what? I don't care how many
times she sucked your cock, or how good she was at it.
There's a BOLO out on her, and if everybody on the force
doesn't know she's a cop killer, they will before end of
third watch today. I guarantee it. Now get the fuck out
of my sight."

We got.

We were almost back to the car when my cell phone rang.

"Markowski."

"So this guy goes to a whorehouse, but he doesn't
know that all the girls working there are vampires, right?
He says to the madam–"

"Lacey, I am really, *really* not in the mood for jokes
right now."

"Suit yourself, Stan. But I'm looking at something I
think you might wanna see."

"Which is...?"

"Another dead vamp."

"Shit."

"Yeah, and it looks like the same M.O. – well, it is, but
it isn't, if you know what I mean."

"No, I don't," I said, "but it doesn't matter. Look, Lacey,
I appreciate your calling, but there's shit I need to deal
with here tonight. Can you just send me the reports and
photos online later tonight, or tomorrow?"

"I probably could, but it's not my case. I'm in Pittston,
the most musical town in the Valley."

"Say what?"

"You ever drive down Main Street? Bar, space, bar, bar, space. You'd probably get the opening song from that musical *Bats* if you played it on the piano."

"Lacey–"

"Okay, okay, but that's where the vic turned up. A Statie I know gave me a call, because he knows about the dead vamp we turned up the other night."

"A Statie?"

"Well, Pittston doesn't exactly have a Homicide squad, you know? So they called in the Staties, and the PBI's taking over the investigation."

"Shit."

"If you put in a request through channels, you might get copies of all the case materials in, I dunno, a week or so. Maybe two."

"Shit."

"You keep saying that, Stan."

"Well, what did *you* say when you found out you were going to have to drive to Pittston tonight?"

"Me? I said *motherfucker*."

"Give me your 20, and I'll see you there in a little while."

She gave me an address along with some directions, then said, "Are you bringing that partner of yours along – the big guy?"

"I was planning to, yeah."

"Good. He's cute."

As I guided the car onto 81-South, I said to Karl, "Four dead vamps. Normally, I'd file that under G for "a good start", but if Vollman's right, that means Sligo, or whoever's behind this, is almost ready to do the Big Nasty."

"Except we don't know what *that* is, either."

"Or when he's gonna do it, or where, or even who this

Sligo is. But other than that, I'd say we're pretty much on top of this thing."

We'd gone about a mile down the highway when Karl said, "Stan. Listen."

"What?"

"If this is none of my fucking business, then just say so, but..."

"But what? Just spit it out, Karl – I won't shoot you. Not while I'm driving, anyway."

"Well... it's pretty obvious that you've got a real hard-on for vamps. Not for other supes, so much. I never heard you bitch about weres, or trolls, or even ghouls – and *those* fuckers creep me out. But you just *hate* vampires. And that's your business, I'm not tryin' to tell you what you oughta think. I was just wondering... how come?"

I thought about making a joke about it and changing the subject. And I thought about telling Karl to mind his own fucking business. Then I thought about telling him the truth.

Since he's my partner, who's saved my ass at least twice, I decided to go with door number three.

I took in a deep breath and let it out slowly. "Okay," I said. "It's like this."

I've been on the force for nine years, and a detective for two, and I want that Detective First Grade shield so bad I can taste it. I can't explain why it means so much to me. Maybe it had something to do with my old man, who said I'd never amount to much, or the Irish nuns, who always treated me like just another dumb Polack – it doesn't matter why. I want that promotion, and the way to get it is to make collars and clear cases. So I'm putting in a lot of overtime, and I mean a lot.

This brings me a fair amount of grief at home, with Rita complaining about how I'm not there much and when I am all I want to do is sleep, or vegetate in front of the TV, stuff like that. But she never complains when I bring home the paycheck, which is pretty fat because of all that overtime.

Once I make First, I'm gonna dial it back a bit, start spending more time at home with my wife and kid. That's what I tell myself, anyway.

So I come home late one Saturday night (weekends are busy times for cops) and my daughter Christine is out with friends, and my wife is in bed, and that's all normal except when I go up there I find Rita isn't breathing.

I call 911, then do CPR until they get there, and the ambulance guys are pretty quick, but none of it makes any difference. They pronounce her about ten minutes after we get to the hospital.

Once I can think again, there are two questions burning in my mind: "How?" and "Why?" I start by demanding a copy of the autopsy report and I finally get one – but it's not brought to me by a doctor, but by another guy from the job. His name's Terrana and he says he works in Supernatural Crimes. In my department we used to make jokes about Supernatural Crimes.

I've seen plenty of autopsy reports, and I try to close my feelings off and treat this one like its about somebody who doesn't matter to me. That works until I get to the part where it says "exsanguination."

I look at Terrana. "She bled out? That's bullshit *– there wasn't a fucking drop of blood on her or on the bed. Not a drop."*

"I know," Terrana says to me. He's got one of those slow, measured voices that reminds me of funeral directors. "But there's more than one way somebody can bleed to death."

I stare at him and I think about what unit he's with and the little light comes on in my head, finally. "Vampire? You saying a vampire killed Rita?"

He just looks at me, which is all the answer I need.

"Wait a second," *I tell him.* "There were no marks on her neck. I'd have seen 'em, count on that."

"That biting on the neck stuff is kind of a cliché spread by the movies, Stan. Sure, it happens sometimes, especially when it's involuntary, such as in cases of surprise vampire attack. But there's lots of veins and arteries all over the body that a vampire can make use of."

"Terrana, will you talk English and stop with the riddles? Please? You're saying a vampire killed her but that she wasn't attacked? What the hell does *that* mean?"

"It means it may have been consensual," *he says.*

I feel my hands form into fists, seemingly of their own accord. "You're telling me she let some fucking bloodsucker...?"

"The M.E. did find fang marks, Stan. And you're right, her neck was clean. He found them on the inside of her thigh, high up, near the... uh, there's a big artery that runs through there, the femoral artery."

"So the blood-sucking bastard raped her with his fangs, the fucking–"

"I'm sorry, Stan, but the M.E. doesn't think there was force involved. If you read the rest of the report, you'll see that there was no evidence of other trauma, and that there was more than one set of fang marks. Some of them were... old."

I run my hand over my face, maybe trying to wipe away the expression that I knew was stamped there. Then I have a thought. "So he snuck in, night after night, like in Dracula. He kept attacking her in her sleep until she–"

"Stan, that book was written before we knew very much about vampires. Stoker got a lot of it right, but there were quite a few things he got wrong."

"Like what?"

"Vampires can't sneak into a house like cat burglars, Stan. Nobody knows why, but they have to be invited in."

A few days later, I apply for the transfer. It works its way through the system, and a week later I get approval. So I go through the special training, then start work as a detective in Supernatural Crimes. And in my time away from the job, I hunt the bloodsucker who had seduced and killed my wife.

It takes me eight months. Eight long months of research, cultivating informants, reading old arrest reports, trading favors with other cops, intimidating and cajoling and bribing members of the local vamp community.

Eight months. And then I find him.

But it isn't that simple anymore, because by then, I've got a bigger problem to deal with. My need for revenge is now mixed with fear – fear for my daughter, Christine.

Anton Kinski's got a job. Most vamps do, I'd learned. Since the undead had made themselves known, along with the rest of the supes, they were able to stop living in graveyards and the basements of abandoned houses. But rent and decent clothes cost money, so Anton has found work (night shift, of course) as a pleater at a small garment factory.

He's a good worker, is Anton. Puts in his time, rarely misses a night (vamps don't call in sick) and pretty much keeps to himself. When he's not off seducing and murdering women, he's got a pretty boring life, or whatever it is that vamps have.

Until the day he wakes up at sunset to find me leaning over him, the sharp point of my wooden stake resting lightly against his chest. My other hand is holding a mallet, and I make sure he sees that, too, along with the silver crucifix hanging on a chain around my neck.

"You don't know how much I want to pound this stake

clear through your body, Anton," I tell him, my voice thick and tight. "And if you so much as twitch, that's exactly what I'm gonna do."

Nothing moves but his eyes, which search my face and see there the truth of what I'd just told him.

His lips barely move when he finally speaks, and his voice is barely loud enough to hear. "Who – who are you?"

"I'm the husband of Rita Markowski, the woman you killed last fall. Remember, Anton? There can't have been so many of them since then that you don't remember Rita."

He closes his eyes for a few seconds. Then he opens them and says, "I don't suppose it will matter if I tell you it was an accident – carelessness, really, on my part."

"No difference, Anton. None at all."

His head moves about an eighth of an inch in a nod. "So, why are we talking? You want to gloat a while before you stake me?"

"No, Anton. It tears my guts out to say it, but I need you."

He looks a question at me.

"You didn't turn Rita – didn't make her... one of you."

"Like I said – accident. Got... carried away."

"But you know how to do it."

"Sure, of course," Anton says. "I've done it before."

"Is it true, what I've heard? You have to exchange blood with the victim before she dies? Is that how it's done?"

"Yeah, pretty much." He swallows. "That it? You want... me to turn you?"

He winces as the stake's point presses harder into his chest. "Don't push your fucking luck, Anton. I'd no more become one of you leeches than I'd volunteer to work in a concentration camp."

"What, then?"

"My daughter. I want... I want you to turn my daughter."

• • • •

Christine's admitted to me that she'd been concealing the symptoms – the weakness, night sweats, joint pain – for as long as she could. She didn't want to be a bother, she said – meaning, I guess, that she saw I was half-crazy with grief and she didn't want to push me the rest of the way. And I guess she also thought that some of it was just her body's way of dealing with the shock of Rita's death.

But when the lumps appeared in her armpits, she'd realized that something more serious was going on. By then, of course, it was too late.

The docs did everything the book says – radiation, chemo, even some experimental medicines. Then one day her primary physician took me into that little room they have at the hospital, just off the intensive care unit. As soon as I sat down, I figured this was the room where doctors give you the Bad News. I was right, too.

I'd suspended my off-hours search for Rita's killer when Christine was hospitalized. But the night they gave me the Bad News, I went back to it. If possible, I pushed even harder than before – and it paid off.

That's how I find myself kneeling over a vampire and telling him that he's going to buy continued existence by making my only child a bloodsucking leech just like him.

I bring Christine home a few days later, promising the hospital people that I'll arrange for twenty-four-hour nursing care. I tell them that I'll make sure she gets everything she needs.

And then, one night, when the painkillers have pushed her to edge of unconsciousness, I tell the night nurse she can go home early. Then I get in touch with Anton Kinski again.

He doesn't have to ask my permission to enter the house. He's been there before.

Even now, I'm not sure if what happened next was the right thing to do, or the worst idea I ever had.

● ● ● ●

Pittston's only about twenty minutes' drive from Scranton, so I gave Karl the short version of the story, but it contained all the essentials.

When I was done, he turned in his seat and looked at me. "Stan – Jeez – I'm sorry, man, I didn't–"

"Forget it, Karl," I said. "You didn't know and now you do, and there's nothing else to say about it. Besides, it's time to go to work."

We had reached the crime scene.

Pittston's a town of about nine thousand, midway between Wilkes-Barre and Scranton. It's got more hills than any other town I've ever seen. I hear San Francisco's worse, but I've got no desire to find out – they can keep their vamp mayor, as far as I'm concerned.

The city's in Luzerne County, not Lackawanna, which explains why Lacey Brennan got the call from the State Police and I didn't. Besides, Lacey's got a much cuter ass than I do.

We parked behind a Pittston PD cruiser that looked like it had a lot of miles on it. I could see yellow crime scene tape fencing off a white duplex with green trim. The place had seen better days. A couple of shingles were gone from the roof, and the paint was peeling in several places. As soon as we were out of the car, Lacey came strolling over, a notebook in her hand and a frown on her heart-shaped face.

"Good evening, as Bela Lugosi used to say," she said to me, then nodded at my partner. "Karl."

"Whatever chance this had of being a good evening went down the tubes hours ago," I said. "You wanna fill us in?"

"I might be able to do better than that, and get you inside for a look," she said. "The Crime Lab guys have been and gone."

As we walked toward the house Lacey said, "Family's name is Dwyer. They've got the upstairs."

"Who's ROS?" I asked her. I wanted to know who the Ranking Officer on Scene was because I wasn't going in that house without permission. Lacey couldn't give it, because this wasn't her case, or her jurisdiction. The last thing I wanted was some Statie calling McGuire to complain that I'd violated procedure.

"Twardzik," she said flatly.

There was silence for three or four paces.

"Of course it is," I said. "Why should God start taking pity on me now?"

I followed her through the small crowd of milling cops and technicians to where the Ranking Officer on Scene was chewing on a couple of guys in plain clothes. Even from the rear, Lieutenant Michael Twardzik was easy to spot. He was the only one around in a State Police uniform who barely topped 5'5". That's the minimum height requirement, and I swear the little bastard must've worn lifts in his shoes when he applied for the academy. His case of short man complex isn't much worse than, say, Napoleon's.

"And if either of you fail to turn in your Fives in a timely manner again," Twardzik growled, "you'll be packing up for your transfer to Altoona before end of shift. Understand me?"

He didn't wait for an answer. "Dismissed."

Every big organization has its version of Siberia – the place they send you when you fuck up not quite bad enough to be fired. In the Army, it used to be the Aleutian

Islands off Alaska. With the FBI, it's Omaha, for some reason. And the Pennsylvania State Police's designated version of Purgatory is Altoona. I wouldn't argue the choice – I've been to Altoona.

I let Lacey take the lead as we came up behind Twardzik. "Lieutenant?" Even in that one word, I could tell that she'd made her voice softer, a little more feminine. This surprised me some, since Lacey's normally a "fuck you if you can't take a joke" kind of gal. She must really want us to see the inside of that duplex. "Would it be okay with you if I give these officers a look at the crime scene?"

Twardzik turned, squinting against the flashing lights from the police cruisers. "Which – oh, *these* officers."

Years ago, before I joined the Scranton PD, I thought I wanted to be a Statie. So I took the exam for admission to their academy. Something like two hundred and thirty guys (it was all guys, back then) took it that year, and I scored fourteenth. Each new class is capped at a hundred, no exceptions, and the test score is what they go by.

Before you can even take the exam, they check to make sure you have a high school diploma and a clean record, and you've got to pass the physical fitness test. So if your score is in the top hundred, you're in, and if not, sorry, Charlie. And they only let you take it once.

The scores are public record, which is how I know my rank – as well as Twardzik's, which was one-oh-one. When I decided not to go (that's pretty rare, I guess), everybody below me moved up one. And that's how Twardzik got into the academy. He owes his career to the fact that I gave up my place in line.

No wonder the little bastard hates me – even though I've never once mentioned it to him.

Twardzik gave me the kind of look you'd give a particularly scuzzy-looking panhandler. "You're a long way from your playpen, Markowski. What'd you do – take a wrong turn on your way to the whorehouse?"

"Patronizing prostitutes is illegal, Lieutenant," I said evenly. No way was he getting a rise out of me. I wouldn't give him the satisfaction – or the excuse.

"I asked these detectives to come down from Scranton, Lieutenant," Lacey said hastily. "It looks like this homicide has some similarities with others that we're currently investigating."

Twardzik looked at Lacey. "Last I checked, Wilkes-Barre and Scranton were some distance apart, not to mention being in different jurisdictions. How is it you two are investigating homicides together? Has a law enforcement romance blossomed?"

That was when I wanted to hit him. But before I could say anything, Lacey got in with "I'm sorry, Lieutenant, I was being unclear. I meant that each of us is investigating separate homicides that seem to have similarities with each other, as well as with the case you have here. I thought it might help both investigations to move forward if these officers had a chance to view this crime scene."

Twardzik looked at me, then back at her, taking his time. I was pretty sure I knew what was going through his mind. If he denied permission, and Lacey and I each sent separate complaints to his Troop Commander, Twardzik would have to give a reason why he'd done it – and it would have to be a better one than his desire to see me in Hell with my back broken.

"Yeah, all right, go on," he said to me, making a head gesture toward the house. "The sooner you do, the quicker you'll be out of my sight." Then he turned away, probably looking for a stray dog he could kick.

We followed Lacey up the creaking steps that led to the second floor apartment. "Snotty little fuck," she said quietly, but with a lot of feeling. "It should come as no surprise that he's got a tiny cock, too."

"And you would know that, how?" I kept my voice casual, as if the answer wouldn't matter.

"I'm friends with his ex-wife, Stan. Jeez, how did you *think* I'd know?"

I didn't say anything, but felt my shoulders lose some tension I hadn't even known was there.

The steps brought us to a small landing in front of a simple wooden door that had plastic numbers "443B" glued to it. The doorway was spanned by a big yellow X of crime scene tape, which Lacey started to remove.

"Careful now," Karl said. Even though he was behind me, I could hear the grin in his voice. "Wouldn't want to upset the lieutenant."

"Are you kidding?" Lacey said. "I'm gonna put that back *exactly* the way I found it. Shit, I was tempted to take a picture, to make sure I get it right."

Once the tape was down, she opened the unlocked door and led us into the living room. I stepped to the side to make room for Karl's bulk and almost knocked over a knick-knack shelf full of little ceramic leprechauns. There'd be hell to pay if I broke any of them.

The furniture and drapes were old, but well cared-for. The floral wallpaper wasn't peeling anywhere, although nails stuck out from it in several parts of the room. The rug we stood on was threadbare in a few places, but it was as clean as you could expect with cops tramping all over it.

The Dwyers didn't have a lot, but they seemed to take pride in what they had. I was betting that Mrs. Dwyer vacuumed every week – probably on Saturday morning, just like my mom had done. On one wall, occupying a place of honor, was a framed faded portrait of JFK that looked like it had been clipped from a magazine. The one in our house had been from *Life*, I remembered.

A short hallway branched from the living room, with a door on each side and a bathroom at the end. One room had its door open, lights burning inside. Lacey led us there saying, "Mom, Dad, and two boys. Dennis is at Penn State, the other one, James, dropped out of high school a little over a year ago. Junior year."

"That must've been when he was turned," I said. "Which came first, I wonder?"

"Was he out to the parents?" Karl asked.

"Dunno," Lacey said, "but, Christ, he'd have to be."

Pretty hard to explain to Mom and Dad that you weren't going outside in daylight any more, and that midnight mass at Christmas was off your schedule for good. Sunday dinner would never be the same, either. They must've known their kid was a vamp. I felt sorry for them.

The bedroom looked like it would make a good set for a remake of *I Was a Teenage Vampire*. The walls were covered with posters of rock stars, although I didn't recognize most of them. Discarded clothes covered the furniture, and the floor was littered with CDs, DVDs, and magazines. The room's two windows had close-fitting boards nailed over both of them, which were covered with black plastic from garbage bags. The edges of the bags were heavily taped around the edges, to make sure no speck of sunlight would sneak in. That was the only unusual thing about the room – unless you counted the bloody corpse on the bed.

The wooden stake must have been very sharp – it looked like it had gone right through the kid's body, pinning him to the mattress like some kind of bug in a museum exhibit. James Dwyer had been wearing white briefs and a gray T-shirt with "Question Authority" printed on the front. Probably what he wore to bed when he'd been sleeping at night, not all that long ago.

The heart contains a lot of blood, so I wasn't surprised at the gore that half-covered the body and bed, and spattered the nearby wall. I'd seen staked vampires before.

"Here's the reason my buddy called me, and why I got in touch with you guys," Lacey said, walking over to the body. She pushed bloody blond hair away from James Dwyer's forehead, and there they were: three of the same kind of symbols that we'd been encountering on corpses lately. In fact, these looked kind of familiar.

I reached into my jacket pocket for my notebook. Even though the case files contained plenty of photos from each of the dead vamp crime scenes, I had still made copies by hand of the symbols that had been carved into each of the victims.

First vic – three symbols. Check. Second vic – three symbols, but different from the first set. Check. Third one – three symbols found on the guy in Wilkes-Barre. Check. Same weird alphabet, but different from the other two. Then James Dwyer, right in front of me. Three symbols. Check. Except...

"Lacey, lift the kid's hair again, will you? Karl, take a close look at these."

Karl stepped closed and leaned in close. Then he straightened up. "They look similar to the ones we been seeing," he said. "Not surprising."

"No," I said, "but here's something that is." I showed

him my notebook. "See?" Each of the first three vics had a different set of these fucking arcane symbols carved on him. But James, here–"

"–has got the same markings as the first vic." Karl's forehead wrinkled. "So, maybe this fucking ritual, whatever it is, requires some kind of repetition, only... Fuck, I dunno."

Lacey was looking at me. "There's something else that doesn't fit," she said. "Now that you mention it. The M.O."

"All the M.O.s have been different," Karl said. "I mean, that's part of the pattern, haina?"

"I think maybe I see what she's getting at," I said to him. "It's not weird enough."

She nodded slowly. "Yeah, exactly. My guy had been done by a silver garrote, and in your two, the perp used–"

"Charcoal bullets and a silver-coated blade," I said. "Wooden stake through the heart, it's, I dunno, too *conventional*."

"Okay, I'm with you now," Karl said, "but it still doesn't tell us shit. We don't know why the perp would all of a sudden start using the tried-and-true method of killing a vamp, but we don't know why the fucker's doing *anything* he does."

"Yeah, but I wonder..." I let my voice trail off. "Look, we should get out of here so the coroner can take the body away. They're probably waiting for us."

As we shuffled back out the door, I said, "Besides, there's something I wanna look at in the car."

"What's that?" Karl asked.

"My laptop."

Karl was just slipping into the passenger side as I reached under my seat for the slim laptop computer. I heard the rear door open and close as Lacey scrambled into the back seat.

I opened up my computer, logged on, then passed it to Karl. "Here," I said. "You're better at this stuff than I am."

"What stuff?" Karl asked.

"Searching the Internet."

"Ah, hell. It's not all that hard to find porn." He glanced over his shoulder at Lacey. "Not that I would know."

"If not, you're the only guy in the world who doesn't," Lacey murmured.

"So what am I looking for, Stan?" Karl said.

"Images of the symbols that were carved into the first victim."

He looked at me. "Scranton PD never released that information. Neither did Wilkes-Barre."

"No, they didn't," I said. "But it's funny how much confidential stuff gets on the Internet without being officially released. I want to know if somebody outside law enforcement could've known what those symbols looked like."

Lacey leaned over the front seat. I could feel warm breath on the back of my neck. "You're thinking copycat?"

"Maybe," I said. "It would sure explain a few things that don't otherwise make much sense."

Despite his modesty, Karl was good at finding stuff online besides porn. His fingers were flying over the keyboard, and I could hear him swearing softly as his search efforts came up empty, one after another. Then he stopped, stared at the screen, and said, "Jesus fucking Christ on a goddamn bicycle."

"What?" I asked, although I thought I knew the answer.

"This," Karl said, and turned the screen to face me.

And there they were.

• • • •

The website described the photo as showing "Actual Occult Symbols Carved into Murder Victim in Scranton PA!!!" The idiot who put it up there explained that this was somehow a sign of the oncoming Apocalypse.

Whoever he was, I hoped he was wrong.

"How the fuck did some asshole get hold of these?" Lacey said from the back seat.

"Lots of possible ways," I said. "Somebody at the coroner's office, a guy doing night shift at the morgue, the funeral home people – could've been anyone. Almost everybody's got a cell phone these days, and almost every one of those has a built-in camera."

"Yeah, be a piece of cake," Karl said. "All you'd need is some decent light and about a minute of privacy."

Lacey had her forearms crossed over the back of the front seat, her chin resting on them. "So some 'fearless vampire killer' decided to make his work look like it was done by Sligo – or whoever's been going around knocking off vamps – to throw us off the scent. That what you're saying?"

It was quiet in the car for a few seconds.

Lacey bit her lower lip for a second or two, then shook her head. "Doesn't make any sense, Stan," she said. "Mostly these Van Helsing types want publicity for their deed, if not their name. See themselves as big holy heroes. They wouldn't want a serial killer to get the credit."

"Yeah, I know," I said. "It doesn't fit the pattern. If it's a vigilante, that is."

"But what's left?" Lacey asked. "If it's not the wizard, or a fucking vampire slayer...?"

I looked over at Karl and raised my eyebrows. He saw me, and nodded slowly.

"Lacey, listen: far be it from me to tell the great Michael Twardzik, Lieutenant, Pennsylvania State Police Criminal Investigation Division, how to run one of his cases."

"Apart from the fact that he'd tell you to fuck off as soon as you opened your mouth," Karl said.

"There's that too," I said. "But he seems to like you, Lacey. Kind of."

"He's got fantasies about getting in my pants," she said, "which should be filed under G for 'Good fucking luck.'"

"Whatever the reason, he at least lets you talk to him," I said. "Which is more than Karl and I can say."

"I know about you and the academy thing," Lacey said, "but what did Karl do to piss him off?"

"Guilt by association," Karl said, with a grin.

"Anyway," I said, "the next time you have the lieutenant's ear, you might whisper in it that he should take a good hard look at the kid's parents."

Lacey just stared at me.

I said, "If it were me, I'd want to know where both parents were at the kid's time of death, whenever the coroner says that was," I said. "I might also check trash cans and storm drains in a ten-block radius, looking for some bloody clothing that somebody might have tried to get rid of. And check the sink traps in the house for blood residue – you know the routine."

"'Course I do," she said, "and I'm aware that in most murder investigations you look at family first. But why...?"

"When we were in there, I counted six nails sticking out from the walls with nothing hanging from them, and those people are too neat just to leave nails there for no reason. That's where they hung the crucifixes, the paintings of the Sacred Heart, the little frescoes of the Virgin Mary, all that. If you looked, you'd most likely find all that stuff stashed in a bureau drawer. And I'll bet that all of it will be back on the wall tomorrow, or the next day."

Lacey shook her head again, but not as if she was disagreeing with me. "I can imagine how hard it is to deal with someone in your family who's been changed," she said. "But to off your own kid in cold blood..."

"You're Catholic, aren't you, Lacey?" I asked her.

"I was raised that way, but I'm in recovery," she said with a tiny smile, which is all that old joke deserved.

Karl turned and looked at her. "You're shittin' me," he said. "How can anybody do this kind of work and not believe in God?"

"I didn't say I don't believe in God, Karl," Lacey said. "Although, if you ask me, all supes prove is the existence of the devil. I just walked away from all the Catholic bullshit. No offense, if that's your thing."

"Even so," I said, "you know the Church's views about supes – vamps, weres, goblins, the whole crew."

"*Anathema*," Karl said. "The pope says they're cursed by God, all of them."

"Yeah, and that's one of the reasons I took a hike," Lacey said. "Give some old man a tall hat, and all of a sudden he speaks for God? I don't think so."

"You may not be with the program any more, Lacey," I said, "but I'm betting the Dwyers were. From all indications, they were hard-core Irish, and, especially in this area, that means hard-core Catholic."

"You think they drove a stake through their own kid because some fucking priest told them to?"

"Possible, but it didn't have to happen that way. If they figured the Church would have wanted him dead, that might have been enough. It would be, for some people I grew up with. They probably told themselves they were saving his soul." I turned my head and looked at the night as it pressed against the car windows. "Who knows? Maybe they were."

We were approaching the on-ramp for 81-North when I whacked the steering wheel with one hand and said, "Damn!"

Karl was bent forward, fiddling with the radio. "What? What's wrong?"

"Just remembered something else the Staties ought to be doing: check the computer in the kid's room."

"For what – to see if he was downloading vamp porn?" I couldn't see Karl's smile in the dark, but I knew it was there.

You can find porn catering to every taste on the Internet – most of it legal, some not. Where there's a niche market, somebody will come up with product to fill it: gay, straight, bi, gimp, albino, human, nonhuman. It's all there someplace, and I guess vampire porn's been around the Internet as long as all the other kinds. I once had to check some of it out for a case I was working. I hope never to have to look at it again.

"No," I said, "I'd be more interested in finding out whether any Google searches had been done for those symbols we found carved on our first vic. If it was Mom or Dad, or both, who carved them in the kid, they had to find them first."

"Yeah, that could be useful," Karl said, "although there's no way to tell who was doing the search, if there is one. Hell, the kid could have done it."

"Not if it took place during daytime, he didn't. Anyway, it's kind of a reach for the kid to be researching symbols that later end up carved on his own corpse, isn't it? I'm pretty sure he didn't carve himself."

"You got a point there." Karl found a radio station he liked and sat back. "But what you did back there with Twardzik was pure fucking genius, Stan."

"Thanks. Too bad they don't give out Nobel Prizes for conniving."

All I'd done was suggest to Lacey that she tell the lieutenant that I was convinced James Dwyer was the latest victim of the serial vamp slayer, and in my opinion the investigation should focus on that aspect of the case and exclude all others.

Which guaranteed that Twardzik, while following the vamp slayer angle, would also spend plenty of man-hours treating the case like just another homicide. If there was any evidence of the parents' involvement, he'd find it. And then figure out a way to let me know about it, bless his little head. Both of them.

We were about a mile out from Scranton when Karl said, "Getting late."

I glanced at the dashboard clock. "Yeah, double shift is almost over. The chief won't pay for triple overtime, even if I had any energy left to do it. Which I don't."

"Yeah, I guess what-his-name, Jamieson Longworth's 'pad' will have to wait until tomorrow night." Karl scratched his chin. "Unless he has his pet wizard drop a boulder on us while we're asleep."

"If he was able to do that, he'd have done it by now."

"You hope."

"Yeah. I hope. But if you think about it, he probably hasn't—"

The police radio crackled into life. "Car 23, car 23, this

is Dispatch. Do you copy? Over."

Whoever's riding shotgun handles the radio, so Karl reached out, snapped off WARM 590 AM, and picked up the mike.

"This is 23," he said. "Copy just fine. Over."

"That isn't Sergeant Markowski, is it? I'd know his voice. Over."

"No, this is Renfer, but Markowski can hear you. He's driving. What's up? Over."

"I've got a phone call just come in for Sergeant Markowski. The lady says it's urgent. Do you want me to patch it through to your vehicle? Over."

Turning my head a little, I could see Karl looking at me. "Ask if she's got a name," I said, "or knows what it's about."

"Did the caller ID herself?" Karl asked. "Over."

"Affirmative. Says her name is Joanne Gilbert."

"Doesn't ring a bell," I told Karl. "Have her leave a number, and I'll–"

The radio dispatcher spoke again. "Caller says she's Rachel Proctor's sister."

I checked the mirror, then put my foot on the brake and began easing us over to the shoulder of the road and a complete stop as I said to Karl, "Tell them to put her through."

"Hello? Hello?"

"This is Detective Sergeant Markowski speaking."

"Oh. Uh, hi. My name is Joanne Gilbert. Rachel Proctor, who I guess works with you, is my sister."

Her voice did resemble Rachel's. Joanne Gilbert sounded like someone who was trying very hard to stay calm.

"Gilbert would be your married name, then," I said.

"That's right. I live in Warwick, Rhode Island, but I've got a... message... for you from Rachel."

"Is she there with you now?" My fingers were suddenly tight around the microphone. "Because I really need to–"

"No, sir. I haven't seen Rachel in a couple of years. We were going to get together at a big family thing last Christmas, but then one of my kids got sick... you know how it is."

"Yeah, I guess I do. So, how did Rachel get in touch – email, phone call, what?"

Silence. I let it go on for a little bit, then said, "Mrs. Gilbert? You still there?"

"Yes, I'm here. It's just that this is a little... what happened was, Rachel got in touch by making me write the message down with my own hand."

This time the silence was on my end. Joanne Gilbert didn't let it last long. "Detective, if you work with Rachel, I guess you must know something about witchcraft."

"More than I ever wanted to," I muttered.

"Excuse me? What?"

"Sorry, Mrs. Gilbert. I got distracted for a second. Yes, I'm pretty familiar with witchcraft."

"Then you know that the basic Talent is genetic. You're either born with it, or you're not."

"Yeah, I'm aware of that."

"But the Talent itself is practically useless," she said, "unless you get training in how to use it."

"Right."

"Rachel made the decision to develop her Talent. I didn't. I wanted a normal life. But we've both got it. The Talent, I mean."

"And all this has something to so with the message you got from Rachel." I was in no mood to listen to lengthy explanations about stuff I already knew.

"It has everything to do with it, Detective. Look, when we were kids, Rachel and I used to play around with our ability. Nothing serious, just for our own amusement. One of the things we could do, anytime we wanted, was what they call automatic writing. We didn't even know it had a name."

"One person writes what the other one is writing, even though they can't see each other."

"Exactly. I gather it's a form of clairvoyance."

"So, this is how you got Rachel's message, through automatic writing?"

"I was sound asleep. What is it now, almost three? This was like twenty minutes ago. Rachel showed up in my dream, which isn't all that unusual. But all I could see was her face, and she was looking right at me. *Wake up, Jo-Jo*, she said, very seriously. *Wake up and get a pen and paper.* She kept saying it over and over, and finally I did wake up."

"I guess 'Jo-Jo' is some kind of pet name?" I asked.

"It's what our family called me when we were kids. So, I got out of bed, put my glasses on, and stumbled downstairs. There were some pens in the kitchen, and a pad of notepaper. I got them, and sat down at the kitchen table. As soon as the tip of the pen touched the paper, my hand started moving – *writing* – of its own accord."

"Do you and Rachel communicate this way often?"

"Not since I was twelve, or thereabouts."

"So, what did you write down?"

"I'll read it word-for-word." I could hear paper rustling, then she said: "*Urgent you call Det. Stan Markowski, Scranton*

P D 717-655-0913. Tell him: Stan, I didn't hurt those poor cops.
Kulick did. I was his instrument. He's very strong. I can only
regain control like this for brief periods. You must stop him.
We're hiding...

"And that's all of it," Joanne Gilbert told me. "As soon
as I wrote *hiding*, the ink line was yanked away, right off
the edge of the paper. I waited a little while, to see if she
was going to come back, but she didn't. So I figured I'd
better get moving and do what she asked me to. Rachel
doesn't use words like *urgent* very often."

"Mrs. Gilbert—"

"I guess you might as well call me Joanne."

"Okay, fine. Joanne, would you please repeat the message again, slowly?"

"Sure." She read it again. It didn't sound any better
the second time around.

In the pale green light from the dashboard, Karl and I
looked at each other.

"Joanne, if you hear from Rachel again, anything at
all, I want you to call me at my private number. It's very,
very important." I gave her my cell phone number. "If I
don't answer, please leave a message in the voicemail
box, and I'll call you back as soon as I possibly can."

"All right, I'll do that," she said. Then, after a moment,
"Detective?"

"May as well call me Stan."

"Stan, she's in trouble, isn't she? Bad trouble?"

I tried to keep the sigh out of my voice, but I don't
think I succeeded, completely. "Yes she is, I'm sorry to
say. It's pretty bad."

"Can you get her out of it?"

"I have to," I said. "I'm the one who got her into it."

• • • •

After four hours of restless sleep, I went back to work. Telling McGuire about my phone call from Rachel's sister was at the top of my to-do list, but when I walked into the squad room I could see that he had visitors.

Two men in gray suits stood in front of McGuire's desk, talking to him. One was middle-aged, and average size; the other one was younger, and bigger. I could tell their suits were expensive – better quality than most cops wear, even the *federales*.

Minding my own business is usually something that I'm pretty good at, but the hairs on the back of my neck were bristling, for a reason I couldn't pinpoint. It could have been the expression on McGuire's face, which made him look like a man who's just had to swallow a medium-sized turd. Or maybe it was the way the two strangers held themselves – still and yet tense, like piano wire stretched tight. And piano wire is what they use in a garrote.

I wandered over to the back of the big room, thinking I'd stick my head into the reception area and ask Louise the Tease if she knew what was up. But before I could reach her desk, McGuire looked up, saw me, and motioned me over.

I stepped inside McGuire's office and closed the door behind me. The two guys in gray had turned to look at me, and that's when I saw that each of them wore a clerical collar.

Priests wear black suits, which meant these guys were Protestants. But my work brings me into regular contact with the local clergy, and I knew every one in the area by sight, no matter what denomination.

What did a couple of out-of-town ministers want with McGuire – or, for that matter, with me?

It didn't take long to find out.

"This is Detective Sergeant Markowski," McGuire said. His voice was flat, as if he had squeezed all feeling out of it. "He's the lead detective on the case."

To me he said, in the same detached tone, "This is Reverend Ferris," with a head gesture toward the older guy, "and his associate, Reverend Crane."

I figured I ought to shake hands – what else was I going to do? I was extending my hand toward the younger guy, Crane, as McGuire continued, "The reverends, here, are witchfinders."

I froze for a second. *Witchfinders.* Fortunately, Crane's hand was already on its way to mine, and I clasped and pumped it a couple of times by reflex. Then came the older guy. I was moving okay by then, but Ferris held the handshake longer than you'd expect, staring at me intently.

After he let go, the stare continued for a moment longer before he said, "You have the odor of witchcraft about you, Sergeant."

Before I could say anything, Ferris gave me a little smile and went on, "But that is to be expected of any guardian of the public order who must deal with these abominations on a regular basis. Certainly it is nowhere near as strong as we find in a true practitioner of the black arts."

"Well, that's good," I said. "For a second there, I thought I needed another shower."

"Witchcraft is no subject for humor, Detective," Crane said. His voice was thin and nasally, like the whine of a mosquito just before it bites you. "Consorting with the devil is a matter of utmost seriousness."

"Peace, Richard," Ferris said, laying a light hand on the younger guy's arm. "I'm sure the sergeant meant no harm." He gave me a wider version of the smile this time, but his gray eyes were as cold as January slush.

"The reverends here were sent for by the chief, on orders from the mayor," McGuire said. "Who is very concerned that a witch cop-killer is still at large." McGuire seemed about as overjoyed to see them as I was, although maybe for different reasons.

He probably didn't like the implication that he wasn't doing his job as head of the Supe Squad. But it was the prospect of these two self-righteous pricks going after Rachel, and what they'd do if they found her, that scared the shit out of me.

"Yeah, about that," I said. "I got an interesting phone call while Karl and I were on our way back from Pittston last night – or, rather, this morning." I ran down for them what Rachel's sister in Rhode Island had told me.

"That supports what you've been saying ever since Rachel disappeared from the hospital," McGuire said thoughtfully, once I'd finished.

The Reverends Ferris and Crane, however, looked as if I'd just told a filthy joke about one of their mothers.

"I hope you're not inclined to treat this... account seriously, Lieutenant," Ferris said.

McGuire looked at him. "Are you saying you think Detective Markowski made this all up?" he said slowly. There was nothing threatening in his voice, but I still saw the older witchfinder swallow a couple of times. Say this for McGuire, he stands up for his people.

"No, of course not," Ferris said, his voice sounding like he hadn't completely ruled it out. "But even if the sister's account of this automatic writing business is true – which it may not be – we can hardly expect anything but deceit from those who have given their allegiance to the Father of Lies himself."

"'Their delight is in lies; they give good words with their mouth, but curse with their heart'," Crane intoned.

"The Book of Common Prayer, 62:4," Ferris said, nodding. "Exactly."

"Wait a minute," I said. "You're saying we shouldn't believe anything Rachel says about not practicing black magic, because everybody knows that people who do black magic lie? I'm pretty sure that's what my Jesuit teachers would call circular reasoning."

"*Jesuits*," Crane said, with a smirk. "We know all about *them*."

Before I was able to get in his face about that, Ferris said, "Regardless of how you twist our words, Detective, the fact remains that the woman is already on record as practicing witchcraft. As I understand it, that's even in her *job description*."

"Rachel Proctor's job title is 'consulting witch', it's true," McGuire said. "But the job position specifies the practice of white witchcraft exclusively."

The two witchfinders looked at each other, their expressions saying as clearly as words, *What are we to do with such idiots?*

"Black witchcraft, white witchcraft," Crane said. "The important word in each phrase is the noun, not the modifier: *witchcraft*."

McGuire leaned forward in his chair, resting his elbows on the desk blotter. "Let me see if I've got this straight," he said. "You fellas don't see any difference between black witchcraft and white? None at all?"

Ferris shrugged his narrow shoulders. "We are aware

that various apologists have argued the distinction, claiming that so-called white witchcraft is somehow less pernicious than the other variety. In practice, Reverend Crane and I have found little difference between them."

This conversation was becoming so ridiculous that I didn't even know what to say. It's true that black witchcraft is exactly what these two clowns had been talking about: you mortgage your soul to Satan, in return for supernatural power to do evil: curses, deadly spells, stuff like that. But white witchcraft, an outgrowth of Wicca, derives its power from nature and can't be used to hurt people, except sometimes in self-defense. The difference is as obvious as, well, black and white.

Fortunately, McGuire wasn't stuck mute by this bullshit. "Well, here's one difference the two of you had best keep in mind," he said. "The practice of black witchcraft is a felony, subject in some cases to capital punishment. But white witchcraft is legal, and protected by the law, just like any other kind of free expression."

Crane drew breath to speak, but again Ferris quieted him with a touch on the arm. The older witchfinder drew himself up and his voice was frosty when he said, "We are well aware of the law, Lieutenant, and it will be followed to the letter. We shall *lawfully* apprehend this witch Rachel Proctor, and we shall then put her to the question as to the nature of her recent activities, just as the *law* allows. And when – excuse me, *if* – she confesses to the practice of black witchcraft, which is both a crime against the state and an offense before Almighty God..."

Ferris turned his head to look at me for a second before returning his gaze to McGuire. "... then we shall *lawfully* show unto her, God's judgment, exactly as Scripture has specified."

He turned away and walked stiffly toward the office door. Crane stood looking at us, however. Maybe he felt the need to add to his boss's little oration, or maybe it was his job to have the last word. Before following Ferris out of the office, Crane looked at us and declared, with the certainly that only the truly self-righteous ever achieve, "Exodus 22:18. *Thou shalt not suffer a witch to live.*"

In the silence that followed, Crane's words seemed to hang in the air like a storm cloud. Before either of us could speak, there was a tap on McGuire's open office door, and Karl walked in.

"I was watching from the squad room," he said. "What the hell was *that* about?"

I quickly ran down for him who the visitors were, and what they intended. When I finished, Karl just shook his head.

McGuire leaned back in his chair. "You know, I've been thinking about Rachel quite a bit lately. Trying to figure how she could do evil shit like that to anybody, let alone a couple of cops. It didn't seem like her, to put it mildly."

"And now we know it wasn't her – well, not really her," I said.

"So you believe the sister?" McGuire asked me.

"Yeah," I said. "I do."

McGuire nodded slowly. "I think maybe I do, too." He moved some stuff around on his desk that didn't need moving. "Well, possession has been used successfully as a legal defense before. Kulick's not a demon, exactly, but the principle's probably the same, under the law."

"She's not gonna get the chance to make her case in court – not if those two sanctimonious bastards get hold of her," I said.

"I didn't know there even were such things as witchfinders anymore," Karl said. "They didn't tell us about it at the academy, and nobody's mentioned it since I joined the squad, either."

"Nobody in law enforcement talks about them much," I said. "They're kind of a dirty little secret."

"Why should they have any better chance of finding Rachel then you and me?" he asked. "Or even as good a chance, since we know the town and they don't?"

"Because they've got a Talent," McGuire said. "Some people, like Rachel and her sister, are born with the Talent for magic, and others are born with a Talent for sniffing it out. It's kind of like the polar opposite of the witchcraft Talent. Most people who have it don't even know they do."

"But what they're doing is fucking vigilantism," Karl said. "And that's against the law, goddammit."

"It is and it isn't," McGuire said sourly. "Their brand of vigilantism is actually legal in Pennsylvania, and most of the New England states."

"That's because when they were colonies, there were laws on the books against witchcraft," I told Karl. "Laws that nobody ever got around to repealing."

"So these fuckers can kidnap Rachel, torture her until she confesses, and then... what?" Karl asked.

"Burn her alive," McGuire said. "Just like in Europe, five hundred fucking years ago."

I looked at McGuire, then at Karl. My throat felt tight as I said, "Unless we find her first."

As we left McGuire's office, Louise the Tease motioned us over. She had the phone receiver in one hand, and she held it out to me as I reached her desk. "It's for you," she said. "Some doctor, says he's at the hospital."

As my hand reached out, I ran down the list of all the bad things this could mean. It's a good thing my mind works fast, because the list was a long one.

I took the phone. "This is Detective Sergeant Markowski. Who's this?"

"Hello, Detective." The voice was male, and deep. "This is Dr Barry Santangelo at Mercy Hospital. Benjamin Prescott, that man from DC who suffered a recent stroke, is a patient of mine."

He's dead, I thought. *Prescott's dead, and they're gonna say it's my fault. And maybe they're right.*

But what I heard instead was, "Mr Prescott has come out of his coma."

A few seconds went by while I got used to breathing again. I hadn't even realized I'd stopped.

"Detective? Still there?"

"Yeah, sorry, Doctor. That's great news, really great."

"Relapse is always a possibility in these cases, of course, but not very likely. I just finished a thorough neurological examination, and it's my opinion that Mr Prescott is going to stay awake – and, quite possibly, recover completely."

"I'm really glad to hear he's going to be okay."

"It's a nice change for me, to be the bearer of good news," Santangelo said, "but that's not why I'm calling."

"Oh? What is it, then?"

"Well, Mr Prescott's still in intensive care for the time being, that's standard procedure with coma patients. Still... I don't see a problem in this case."

"I'm sorry, Doctor, you lost me. Problem with what?"

"Prescott wants to see you. You and your partner."

I'd first been to Mercy's Intensive Care Unit when Christine was a patient there. That was before I took her home and... did what I did. The place doesn't exactly have happy associations for me, but I suppose that's true for most people.

In my case, the creepiness factor was ramped up by the fact that I'd recently been looking at video of this very area, trying to figure out what had happened to Rachel Proctor. I thought I knew the answer to that now, but the knowledge didn't keep me from a mild case of the willies as Karl and I took turns rubbing foamy disinfectant over our hands from the dispenser they keep just outside the door.

"I hate this place," Karl said softly. "But maybe not so much today as usual. You ready?"

I nodded, and he used his hip to nudge the saucer-sized metal plate that was set into the wall. The double doors opened, and I followed him through.

I've been in a few hospital ICUs, and they're all laid out essentially the same: a big circular chamber, with glass-enclosed patient rooms along the outer ring and a monitoring station in the middle that looks like something you'd find on the bridge of a battleship. The thin, middle-aged nurse behind the desk facing the door had the same calm face and emotionless delivery you find in ICU nurses everywhere. "Can I help you?"

"We're here to see one of the patients," Karl said. "Ben Prescott."

She glanced at one of the three monitors in front of her, then looked up and said, "Visitors in Intensive Care are restricted, sir. Are you members of the immediate family?"

I had the ID folder with my shield ready, and I flipped it open so she could see it. As she was taking that in, I said, "Dr Santangelo called us. He said it would be okay."

I spoke softly. An ICU has that effect on people – like a funeral home, which my mom's generation used to call a "corpse house."

She pressed something on her keyboard a couple of times, then looked at the screen again. "Mr. Prescott is in Room 9, officers," she said calmly. "To your right."

We thanked her, and went to see the guy we had almost killed.

Prescott didn't look bad, considering what he'd been through. But he wasn't as elegant as he'd been behind the podium. The well-tailored suit had been replaced by a hospital gown, of course. I was momentarily surprised that they'd had one to fit him, but I guess hospitals are prepared for a wide range of patients. Prescott's hair was greasy-looking, and he had a pretty good beard stubble going. I guess the ICU staff had been more concerned with keeping him alive than well-groomed.

"You two look familiar," he said. "And since you're not dressed as priests, I assume you're the two detectives who, they say, saved my life." His mellow tenor was scratchy and hoarse now; he'd probably had a breathing tube down his throat for a long time.

He doesn't remember! The stroke must've killed the brain cells where his most recent memories were stored. He doesn't know that it was me who caused him to inhale the piece of shrimp, which brought on the stroke – which nearly sent him to that Great Lecture Hall in the Sky, or so the doc said.

"All cops receive training in CPR and the Heimlich maneuver, Professor," I said. "I'm just glad we were nearby when you started to choke."

I walked close to the bed and put my hand out to shake. "Stan Markowski, Scranton PD, pleased to meet you." I gestured behind me. "And this is my partner, Karl Renfer. He's the one who did the Heimlich on you." Karl came over and shook hands.

"Well, I'm grateful to you both," Prescott said. "Thank you for saving me. Thank you very, very much."

Strokes sometimes change people's personalities. If that's what happened here, I figured I was going to like Prescott 2.0 better than the original version.

"What's the last thing you remember?" I asked him. "At the reception, I mean."

Prescott shook his head slowly. "I remember shaking hands and smiling at a lot of people, all of whose faces are just a blur to me now... And I remember there was a bowl of iced shrimp nearby that I was hitting pretty hard. I *love* shrimp – or, at least I used to. They tell me that's what I was choking on. Must've swallowed too fast." He frowned. "I'm not sure that shrimp, iced or otherwise, will ever be on the menu for me again. We'll see."

"Detective Renfer and I were close by, because we hoped to have a word with you, about a case we're working on," I said, with a straight face. "But you... got into trouble... before we had the chance."

I saw Prescott's eyes narrow as he looked at me.

Uh-oh. It is starting to come back to him?

"Markowski..." he said thoughtfully. "We had a phone conversation, didn't we, a few days before I came north?"

"Yes, sir, that's right. We did."

"I don't remember what we talked about, but I have the vague impression that I was pretty snotty to you." The frown of concentration gave way to a smile. "If so, please accept my apologies. I'm often rude to people, I'm afraid." He was silent for a couple of seconds. "Maybe it's time I stopped."

Karl and I looked at each other. The raised eyebrows he was showing were reflected on my own face.

"Well, I gather it's been a while since your last attempt to talk to me, Detective," Prescott said, "but if it's not too late to help your case, let's give it another try. I believe I owe you, and" – he made a gesture that took in the whole room – "my secretary seems to have cleared my calendar for the rest of the morning."

He started coughing then, a dry hack that sounded loud in the small room. I started toward the nightstand next to his bed, but he waved me away, reached over himself and grabbed a red plastic tumbler full of ice water. After several long sips through the bent straw, he put the tumbler down. The coughing had stopped.

"Sorry," he said. "Throat's still a little raw." Prescott leaned back against the pillows behind him. "So, what is it you wanted to know about?"

"A book that you've translated," I said. "Parts of it, anyway. It's called the *Opus Mago*."

Prescott looked at me and blinked a couple of times. Then he slowly turned back toward the nightstand, got the tumbler again, and took a long sip of water. I didn't know if he was still thirsty or just buying time.

He put the tumbler back. "Well," he said. "I suppose that explains my rudeness over the phone earlier, not" – he waved a hasty hand – "that it constitutes an excuse."

Prescott stared at me some more. Then he gave a long sigh and said, "Can you tell me why you need to know about this... book? Forgive me if it's ground we've already covered, but..." He made a gesture toward his head.

"No, that's not a problem," I said, then ran it down for

him again – the symbols on the corpses, what we'd learned from Vollman, all of it.

Prescott had been studying the backs of his hands during most of my recitation, and he was still looking at them when he said, "I owe my life to both of you. It could have all ended for me on the floor of that banquet room, and what an embarrassment *that* would have been."

He looked up then – first at Karl, then at me. "So, in a very real sense, every moment of my life from that point forward is a gift from the gods." A smile came and went. "By way of the Scranton Police Department. And, despite my other failings, I'm a man who pays his debts."

He looked at his hands again, then back at me. "All right, Detective. It doesn't amount to much, but I'll tell you what I know about the *Opus Mago*."

"Although the book was published in 1640, by a man who was burned at the stake for his trouble, most of its contents are far older. The pages I worked with have passed through who knows how many hands, over who knows how many centuries. Nothing is numbered, so it's difficult to tell what order they are supposed to be in. So I just picked one, more or less at random, and began work.

"It was slow going. Despite the Latin name by which it's known today, most of the book is written in an obscure dialect of Ancient Sumerian that, if I may flatter myself, very few scholars are capable of working with.

"The fragment that came into my possession consists of sixteen pages. I got through six, then stopped. Of the material I did translate, I believe some of it does pertain to this spell or ritual that you've described, which some madman is apparently trying to perform.

"The section I worked on reveals that the total number of sacrifices required is five, and that they all be vampires – although the term used in the text is *ghosts who suck blood*. And the fifth, final sacrifice must take place as the ritual itself is being performed. A sort of culmination of the vampire bloodletting, if you will. I also get the impression, although the text is ambiguous on this point, that the rite can only be performed successfully by someone who is a worker of magic – which is the Ancient Sumerian term for wizard, and also a ghost who sucks blood. Someone who combines the attributes of both wizard and vampire, if such a thing is even possible."

I looked at Karl, who returned my gaze and probably my expression. "Oh, yeah," I said. "It's possible, all right."

Vollman.

"And that's as much as I know, based on the fragments I've translated," Prescott said.

"Why did you stop?" Karl asked him.

Prescott studied the backs of his hands again, as if he hoped to find the answers to all of life's mysteries written there. Eventually, he looked up.

"I stopped at the sixth page, because of a passage I found there, near the bottom. I believe I can recite it verbatim – God knows I've read it enough times. My little cerebral episode hasn't erased that part of my memory, more's the pity."

Prescott closed his eyes, and when he spoke it was in a different tone from his usual conversational voice.

"Let any man who reveals the secrets of this sacred book to strangers be accursed for all time. He shall be blinded, then castrated, then dismembered, then burned, to serve as instruction

and example to any who would dare let these words become known to those uninitiated in our rites."

Prescott opened his eyes again and spoke in his normal voice. "Scary stuff, huh?"

"I guess you took it pretty seriously, then," I said.

"Detective, this is a world in which we find were-wolves, vampires, witchcraft, goblins, and I don't know what else. What's in that book is a curse, and yes, I took it seriously."

I nodded. "And yet you just told us everything you found there – all that bears on our case, anyway."

Prescott leaned back and spread his hands. "I'm on borrowed time, remember? By rights, I should be dead and buried by now. That, or a vegetable hooked up to some machine for the next thirty years, until my heart gives out." He put his hands back in his lap. "Besides, it looks as if you've got something pretty nasty brewing here in Scranton. I can't sit by and let it happen – not if I have information that will stop it."

I started to speak, but he held out his hand, like a traffic cop. "I know what you're going to say. What I've given you *won't* stop what's being prepared by this lunatic Sligo. And you'd be right. But maybe there's something in the rest of the *Opus Mago* fragment that will."

"Look," I said, "I appreciate the offer, more than you know. But even though you woke up from the coma, you're probably still a sick man. Flying back to Washington–"

"I have no intention of flying back to Washington, at least, not in the near future. The good Dr Santangelo made it very clear that he wants me to stay under obser-vation, for at least a week. And since I have no desire to suffer another stroke, I'm inclined to agree with him."

Prescott ran a hand slowly through his greasy hair. "But if I call my research assistant at G-town and describe what I need, she'll get it all together, and send it FedEx overnight. That's likely to be expensive as hell–" he grew a little smile "–so I'll let the university pay for it."

The smile became a grin, even if it seemed a little forced. "By tomorrow, or at latest the day after, I should have those fragments here – or rather in my regular hospital room, where I gather I'm headed shortly. I will also have her send the proper dictionaries and any other research tools I can't get off the Internet. I assume they have wi-fi here at the hospital?"

"If they don't, I will personally have it installed for you," I said.

"This kind of work is slow going," he said, "but I'll push as hard as I can, given–" he made the gesture toward his head again "–everything. I know there's a time factor, so we'd best not waste any. In fact, my phone should be in my jacket pocket, which is probably hanging in that little closet over there. If one of you gentlemen would be so kind…"

As we pulled out of the hospital parking lot, Karl said, "I'm not too well up on curses. Missed the two lectures on them at the academy, because I got the flu, and never made them up. There was some stuff I was supposed to read on my own, but you know how it is."

"Yeah, I do. There's always something else to think about."

"If the curse Prescott told us about is the real deal, who's gonna carry it out? I mean, the fucking pages aren't gonna grow arms to cut him up and burn him with, are they?"

"Probably not," I told him. "A curse – a real one, not the crap that some gypsies deal in – usually involves a pact with a demon, one that's pretty low in the infernal pecking order. The lower they are, the weaker, and that much easier to summon and control."

"Yeah, I didn't miss Demonology. I know that part."

"Okay, then. So a curse, if it's legit, sets up preconditions for the demon to operate under. It's like one of those old mummy movies you see on TV late at night. A bunch of archeologists find Ramah-Ho-Haina's burial chamber, and go in for a look-see. And the usual looting, of course."

"'Course," Karl said. "Can't have a mummy movie without looting."

"So, say that back when old Ramah-Ho-Haina dies, the burial party includes a pretty powerful wizard. He puts a curse in place that automatically summons the demon if anybody messes with the tomb. Doesn't matter if it takes like three thousand years to kick in – demons don't give a shit, they're not going anyplace."

"Yeah, I've seen those movies," Karl said. "The evil spirit follows the scientists home, then does a number on them, one by one."

"Right, and the kind of number it does is one of the things that the wizard set up thousands of years ago."

"So Prescott could be letting himself in for some serious shit, helping us."

I shrugged. "Maybe. Just because some dude writes down that there's a curse doesn't mean there really is one. Still, we better assume the worst."

"But, the hospital's already protected, Stan. It's gotta be. People die in there all the time, and they sure don't want demons hanging around, waiting to grab up somebody's soul."

"Sure, it's protected. But I don't want to take any chances with something like this. We need to get some additional wards placed around Prescott's hospital room. Normally, that would be Rachel's job."

"Yeah, I know. So, we'll have to subcontract it out," Karl said. "I know a couple of first-class witches..."

"Call one of them," I said. "Now."

"We don't have authorization yet, Stan."

"Fuck it – I'll pay for it myself, if McGuire's feeling stingy. Now *call*, will you?"

Karl opened his phone, but then stopped to look at me. "You really worried about this curse thing?"

"Some," I said. "But it's more than that."

Karl was squinting at his phone's directory. "Like what?"

"I'm thinking about what might happen if Sligo gets wind of what Prescott's up to."

Karl thought for a moment. "He'd probably want to do something about it, wouldn't he?"

"Yeah. Shit, I would, in his place."

"And since we know that, if we were ready for him..."

"Uh-uh. No way, no how. I'm not using the guy as bait. We fuck it up, and Prescott's toast. There's got to be another way to get this fucking Sligo."

"Hope we think of it soon," Karl said, and began to tap in numbers.

At certain times of the day, getting around Scranton is quicker if you use side streets and stay away from the main thoroughfares, such as they are. That's what I was doing, and I managed to get the speed up to about forty while Karl tried to track down a witch who had apparently changed her phone number a couple of times.

A hundred feet or so ahead, a black cat was just start-ing to lead three of her kittens across the wide street. I'm fond of animals, so I figured I'd better speed up a little – that way, I'd be past them and gone before they reached my side of the road. I could've just slowed down and let then go first, but that would mean a black cat – hell, four of them – would be crossing my path. I'm not supersti-tious or anything, but I still thought that was a bad idea.

Turned out I was right.

Because if I hadn't speeded up right about then, the dead body that fell on top of us would have gone right through the windshield, instead of just putting a humon-gous dent in the roof.

Close to two hundred pounds of dead weight moving that fast – it might well have killed one or both of us if it had gone through the glass, or at least hurt us pretty bad.

But we were fine. Being scared shitless doesn't count. Or so they tell me.

I've been around plenty of crime scenes, but this was the first time I found myself the focus of one. Since there was no high place nearby – either man-made or natural – that the guy could have jumped, fell, or been pushed from, the first uniforms on the scene started kicking around the idea that maybe I'd hit a pedestrian who'd been crossing the street – him hard enough with the front bumper to toss his body onto the car's roof. The pricks.

The doc from the M.E.'s office put the kibosh on that pretty soon, though. Even without an autopsy, body temperature showed the dude had been dead for at least two hours.

The M.E.'s guy wasn't a guy this time, but a gal. In-stead of Homer, they'd sent a thin, I mean *really* thin young woman named Cecelia Reynolds. Fine with me – she's as good at pathology as Homer, maybe better. I'm always telling her, in a kidding way, to go eat a cookie, and she usually responds, in an equally joking way, by telling me to go fuck myself.

I was explaining, to the third pair of my brother officers – these two from Homicide – what had happened to Karl and me, when Cecelia called me over. She was squatting over the dead guy, who had come to rest on the asphalt after sliding off the car's roof.

"We're just about to bag him," she said to me, "but I thought you'd be interested in this."

Cecelia tugged on a fresh pair of latex gloves. "It was just a hunch I had," she said, "and turns out, I was right." She leaned forward and used her fingers to peel back the corpse's upper lip.

Fangs. Two nice long, sharp vampire canines.

"Thanks, Cecelia," I said after a moment. "And, listen: I realize you can't undress him here, but when you get him on the table, I'm betting you'll find some weird symbols, probably three of then, carved into the body someplace. If you do, I'd be *real* grateful if you'd give me a call, okay?"

She looked at me for a couple of seconds before nodding slowly. "Okay, Stan, I'll be sure to do that."

I straightened up and headed back to the Homicide cops to answer more questions. There wasn't any doubt in my mind that Cecelia would find three more of the arcane symbols carved into the dead guy. Because now that I knew he was a vamp, I was also pretty sure I knew something else about him, too.

He was the fourth sacrifice.

● ● ● ●

Whenever a cop is involved in anything where somebody gets killed, whether it's an officer-involved shooting or something more unusual, like having a dead guy drop out of the sky on you, Internal Affairs takes over – and the only reason we don't call them Infernal Affairs is that we don't want to be insulting to Hell.

I had to relate the details of my current case, over and over, to a couple of IA cops named Famalette and Sullivan. Karl was going through a similar routine down the hall with another pair from the Rat Squad. Maybe my two interrogators figured I'd get sick of the repetition sooner or later, and confess to something, just to make it stop.

But they didn't get any confessions out of me, because I hadn't done anything. And I kept bringing the conversation back to the central fact that the undead guy had been truly dead for at least two hours before he ended up on top of my car, however the hell he got there.

"How do you know the vamp had been iced two hours earlier?" Famalette asked, as if he'd just caught me in a slip-up. He had a rubber band wrapped around the spread fingers of one hand and he kept twanging it with the other. I think Internal Affairs training must include lessons on how to be annoying.

"Because the M.E. doc said so. What's her name – Reynolds."

"The M.E.'s report hasn't even been filed yet," Famalette said, in an *a-ha* tone.

"She told me at the scene. She knew from the body temp."

"What's she doing revealing confidential information like that to you?"

"She thought I'd be interested," I said, "since I'm the one who had the dead guy dropped on top of him, and all.

Well, me and my partner. And who says it's confidential?"

"All M.E. reports are confidential, Markowski, you oughta know that," Famalette said.

"Yeah, but the M.E. report hasn't been filed yet – you said so, yourself."

His face started going red, and he turned away.

"You real chummy with this chick from the M.E.'s office?" Sullivan asked me. He had a Brillo pad of curly hair that reminded me of that singer from the Seventies, Art Garfunkel. I hoped that he wasn't going to break into "Bridge Over Troubled Water" – although even that would have been better than the crap I'd been listening to for the last two hours.

"Chummy?" I said. "I dunno – the last thing she said to me was 'Go fuck yourself.' Draw your own conclusions."

"You sure the one you're fucking isn't her?" Sullivan said with a leer.

"Not me," I said. "I like women with some meat on their bones." Like Lacey Brennan, for instance, but I kept that thought to myself.

Famalette turned back from some graffiti on the wall he'd been pretending to read, still twanging that damn rubber band like a Spaghetti Western soundtrack. "You don't like vampires much, do you, Markowski?"

"Vamps aren't so bad," I said. "At least, I never heard of one working for Internal Affairs."

"Word is," Sullivan said, "you'd just as soon stake a vampire as have lunch."

I shrugged. "Depends on what's for lunch."

Sullivan leaned close, and his breath should have been banned by the Geneva Convention. "Face it, Markowski, you're not exactly broken up over this vamp's death, are you?"

"I wouldn't be broken up if you two walked in front of a truck tomorrow," I said. "Doesn't mean I'd be the one behind the wheel."

"Are you threatening us, Markowski?" Famalette said, trying for indignant and failing.

I just shook my head slowly and wondered how much longer it was going to last.

Eventually they turned me loose. Karl, too. The rat fuckers had no case, and no choice. McGuire agreed with that assessment, and he told Karl and me as much in his office. By then it was end of shift – the double shift that Karl and I had pulled, again. I'd planned to spend the time doing something more useful than answering questions for morons, but McGuire was philosophical.

"They're like the clap," he said. "The best you can do is take precautions and try to avoid them."

Karl and I laughed at that. Then McGuire said, "None of which answers the question of who dropped a dead vamp on top of you guys – and why?"

"Not to mention how," Karl said.

"Had to've been magic," I said.

"I wonder." McGuire leaned back in his chair. "I've been thinking about this. Let's say the vamp is in bat form, and he's flapping along, on his way to Joe's Blood Bank, or someplace. But there's a guy on the ground, or maybe on a roof, who's got a rifle loaded with silver, or that charcoal stuff we've been seeing lately. *Bang*! He nails Mr Bat, who turns back into human form upon death, like they do, whereupon gravity takes over and he drops like a rock – right on top of you."

I glanced at Karl. I was pretty sure we had the same

thing in mind: this is what happens when the boss has too much time to think about stuff.

"Be a hell of a shot," I said. "Especially at night."

"More than that, it fails the test of Occam's Razor," Karl said.

"*Whose* razor?" McGuire asked.

"William of Occam, big philosopher dude in the Middle Ages. He said that 'The simplest explanation that fits the known facts is probably true.'"

McGuire and I both stared at him.

Karl shrugged. "Just something I read in a magazine, is all. But it makes sense. No disrespect, boss, but that thing with the rifle is just too complicated to be real likely."

McGuire didn't get mad. "I wasn't pushing it," he said. "It was just a thought. And if that's not what happened, then why is some magician dropping a dead vamp on a couple of cops?"

"We might have the beginning of an answer once I hear from Cecelia Reynolds," I said. "She's doing the post on the vamp and I asked her to look for those symbols carved on the body."

"Oh, right," McGuire said. He rummaged through the mess on his desk and came up with a phone message slip, which he handed to me. "She called while you were in with the Rat Squad. Wants you to call back."

I got out my cell phone. "You mind?" I asked him.

"Nah, go ahead."

I called the number that Cecelia had left. It rang five or six times, and I was just thinking that I was going to have to leave a voicemail message when she came on the line.

"This is Dr Reynolds."

"Stan Markowski, Cecelia. I'm calling–"

"–about your vamp, right." Cecelia's phone manner tends to be kind of brusque.

"You called, so I'm assuming you found–"

"–weird symbols carved into the corpse. Yeppir, we got 'em. In the back, between the shoulder blades. Almost certainly post-mortem."

"Were there–"

"Three of 'em? Yep, just like you predicted, Stan."

"Okay, I'll need–"

"Photos, check. Ronnie already took 'em. Close up, middle distance, side angles, the whole nine yards. Give me your–"

"Email address?" Two can play this game. "Sure, here it is."

I gave her the address I use for official business. Cecelia promised to get photos to me within the hour, then hung up.

I told McGuire and Karl what she'd said.

"Which means that's number four," Karl said. "Just like you figured, Stan."

McGuire looked at me. "Somebody was trying to send you guys a message."

"That's not all they were doing," I said. "Remember, I sped up kind of sudden, to avoid hitting a cat that was crossing the street."

"Yeah, that's right," McGuire said. "I hope you told Internal Affairs about the cat – they'll probably wanna interview it."

"So it was a hit," Karl said. "The body was intended to go through the windshield, right on top of us – along with all that broken glass."

"Yeah," I said, "and that's where this gets really fucked up. The esoteric marks on the corpse means it's Sligo –

or whoever's been offing all these vamps." I hadn't forgotten about Vollman – not after Prescott said this hard spell had to be carried out by a vampire/wizard.

McGuire nodded, then made a "Go on" gesture with one hand.

"But now we've got another hit attempt, using magic. We've been operating on the assumption–"

"–that Jamieson Longworth was behind that shit, to get even for his brother," Karl said. I wondered for a second if he'd been banging Cecelia Reynolds and picked up her manners, or lack of them, as Karl added, "We figured he's hired a black wizard to do the dirty magic for him."

"But somebody who's involved in the vamp sacrifices just tried to kill us," I said. "And that means, one of our assumptions was wrong, either about Sligo or Longworth..."

There was silence in the little room before McGuire finally put it into words.

"Or the two of them are working together."

I needed sleep badly. My skull felt like it was packed full of wet cotton, and I knew that any heavy thinking was out of the question before I grabbed some z's. And in light of what we'd been discussing in McGuire's office, some very heavy thinking was going to be in order.

Karl and I left the building together, like we usually did. There wasn't much conversation along the way. We were both beat, and besides, whatever there was to say, we'd already said it in McGuire's office.

As we reached the cracked asphalt of the parking area I said, "I can probably function okay if I get six hours – how about you?"

"That seems about right, I guess." Karl didn't sound happy about it, and I didn't blame him.

"Then why don't we plan to come back on shift at–"

"Stan." Something in Karl's voice brought me to full alertness in the space of a quick breath.

"What is it?"

"There's somebody near your car, but on the other side of the fence."

I slowly pushed my sport coat back and reached for the Beretta on my right hip. A second later, I heard the soft *click* as Karl thumbed back the hammer on the Glock he carried.

"What're you packing?" I asked softly.

"Silver, cold iron, and garlic-dipped lead, alternating," he said. "You?"

"Straight silver," I told him, "but it's been blessed by the bishop."

Now that Karl had warned me, I could dimly see a single figure standing in the street, practically pressed up against the fence just opposite my Toyota. Whoever it was must have seen us notice him, but didn't try to hide or run away. He just stood there, waiting.

As we walked forward, Karl and I separated, so as not to give whoever it was a twofer target. The parking area was warded, and those wards had been amped up considerably since somebody had gotten in with a couple of Medusa statues. But it's impossible to guard against all possible spells, and the wards might not stop someone outside the fence with a gun. No system's perfect.

We had almost reached my Toyota when I realized who it was, standing on the other side of the fence. "It's all right, Karl," I said, and holstered my weapon. The still figure spoke for the first time.

"Hello, Daddy."

• • • •

"You know, you could've come into the fucking station house if you'd wanted to see me, instead of lurking around the parking lot like this," I said. "It's a public building – you don't need to get permission." I'm not sure if I was being pissy because I was tired, or because of the momentary fright she'd given me.

"Oh, I wouldn't want to embarrass you in front of your brother officers," Christine said, the sarcasm more in her voice than in the words. "And as for lurking, that's what we undead do best – but I guess you know that."

I took a breath and got better control of myself. "Well, if you want to talk, meet me at the gate. Or I'll go out there, if you'd rather."

"Let's talk like this," she said. "Sunrise in less than ten minutes. Thanks to you, I haven't got much time."

Well, if you'd let me know you were out here... I kept the thought to myself. There was no point in getting into one of our arguments now – not with dawn so close.

I remembered that Karl was standing a few yards to my right. "It's okay," I said. "Go on home, get some sleep. I'll see you about 1:00, okay?"

"Is this your partner, Daddy?" Christine asked. "Aren't you going to introduce us?" I saw a glimmer of white in what could have been a smile.

Without voicing the sigh that I felt, I said, "Karl, meet my daughter, Christine, who you've heard me talk about. Christine, this is Karl Renfer."

I saw Karl nod. "Hiya. Hard to shake hands through the fence, but, anyway – hi."

"He's *told* you about me? The vamp daughter?"

"Yeah, he has," Karl said in a neutral voice.

"And did he tell you *how* I came to join the ranks of the bloodsucking undead?"

"Christine," I said, "there's no fucking time–"

Karl spoke over me. "Yeah, he did. And he told me why, too. He couldn't stand to watch you die, because he loves you so much."

I thought I heard Christine draw in a breath, but I must have imagined it, since she doesn't need to breathe. She looked at me a moment, then turned back to Karl. "Then why doesn't he–"

"Christine!" It was the voice I'd used to show I was serious, back when she was... human. "Unless you want to find out the hard way what sunlight does to vampires, you better say what you came for, and quick."

When she spoke again, her voice was emotionless. "Okay, then, I will. There's a rumor that you killed another vampire. Ran him down with your car, like a dog in the street."

"And you believed that bullshit?" I said.

"No, I didn't. That's why I'm here. Wanna tell me what happened?"

What the hell, it can't do any harm. And I'd rather not have every vamp in town looking for a piece of me. Not now.

Being as concise as possible, I ran it down for her. When I'd finished, Karl said, "For whatever it's worth, I know he's telling the truth. I was there."

I saw Christine nod at Karl. "I know. I believe him."

The fact that I could see her better meant it was getting lighter out. False dawn, probably, with the real thing not far behind.

"I'll put the word out," she said to me. "I *had* noticed the unmarked car at the end of the lot with a huge dent in the roof, but it's nice to hear it from the source."

"Good," I said. "I'm glad you don't just have to take my word for it." Sarcasm was slipping out, and I reined it in, hard. "One thing before you go: a guy who would know says that the only one who could pull off this spell would be a vamp, uh, vampire who is also a wizard. You hear of anybody like that?"

After a moment she said, "Mr Vollman, of course."

"Yeah, him I know. Questions is: can you think of anybody else?

"The vamp community seems to thrive on rumors as much as we do on blood," she said. "I did hear something about a guy new in town who plays for both teams, but I didn't pay it any mind."

"Did you maybe hear where he spends the day?"

"Well, one chick told – oh, shit!"

Thin smoke had started to rise off her head and shoulders. I could see it clearly in the growing light.

"Get out of here! Go!" I shouted.

She turned and ran, shouting over her shoulder, "Tonight, sunset, right here!"

A second later, she was out of sight.

I went home. What else was I gonna do? I ate, showered, and got into bed. Despite being exhausted, I didn't get a lot of rest. My mind was like a madhouse in an earthquake – each inmate demanding my attention – Karl, McGuire, the IA clowns, Prescott, Rachel, the witchfinders – and Christine. Especially Christine.

Had she made it back to her resting place, before the sun turned her into a screaming torch? I'd had the police radio in the car on while driving home, and there'd been no reports of unexplained combustion anywhere. She was okay. Probably.

But what if she had stayed a minute longer this morning? Would she have burned, while I stood helpless behind the chain link fence and watched? Would her screams be echoing inside my head right this second? Is that why I saved her from leukemia – so she could die like that today, or tomorrow, or next week?

I guess I've spent worse mornings trying to sleep. But not recently.

After a while I got up. I changed the sweaty bedding, did a load of laundry, and cleaned Quincey's cage. As I did that last chore, I told him about the latest developments in the case. Quincey doesn't say much, but he's a good listener. And sometimes it's good to talk about stuff out loud – helps me organize my thoughts, and lets some of the psychological pressure off. And I know I can trust Quincey to keep it to himself. As a reward for letting me bounce some of that stuff off him, I put some raisins in his bowl along with the food pellets. He really likes raisins.

Around noon, I made some scrambled eggs. I wasn't hungry, but I didn't want low blood sugar making me slow and stupid later on. I'd been slow and stupid enough already.

I left for work about 12:45, and I was two blocks from headquarters when I noticed the woman standing on the corner. She drew my eye because she wasn't staring across the street at the crossing light, like people usually do. She was turned sideways, looking into the oncoming traffic stream, which included me.

Driving a familiar route doesn't require a lot of concentration. I was thinking about the case, but a tiny part of my mind whispered, "Hey, I know her."

Which was of no particular importance, but it aroused my curiosity. I focused my attention on the woman and suddenly realized that I was looking at Rachel Proctor.

I hit the brakes, which meant that the blue SUV behind me damn near ended up in my trunk. The driver stopped in time, but his blaring horn was designed to show me he wasn't too happy about it all.

All of that registered dimly, like a voice you hear from three rooms away. I was focused on Rachel.

She locked eyes with me and nodded, once. Then she turned and walked away.

Rachel had gone down a side street, so I put on my turn signal and waited for the traffic flow to take me to the corner. I've got a portable flashing red light that I could have put on the roof – that would have allowed me to cut around, as well as shutting up the honking, bird-flipping idiot behind me, but I didn't want to draw attention to myself, or to Rachel.

I finally made the turn, and saw Rachel a couple of hundred feet ahead, walking along at a good clip. I came up alongside her and tapped the horn, but she ignored me. I was looking for a parking space when she turned into the big parking garage that serves that part of the city. At least that solved my problem of what to do with the car.

I had to stop and get a ticket – even a badge won't impress an automated gate – and by the time I was inside I'd lost sight of her. I cruised the ground level slowly, my eyes darting everywhere. No Rachel.

Nothing to do but go up. Second level – nothing. Third level – *nada*.

Only one more place to go.

I saw her as soon as I reached the roof level. She was leaning against the retaining wall that stops careless drivers, or suicidal ones, from driving off the top of the building.

Plenty of room up here; most people parked on the roof only as a last resort, since it's not sheltered – maybe that's why Rachel had chosen it. I slid the car into a parking slot, got out, and walked toward her. She stood, arms folded below her breasts, watching me approach.

"Rachel, you took one hell of a chance, showing yourself like that," I said. "The police think you're a cop-killer, and you've been around the force long enough to know what that means."

"It means they will shoot first, and ask questions probably never," Rachel said.

Except it wasn't Rachel.

The voice was deeper than Rachel's, the intonation somehow different. I looked closely at her face and saw subtle differences in its shape and form from what I remembered. But the big difference was the eyes.

The gentle gray eyes of Rachel Proctor were gone, replaced by the bright blue eyes of a madman.

I swallowed a couple of times and tried to keep my voice under control as I said, "George Kulick, I presume?"

Rachel's head inclined a few inches. "None other."

Getting emotional about what he had done to Rachel, and might yet do, was a waste of time, so I just said, "What do you want?"

The eyebrows went up in an exaggerated show of amazement. "A man who gets right to the point, and a policemen, no less. How unusual!"

I had nothing useful to say to that, so I kept quiet. But wizards are sensitive, so I wouldn't have been surprised if he could feel the hatred coming off me, like heat from a freshly stoked stove.

He nodded slowly, as if confirming something for himself. "As to what I want: I want the man who killed me."

"Sligo, you mean."

"He did not bother to tell me his name. But I will know him, when we meet again. I want him in my power, so that I can make him suffer as I did. When I have paid him back in full measure for my pain, plus considerable interest, then perhaps – *perhaps* – I shall allow him to die."

"I want pretty much the same thing," I said. "Without the histrionics."

His eyes narrowed. "Why? Because it is just another *case* you must solve?"

"That would be enough," I said. "But it's a lot more. Sligo is planning to work a spell from the *Opus Mago* to do... I don't know what. But it's gotta be pretty powerful, because the recipe calls for five dead vampires. That ring any bells with you?"

He shook his head, which was now Rachel's head. "My responsibility was not to read the book, even if I could have, but to safeguard it."

I thought about saying, *Yeah, and you did a hell of a job.* But a cheap shot like that would just piss him off, and I expect he'd been thinking about it, anyway. Maybe that was part of what was fueling his rage: the knowledge that Sligo had made Kulick betray his trust.

"Well, he's got something big and bad in the works, and I have to stop him," I said. "Oh, and he keeps trying to kill me."

He made with the eyebrows again. "Does he, indeed? How many attempts?"

"Two – so far."

"And yet, here you are before me. Good – that means you are resourceful. You will be a useful ally."

"I'm not your ally, pal – not until you let go of Rachel."
And not even then, fuckwad – but I thought it best to keep that last thought to myself.

Kulick/Rachel looked at me as if he'd suddenly realized he was conversing with the village idiot. "What would you have me do? Simply leave this body and float away into eternity, my revenge unfulfilled? I am curious about what comes after this life, and I shall satisfy that curiosity, once I have exacted vengeance. But for now, this woman is useful to me, and I will not leave her. But you can speak to her, if you wish."

The face changed in small ways, to become completely Rachel's. She blinked a couple of times, then said urgently, in Rachel's voice, "Kill me, Stan – do it now! It's the only way. He's got to be stopped, before he destroys–"

Her mouth closed, and after a moment the face began its subtle transformation again.

"'Kill me, Stan'?" The deeper voice was mocking. "Is that what you intend to do – assuming I would permit you?"

I didn't know whether I had it in me to carry out Rachel's plea or not, but I couldn't do it now, anyway – Kulick was ready for me to try. He probably had a defensive spell set to go at an instant's notice.

"No," I said, keeping most of what I felt out of my voice.

"Good," he said, putting a tiny smile on Rachel's face. "Then we are allies, after all."

He reached into the pocket of Rachel's wide skirt and removed something shiny that he tossed to me.

It looked like half an amulet. Whole, it would be the size of a half-dollar. It had words engraved on it that looked like ancient Greek, and part of a symbol that I didn't recognize.

"It is imbued with a finding spell," Kulick said. "I retain the other half. When you have located this Sligo, or whatever his name might be, hold this between your thumb and forefinger. Say my full name – George Harmon Thraxis Kulick – aloud five times. At the fifth utterance, I will join you."

I studied the half-amulet a second longer, then slipped it into my pocket. "All right," I said. "Anything else?"

Kulick stared at me with those insane eyes. "Give me what I want, and I will return this woman to you, unharmed. But you may think to deny me my vengeance, perhaps by refusing to use that amulet at the crucial hour. Understand this, policeman: if Sligo escapes, or dies by any hand but mine, I shall have no further use for this woman's body."

He touched one of Rachel's breasts, and I wondered if he was enjoying feeling himself up.

"I will depart her, to see what awaits me on the other side. But before I do, I will soak her in gasoline. And my last act in this vessel will be to light a match. Do we understand each other?"

God almighty, just let me kill this fucker right now. All I said was, "Completely."

Then the ugly image of Rachel burning stirred my memory of something else. "You should know, there are a couple of witchfinders in town, hired by the mayor. I guess you realize what'll happen, if they get their hands on you – her."

A smile crossed the face that was and was not Rachel's. "Witchfinders? How quaint. Well, if they should succeed in locating this particular witch, they will have scant time to wish that they had failed to do so."

Rachel's body detached itself from the retaining wall and headed toward the elevator. "Goodbye, detective," Kulick's voice said. "I'm sure that you will be in touch."

Once the elevator doors closed, I dashed for my car and headed for the exit. Driving as fast as I could without the telltale noise of tires squealing, I made it to the exit gate and showed my badge to the sleepy-looking teenage attendant. "Open it! Now!"

As soon as I'd made my turn out of the garage, I was scanning the street for Rachel. If I could follow her to where she and Kulick were holed up, I might... oh, hell, I didn't know *what* I could do. But knowledge is power, and I'd had damn little power in this situation from the beginning.

I didn't gain any more this time, either. I circled the block twice, then checked the side streets and alleys, with no sight of Rachel.

It was then I realized that the phone in my coat pocket was vibrating, and had been, off and on, for quite some time.

As I pulled into the nearest parking space, I realized that I had actually gained two things from the encounter on the roof. One was that I now held half of an amulet with a finding spell connecting me to George Kulick. I don't know much abut finding spells, but I was betting the connection ran both ways. A good witch could tell me whether that was true, and what to do if it was.

The second thing is that the bastard had given me his true name: George Harmon Thraxis Kulick. "Thraxis" must have been the name he took when they put that tattoo on his hand. It had to be legit, or the finding spell wouldn't work. Names are important in magic, I knew that much – and now I had his.

• • • •

I opened my phone and put it to my ear. "Markowski."

"Stan, are you all right?" It was Karl's voice.

"Yeah, I'm okay. Sorry I'm late getting in to work, but something pretty weird happened."

"I was startin' to get worried, since you'd made a big deal of wanting to start our shift at 1:00, and it's almost 2:00. When you didn't check in by 1:30, I started calling you, but got no answer – until now, anyway."

"I didn't have a chance to call in," I said. "I encountered something interesting on the way to work – look, I'll tell you when I see you."

"Something about our case?"

"Yeah, kinda. I don't want to discuss it on the phone, okay?" Not with the witchfinders after Rachel, I didn't.

"Okay, sure. As long as everything's cool."

"I'm fine, Karl. See you at the squad in ten minutes."

"No, you won't."

"Say again?"

"I'm in our new unmarked car – well, new for us, anyway – on the road, trailing behind the SWAT van."

"What? Why? What happened?" I asked.

"The arrest warrant for Jamieson Longworth finally came through, that's what happened. Since the little bastard may have been associating with a black magician, McGuire figured that SWAT ought to serve it. But I wanted to be there when they do, and I figured you would, too."

"Fuckin' A right, I would."

"So I'll meet you at the staging area, which is gonna be one block south of Longworth's crib, at the Rite-Aid lot. You remember the address?"

"It's 157 Spruce, right? I'm on my way."

"Ten-four."

Ten-four. Yeah, Karl loves shit like that.

I turned into the parking lot of the Rite-Aid drugstore just as the black, windowless SWAT van was coming to a stop. I parked nearby and walked over.

Scranton PD can't afford to maintain a full-time Sacred Weapons and Tactics unit. It just isn't needed often enough to be cost-effective. So, when there's a mission, the commander has to send out a call-up. All SWAT-trained officers on duty, and several affiliated members of the clergy, leave whatever they're doing to convene at police HQ. There they strap on their gear, receive a situation briefing, and get their orders.

SWAT doesn't roll for just any dicey set of circumstances. Black-and-white units can handle 90 percent of what happens, and if there's an extraordinary situation involving human perps, they send the TRU (Tactical Response Unit). But if you've got a barricaded ogre, or a hostage situation with werewolf involvement, or you have to serve a warrant on a powerful witch or wizard, then the SWAT team will get the job done. One way or another.

The back of the van opened and a tall, lean guy in black fatigues and a matching baseball cap stepped out. Lieutenant Frank Dooley has been SWAT commander for the past four years. To look at him, you'd never know that he did a year and a half at the seminary before realizing he had a different vocation. Come to think of it, the outfits of both jobs are pretty similar, give or take the hat.

I saw Karl come around the van from the other side. Inside, several black-clad figures were moving around putting on spell-dispelling body armor, checking their weapons, and probably saying last-minute prayers. Even the non-clergy SWAT guys are a religious bunch. I guess they have to be.

"I devoutly wish we had better intel about what we're likely to be facing in there," Dooley said to Karl and me.

"I told you what we know, Lieutenant," Karl said. "I admit it ain't much."

Dooley unbuttoned the flap on his breast pocket and pulled out a notebook. He opened it, flipped past a couple of pages, then frowned at the page he'd stopped at.

"Condo's owned by one J. Longworth." He looked up. "Any relation to *the* Longworths? The rich ones?"

"Their son," I told him.

"Oh, good," he said with a smile. "I just love busting me some rich bitches." Dooley grew up shantytown Irish, and never quite got over his resentments. "Hmmm. Cultist." He was looking at the notebook again. "Busted for summoning demons and murder of a known prostitute." He looked at me. "That what you figure we're likely to be up against? A demon?"

"No reason to think so," I said. "But Longworth is believed to have been associating with a vampire/wizard named Sligo. There's no way of knowing if he's taught young Jamieson any tricks, or even if he's in there with him. But both those things are possible."

"Um." Dooley wrote something in the notebook and put it away. "If the wizard's also one of the undead, we know what he'll be doing at this hour." He glanced up at the sky, where the sun was shining through a nearly cloudless sky. "And we've dealt with wannabe wizards before, too. Excuse me." He turned and went back into the van.

"Took that warrant long enough to come through," I said to Karl.

"McGuire thinks that Mrs. Longworth tried to stop it. Maybe she put out the word that any judge who signed the arrest warrant on sonny-boy was going to be running against a very well-funded opponent next time out."

"Olszewski would've signed it," I said. "He doesn't give a shit. Anyway, he's what Rachel calls my *paisan*."

"You're probably right. But his mother, who's in Florida, had a heart attack, or something. He just got back last night – and signed the warrant this morning."

"Speaking of Rachel reminds me," I said, "you need to know what went down while I was on my way to work today."

I took Karl aside and gave him the short version of what had happened at the parking garage.

"Well, doesn't that just suck dog cock," he said. "You either tell him where Sligo is, assuming we ever find the motherfucker, or he turns Rachel into a human torch."

"Yeah," I said, "but there's a couple of other–"

I stopped because Dooley had come out of the black van again, and this time the rest of his team followed him. SWAT was ready to rock and roll.

The first black-clad figure out after Dooley was Heidi Renfer, who was Karl's cousin. She had the same long, lean build, although I sometimes wondered if her supe-proof vest had to be custom-made to accommodate those formidable breasts. She was carrying a Benelli combat shotgun as her primary, and I knew it was loaded with a mixture of double-ought buck, rock salt, and BB-sized balls of silver, all blessed by a priest.

Like everybody on the team, she wore a set of vision-enhancing/protective goggles around her neck and a wide belt encircled her hips. The belt held the holster for her backup weapon – Heidi favored a big .50 magnum

Desert Eagle loaded with explosive rounds. It also held a can of Supe Repellant Spray (silver nitrate suspended in holy water), silver-plated handcuffs made of cold iron, a tactical radio, and a couple of pouches that might contain anything – from extra ammo to field dressings imbued with a healing spell.

Heidi smiled and waved at Karl, but ignored me, which good-looking women have a habit of doing. Give or take Lacey Brennan.

Next out was a blocky guy in his thirties named Van Cleef. He looked like he had barely made the minimum height requirement of 5'8". Seeing him next to Heidi Renfer's 6'1" was enough to make you smile, but something about Van Cleef's face discouraged you from making jokes about it to him. Maybe it was the long puckered scar that ran from his forehead almost to his chin. He had an H&K MP5 assault weapon slung over his shoulder and carried the big door-busting sledge that was a vital part of SWAT's equipment. I'd heard that, during a breach, he always volunteered to be the first one through the door, and the others were happy to leave that hazardous job to him. I'm pretty sure if he was 6'4", he wouldn't feel he had so much to prove.

He was followed by a Jesuit named Garrett who taught theology at the U. Garrett could have served on the prayer team and done a lot of good that way, but he'd volunteered for the combat training, and come out near the top of his class.

A lot of Jesuits are badasses – I think it's part of their image. Their founder, St Ignatius of Loyola, was a soldier before he got religion, and the Jebs have never completely abandoned that military mindset.

Garrett carried a mini-flamethrower strapped on his

back, the nozzle held in one asbestos-gloved hand. Some supes are vulnerable to silver, others to holy water or garlic, or cold iron. But fire will stop practically anything.

Then came Shiro Kyotake, who was born in Yokahama and speaks better English than I do. He studied the sword under a master in Japan and was the team's edged-weapons specialist. There aren't too many supe species that can survive decapitation, and Shiro can take the head off an ogre so fast the thing will be almost too surprised to fall down. He makes jokes about being descended from a long line of ninjas. But I've seen him at work with that long, curved blade, and I'm not sure he's really kidding. And he can throw a knife better than anyone I've ever seen.

After that came someone I didn't know. Make that two someones. The human, who was dressed like the rest of the team, had wavy blond hair and a muscular upper body. I couldn't see his eyes, since they were hidden behind a pair of wraparound sunglasses. The backup weapon in his belt holster looked like a Colt Python .357 Magnum, the only revolver I'd seen among this crew. The guy wasn't carrying a heavier weapon, but I knew he wasn't unarmed. His primary was the dog.

Instead of a leash, the blond guy had attached to the animal's collar a four-foot length of chain that would not have looked out of place attached to a tow truck. He had the other end wrapped a couple of turns around his left hand, which was encased in a heavy leather glove.

Far as I know, the dog breed that comes closest to resembling what I was looking at is the Neapolitan mastiff. A cousin of mine used to own one, although he always used to say that *it* owned *him*. The SWAT dog, which must have weighed close to two hundred pounds, had the same black fur, floppy ears, and wrinkled face that you find with Neapolitans. But this animal also had a tuft of red fur that ran from its neck along the spine and all the way to its tail. Its teeth looked to be about twice as long as an ordinary dog's, and three times as sharp. And I saw that the eyes atop its huge muzzle glowed bright red, which you never see on anything that comes from this world.

Without taking my eyes off this apparition, I quietly said to Dooley, "Since when did you guys start using a Hellhound?"

"She's been on the team about six weeks now," he said.

"*She*?"

"Yeah, you have to use females," he said. "The males are just too big and dangerous."

I tried to imagine one of these things that would be even larger and more frightening than what I was looking at now.

"Kind of an experiment," Dooley went on, "but it's working out pretty well, so far. They can sniff out any species of supe, no matter what kind they are, or where they try to hide. We were using electronic detectors before, and the fucking things just weren't reliable. But Daisy never lets us down."

"*Daisy.*"

Dooley shrugged. "That's what Sam named her," he said. "He's her handler. Bought her from some wizard and raised her from a pup."

"I'm sure he did." *And I bet she gets to go outside whenever she fucking well wants, too.*

The last SWAT team member out of the van was Spencer, one of the few African-Americans on the Scranton PD. I don't think it's racism – the Wyoming Valley just doesn't have a real big black population. Spencer was a sniper, a skill he'd picked up in the Marines, and the USMC Scout Sniper Program sets their standards high. I'd once asked him if that was why he'd been drawn to SWAT and he'd replied, "Nah, don't you read the comics, man? You ever seen a bunch of badass superheroes like this without a brother on the crew? Shit, it'd be un-American." Spencer likes to talk street, but I knew that both his parents were doctors. He went to some exclusive prep school before graduating to join the Marines, much to Mom and Dad's disappointment. He's about as ghetto as the Prince of Wales.

After the tactical people came the prayer team. Their job it was to counter any black magic that was operating, or might be invoked, within the team's perimeter. Reverend Greene was a Baptist minister, O'Connell was another Jesuit from the U, and Rabbi Zimmerman could usually be found at Temple Beth Shalom, until there was a SWAT call-up. A Buddhist monk, Quan Tranh Han, had been part of the team until last year, when he died of cancer.

As members of the Supe Squad, Karl and I were authorized to go along on the raid, as long as we didn't get in the way. As Dooley liked to say, "We'll send for you when it's safe."

I guess Dooley must have given his briefing inside the van, because Spencer immediately picked up his long hardshell rifle case and jogged off. I watched him cross the street and disappear down a nearby alley. I figured he was heading for the building directly across the street from Longworth's condo. There he'd set up on the roof, ready to provide a diversion, covering fire, or a one-shot kill, as directed.

Dooley had been on his tactical radio for the last few minutes. Now he put it back on his belt and announced,

"Surveillance confirms that the subject entered the building at approximately 1900 hours last night, and he hasn't left. Plainclothes officers have just finished going through the building. Only one of the other condos was occupied this time of day, and they got the owner out the back way, nice and quiet. The field of operations is all ours, gentlemen." He nodded toward Heidi Renfer. "And lady."

"Haven't been one of those since I was sixteen, Loot," Heidi said with a grin. "But thanks for the thought."

A couple of the guys grinned at that, but nobody laughed out loud. I knew that, on the team, pissing Heidi off was widely regarded as a bad idea.

"All right," Dooley said. "You know the order of march, and you each have your assignments. Questions?"

Everybody on the team tried to look nonchalant, if not outright bored. Just a walk in the park.

They didn't fool me, and I bet they didn't fool their commander, either. Each one was amped up to the eyebrows. You could see it in their eyes, their hands, and the rapid jaw movements as three of them chewed gum.

"Okay, let's move out," Dooley said. Turning to the three clergy he said, "Prayer Team, whenever you're ready."

The three clergymen formed a rough triangle, a few feet separating them. Each would read or recite prayers in his own tradition designed specifically to dispel black magic. Supposedly, having them pray together produced a "synergistic effect" greater than the sum of their individual efforts.

How somebody figured that God would pay more attention to a group effort than if each of these guys prayed separately wasn't real clear to me, but I'm just a simple cop, not a theologian.

As the members of the SWAT team left the parking lot, single file, Dooley turned to Karl and me.

"You're not armored, so hang back a bit. But come in fast if I call for you."

We both nodded, and he went to catch up with his crew.

Dooley led us into an alley that ran along the rear of Jamieson Longworth's building. Karl and I followed the team as they made their silent way through the back door and up the stairs to the third floor. Then it was through a service door and down a hallway to number 304.

I watched them "stack" along the wall just outside Longworth's door – bunching close together in a line so that they could get everybody inside very fast once the breach was made. Sam and the Hellhound brought up the rear, followed by Karl and me.

Dooley was first in line. I saw him reach forward and slowly try to turn the knob, on the off chance that it might open. It didn't, but it's always good to check. More than one cop has gone to the trouble and risk of kicking down a door that wasn't even locked to begin with.

Dooley turned to Van Cleef, and took from him the big sledgehammer and stepped with it to the opposite side of the condo's door. Van Cleef unslung his weapon. I saw him click off the safety and then, a true professional, look to be sure the switch was really disengaged.

Behind Van Cleef, Garrett had ready two of the "Splash-Bang" grenades that he would throw into the condo as soon as the door was breached. The grenades looked like motorcycle handlebar grips made of cast iron, with holes drilled in them. Each one would explode with a loud noise, a bright flash, and a dispersal of four fluid ounces of holy water.

I could hear my pulse pounding in my ears. Sligo, being a vampire, ought to be dead to the world, literally. Assuming he was in there at all. But that didn't mean he hadn't set up magical protections or booby traps throughout the condo. The work of the prayer team should nullify those, but everybody in that hallway had been around long enough to know what "should" is worth.

Then there was Longworth himself. Normally, a pampered rich boy/cultist would pose no threat to these guys, but there was no way to know whether Sligo had taught him any dark magic, or whether Longworth had the Talent to use it.

It had the potential to get pretty dicey in there. That's why every cop serving in SWAT receives the extra pay that all of them like to call "danger money." They get excellent life insurance policies, too.

Van Cleef nodded at Dooley, who set his feet, gripped the sledge's handle tightly and lifted the head back and over his shoulder. With a barely audible grunt he smashed the sledge hammer into the door, just below the lock.

The *bam* of impact was jarring after the silence, even though I had been expecting it. The wood splintered where Dooley had struck, and the lock mechanism came free of the door jamb. It looked like the door might be hung up on something – a security chain, maybe. But it was no match for Van Cleef's size 12 boot, as he delivered a vicious kick above where the lock had been. The door flew open and Van Cleef instantly crouched down to give Garrett a clean line of sight into the condo.

The pins of the grenades had already been pulled. Garrett held one in each hand and flung both inside at the same time.

One thousand one. One thousand two.

Each of us squeezed our eyes closed. That's a risk in a tactical situation, but you've got no choice, unless you want to be temporarily blinded by the million-candle-power flash, just like whoever was inside the condo would be.

WHAMWHAM!

The two explosions were almost simultaneous, and they were fucking *loud*. The grenades contain magnesium instead of explosives – high on noise, but low on destructive power. And the cast-iron body won't fragment, so there's no shrapnel, which is why you can safely use them in hostage situations.

Van Cleef, clutching the H&K against his chest, dived through the door. I couldn't see inside from where I was standing, but I've seen enough SWAT training to know that he would land face down, do a quick hip roll to the right, and come up on one knee, weapon ready to fire. The next man through the door would break left, then the others would follow, going alternately right and left. All of this usually took about three seconds.

Once the team was inside, I waited for the rattle of gunfire, but it never came. Instead, I could hear voices, one after another, yelling "Clear!" as each room was checked in turn.

Then there was silence for a little while, then Dooley appeared in the doorway. "Come on in," he said.

We followed him into the sparsely furnished living room, its cream-colored walls and modernist furniture now stained with soot from the grenades and damp from the holy water.

"Nobody home, Goldilocks," Dooley said to me. "You can have your choice of chairs, beds, and porridge."

The other team members, who were leaning against walls and doorjambs, laughed loudly. I didn't mind – they had a lot of tension to get rid of.

"So, no Longworth," I said. "I take it you guys didn't turn up any slumbering vampires, either."

"Not a one," Heidi Renfer said. "But there's a pretty nasty-looking mouse in the kitchen that you guys might be interested in."

More laughter.

Karl shot his cousin a dirty look, then said to Dooley, "Lieutenant, didn't you say that surveillance had reported Longworth coming in the building, and didn't see him leaving?"

"Yeah, you've got a point," Dooley told him. "I wonder if the guys watching this place fucked up, or... just a second."

He pulled the tactical radio from his belt and thumbed the switch. "S-4, this is S-1. Do you copy? Over."

"Loud and clear, skipper." Spencer's voice came through crisply. "Hell, I can even see you through the window. Got the crosshairs right on you."

"Make sure your finger's off the trigger, then," Dooley said. "Did you see anyone leave the building from your side since we went in?"

"Negative, skipper. Nobody in or out. What's up – you missing a suspect or two?"

"Stand by."

Dooley scratched his cheek. "I suppose he could've made us somehow, as we came up the stairs, and went up or down the front stairs to another floor. All the other condos are locked up tight, but nothing's stopping him from roaming the hallways – or even breaking into somebody else's place, if he's got the right tools and know-how.

We didn't have the manpower to put a man on each floor, dammit."

Then I noticed that the Hellhound was acting strangely. She'd been sitting obediently next to Sam's leg, but now she was up, whining softly as her nose quested around the room.

"Daisy's got something, Loot," Sam said. "Don't know what it is, though."

"Look alive, people!" Dooley snapped. "There may be a bear at home, after all."

The rest of the SWAT team assumed alert postures, weapons ready. A couple of them started walking slowly around the big room, looking closely at the walls, the floors, the ceiling.

"Priest hole, do you think?" Garrett asked.

I knew the term. Used to refer to small hidden closets built in English houses during Henry VIII's time, after Catholic clergy were expelled from the country. Some stayed behind, and had to be hidden by Catholic families when Henry's goons came searching.

I wondered if Garrett the Jesuit saw the irony.

"I need him, or them, alive, if at all possible," I said, my own eyes roaming the room.

"It's always their choice," Dooley said softly. "Now shut the fuck up."

"You want us to check the other rooms again, boss?" Kyotake asked. He held the big samurai sword at guard, both hands on the custom grip.

"Let the dog show us where to go," Dooley said, and nodded toward Daisy's handler. "Sam."

The blond guy, still wearing his shades indoors, released his grip on the Hellhound's chain, which hit the carpet with a muffled *clank*.

Continuing to sniff the air, Daisy began moving around the room, dragging the chain behind her. Her nose led her toward the big window overlooking the street. She approached it slowly, then became still, growling softly – a sound that made my asshole pucker, even though I wasn't the focus of her attention.

Heidi Renfer was standing maybe ten feet from the window, with her back to it. I was looking in her direction when I saw the air *ripple* behind her, something that I wish I could say I'd seen only in the movies.

Then a man was standing there, where nobody had stood an instant before. At the same moment he appeared, I heard a male voice I didn't recognize snarl, "*Aw, shit!*"

The bastard was fast, I'll give him that. As he materialized, his left arm snaked around Heidi's slim waist and pulled her right up against him, while his right hand brought a black-bladed knife up to the side of her long neck, the point an inch away from her flesh.

The young guy's face was flushed and sweaty and tight with tension, but I was pretty sure I recognized it from mug shots, as well as an evening I once spent in a certain warehouse.

It looked like Jamieson Longworth was home, after all.

For a few seconds, we all stood in a tableau, like wax figures at Madame Tussaud's – maybe an exhibit titled "Hostage Situation."

Then the Hellhound lowered her haunches, preparing to spring.

"Daisy!" Sam's voice was a whipcrack. "Sit!" Then: "Stay!"

The dog obeyed, but you could see she was reluctant, not understanding why she wasn't being allowed to tear the intruder's throat out.

I knew exactly how she felt.

"Everybody stay right where you are!" Longworth shouted – unnecessarily, since that's exactly what we were all doing.

I saw Heidi wince when he yelled that, since his mouth was just a few inches from her ear. In response, Longworth squeezed her even tighter. "Keep still, bitch!" Longworth gasped a couple of breaths, then said to her, "Keep hanging on to your gun, honey. But if I see that barrel move an inch, in any direction, you're fuckin' dead! Understand?"

"Yeah," Heidi said hoarsely. "I understand."

"Something all of you should know!" Longworth said, still gasping for breath. He must've had enough adrenaline rushing through him to fuel an Olympic track team. In an older man, I might have hoped for a heart attack. "This is a Death Dagger," he went on. "One scratch, anywhere on her, and she's dead meat."

I believed him. Putting a spell like that on a weapon was pretty basic black magic. He might've done it himself, or had Sligo do it for him – if Sligo had been here, and I was betting he had.

It also explained why Longworth didn't have the blade pressed against her flesh, the way they usually do in situations like this. He didn't want to kill her – by accident. The Prayer Team's efforts might have neutralized the effects of the dagger's magic – but I don't think there was a man in the room willing to gamble Heidi's life on it.

Sligo must have taught Longworth how to work the Tarnhelm Effect – an invisibility spell, and not easy to do. That one's not black magic, but it's still pretty good work for a novice. He had fooled us all – except for Daisy.

"Okay, we hear you," Dooley said – pretty calmly, under the circumstances. "We'll all get this worked out somehow. Just stay cool."

Cool? Longworth was being about as cool as the Fifth Circle of Hell. But Dooley was handling it right.

I turned my head, very slowly, to take in the rest of the room. The other members of the SWAT team were utterly still, but each was coiled, like the dog had been, ready to spring.

I'd wondered if any of them had a shot at Longworth from the side, and whether he'd have the nerve to take it. But the only one with anything like the right angle was Garrett, holding his useless flamethrower. Like the others, he had a pistol on his belt – but there was no way in hell he'd be able to drop the flamethrower, draw, and get off an aimed shot without giving Longworth plenty of time to stab Heidi.

"Something for you to keep in mind," Dooley went on in that same, almost-calm voice, "is that if you *do* kill her, you're standing there naked, without protection. And I guarantee you won't live long enough to disappear again."

Longworth's voice went up a couple of notches. "Are you fucking *threatening* me, you cocksucker?"

Dooley shook his head slowly. "Nope, not at all. Just pointing out a good reason for you to keep that knife-point from getting too close to her neck. Be a shame to have people die today, just because of an accident."

"Don't fucking worry about me – worry about this bitch right here."

Then Longworth's gaze shifted to me, and something changed in his face. It only lasted a second or two, but it might almost have been the beginning of a smile. He added, "And you can worry about your bitch, too, you

Polack assfuck. You and that depraved motherfucker next to you threw my brother to a fucking demon! Did you think you can do that and just walk away, laughing? Did you?"

I remembered my laughter in the warehouse after Karl had saved my ass from the demon. I didn't think trying to explain to Longworth that it had been an hysterical reaction would be likely to improve the situation, so I kept quiet.

But I was confused by his reference to my "bitch." My poor wife was in the ground, and I didn't have a girlfriend – the closest thing to that in my life was Lacey Brennan, and she wasn't all that close, anyway.

Did Longworth realize that? Or was Lacey in trouble?

I was trying to phrase a question that wouldn't set him off, when he spoke again. "You'll see what it's like, motherfucker, lose somebody you really love. Then maybe I'll be the one to laugh."

Someone I really... Christine? Did this crazy bastard mean Christine?

Longworth was talking to Dooley again. "Okay, here's how this is gonna work. Me and sexy here are walking out, real close together. You boys are gonna stay right here. I see anybody follow me out, she's dead. We're gonna get my car, then she's gonna drive us wherever I wanna go. I see one cop car or helicopter or police dragon along the way, and she's dead. We get where we're going, I'll turn her loose, unharmed. My word of honor. Got that?"

Sure, we'll be happy to take the word of a wannabe black wizard and cult murderer. And right after that, we're gonna see if Charlie Manson is free to babysit the kids Saturday night.

Dooley nodded a couple of times. It was then I noticed that he still held his tactical radio down by his side, and a couple of his fingers were moving, ever so slowly, toward the "Transmit" button.

Who had he talked to last, on that radio?

"I'll even help you out with that," Dooley said. "If you want, I can make sure that all the traffic signals go your way, no matter where you're headed. No reds or yellows to slow you down. You'll see nothing but–"

Spencer. He'd been talking to Spencer.

Dooley had paused, just for a second, and I saw his finger depress the "Transmit" button before he continued, "Green light, green light, green light. All the way home."

Maybe my concern for Christine was distracting me, but it took me a heartbeat too long to realize what Dooley had just done.

Longworth was saying "I don't need your fucking–" as I opened my mouth to tell Dooley to call it off, that we needed Longworth alive–

There was a loud *click* as a small hole appeared in the window behind Longworth, who grunted once, then stopped talking because he was already dead and falling to the floor, the dagger tumbling harmlessly to the carpet as the sound of the rifle shot that had killed him echoed back and forth across the street like lost hope.

There were sirens in the distance and drawing closer – lots of them. Spencer had joined us, the big rifle case in one hand, after Dooley had given him the all clear. He was instantly exchanging high fives with the rest of the team, except for Heidi Renfer, who stepped so far out of character as to kiss him on the mouth, hard.

I knew she and Spencer would be kidded by the team about that kiss, along with Spencer's rescue of the "damsel in distress," for years to come. But they'd both get over it. And I was glad that Karl's cousin hadn't died today.

The first thing Dooley had done after the shot was to quickly check Heidi's back for a gunshot wound, although the fact that she was still standing under her own power was a good sign. Her Kevlar body armor had stopped the round from penetrating the skin, although she was going to have a painful bruise between her shoulder blades later.

"I figured her armor would stop the round," Dooley said to me, as we stood a little ways off, watching the SWAT team, along with Karl, congratulating Spencer. "Especially after being slowed by the window and Longworth's body. The odds were good."

"And what if the odds didn't pay off today," I said, "and the bullet kept on going? What then?"

"She still might've survived, if it missed a vital organ. Besides," he said, and his hard eyes bored into mine, "what odds would you give her if we just let Longworth take her out of here? Huh?"

I looked away from his stare. "Between slim and none," I said. I felt a deep sigh come out of me before I said, "I'm not questioning your order, Lieutenant. It was the right call, and I'd have made the same one myself, in your position. It's just that I'd have preferred him alive to question, that's all. But I agree the situation didn't make that possible."

"Yeah, okay, then. All right." Dooley's lean face softened a little. "Question him, you mean, about that shit he was talking – about you losing a loved one? You worried about somebody, Stan? Because I can get twenty-four-seven protection assigned as soon–"

I held up a hand. "No, that's all right. It wouldn't work in this case, although I appreciate the offer – I do."

Dooley looked at me for a bit. "Who are we talking about, anyway, Stan? I know about, uh, your wife, God rest her. You seeing somebody these days? Is that who you think Longworth was talking about?"

"No, no girlfriend," I told him. "The only realistic candidate... is my daughter Christine."

The silence was even longer this time. I listened to the sirens reach a peak, then stop outside the building. "I remember Christine," Dooley said. "And I also thought I remembered that she, uh, had died a while back."

"You're right," I said. "She did."

Given the Longworth family's social prominence (and big fat bank account), the chief had sent a captain down to supervise the cleanup. I bet Internal Affairs was going to spit blood over that.

Captain D'Agostino brought a team of eight detectives with him. He said it would be a while before they got to me, so I spent the time wandering around the condo, being careful not to touch anything or disturb the forensics techs.

Like the rest of the place, Jamieson Longworth's bedroom didn't look especially lived in. It contained a king-sized bed (where I guess he fucked all those nice girls his mom had mentioned), some new-looking furniture, and a big, elaborate computer, but not much of his personality was imprinted on the room. Considering what I knew about his personality, the room should've considered itself lucky.

I wandered over to the huge computer desk that looked like it was made out of teak. It had drawers, cubbyholes, paper trays, and even a cup holder. *Wouldn't want to spill any cappuccino on the keyboard, would we?*

The machine itself was a Dell PC that I assumed was top-of-the-line. It looked like it had everything but warp drive, and I decided not to bet against that feature either. I would have loved to go through its files to see if I could shed any light on Longworth's threats, but Captain D'Agostino would probably boil me in oil for messing around with his crime scene.

I'd have to see about getting access to the computer through channels later, assuming it was even impounded as evidence and the Longworth family didn't demand its return immediately. The Longworths, I was learning, tended to get what they wanted. But even they couldn't fetch sonny-boy back from Hell, where I hoped he and some especially sadistic demon were having a nice chat right about now.

Some scraps of paper and index cards were strewn around the keyboard and mouse pad, and I bent over them to see if Jamieson Longworth had obligingly left all his secrets written down for me, just like on TV. I took out my pen and used its blunt end to move some of the stuff around a little for a better look, but all I learned was that Longworth wanted to remember to "Call Mom," had a dentist appointment next week he was unlikely to keep, and was running low on pineapple juice and cottage cheese.

From the living room, somebody called my name. I started a little, and my hand brushed the computer's black and silver mouse, where it lay on a rubber pad that had "Carpe Noctem" printed on it in spooky-looking letters.

The machine must have been in sleep mode, because that slight movement of the mouse woke it up. I heard my name again, and it sounded like the voice's owner was closer now, and getting pissed.

As I straightened up, I saw that the monitor was now showing a professional-looking photo of a small stone building with water around it. It looked like it belonged on a calendar from Ireland, or someplace. You'd think Longworth's tastes would run more toward splatter porn. Go figure. I didn't recognize the image on the screen, but there was something...

"What are you *doing*, Detective?"

One of D'Agostino's guys, in a blue pinstripe suit and hundred-dollar haircut that made him seem more like a corporate lawyer than a cop, stood in the door. He looked like he'd caught me buggering a donkey right here in the bedroom.

"Just killing time," I said. "Sorry I didn't hear you at first – daydreaming, I guess."

He stepped into the room and glanced at the computer screen, then looked at me hard for a few seconds. But when I didn't turn into a weeping puddle and confess to the Lindbergh kidnapping, he jerked his head back in the direction he'd come from. "Come on – you're up."

"You bet," I said, and followed him out of the room. The photo on Longworth's monitor wasn't either significant or sinister. Just a little pastoral art, unlikely as that might be. But I was irritated that it had some kind of association for me that I couldn't put a finger on.

I didn't get to dwell on it for long. I soon had other irritations to replace it, all of them wearing expensive suits and power ties.

I didn't have a lot to talk about, since my role in both the raid and the shooting was one of observer. I told two of D'Agostino's detectives what I'd seen, and agreed to provide sworn testimony at any proceedings, departmental or legal, that might stem from today's tragic events. Then I got to say the same thing to two more of them. Then two more. Karl, I found out later, went through the same fucking round-robin. Then, when they finally ran out of idiotic questions, and big words to ask them with, they cut us loose.

"I wonder who's gonna get the job," I said to Karl, as we walked back to the Rite-Aid lot.

"Who, Dooley's? He won't get fired, Stan. I don't care who the fucking kid's family is. It was a righteous shoot, with lots of witnesses."

"No, I mean the job of bringing the bad news to Mrs. Longworth. Glad it won't be us."

We'd walked another three or four paces before Karl said, "Maybe they can tell her it was done by werewolves."

Karl had made a light on yellow that I hadn't, so he was just getting out of his car as I pulled into the police department lot. He walked over and waited while I locked the Toyota. "You heard what Longworth said back there," I said.

"About your loved ones? Yeah, I heard the fucker. You think he meant Christine?"

"I don't see who else he could've been talking about. I mean, I kinda like you, Karl, but you don't really qualify as a 'loved one,' you know?"

"I guess that means no flowers on Valentine's Day," he said. "How about Lacey?"

"No, she doesn't quite make the list, either."

"Okay, so it's Christine," Karl said. "You got a plan?"

"Not much of one. But I'm for damn sure gonna be right here, come sunset."

We started walking slowly toward the station house.

"Think I'll tag along, if that's okay," Karl said.

"Sure, the more the merrier," I said, then, "Thanks, man."

"No prob. Anyway, if you don't mind me saying so, I think Christine's kinda cute."

"For a vamp, you mean."

"For anybody. So, okay, assume she shows, what then?"

I shrugged. "I'll find out if she knows anything about Sligo. Then I'll tell her what I find out, which doesn't amount to a hell of a lot. Suggest she move her daytime resting place, just as a precaution. Remind her to watch her back. Stuff like that. Just... fatherly advice." My voice might have gotten a little funny as I said those last two words.

Fatherly advice? I haven't talked about Christine that way since she was changed. Since I had her changed.

"Think she'll believe you?"

"I've got no reason to lie," I said. "She'll understand that."

"Okay, sure. But what if she doesn't show at sundown?"

"I'm still working on that part of the plan."

We'd kept McGuire informed by radio of where we were and what we were up to, but I wanted to fill him in on some of the details before Karl and I hit the streets again.

As we walked into the squad's tiny reception area, I asked Louise the Tease if there'd been any word from Vollman.

She shook her head, the blonde curls bouncing a little. "Not a peep since last week."

To look at the hair and that body of hers, you'd never guess that she's a member of Mensa, but I knew she had been for years. She's also deadly at Scrabble, I hear – plays in tournaments, and stuff.

"If he calls when I'm away from the squad," I said, "give him my cell phone number, patch him through on the radio, or do whatever else it takes. I have *got* to talk to that creepy old bastard, and the sooner the better."

"Will do," she said. Then she glanced toward the squad room door and said, "Those two witch sniffers are in with the lieutenant."

An icy finger traced its slow way down my spine. "They haven't found Rachel, have they?"

Louise shook her head. "I'm pretty sure not. I think that's what they're in there bitching about."

"Okay, good."

I turned to Karl. "Let's go in, sit down, and catch up on paperwork or something." We still call it paperwork, although most of that crap is digital now. "Once those two bozos leave, we can talk to McGuire."

"Works for me."

I went into the squad room and could see, through the glass panels in McGuire's office, the two witchfinders in there with him. They were standing, and the older one, Ferris, was gesturing the way people do when they are seriously pissed off. The other guy, Crane, didn't look real cheerful, either, and that was fine with me. The unhappier those assholes were, the better I liked it. Or so I thought.

Aquilina and Sefchik were at their desks, the ongoing argument apparently suspended for the time being while they each worked at their computers. They looked up as Karl and I came in, nodded "Hi," and went back to work.

Any hope I had of doing the same was crushed when McGuire appeared in his office door, pointed at me, and made a summoning motion. Guess I wouldn't have to wait to see the boss, after all.

As I walked through the door, McGuire said, "The reverends here have filed a complaint about the lack of cooperation they say they've received from the department as a whole, and our unit in particular. Therefore, Sergeant Markowski, I'm appointing you liaison, so that – what's the matter?"

Ferris and Crane were looking at me as if I'd come in covered in shit. A kind of horrified fascination was in their stares; they recoiled as if I might get it all over them, and even the way they were sniffing gave some credence to the metaphor.

"Anathema," breathed Crane, the younger one, who then said it again, louder: "Anathema!"

"Cursed of God," Ferris said slowly, nodding, then he pointed an index finger at me like it was a loaded gun and he was getting ready to open fire. "Abomination!"

I looked at McGuire if he knew what the fuck was going on, but he seemed as baffled as I was. I opened my mouth to demand some answers, but before I could speak, Ferris turned to McGuire and said, "This man" – still pointing at me – "reeks of accursed black magic. He has been consorting with the minions of the Evil One, and I demand to know why you have allowed such a person to remain not just in this city, but on the *police force*, for the love of Almighty God!"

I noticed that Crane was nervously touching something through his suit coat. It appeared to be underneath the material, near his right hip.

He's packing? There's metal detectors at every door to the building, the best ones they make – no way could he get in here with a gun.

Or could he?

"All right," McGuire said, "let's everybody just calm down." I assume he meant the reverends, since I hadn't had the chance to get a word in yet.

Once Ferris and Crane had stopped acting like nuns at a strip club, McGuire said to me, "Stan, you got any idea what these... *gentlemen* are talking about?"

"That's what I came back here to tell you about, boss," I said. "I was approached by Rachel Proctor today – or, rather, Rachel's body with that bastard Kulick in charge."

Crane made one of those snorts that means "Likely story," but at least he didn't start yelling again.

"I'd like to hear about it now," McGuire said. Looking toward the witchfinders, he went on, "*without* interruption."

They didn't like that, but at least the two of them kept their mouths shut while I ran down my encounter with Rachel/Kulick. As far as I was concerned, I was reporting to McGuire; the witchfinding assholes could listen if they wanted to.

When I'd finished, McGuire asked, "Got that amulet on you?"

"It's half an amulet," I said, "but yeah."

"Let me take a look."

I dug it out and handed it over. McGuire rubbed the metal gently between his fingers, as if he was expecting a genie to appear. "So Kulick gave you his true name, along with this little trinket."

"Had to," I said. "The spell wouldn't work, otherwise."

"You're supposed to hold this, say the name five times, and *poof* he appears?"

"I don't know if there's a *poof* involved, but that's about the size of it. Except he'll still be in Rachel's body when he shows up."

"Ridiculous!" Ferris said, as if he couldn't hold himself in any longer. "Lieutenant, your man has obviously fabricated this fairy story to conceal his own involvement with the witch, Proctor. He is probably in league with her – even after she murdered one of his brother officers, and drove the other insane."

He actually said "in league with her." I didn't think anybody talked like that any more.

"Oh, I don't know," McGuire said slowly, and I could tell he was working to keep his temper under wraps. "The sergeant's story is consistent with the other facts we have, such as they are. And he's had an exemplary record of service in this unit. I'm inclined to believe him."

That was the first time he'd ever called me "exemplary" – in a good way, that is.

Ferris glared at McGuire. "All right, Lieutenant. Your faith in your subordinate is touching – so, let us test it."

He looked at me. "Take hold of the amulet, then recite the so-called true name of this wizard-in-a-witch's-body. Make him appear here, in this office. Right now."

"Can't do that," I told him.

"*Can't*, or *won't*?"

"Both," I said. "If I bring Kulick here, where Sligo obviously isn't, he's gonna be pretty pissed off. He's a powerful wizard, and there's no way to know what spells he's got prepared and ready to go. He could wreck this whole place – and us along with it. I think we can maybe use this thing to trap him, but it's gonna take careful preparation to control him once he shows up."

"What a steaming pile of self-serving–" Crane began, but I kept talking, right on over him.

"Besides, if we tried to take Kulick into custody now, Rachel could be hurt, even killed. I'm not willing to risk that – not even for two people I like and respect the way I do you guys."

I wondered if these clowns even understood sarcasm.

"An interesting story," Ferris said. "It neatly covers all your transgressions – or it would, if Reverend Crane and I were just a little more gullible."

Ferris turned to McGuire. Speaking formally, as if making a public proclamation, he said, "Lieutenant, we believe this man to be willfully withholding information vital to our investigation, which we are undertaking as lawfully constituted witchfinders. We shall therefore take him into our custody and question him at length, until we are satisfied that he has spoken the truth of this matter."

I felt my testicles try to pull up into my body. I'd heard stories about the "questioning" techniques of witchfinders. Word was, they were modeled on the Spanish Inquisition – which was one of the reasons I didn't want Rachel falling into their bloodstained hands.

Crane reached under his suit coat, and produced a pair of police-grade handcuffs. So that's what he'd been fondling under there. Then he gave me the nastiest smile I'm seen in quite some time. Maybe he did recognize sarcasm, after all.

"Question him?" McGuire said. "Is that a polite term for 'torture'?"

"Torture?" Ferris pretended indignation. "Heaven forefend, Lieutenant. We simply apply proven methods of... vigorous interrogation."

"Taken from the *Malleus Maleficarum*?"

The Hammer of Witches is a fifteenth century book describing how to torture confessions out of witches. The two guys who wrote it, Kramer and Sprenger, knew nothing about real witchcraft. They were just a couple of sick fucks who liked listening to women scream.

"The source of our methods is irrelevant," Ferris said loftily. "They are all quite legal."

"So's waterboarding, in some circles," McGuire said. "Doesn't make it right." Without taking his eyes from Ferris, McGuire said to me, "Detective Sergeant Markowski, do you willingly agree to accompany these men, and undergo interrogation at their hands?"

I tried to speak, but failed. So I cleared my throat and tried again. "No, Lieutenant, I'd really rather not."

"It seems the sergeant doesn't want to go with you, gentlemen," McGuire said. "And I'm afraid I couldn't spare him, anyway. His caseload is far too heavy."

Ferris drew himself up. "It is not your choice to make, Lieutenant. This man is coming with us. We have the full authority of the law behind us."

McGuire stood up slowly. He pushed his chair back, came around his desk, and stood next to me. He folded his arms across that barrel chest and said, "No, Reverend – you've got the full authority of the law in *front* of you."

"It's over here, too," a familiar voice said. Karl was in the doorway, and he slowly pushed back the right side of his jacket to reveal the holstered Glock on his belt. He held the jacket back with his forearm, and just stood there, like an Old West gunfighter ready to take care of business.

Karl gestured in the direction of the squad room. "And I think there's some more of it out there, too."

I slowly turned my head to look through the glass. Sefchik and Aquilina were both on their feet and facing us, maybe ten feet apart. As I watched, Aquilina slipped off the blazer she wore on the street to reveal the wide brown leather belt underneath, and the holstered automatic on her right hip. She dropped the blazer on a nearby desk then just stood there, hands on her hips, calmly looking at us. Sefchik left his suit coat on, but he slowly and deliberately hooked his thumbs in his belt, and kept them there, close to the gun you knew he had under the coat. He stood looking our way, too.

I glanced at McGuire and saw a tight smile appear on his face. "Don't let us detain you, gentlemen. I'm sure you have a number of important appointments – elsewhere."

Ferris's pale face had turned dark red, and I noticed that Crane had lost that mean smile of his. "This is – this is–" Ferris seemed to be having trouble getting the words out. He stopped, swallowed a couple of times, then said, more calmly, "Stay near your phone, Lieutenant. You'll be hearing from your superiors, shortly. Enjoy your early retirement from the police force."

Ferris looked at the handcuffs Crane still held and snarled, "Put those away and come on!" Then he stalked toward the office door, and Karl moved away to let him pass. Crane dropped the cuffs in his suit pocket and hurried after him. I saw that Aquilina and Sefchik didn't bar their way, but they didn't step aside, either.

My chest was tight, and I took a big, deep breath to loosen it a little. "Thank you, sir," I said to McGuire, which may have been the first time I ever called him that.

I looked through the glass at Sefchik and Aquilina and

nodded at each of them. They returned the nod. Aqulina put her blazer back on, then she and Sefchik returned to whatever they'd been doing.

I turned back to McGuire. "Are you screwed, Lieutenant?"

He went back behind his desk and sat down again. "Maybe, but I don't think so. I know several city councilmen who are none too happy with this witchfinder bullshit, and a couple of local religious leaders who feel the same way. I'll make sure the mayor and the chief both hear from them. Now get out of here, both of you – I've got some phone calls to make."

"I don't know about you," I said to Karl, "but I've probably got a shitload of messages that've come in since yesterday. Email and voicemail both."

"Yeah, I've got a bunch, too." I didn't know if that was true, or if he just understood that I wanted to spend a few minutes letting my guts unclench. "Might as well take ten or fifteen, catch up a little," Karl said.

"When do you figure the department's going to start issuing those fancy phones where you can check all that stuff from anywhere?"

He pretended to think about it. "Dunno. What's the latest estimate for Hell freezing over?"

"Beats me," I said. "But if it does, I bet we'll catch the complaint."

Karl laughed and turned toward his desk.

"By the way..." I said.

He looked back at me.

"Thanks," I told him. "For... you know. Thanks."

He gave me a fat grin. "Ahh, I fuckin' loved it. Felt like John Wesley Hardin there, for a minute."

"Is that better than 'Bond, James Bond'?"

"No," he said, "but it ain't half bad, neither."

I started with my email but only got through about half a dozen messages when McGuire came to the door of his office.

"Sefchik! Aquilina!" he called. "You got one!"

Once I knew that it was somebody else's problem, I brought my focus back to the computer monitor. But you know how it is: if somebody uses your name, even in a conversation that you're not really listening to, you're going to notice. The name that caught my attention wasn't my own, however. It was *Mercy Hospital*.

It's impossible to measure stuff like this, but after the hospital's name was mentioned, I'd say the conversation at McGuire's door had maybe 25 percent of my attention. Then I heard *patient was incinerated*, and that brought my focus up to around 75 percent. But it was the word *dismembered* that got me to my feet.

I walked quickly to where the three of them were standing. "Don't mean to kibbitz, boss, but did you say something about burning and dismemberment? At Mercy Hospital?"

From the corner of my eye, I saw Karl get up from his desk and head over.

McGuire stared at me for a couple of beats, then said, "Yeah, it's at Mercy. There's a report of a patient in his room found burned to a crisp, arms and legs hacked off. Since there was no fire damage elsewhere in the room, the first responders are thinking black magic as a COD."

My guts, which had just started to relax, were a big clenched fist again. "Did you get a name on this patient?" I asked, dreading the answer.

"No name," McGuire said. "Just the room number: 333."

I glanced at Karl. His expression said he was thinking the same thing that I was.

"Boss, can you let Karl and me take this one?" I turned to Aquilina and Sefchik. "That okay with you guys?"

Aquilina said, "Sure," and Sefchik shrugged. They didn't much care – there would be other calls; they'd catch the next one.

"What's your interest?" McGuire asked me.

"I'm thinking that the vic might be–" I took a second to swallow, even though my mouth was suddenly very dry. "–Benjamin Prescott."

"Prescott?" McGuire's eyebrows dipped in a frown. "Oh, that professor, right? The one who was choking, and you two got to be heroes over. I thought he was in a coma."

"No, he's out of it, and doing some translation work for us. On the *Opus Mago*."

"Then what the fuck are you two standing here for?" he said. "Get moving."

It's not unusual to find flashing red lights around the back of Mercy Hospital. That's where the ambulances deliver emergency cases to the ER. But flashing lights clustered around the hospital's front entrance – that's something you don't see every day.

I took some doctor's parking space, then Karl and I made our rapid way toward the front door. I made sure that the ID folder with my shield on it was hanging over my breast pocket, since I was in no mood to be stopped by some rookie who didn't know us by sight.

I'd planned to stop at the information desk and get the name of the patient who'd been in room 333, but the harried-looking woman behind the counter was trying to talk to five people at once, and every one of them look pissed off, or scared, or both.

At the elevators, I mashed the call button and we waited for a car to show up. About half a minute later, I was about to say "Fuck it" and look for the stairs when one set of elevator doors slid open with a muted *ping*.

The only one inside was a middle-aged nurse who quickly left the car before Karl and I got in. I got a glimpse of her face as we passed each other. Being strong, controlled, and emotionally resilient are all part of every nurse's unofficial job description, which is why I was surprised to see that this one had almost certainly been crying.

The elevator brought us to the third floor, and a sign said that those with business in rooms 320 to 340 should turn left. We did, and a hundred feet farther down rounded a corner and that's when I knew we were in the right place – or the wrong one, depending on how you look at it.

Part of the hallway was blocked off by yellow crime scene tape in two places, with one room in the middle. I didn't really need to look and see if it was 333, but I did, and it was.

A uniform named Klein was stationed at the barrier. He nodded at me and lifted the tape up so we could duck under it.

I waited for Karl to say "What do we got here?" but he didn't. I glanced at him and saw that his face was pinched and gray, and we hadn't even been inside the room yet.

A few yards down the hall, another uniform was interviewing a nurse who kept waving her hands around as she talked. I walked up to them. "Excuse me," I said. "Anybody know the name of the vic?"

The cop, a redheaded beanpole named Sadler, flipped back a page in his notebook. "Prescott, Benjamin R," he said. "Moved down here from the ICU earlier today."

I wish I could say that the news surprised me, but by then the surprise would have been if he'd said a different name. My guts weren't clenched, the way they'd been with the witchfinders. Instead they were cold, freezing cold, as if a big ball of ice had formed there and was planning to stay a while. Like maybe the rest of my life.

I asked Sadler, "Witnesses?"

"Nah. Couple of nurses heard screaming and ran over, but the guy's door was locked – from the inside. One of them had to go back to the nurse's station to get a master key. When they got the door open, nobody was in there but the vic, or what was left of him." He shook his head. "Sounds like your kind of thing, huh?"

"Yeah, sure. My kind of thing."

I turned away and went to the doorway of room 333 and stood there while a couple of forensics techs inside went about their business.

I let my gaze wander around. Standard-looking hospital room: green walls, patterned linoleum floor, a single window open wide; I didn't know if the window had been like that earlier, or if a cop was hoping to let out some of the stench. If that was the point, it hadn't worked real well so far. The sickly-sweet smell of burned flesh was so thick, you could almost see it in the air.

The rest of the room was pretty much what you'd expect. Narrow bed with mechanical stuff underneath it for raising and lowering; a small wooden armoire; a nightstand; one of those rectangular tables on wheels that they use for meals; a couple of uncomfortable-looking chairs.

There were a couple of differences from the average hospital room, though. Like the four bloody, naked limbs – arms and legs, two of each – stacked neatly in one corner, and the charred thing that lay in what was left of the bed.

Some of Prescott's abundant body fat had been liquefied by the intense heat. You could see it, runny and yellowish, sticking to parts of the bed frame. There were a couple of congealed pools of it on the floor, one on each side of the bed.

I stepped closer to the monstrosity on the bed. Might as well drink from this cup all the way to the bottom. A quick look at what had once been Prescott's head didn't tell me anything useful. A really hot fire will explode a corpse's eyeballs, so there was no way to tell whether the empty sockets that stared accusingly at me had been victims of the fire, or maybe the claws of something right out of Hell. I couldn't bring myself to check Prescott's crotch, to see if his balls were still there. I just couldn't.

Apart from some scorch marks on the wall behind the bed, the rest of the room had been untouched by the flames. The blaze had been localized and focused, no doubt because that's what a very old and deadly curse had specified.

The curse that I had invoked.

Sure, Prescott did the translating, but that's not what caused the curse to kick in – it's *revealing* to somebody what you've learned that does it.

Which is exactly what I asked Prescott to do.

Which is why Prescott died, in agony and horror.

I think Karl said something to me, but I waved him off. I stood there, looking at the remains of what had been a pretty good man and wondered if he'd damned Stan Markowski in his final moments. If he did, I wouldn't blame him.

But even he couldn't have damned Stan Markowski nearly as hard as I was right now.

After a while, I went back to acting like a cop. What else was I gonna do?

As I turned, my foot knocked against something metal. A wastebasket. I looked and saw some used Kleenex, the remains of a tube of Life Savers, a bent straw, a couple of used cotton balls. And a big FedEx overnight envelope. It was addressed to Prescott, care of the hospital, with a return address at Georgetown University. Looked like his assistant back on campus had sent the stuff that Prescott wanted. Like the remaining untranslated pages of the *Opus Mago*.

Then what the hell happened to them?

I turned to one of the forensics guys, Billy Santoro. "You come across any paper around the corpse, maybe something written in a foreign language?"

"No, no papers, Stan. Some ashes that might've been paper, but nothing that's got any hope of recovery. Fire was just too hot, you know?"

"How about a laptop?"

"We found something, was probably a laptop once. But now it's just a bunch of warped metal and melted plastic. You can look at it, if you want."

"No, I guess not. Thanks."

Well, so much for that brilliant idea. If Prescott had learned anything useful from the *Opus Mago* fragments, it had died with him. Even if my hunch had panned out, what would I do with a bunch of papers written in Ancient Sumerian?

Find another translator, who can get dismembered, blinded, and burned alive for his trouble? One's not enough?

I looked at the corpse one more time. Just punishing myself, I suppose. I didn't need to see it again – that charred mound of gunk and bone was going to have a starring role in my nightmares for a long time to come.

As I turned away, something glittered in the corner of my vision.

It came from the corner where Prescott's severed arms and legs were stacked. They hadn't bled much, without a heart to provide pumping action. I walked over, and tilted my head a little. There it was again.

I squatted next to the pile of flabby, pale flesh, careful not to touch anything. I looked closer.

A cell phone. Prescott had been holding the phone in his hand when the arm was severed. Not surprising, then, that his big paw was squeezed tight around it.

I looked over my shoulder and saw that Billy was still taking samples of Prescott's ashes and putting them into small plastic bags.

"You do these yet?" I asked him. "The arms and legs?"

"Not yet," he said. "Thought we ought to concentrate on the torso first. We'll get to the rest of him pretty soon. I figure there's no hurry."

"No. No hurry at all."

He went back to work. Using my body to hide what I was doing, I slowly leaned forward, got two fingers around the phone, and carefully worked it loose from Prescott's grip.

I knew I was tampering with evidence in a homicide investigation. But the cause of death wasn't exactly in dispute, even if nobody but me and Karl would ever know for sure what had happened here.

I slipped Prescott's phone into an inside pocket of my suit coat, then stood up. Walking over near the window for better light, I casually pulled the phone out again. As far as anybody could tell, I was messing around with my own phone, just like millions of people do every day.

I opened the phone and, with a little work, found the list of outgoing calls. The last one Prescott ever made had been to a number I knew well – it was my phone, at the squad room. Length of call: 11:46.

Sweet Mother Mary on a motorcycle.

"Come on," I said to Karl, who'd been staring at the body from another corner of the room.

"Where we goin'?"

"Back to the squad, so I can check my voicemail."

As I drove us out of the hospital parking lot, Karl said, "It's my fault."

I turned and looked at him, and his face reminded me of a man I'd once seen at the funeral of his three children. They'd been murdered by his wife, before she killed herself.

"What the fuck are you talking about, Karl?"

"Prescott. What happened. It's my fault."

"You're wrong about that, partner. You are totally fucking off base. *I'm* the one who roped him into all this shit."

"Doesn't matter. You *told* me, Stan! You said to get additional warding for his room. I called two witches I know. One's moved out of town, I left a message with the other one's answering service. She didn't call back, and I *forgot*, Stan. I should have tried somebody else, even looked in the fucking Yellow Pages, if I had to."

"Karl, listen, you didn't–"

"But I just *forgot*. With people dropping dead bodies on us and Internal Affairs and the SWAT raid, and the rest of it..."

"Listen, man, don't be–"

"It could've made the difference, Stan! It *could*. If the protection was stronger, the fucking curse might not have been able to get him. Instead, he went out as hard as any motherfucker I ever saw, or even heard of. The dude was trying to help us, and for that he had his fucking *eyes* gouged out, and got his *arms* and *legs* chopped off, and then he was *burned alive*..."

Karl buried his face in his hands and started to cry.

If I wasn't driving, I just might have joined him.

Back at the squad, we reported to McGuire what we'd seen, what we knew, and what we suspected.

He sat back and ran a hand slowly over his big jaw. "All right," he said. "I'll assign a couple of other detectives to it, just so we can say we investigated and filed a report. I'll need you to brief them before they go out, so that they don't waste a lot of time reinventing the wheel."

Fine. Now I'd have to explain to a couple of other cops just how bad I had fucked up. McGuire was right to do that – I just wasn't looking forward to it.

"You figure this was Sligo, shutting Prescott's mouth?" McGuire asked. "He's got a copy of the *Opus Mago*. He'd probably know about the curse, and how to make a murder look like one."

I thought about that, then shook my head. "No, if it was him, he'd want us to know it – he wouldn't try to hide his work by imitating the curse, the arrogant prick."

"Besides," Karl said, "it happened in broad daylight. Sligo's a vamp, remember?"

"Yeah, you got a point there." McGuire looked closely at me, then gave the same scrutiny to Karl. "You guys need some time off?" he asked quietly.

Considering everything that was going on right now, he was being extremely generous. But there was no way I wanted to spend the next few days sitting around my house thinking – or worse, drinking myself stupid.

I looked at Karl, who gave me a small headshake. His face had lost a little of the stricken look it had worn at the hospital, but only a little.

"We'd just as soon keep busy, boss, but thanks," I said.

McGuire took a case file from a stack sitting on his desk and put it on his blotter. Opening it, he said, "Then get back to work and catch this motherfucker, before he kills anybody else."

I'd told Karl I wanted to check my voicemail, and why. He said he'd start going through the files, to see if he could find a connection between Sligo and Jamieson Longworth. Then he reminded me that sunset was about an hour away. "You've got an appointment, in the parking lot," he said.

"Yeah," I said, "if she shows up."

"She seemed pretty definite about it this morning. Think she'd change her mind?"

"No, I'm just hoping that Longworth's threat turns out to be empty bullshit, that's all."

"Yeah, I know," he said. "Don't forget, I'm going down with you when it's time. Help you wait."

I nodded my thanks. "I wouldn't have it any other way."

● ● ● ●

"To access your voicemail messages, please press 8."
The computer's recorded voice was as polite as ever. I
touched 8.

"Please enter your four-digit extension number."
4294

"Please enter your security code."
3475833

"You have eight new messages. These are your options
while listening. To listen to a message, press 5. To go back
to the beginning of a message, press 7. To delete a message, press 2 twice. To save a message, press 4. To
advance to the next message, press 3. To end this session,
press 9 twice. Ready."
5

"Going to the first new message."

"Sergeant, this is Sonia, over in Human Resources.
Your leave record for last month hasn't been–"
22
3

"Stanley, this is Father Cebula at St Casimir's. We've
got the annual Corpus Christi banquet coming up–"
22
3

"Hey, Stan – Lacey. What do you get when you cross
a female ogre with a werewolf? You–"
4
3

"Mr Markowski, this is Rob at Nationwide Insurance.
I see you've got a birthday coming up soon, and I'd like
to talk–"
22
3

"Sergeant, this is Ben Prescott, calling from my lovely

new digs – let's see, it's room 333. The material I asked
my assistant at G-town to send me arrived via FedEx
early this morning, including the remaining fragments
of the *Opus Mago* that I had yet to translate. I went right
to work, and I'm pleased to say that it went faster than
I'd anticipated. Maybe my brain is a little sharper from
its long rest while I was comatose.

"I should probably wait until you get over here to fill
you in on what I've been able to make of this, but I'm
pretty excited – and more than a little disturbed, frankly.
Anyway, I thought I would get the gist of it to you now,
in case that curse we talked about earlier turns out to be
real, ha ha.

"Most of what I've learned about this spell you're interested in deals with the final stage. By the way, the fifth
sacrifice, the final vampire killing, is supposed to take
place as part of the actual ritual. The other four are pro-
logues, as it were.

"All right, let's see here. The book specifies that the
spell must take place near water. Still water, that is not
of the sea. Meaning, not salt water. The other requirement is that the ritual be carried out on the first night of
the full moon, at the 'turn of time' – which, given the
context, I would say refers to midnight.

"Um, that's followed by a long incantation the practitioner is supposed to recite, that's probably of little
interest to you... Okay, here's something: I expect you'll
want to know what all of this is in aid of – the purpose
of the spell, as it were. Well, that would be, in a word:
transformation. If the ritual, which is supposed to be one
of extreme difficulty, by the way, is carried out in the
proper manner, all the magical I's dotted and T's crossed,
and so on, the vampire/wizard conduct–"

"The disk space allotted for this message has been filled. To listen to the next message, press 3."

Goddamn motherfucking cocksucker shit!!

3!

"Advancing to the next new message."

"Prescott again, Sergeant. Sorry about that. Long-windedness is an occupational hazard of academe.

"All right, now, where was – oh, right. Transformation. According to this, the practitioner will be transformed into... this next word is a double compound, and the grammar is confusing, but I've rendered it as 'a creature of both night and day.' The fragment says the one casting the spell will 'walk under the sun without fear.' I suppose if you were a vampire, that would be a pretty desirable thing, wouldn't it?

"Oh, and it gets better – better, I mean from the perspective of the vampire. It says that, after the transformation, the practitioner will 'fear not holy things, nor fire, nor sharp branches.' Would that be wooden stakes, do you suppose? I guess that would make the guy some sort of 'super-vampire,' wouldn't it?

"That goes on for a while, then four lines further down it says that this one who 'walks under, or beneath, the sun without fear,' can drink the blood of others and thereby make them 'brothers, or brethren, like himself.'

"I'm not sure what to make of that one – you're probably a better judge than I, since you deal with this kind of thing all the time. I mean, everybody knows that vampires can reproduce by exchanging blood with one of their victims, presumably willing ones. Nothing new there. Or could it mean that once transformed, this 'super-vampire' can make others like himself, just by biting them? I suppose the blood exchange is assumed there, too.

"Quite the spell this guy's got here. No wonder it's supposed to be so hard. He turns himself into a vampire without vulnerabilities, then can pass that on to others in the usual vampiric way? Sounds like a bad James Bond movie, if that's not redundant, but with fangs. You could create a whole army of – *Jesus Christ, what the fuck? Who are you? How'd you get in here? Stay back! The... the power of Christ compels you! Get away from me, get away get awayyyyy...*"

Then there was nothing but the screaming.

99

"Session terminated. Goodbye."

"How'd you get in here? Stay back! The–"

"You can stop there and log out," I said to McGuire. "The rest is... just screaming." I tried to keep what I was feeling out of my voice, and off my face. I'm a cop – we're supposed to be good at that.

I may not have succeeded completely, because McGuire looked at me closely before he disconnected from my voicemail. I'd told him about Prescott's messages, so he'd asked me to retrieve them again but from his phone, to play over the speaker.

I glanced over at Karl, who was in McGuire's other visitor's chair. He looked like a guy with a bad stomachache – but whether that was from Prescott's discovery or from his screams, I didn't know.

McGuire was staring at the phone as if it were his worst enemy. He didn't look away from it as he said, "Super-vampire, huh?"

"It sounds kind of stupid when you call it that," I said. "But, still..."

"Yeah," McGuire said. "But, still..."

"And first night of the full moon," Karl said.

I hadn't had to look it up – none of us had. Everybody in the Supe Squad always knows when the full moon is due.

"Tonight," I said.

A good piece of the squad room's west wall is taken up with a map of the city and surrounding area. McGuire, Karl, and I stood looking at it, and what we saw did not make us happy.

All those lakes.

"Fuck," Karl said.

All those ponds.

"Fuck," McGuire said.

All those swimming pools.

"Motherfuck," I said.

"There's no way we're going to get surveillance of all those bodies of water," McGuire said. "We couldn't do it even if we knew what to look for, which we don't – or even if we had the entire U.S. Air Force at our disposal, which we sure as shit don't."

"So we can't find him by air," I said. "That's a fact. We'll have to approach it some other way."

"If you've got any ideas, you'll find me an eager audience," McGuire said.

I just shook my head, but Karl said, "There is *one* thing."

McGuire and I both turned to stare at him.

"Seems to me that Stan here has an appointment with a certain young lady, in about..." Karl looked out the window, at the setting sun. "...ten minutes or so. She said something just before dawn today, gave us the impression she might know where Sligo's daytime crib is."

McGuire looked at me with raised eyebrows. "You've got a snitch – somebody who'll give up Sligo?"

"Not exactly," I said. "But sort of."

"Who do you–" McGuire started, then I saw the light dawn. "Oh. You mean..." He flipped a glance toward Karl.

"It's all right," I said. "He's met Christine." There are some secrets you shouldn't hide from your boss, and Christine was one I hadn't kept from McGuire. I'd trusted him to keep his mouth shut about her, and he always had.

"We were talking to Christine this morning, and it occurred to me to ask her about Sligo. It seemed like she knew something, but then she had to leave, pretty quickly." I made a head gesture toward the window, where a sliver of sun could still be seen.

"You know," Karl said, "it occurs to me that even if she can give us Sligo's resting place, the motherfucker'll be gone by the time anybody could get there, and we can't wait until he comes back for beddy-bye at dawn. It'll all be over by then, one way or another."

"But if we know where he's been, maybe we can figure out where he went, if we move fast," I said.

McGuire nodded. "Then you'd better get your ass downstairs," he said. "Don't you think?"

Karl and I stood quietly near the fence in the gathering dark, listening to the crickets and trying not to think about the ugly death of Benjamin Prescott, PhD. I don't know about Karl, but my efforts weren't exactly a howling success – more like a screaming failure.

"So," I said after a while, "how 'bout those Mets, huh?"

Karl doesn't follow baseball, and neither do I. He likes hockey, and I've been a Knicks fan since I was a kid and got to watch the team hold their pre-season training camp at the U.

That thing about the Mets is just something I say to fill awkward silences, and Karl knew it. He came back with his standard response: "Get a couple of good trades, and they could go all the way this year."

We waited some more, not talking, until Karl said, "I'd say it's full dark, Stan."

"Yeah."

"Probably has been, the last ten minutes or so."

"Yeah."

We listened to the crickets for a while longer.

Karl said, "Could be she's not coming, Stan."

"Yeah."

More crickets.

"Maybe we oughta go back inside, tell McGuire."

"Okay." I still didn't move.

"Could be lotsa reasons she didn't show," Karl said. "Doesn't have to mean she's in trouble."

I whirled to face him, and my voice was ugly when I said, "Jesus, what do you *think*, Karl? That maybe she found herself a nice *boyfriend*? That she couldn't make it because tonight's the junior fucking *prom*?"

Karl didn't tell me to go fuck myself. He didn't even turn and walk away. He just stood there, looking at me. It was too dark to see his expression, but his posture didn't look like somebody who's pissed off and ready to fight.

I stood there and listened to myself breathe for a while, a sound I used to be pretty fond of.

"I'm sorry, man," I said quietly. "I got no right to talk to you like that. I guess I'm just …"

"I know," Karl said. "Forget it." He gave me a few more seconds, then said, "You feel like going inside now?"

"Yeah, might as well," I said. "She isn't coming."

We went back to the squad and found that we had a visitor.

It was Vollman.

I turned to Louise the Tease. My voice rising, I said, "I thought I *told* you–"

Vollman held up a hand, palm toward me. "Please, Sergeant, do not chastise this beautiful young woman. I have literally arrived within the last minute."

I looked back at Louise, who nodded quickly. "I was just looking up your cell number," she said. "Honest."

"Okay. Sorry, Louise," I said.

I politely asked Vollman to accompany us back to our part of the squad room. I was going to be very courteous to the old vampire/wizard – right up to the moment when I found an excuse to pound a two-foot stake deep into his aged, undead heart.

I was in kind of a bad mood.

As we approached our desks, McGuire came to his office door and looked our way. I shook my head, but then used it to gesture in Vollman's direction. McGuire nodded and went back to his desk. He'd understood what I meant: we'd missed one source of information, but just gained another one. Maybe.

Everybody sat down, Karl and me facing Vollman from maybe ten feet apart. He looked pretty much the same as last time, although the shirt was different – a pale green number with little roses all over it that had probably been the height of fashion just after the war. The Civil War, I mean.

"Been a while, Mr Vollman," I said. "We were beginning to think you didn't like us anymore."

The old face grew a tiny little smile. "Two charming young gentlemen such as yourselves? The very idea is absurd."

Never try sarcasm on a five hundred year-old vampire.

"We haven't got time to fuck around," I said, "so I'm going to take a risk and be totally honest with you about the situation we're facing here – as much as we know of it. I say it's a risk, because I'm pretty damn sure you haven't been honest with us, so far."

Vollman's bushy eyebrows made a slow climb toward his hairline.

"I'm not saying you actively lied to us, but you've withheld information, for reasons of your own. I'm pretty sure if we knew everything you could have told us a week ago, we would have closed this case already, and a pretty good man would have been spared a really ugly death."

"Indeed?" Vollman said softly. "I am sorry to hear of that."

"Maybe you are, maybe you're not. For all I know, you think of humans as nothing more than blood bags with legs. Some vamps do, I know."

Vollman frowned at that, but kept quiet.

"But it doesn't matter," I said. "Because a wizard named Sligo, who is also a vampire – you know, like you – is probably going to attempt a complex and nasty ritual at midnight, near some body of still water."

"And if he pulls it off, the result could be very, very bad," Karl said.

"*Very bad* is an understatement," I said. "The bastard will have the power to create a whole new race of vampires that'll be invulnerable to everything – sunlight, stakes, crucifixes, the whole nine yards."

"And that will fuck up the world for everybody, Mr Vollman," Karl said. "Old-style *nosferatu* like you will probably become an endangered species – just like humans."

Vollman nodded gravely. "I will give you my pledge to listen closely to all that you gentlemen have to say. Beyond that, I can make no promises."

I sat there, and if looks could kill, the old bastard would have a long sharp piece of polished oak sticking out of his chest right that second.

I wasn't sure what I hated more – the old vamp, or the fact that at this moment, we needed him. Needed him bad.

Vollman let out the little smile again. "I understand, Sergeant. You despise me, and you despise having to depend on me – for anything, even information. It is a very... human reaction, and one that I am not unused to."

I blinked a couple of times, and my voice was husky with anger when I said, "You read minds, do you? I wasn't aware that was one of the vampire talents."

"Not minds, Sergeant – merely faces." Vollman shrugged. "I wonder if it has occurred to you that I am here this evening precisely because I am, however unfortunately, dependent on *you*." He leaned forward in his chair, and I swear I heard those old bones creak. "And in at least one respect we are in agreement, gentlemen: we do not have time to fuck around."

He sat back, hands folded in his lap, waiting.

I took one very deep breath, and tried to imagine that all the hatred and fear and frustration would leave my body with the air I was going to expel. Then I breathed out, told myself that it had worked, and got down to business with the vampire.

• • • •

Karl and I took turns running it down for him, as quickly as we could without leaving out any essential facts. Once it was all out there, I said, "So we've got to find Sligo, and stop him, before midnight which is–" I checked my watch "–about four and a half hours from right now." It occurred to me that my last sentence sounded like something from a bad Fifties horror movie, accompanied by a melodramatic soundtrack riff. In my job, reality is sometimes like a bad movie – and sometimes it's worse. At least the movie usually has a happy ending.

Vollman had been leaning forward in his chair, folded hands between his knees, looking at whichever of us was speaking. Now he sat back, intertwined fingers beneath his chin, the classic pose of Man Thinking. I wondered if he'd been on the stage at some point during his long life – no matinee performances, of course.

Now he lowered the hands, signaling that he had reached a decision. "I told you once," he said, "that I had become a vampire, unwillingly, in the year 1512. That was the truth. I neglected to mention that, at the time of my... transformation, I had a son, Richard." He pronounced it *Reek-ard*, the way the Germans do.

"I had raised him myself," Vollman went on. "His mother died in childbirth, not an uncommon occurrence at that time. I was a skilled wizard, and might have saved her, but she gave birth earlier than expected, while I was away on business.

"So, I raised the boy alone, with the assistance of a series of paid wet nurses, nannies, and tutors. When he reached his majority, he told me that he wished to learn the art of magic, under my tutelage."

Vollman made a wry face. "What father would not be pleased to find that his son wished to emulate him by choosing the same profession? So I began his instruction – which, to do properly, takes several years. We were already well along, when I fell victim to attack by a *nosferatu*. And you should understand this about our kind, Sergeant, if you do not know it already: an honorable vampire, when he turns another, becomes in effect a Father in Darkness, incurs certain obligations. He must stay to teach the newborn *nosferatu* how to live his new, and very different, life."

"From what I've heard," Karl said, "it doesn't always happen that way."

"Sad, but true, Detective," Vollman said. "But, in defense of my kind, how many humans do you know who behave honorably – at all times?"

"Well, you've got–" Karl began.

"Guys, excuse me," I said. "Mr Vollman, this is fascinating, and I mean that. But the clock is ticking, and if you could possibly move this along...?"

Vollman nodded. "I enjoy intelligent conversation, but you are correct, Sergeant, this is not the time." He leaned forward again.

"Because my Father in Darkness did not mentor me in the ways of the undead, I did not learn to control my appetite for blood. Because I had not learned control, I fed indiscriminately. One of those upon whom I fed, to my everlasting shame, was my own son, Richard. And because my bloodlust was seemingly without limit at that stage, I fed on him until he was near death – at which point, overcome with remorse, I decided to make him *nosferatu*, like me."

Vollman stopped speaking, and his eyes lost some of their focus, as if he was examining some bleak inner landscape. I knew that territory very well. I've lived there for years.

"All right," I said, keeping most of what I felt out of my voice. "you made your son a vampire. What then?"

"Unlike my own Father in Darkness, I fulfilled my responsibility to the one I had created. Although, in truth, because I was myself so inexperienced as *nosferatu*, there was much I did not know. But I did my best, even though my son, who was now also my Son in Darkness, hated me."

"The two of you fought, you mean?" Karl asked him.

"No, never," Vollman said. "He was too smart for that. But I knew my own son. In every word, every gesture, he showed how much he despised me. And I cannot in truth say that I would blame him."

I noted his shift to present tense, but didn't say anything about it. Instead I asked, "So, you taught him how to be a vampire – and a wizard, too?"

"I did not finish his course of instruction in magic," Vollman said, "although I had taught him a great deal by the time he attempted to kill me."

"How'd he do that?" I asked. "Come at you with a wooden stake?"

"No, he would not have been so foolish. I was stronger than he, you see. Stronger as a man, a vampire, and a wizard. Instead, he hired men. Thugs, really. As I determined later, he paid them well – with money stolen from me – to carry out three tasks." Vollman ticked them off on his fingers. "To transport an armoire containing his insensate form to a location far away; to seek out my resting place and drive a stake through my heart; and, finally, to burn down my home, which was also my magical laboratory."

Vollman made a face like he wanted to spit on the floor. "The first and last of those tasks they accomplished very well. They spirited my son away, and before leaving, set fires that turned my home, and all my work, to ashes."

"Obviously, they didn't manage to kill you," Karl said. "How come?"

"Because I did not spend the daylight hours in the basement of that house, as I had given Richard reason to believe. I was not, even then, a complete fool."

"I've got a feeling I know where this is going," I said, "but it would be good if we could get there soon."

"Of course," Vollman said. "My son, I have since learned, journeyed throughout Europe, studying magic, learning the ways of the undead, and sucking the blood of innocents. In time, he found his way to Ireland, where he stayed for many years – a strange choice, in a place where the Church is so strong. And there he took for himself the name Sligo."

Neither Karl or I exactly fell out of our chairs at that point. Like an inept comic, Vollman had telegraphed his punchline from some distance away. Still, his admission raised a lot of questions. With the time factor we were facing, I tried to decide which ones I needed answered right now.

"Why did you wait until now to share this interesting information with us?" I asked. "Didn't you *care* that vampires were being killed? Shit, and people accuse *me* of being callous."

Vollman studied me before speaking. "I do not think either one of us is callous, Sergeant. But I was forced to make a choice. If I helped you, and you found my son, you would probably kill him. He might well leave you no choice. And even now, after everything, I would have preserved his life, if I could."

"So you did nothing," I said.

"On the contrary. Ever since you gave me the name Sligo, I have been searching for him, day and night. Well, night, at least. I have used my considerable influence among the local community of supernaturals. But all my efforts have turned up nothing – he has learned how to hide himself well."

"Say you *had* found him on your own," Karl said. "What then?"

Vollman shifted a little in his chair. "I would have stopped him from completing this insane ritual – without killing him, if at all possible."

"But here you are," I said. "What's changed?"

"What has changed is the passage of time," Vollman said. "Like you, I believe that tonight is when he will attempt to consummate the ritual, and that cannot be permitted. Should he fail, he will almost certainly die. And if he succeeds, as you have pointed out, Sergeant, many others will die, in the near future."

"So now you wanna work with us," I said, "and about fucking time, too. But knowing that Sligo is your son doesn't help us catch him. I'm not clear about what you're bringing to the table."

Vollman studied his hands for a few moments. "In truth, not as much as I had hoped," he said. "I had planned to share with you the information contained in the *Opus Mago* about the ritual – its purpose, and its requirements. I was going to tell you that tonight is when he will probably make the attempt – at least, I can think of no reason why he would wait another month, given the ever-present risk of discovery."

He looked up then. "But it seems you already have the information that you need about that evil book.

Courtesy, I assume, of the professor who was killed at the hospital today."

"You got that right," I said. "So, I'm asking you again – what have you got to offer?"

"As we speak, my agents are combing the city, and its environs – not only in search of my son, but of any information about the planned ritual. If any of them learns something useful, they will contact me at once."

Vollman reached into a pocket and produced a cell phone. "Even *nosferatu*," he said, "must change with the times."

"And anything these guys tell you, you're gonna share with us?" Karl sounded skeptical, and I can't say that I blamed him.

"Yes, I will," Vollman said. "Things have gone too far for gentle methods. He must be stopped, even if it means his life. And I am no longer sure I can do it alone."

"And what are you asking from us?" I said.

"Any information you may uncover in the interim – and of course, your vigorous efforts to prevent this tragedy from happening. Which you would have exercised, anyway."

"All right, Vollman, we'll work with you," I said. "But I want something more."

"What might that be?"

"My daughter, Christine, is one of... you."

"Yes, I was aware of this."

"Do you know where she is tonight?"

"I do not attempt to keep track of all the city's creatures of the night," Vollman said. "But I can find out, if it is important. I assume it is, or you would not be asking."

"A threat was made against her," I said, "by a guy named Jamieson Longworth, now deceased. We believe he was somehow mixed up with your son."

"Indeed?" Vollman's tone was frosty. "Had I possessed that information earlier, I might have been able to use it and locate my son, thus saving us all considerable time and trouble."

"We only got the information that allowed us to figure it out yesterday," I told him, trying not to sound defensive.

"And you didn't exactly make yourself easy to find, did you?" Karl said.

"Point taken." Vollman inclined his head forward a little. "Very well, Sergeant. I will have your daughter Christine located. What then? Do you wish her brought here?"

"No, I'm expecting to be pretty busy. Just get her someplace safe, at least for tonight."

"I can do that," he said, "and I will." He stood up. "I should lend my efforts to the hunt for my son. There are those in the city who will not share information with my minions, but who might nonetheless talk to me–" Vollman gave us a humorless, fang-filled smile, "–especially if I ask nicely."

"We should trade phone numbers before you go," I said. "We can't afford any communication delays tonight."

"I agree entirely," he said.

The three of us exchanged cell phone numbers. I wrote Vollman's down, then looked up to tell him "Stay in touch."

He was gone.

"I hate it when he does that," I muttered.

"I don't know," Karl said. "I think it's kind of cool."

Over the next few hours, I looked at that wall map so many times I'm surprised I didn't burn a hole through it. Karl downloaded and printed some aerial photos from

Google Earth and had them spread out on a table. My eyes just about wore them through, too.

We'd put the word out to every snitch we knew, human and otherwise. Anybody who could come up with reliable information about where Sligo was going to perform the ritual tonight would earn so much good-will with us that he could probably knock off a dozen liquor stores without fear of arrest – although we didn't put it quite that way.

The other detectives in the squad knew the situation now, and they'd promised to work their own sources hard and to call in if they picked up anything useful.

Everybody was out on the street, except Karl, me, and McGuire. All three of us were so far past overtime that we probably weren't even getting paid anymore.

The silence in the squad room was like a vice pressing against my skull, squeezing tighter every minute. I willed one of our phones to ring, no matter who was calling – Vollman, one of the squad, a snitch, or even Christine letting me know that she was shacked up with a cute A-positive in Dunmore and wouldn't be home until dawn.

McGuire was at his desk, doing paperwork or pretending to. Karl stood in front of the wall map, staring like a desert traveler hoping for an oasis to appear. I was pacing around the room like an expectant father – exactly what I had done when Christine was born. I looked at my watch, for the thousandth time: 10:03.

"I bet the motherfucker is going to pick a yard with a big old swimming pool," Karl said, without taking his eyes off the map. "Then, once the spell's done, he can jump in and take a dip. Cool off a little. Black magic is hot work, I hear."

"The arrogant prick probably doesn't even–" and that was as far as I got.

I stopped pacing and stood utterly still, while images and sounds flashed through my brain:

–*Sligo, swimming, with a conical cap on his head, like the wizard in* Fantasia...

–*Prescott's voice saying, "Still water, it has to be still water"*...

–*The photo on Jamieson Longworth's computer of a square, stone building near-surrounded by water...*

–*My cousin Marty, when I was fourteen: "Come on, Stan. Nobody goes up there, and the lock on the gate is a joke. You, me, and those two chicks from down the street. Whatdaya say? We'll have a cool swim on a hot night, and maybe we'll even get to see 'em naked!*

"Well, fuck my ass and call me Shirley," I said softly.

"Stan?" Karl's voice. "Stan? Can you hear me? What is it, man?" I think he might have been speaking for a while.

I turned to face him. "Lemme borrow your pen."

I took the pen, ignoring the look on Karl's face, and went to the wall map. It took me only a few seconds to find the dot I was looking for. I circled it once, then again, and again, and stepped back. "That's where he is," I said. "Right there. He's right fucking *there*."

Speaking as fast as I could without becoming incoherent, I told McGuire and Karl what I had just figured out: Sligo was going to cast his spell in the pump house on top of the dam at Lake Scranton.

"He wants still water, and there's a shitload of it up there, and the place is isolated. It's not supposed to be for swimming – that's where the city drinking water comes from. But my cousin Marty and me and a couple of girls went skinny-dipping there one summer when I was fourteen. I saw the pump house close up, although we didn't go inside – it was locked. And the pump

house is what's in that photo on Jamieson Longworth's computer – sure as I'm fucking standing here."

"That's good enough for me," McGuire said, and picked up the phone.

"Who're you calling?" I asked.

"SWAT. Dooley's supposed to be on call, twenty-four-seven."

"Good," I said. I went to my desk and started rummaging through the pile of papers on top of it.

"What're you looking for?" Karl asked me.

"That phone number Vollman left us. Here it is."

A few seconds later, I was listening to the phone ringing in, I hoped, Vollman's pocket. It rang. And rang. Then after the seventh ring, one of those synthesized computer voices that I hate said, *"No one is available at the moment to take your call. Please leave your name and number, and your call will be returned as soon as humanly possible."*

I wondered whether "humanly" was Vollman's idea of a little joke.

At the *beep*, I said, "Vollman, this is Markowski. It's going down at the pump house, at the top of the Lake Scranton Dam. I need to know if you've located Christine, because that's gonna determine our tactics. Call me, or get over here, fast!"

Karl had just finished checking the loads in that big Glock of his. He looked at me. "Determine our tactics?"

"If we know Christine's safe, we can go in there with all guns blazing – or SWAT can. But since she's still missing... don't you think Jamieson Longworth would get a giggle in Hell, knowing that Christine was going to be Sligo's final vampire victim?"

"But we don't know for sure that Longworth and Sligo were even in cahoots, Stan."

"Do you believe in that many coincidences?" I asked.

That brought a little smile to Karl's face. Before I could ask what was so damn funny, he said, the way you do when you're quoting somebody, "'Once is happenstance. Twice is coincidence. The third time it's enemy action.'"

"Who said that? Although he's right, whoever it was."

"Auric Goldfinger – to James Bond."

McGuire came out of his office, scowling. "Problem. Big one. The SWAT unit, every one of them, is on administrative suspension, pending investigation into possible wrongdoing in the death of one Jamieson Longworth."

"What kind of fucking bullshit is *that*?" Karl said.

"Mrs. Longworth again," I said to McGuire.

"Yeah, most likely. Dooley says the union's fighting it, on the grounds that SWAT's vital to public safety – but they're not gonna get it overturned in–" he looked at his watch, "–the next eighty-five fucking minutes."

"If this is a nightmare, I hope I wake up soon," I said quietly. "We don't have SWAT, we don't have a warrant for the fucking pump house–"

"Isn't that city property?" Karl asked. "Don't need a warrant for that."

"No, the water company owns it," I said. "Don't interrupt me when I'm bitching – no SWAT, no warrant, no Vollman..." I stopped, and just shook my head.

"You've got these, though." McGuire held out a key and a slip of paper.

"What?" I asked impatiently.

"A master key, which will open any office in the building, including SWAT's, and–" he held out the paper to me, "–the combination to the SWAT weapons room. The key is from me, who will have no idea how you got it.

The combination's courtesy of Dooley, who says 'Kick some ass for us, too.'"

I took the paper and key and looked at Karl. "You heard the man – let's go kick some ass."

It was quiet in the part of the building that SWAT called home, so nobody asked us what the hell we were doing. Just as well. The mood I was in, if somebody had, I might have shot them.

As Karl unlocked the SWAT team's door, I said, "You know, vampires and wizards and shit – that's weird enough. But now, we're in the middle of a fucking 'buddy cop' movie."

Karl pushed the door open and felt around for the light switch. "Is that what it is? Sure hope you're right, Stan."

"Why – you like that stuff?"

"Yeah, but that's not why I said it."

"I think the weapons room is back there," I said, pointing. "Okay, I give. Why do you want this to be a buddy cop movie?"

"Because the good guys always win," he said, as we walked to the back of the big room. "And neither of the cops ever gets killed. Maybe a flesh wound, arm in a sling in the final scene – but nothing worse. I could handle that. Here – gimme that combination."

Consulting the paper, Karl carefully turned the big dial back and forth a few times, then tried the handle. The steel door unlocked with a *click*. I gave the handle a pull, and the door opened smoothly on well-oiled hinges. A couple of bright florescent lights in the ceiling came on automatically.

"Holy fuck," Karl said softly. "Will you *look* at this shit!"

• • • •

We were bleeding time faster than a vampire's victim loses blood, so within ten minutes of opening the SWAT unit's weapons room, Karl and I were in the parking lot, heading for a brown Plymouth – the car the department had assigned us to replace the one with the man-sized dent in its roof

We walked as fast as we could with all the stuff we were carrying. Stopping behind our new ride, I was fishing for the keys when I heard the sound of a car door opening in the row behind us, then heard it again. Part of my mind noticed that I didn't hear those doors slam shut.

I wasn't worried. Jamieson Longworth was dead, and his buddy, Sligo, was up at Lake Scranton, getting ready for the biggest night of his life – which I hoped would also be his last.

I should have worried.

I realized that when I heard, from behind us, the distinctive *clickety-clack* of a shotgun being racked.

Both of Karl's arms were full; so was one of mine, while my other hand was deep in my pants pocket, digging for the car keys. We had no chance at all.

Then a familiar man's voice told us, "Stand very still, gentlemen."

We froze like Gorgon statues.

After a few seconds, he said, "Good. Now, without unburdening yourselves, turn this way. Slowly."

Once I'd heard that voice, I was pretty sure we were fucked. Then we turned around, and I knew it for certain.

The Reverends Ferris and Crane, still wearing their elegant gray suits, stood thirty feet away, next to the open doors of a big black Caddy. Crane held the shotgun barrel pointed right at Karl and me, and we were so close together, I knew one blast would nail us both. The nasty smile was back on Crane's schoolboy face. The Reverend Ferris was smiling, too, and it wasn't hard to guess why.

"How good to see you both again, Detectives," he said. "Reverend Crane had started to wonder if you were *ever* going to join us out here, but I reminded him that the Lord provides those who serve Him with what they need, all in due time. And here you are."

"We have unfinished business," Crane said. I guess he felt he should contribute something besides firepower.

"Indeed we do." Ferris looked as happy as a little boy with a new kitten – a kitten he planned to torture to death, as soon as he could get it alone. "The sergeant has some questions to answer for us. And do you know, Detective Renfer, I believe I smell the taint of witchcraft on you, too. I'm afraid you'll have to come along with us, as well."

I thought about the surveillance cameras trained on the parking lot. Although always recording, they weren't monitored regularly. It would be hours before anybody inside the building learned that we had been abducted by the two witchfinders. By then, of course, it would be too late. For everybody.

Ferris's smile faded, to be replaced by a solemn look, the kind you associate with a hanging judge. His voice was all business as he said, "All right then: one at a time, you will bend forward slowly, and deposit that junk you're carrying on the ground. You won't be needing it, I'm sure. Detective Renfer first. *Now*."

Karl bent over and gently laid down his share of what we'd taken from the SWAT weapons room. But I saw that as he straightened up, he managed to take a half step away from me. The reverends apparently didn't notice.

"Very good," Ferris said. "Now you, Sergeant Markowski. Slowly."

As I finished putting my stuff on the cracked asphalt, I managed to emulate Karl with a sneaky half step in the other direction.

One thing I knew for certain: we were not getting into the Caddy with these two righteous sadists. What would happen to Karl and me would be bad enough. But if nobody stopped Sligo, and his spell was successful...

Karl and I would have to make our stand here, win or lose. And the next thing we needed to do was get more distance between us. I took another slow half-step to my right.

"Stand still!" Crane barked. "Don't move!"

"I'm sorry, Reverend," I said. "I didn't mean to be disobedient, but you didn't say anything about standing in place, before."

As I spoke, I saw Karl move a little further to his left. The shotgun barrel shifted in his direction, and I took the opportunity to slide my feet a little more to the right. Crane turned the gun back on me.

"I said don't move, damn you!" While Crane yelled at me, I saw, from the corner of my eye, the additional step that Karl got in.

"*Stay still, or I'll shoot you right here!*" Crane said, hysteria rising in his voice.

"I would do what Reverend Crane says," Ferris said sternly. "Taking you for questioning is our ideal outcome, but if we must leave your corpses here, that is acceptable, as well. Sinners must pay for their sins, one way or another."

Karl and I had gained what we wanted. We were now too far apart for a single blast from that shotgun to get us both. One of us would live to put three or four rounds into Crain's chest before he could rack another round into the firing chamber. And since Ferris appeared unarmed...

"What makes you so certain that we're sinners, Reverend?" I asked. "Isn't there something about letting he who is without sin cast the first stone?"

I didn't dare look toward Karl now, but I was sure he'd taken advantage of the couple of seconds their attention was on me to push his jacket back a bit on one side, making for quicker access to his holstered weapon.

"Yeah, Reverend, are you guys that pure yourselves?" Karl said loudly, and when they looked his way, I moved my right forearm back slowly, taking the suit jacket with it. The fabric was almost clear of the holster now.

The clock was ticking towards midnight, and we had exactly zero time to waste with these clowns. At least one of us had to get to Lake Scranton, and fast.

Might as well throw the dice, and see whose number came up.

I was tensing my gun arm as Ferris snapped, "I have no intention of debating theology with the likes of you." He produced two pairs of handcuffs. "Now, you are going to–"

There was movement in the air behind them, something so fast I couldn't tell what it was. Then a shadow appeared directly behind Crane, a black form that reached out and grasped Crane's jaw in one hand, his head in the other, and twisted, hard. Crane was dead before he even knew he was dying.

The shadow blurred again, flowing over the roof of the Cadillac and the dark figure became Vollman, in front of Ferris now, grasping his throat with one hand, lifting the witchfinder off his feet, seemingly without effort...

"*Vollman!*" I managed to yell. "*Don't!*"

The words were barely out of my mouth as Vollman shook Ferris hard, once, the way a terrier shakes a rat – and with similar results. I didn't hear Ferris's neck break, but I saw the way his head lolled before Vollman dropped the limp form to the ground.

Vollman quickly walked over to us and said, "I received your message, and came here as quickly as I could. Fortunate that I did not arrive a minute later – I need both of you alive tonight."

Karl was unlocking the trunk of the Plymouth. I stood there, torn by more conflicting impulses than I've ever had to deal with at the same time.

If you want to imagine one of those internal dialogues that people in the movies sometimes have – you know, with an angel perched on one shoulder and a devil on the other – mine would have gone something like this:

Angel: You've just seen Vollman commit murder. Maybe not with Crane, but Ferris was unarmed. That's murder – arrest him!

Devil: Vollman just saved your life – either yours or Karl's. You were about to throw the dice, remember? You knew that either you or Karl was gonna catch that shotgun load right in the chest. And Ferris might even have had a piece under his coat. If he'd gone for it, one of you would have had to kill him, anyway.

Angel: It doesn't matter – the law's the law. Besides, Vollman's a vampire, an evil creature of the night. He doesn't *deserve* a break.

Devil: Aren't you getting ready to risk your life at least partly to save a vampire you think is in danger, who happens to be your daughter – the daughter who's a vampire because of you?

Angel: Be pragmatic. Remember the surveillance cameras! They've recorded what Vollman just did – and that you were there, and saw it. If you don't arrest Vollman, you'll be charged as an accessory to murder, you and Karl both.

Devil: They only check the video if something's reported as happening in the parking lot. If nothing's reported in seventy-two hours or so, they wipe the memory and reuse the hard drive space.

Angel: Well, when somebody finds those two bodies, don't you think that would count as "something happened"?

Devil: So, make sure the bodies aren't found. Vollman can probably help you there.

Angel: Do that, and you're making a deal with the devil, Stanley.

Devil: Wouldn't be the first time, Stan. And besides, you need this particular devil on your side, tonight, up at the dam. And the clock is ticking, dude, toward midnight and the End of the World as We Know It.

Angel: It's not really *that* bad.

Devil: It's fucking *bad enough*!

All this took place in maybe three seconds. Standing there, you'd never know the convoluted mental process that led to me telling Vollman, "Those bodies are going to be a problem, if they're found."

Vollman thought for a moment. "Very well – I will attend to it. Finish loading your equipment – and hurry!"

Karl and I put the SWAT stuff into the trunk as fast as we could. We closed the trunk lid and turned to find Vollman standing there. "The bodies are in the trunk of their vehicle. I have left the keys in the ignition. One of

my people will move it before dawn, and those two fools
will not be seen again. Satisfied?"

I wanted to ask Vollman how one of his "people" was
going to get in to what was supposed to be a secure parking area. The witchfinders probably had a pass from the
mayor's office, but... what came out of my mouth instead was, "Fine. Get in."

Lake Scranton is at the southern edge of the city, just off
Route 307. Seen from the air, it resembles a bat with its
wings spread wide. It's an artificial lake, created by di-
verting a tributary of the Lackawanna River, then
building a dam to hold the water in. The distance around
the perimeter is something like three and a half miles
and the dam, with the pump house on top, is at the
lower edge of the bat's left wing.

You'd think the pump house would be dead center on
the dam. But it actually sits about two hundred feet from
the northern end, with another couple of thousand feet
of dam beyond it until you reach the other shore. The
stone and cement platform it's built on is perpendicular
to the top of the dam, so the little building appears to be
sitting on top of the water.

If you were interested, for some reason, in launching
an attack on the pump house, you could come in either
on the short side, with two hundred feet of concrete dam
to cross, or the long side, which is about ten times the
distance. If you were a team of Navy SEALs, you'd probably come in by water, climb to the top of the dam with
ropes and grappling hooks, and catch everybody in the
pump house by complete surprise.

I could have used me a team of Navy SEALs, right
about then.

One thing that I didn't need any commandos to teach me: you plan for the enemy's capabilities, not his intentions – because you can sometimes figure out the first, but never be sure about the second.

As we followed the short stretch of Route 307 that would take us to the dam, I asked Vollman, "What kind of spells is he likely to have prepared? Any idea?"

Despite what you see in the movies, wizards and witches can't just wave their hands and make magic happen. It looks that way sometimes, but in fact any hand waving or magic words are used to activate pre-prepared spells. And those take some time, effort, and skill to get ready.

It's kind of like using a gun: you have to load it to make it dangerous. And although you have your choice of ammunition, the piece will hold only so many bullets, and you can only carry so much ammo with you.

"Impossible to know," Vollman said from the back seat. "He is so sure of his own invincibility, that he may have prepared nothing at all, on the assumption that he will face no opposition tonight."

"But we can't count on that,"

"No," Vollman said, "of course not. I only mention it as a possibility."

Enemy capabilities: unknown. Terrific.

We were approaching the exit that would take us to the access roads for the dam. "Does it matter which side we go in on?" I asked Vollman. "The short end or the long end?"

"The faster our final approach, the less chance of detection," he said. "I see no advantage to the long way."

"Short end it is, then."

I turned off the lights as we followed the narrow access road that led to the dam. No point in begging to be noticed. Anyway the full moon, shining down through the scattered wispy clouds, gave all the light I needed.

It was a beautiful night. I wondered how many of us would survive it.

"Vollman," I said, "can you scry the place before we go in – find out the layout, so we know what to expect?"

He didn't respond right away, and I glanced over my shoulder in time to see him shake his head slowly. "I can do so," he said, "but as soon as I commence, Richard will sense the presence of magic close at hand. He will then be alerted to our whereabouts."

Karl turned in his seat and looked back at Vollman. "If you don't scry, or use some other kind of magic, is he gonna know we're coming, anyway?"

"Ordinarily, I would say 'yes.' Wizards are very sensitive to the presence of potential enemies. But tonight he is giving so much of his attention and energy to the ritual, he may be too preoccupied."

"*May*," Karl said sourly.

"*May* is the most accurate assessment possible under these circumstances," Vollman said. "I regret that I cannot offer you certainty, Detective. For all our sakes."

There was silence as I braked the Plymouth to a slow halt about fifty feet from the chain link fence and gate that guarded this end of the dam.

Then Vollman said, "But one thing that I *can* do is to counter any magic he uses against you, allowing both of you the freedom to disrupt the ritual and, if necessary, effect the rescue of Miss Markowski."

"Well, that's a relief," Karl said, with no sarcasm at all.

"It might be best," Vollman said, "if I were to remain out of sight for as long as possible. I can counter his spells from outside that little building as well as I could from within it."

"So you can stop his magic," I said. "Can he stop yours?"

"That depends on whose is the stronger."

"And that's you, right?" Karl said.

"As they say in those awful television programs I some-times find myself watching, *There is one way to find out*."

Karl and I had each taken from the SWAT armory a pump shotgun, a selection of ammunition, and several of the "Splash-bang" grenades we'd seen the team use at Jamieson Longworth's place. We hurriedly loaded the shotguns, making our best guess as to what we would need in there.

"Double-ought buckshot for the door," I said. I once saw a guy use some to make a very large hole in a brick wall.

Karl rummaged through the boxes of shotgun ammo. "Zap the lock? Like the SWAT guys did?"

"The door's probably made of iron," I said. "We take the hinges. It's more certain."

Karl looked at Vollman. "Can't you take the door down for us, with magic?"

"I could," Vollman said. "But since you have the means on hand yourselves, it is perhaps best that I con-serve my energies."

That was Vollman's fancy way of saying "Save my strength." It didn't exactly inspire confidence.

The shotguns held five shells apiece. "For the rest, load whatever you want," I said. "We don't know what we'll be dealing with in there. And don't assume you'll get the chance to reload, because you probably won't."

I loaded two shells filled with blessed silver pellets, then one of garlic-soaked rock salt, then another double-ought buck, and one more silver for luck. I didn't pay attention to what Karl picked.

Once we reached the chain link fence at the dam's entrance, I saw that the gate was secured with a chain and a big Yale padlock. Maybe Sligo had come in the long way; or it could be he just floated over it.

A shotgun blast would take care of the lock, but I didn't want to announce that we were here until I had to. I looked at Vollman and said, barely above a whisper, "Can you...?"

The old vampire nodded, took hold of the lock, and said something under his breath. It sprang open, and I watched him remove and toss it aside. I was sure glad he was willing to expend the energy.

The three of us began the short walk along the top of the dam to the pump house. Ahead, I could see light coming from behind the two windows, brightly illuminating the cracks of the tightly closed shutters.

I kept waiting for all hell to break loose, although I had no idea what form it might take – alarms, devil bats, automatic weapons fire – who knew what kind of shit Sligo might have prepared?

With every step I heard from my guts, which were caring on an ongoing monologue with my conscious mind. *This is a bad idea, Stan. We could die here, Stan. Get us out of here, Stan – before it's too late*.

I kept putting one foot in front of the other. Call me brave, optimistic, or stupid. I was leaning toward the third explanation, myself.

Nothing happened. I didn't know if Sligo was indifferent or careless, but for most of the short walk all we heard was the chuckling of water in the dam and a few night birds in the trees behind us.

Then inside the pump house a woman started screaming, and suddenly I was running.

● ● ● ●

Karl was only a couple of steps behind me when I reached the door. As I'd figured, it was steel. I tried the knob, in case Sligo was *really* confident, but it seemed he'd at least locked the door.

I backed up as far as I could, looked at Karl and pointed at the lower hinge. Then I said, "On three," and took careful aim at the upper one. Inside, the screaming continued.

Part of my brain was wondering if I was going to get a face full of ricocheted buckshot as I said, *"One, two–"*

The two shots melded into one big *boom*. The hinge I'd fired at was in pieces, and a quick glance showed me that Karl's was, too. The metal itself had buckled around the impact areas.

I grabbed the edge of the door where it was protruding and yanked, hard as I could. That pulled it loose from the frame a little. Then Karl got a grip further down, and together we tore that thing free and slammed it to the concrete at our feet with a *clang* that I could feel more than hear, since I was temporarily deaf from the shotgun blasts.

As soon as the door came down I became almost blind, as well as deaf. My God, it was *bright* in there, and my eyes were still adjusted to the semi-dark of outside. But if I stayed put, I was a dead man, so I dived at an angle where I hoped the doorway was, rolled, and came up on one knee – which hurt a lot more than it used to. I felt more than saw Karl do something similar in the other direction.

If Sligo threw any magic at us in the next few seconds, we'd never know it until too late. But either Vollman was on top of his game, or Sligo wasn't, since nothing came our way as my eyes adjusted. Now I could see that the glaring light came from at least a dozen glowing globes hanging from the ceiling, supplemented by several portable spotlights whose glare bounced off the walls and ceiling every which way. Sligo must have installed all of this; I was pretty sure it wasn't part of the original pump house blueprint.

I didn't take time to gawk around, but your eyes can take in a lot of information really fast, especially if you're as keyed up as I was. As I scanned the room in search of something to kill, I was dimly aware that the usual spell-casting paraphernalia was all over the place: incense burners, gongs of different sizes, tall candles in metal holders, the whole nine yards. But the real show was up front.

The building seemed at least twice as big as you'd think from looking at the outside, which I assumed was more of Sligo's magic. At the far end of the room, three long tables were set up, forming an open rectangle with the open end facing the back wall. They were covered with cloths of black and red with arcane symbols woven into them, and on top of those were all the tools and toys the modern occultist can't seem to do without: bowls, flagons, more candles, knives, and so forth. But you could tell the middle table was special. That was where he'd placed, in an ornate brass holder, a thick, old-looking book with a cracked leather cover.

Looked like I'd found the *Opus Mago* at last.

Taking in all that took only a few seconds, and then my attention was riveted to what was dangling from the ceiling. Or rather, who.

A length of chain was suspended over the middle of the open rectangle, tied around a rafter. From the chain hung, head down, the nude, bleeding form of a woman. Her legs were tied at ankles and knees with rope that sparkled in the light, as if shot through with some kind of metal filings. The same stuff had been used to bind her wrists, and a length of it ran from there to attach tightly to a ring affixed into the stone floor.

The woman had fallen silent when Karl and I burst in, but it wasn't hard to figure why she'd been screaming. She looked to be bleeding from three points, in a line between her groin and breasts. The wounds were three symbols carved into her body, probably by the silver-bladed knife in the hand of the man who stood nearby. He was giving Karl and me the kind of look that most men reserve for Jehovah's Witnesses who show up during the Super Bowl.

I assumed the man was the one I'd started calling the Evil Wizard Sligo. But the woman I knew for certain: it was Christine.

I brought the shotgun up to aim, but Sligo took two fast steps sideways that put Christine's body between him and my gun barrel, using her as a shield. Well, nobody said that Evil Wizards have to be brave. Off to my left, I saw Karl moving forward slowly and at an angle, probably maneuvering for a clear shot. I shuffled to the right, with the same idea in mind.

Then Sligo shouted a couple of words in a language I didn't recognize and brought enough of himself out from behind Christine to make a quick throwing motion in my direction, before ducking back.

Motherfucker throws like a girl.

But I guess form doesn't count for much in magic, because an orb of fire about the size of a beach ball appeared in midair, moving fast and coming right at me. I had just enough time to realize that I was about to die when the fireball dissolved into nothing, about twenty feet from me.

It seemed that Vollman was on the job.

I took another couple of slow steps, waiting for Sligo to expose enough of himself for a shot that wouldn't endanger Christine.

Don't look at her. Focus. Focus on sending this bastard to Hell, then you can help her. Focus.

Sligo stuck his head out from the other side of Christine's dangling form and repeated the throwing motion, with the identical result. The ball of fire flew at Karl, but dissipated before it reached him.

Sligo wasn't done yet. He made a cryptic gesture at me while muttering something I couldn't hear, and then a dozen knives were in the air, as if they'd been thrown by twelve expert hands, all right at me.

But then that wave of edged steel suddenly parted, and I heard the knives bounce and clatter harmlessly off the stone wall behind me.

I was closer to the altar now.

He sent Karl a swarm of what looked like hundreds of bees, buzzing like a madman's dream – I assumed they were the African killer variety. By the time they reached Karl, the vicious insects had been transformed into drops of water. The only harm he suffered, far as I could tell, was getting a little of it in his eyes.

Then Sligo dispatched a blast of hurricane-force wind at both of us, which, just for an instant, was strong enough to drive me back a step, before it turned into a gentle breeze.

Go, Vollman.

I'd made a couple more steps forward when Sligo's arm snaked out from behind Christine. His hand held the silver-coated dagger, and he placed the point right over her heart.

"Hold! Both of you!" he yelled. I stopped at once, and saw Karl do the same.

After a few seconds, Sligo slid out from behind Christine, but the dagger point never lost contact with her flesh. I noticed she was still bleeding from the three wounds he'd inflicted on her earlier.

Now I got my first good look at Sligo, aka Richard Vollman. He didn't look anything special, but I knew from experience that Evil Wizards are rarely nine feet tall, and they hardly ever have horns and a tail. Sligo looked to be about twenty, which I guess was his age when Dad lost control of his appetite and turned him. Apart from the hair, which was the same slicked-back widow's peak as his old man, I didn't see much family resemblance. He was slim, maybe six feet, dressed in tight jeans and a white dress shirt with the sleeves folded back a couple of times. Guess he hadn't figured that becoming the world's first super-vampire was a fancy dress occasion.

Sligo was breathing like someone who's just sprinted a hundred yards. He pointed a finger at me, and I noticed his hand was shaking a little as he said, "You! How is it that a couple of miserable fucking blood bags like you two can suddenly work magic? If you had the Talent, either of you, I'd have smelled it on you earlier. *How*?"

Then a voice I recognized spoke from behind me.

"They do not *perform magic. But* I do.*"*

Sligo's eyes widened for an instant, before narrowing into slits.

"I should have known." He nodded slowly. "I should have known you'd interfere, even find some pathetic warmbloods to do your bidding."

Sligo gestured with his free hand toward the central altar, the book resting atop it like a big, poisonous toad. "But not this time, old man. You can't stop me! And when the transformation is complete, the first thing I'm going to do is come for you – at high noon. I'll find you, cowering from the sun in your pathetic box of earth, and then I'll drag you outside and watch you burn!"

"No, Richard," Vollman said. His voice sounded as full of sorrow as his son's was full of hate. "It must stop here. It must stop tonight."

Vollman walked briskly forward, spreading his arms like wings. Sligo withdrew the knife from Christine's breast and began to walk toward his father.

I realized he'd just given me a clean shot, and I wanted to end this fucker's life more than I wanted my next breath, and I brought the gun up to kill him, but Sligo, even while moving toward his father, made a complex gesture in the air – and this time *Vollman was too preoccupied to block the spell.*

What I can only describe as a blast of pure magical energy blasted me off my feet and sent me careening backward, like somebody in a wind tunnel – until I was stopped by my impact with the pump house wall.

Karl was hit by the same force, but his luck was even worse. Instead of slamming flat into the rear wall as I was, his body slammed into one of the broad stone pillars that held up the roof, and I thought I saw his spine bend backward with the impact just before the wall of the pump house hit me like a train.

I'd had enough sense to try to break my impact the same way you break a fall in judo: arms spread, palms flat and a little behind me. Maybe it helped a little, I don't know. But that stone wall hit me harder than I've ever been hit in my life and the shock and sorrow I felt for Karl was lost in the wave of unconsciousness that grabbed me and squeezed me and bore me down into the blackness.

I don't know how long I was down there in the dark. I opened my eyes and tried to get them to focus. I was sitting on the stone floor, my back against the wall that had so abruptly stopped my little journey through the air. I hurt in places I hadn't even known I had.

My vision came back into focus slowly. The first thing I saw were my hands. One was in my lap, and the other was limp on the floor next to me. Both palms were scraped and oozing blood. I remembered something about trying to break my fall, except I hadn't been falling, exactly. Something about judo. Whatever my bright idea had been, it didn't seem to have worked real well.

I tried to raise my head, and my vision blurred again. A word floated out of the part of my brain that was still functioning: *concussion*.

Every street cop gets knocked around some while on the job, and I'd been concussed before, according to a couple of ER doctors. But this concussion, if that's what it was, compared to the earlier ones the way a car crash is like falling off your tricycle.

I tried to keep my head from flopping back down, and succeeded, more or less. When I could see again, I found that I was looking at Karl. He was lying on his side, maybe fifty feet to my left, one arm outstretched, fingers hooked into a claw. The middle of his body was blocked from my vision by the pillar that he'd slammed into. Karl didn't move at all, and I was too far away to tell if he was breathing.

I turned my head, which not only caused another loss of focus but brought on a wave of vertigo that was more like a tsunami. I'd have puked, if there'd been any food in my stomach. When had I last eaten – breakfast? Was that today, or yesterday?

After a while I thought I could see again, but maybe I was just hallucinating. At the far side of the room, in front of that three-sided altar, two figures were struggling. They should have been Vollman and Sligo – I mean, who else could they be?

But what I was seeing, or imagining, didn't look like the two vampire/wizards – not as I remembered them. My brain must have been scrambled but good, because it seemed like I was looking a couple of Roman-style gladiators, shuffling around on the blood-soaked dirt of some arena, hacking at each other with big, heavy swords and defending with manhole-size shields. Roman fucking gladiators – *but their faces were those of Vollman and Sligo*.

I closed my eyes, not wanting to take in any more evidence that I'd gone totally fucking insane. But then I opened them again, and found that I was still seeing things that weren't there – that *couldn't* be there.

How else to explain that dusty Western street, with Sligo and Vollman dressed in outfits that belonged in some particularly gritty Spaghetti Western? They stood maybe thirty feet apart, eyes narrowed, tense hands hovering over the handles of their holstered guns, while the wind blew a single, forlorn tumbleweed between them.

I went away again for a while, and when I returned, it looked like the Western theme was still clinging to my subconscious. That would explain why I could see Sligo, in breechcloth and war paint, razor-edged tomahawk in one hand, locked in combat with a saber-wielding U.S. Cavalry trooper who looked an awful lot like his old man.

I closed my eyes once more, and started to wonder if maybe I'd died from hitting the wall, and Hell was a series of bad TV reruns. When I looked again, at least the channel had changed, because a U.S. Marine resembling Sligo was desperately trying to drive the bayonet on his M-1 through the body of Vollman, who was dressed as a soldier of the Rising Sun, a samurai sword held high in both hands.

This series of fantasy visions seemed to go on forever, lending further support to my I'm-dead-and-in-Hell theory. I remember Vollman and Sligo, in gray and blue, respectively, going at each other on a Civil War battlefield, then it was on to a bloody no man's land of World War I, followed by a vicious gang fight in some urban jungle, and I'm pretty sure we all ended up at the Alamo, with Mexican soldier Vollman contending viciously with Sligo, who was wearing a coonskin cap and swinging a Kentucky rifle like a club. Then, mercifully, I passed out again.

I was brought back to reality, if that's what it was, by the scream. I forced my eyes open and saw Sligo, dressed as he'd been when we first broke in, standing over the still form of Vollman. There wasn't a mark on either one of them that I could see.

The scream was coming from Sligo. Fists clenched, head thrown back, face gleaming with sweat, he stood over the body of the father he'd hated for so long. It went on for what seemed like long time, the scream did; it combined elation with rage and, if I'm not mistaken, a pretty fair dose of grief, too. All in one great bellow.

Then he was done. Panting, he wiped his face with his sleeve, then looked at his watch. At once, he turned back to the altar.

I tried to concentrate on what he was doing. At the moment, I didn't give a shit if he became a super-vampire or the world tiddlywinks champ, as long as he didn't do anything more to hurt Christine. But I kept remembering that the other four vampires who'd been material for this ritual all had to die. First he'd carved his magical symbols on them, as specified by the *Opus Mago*, then he'd killed them. I assume the book said to do that, too.

Sligo stood behind the altar and went through the ritual. He read aloud from the *Opus Mago* sometimes, he rang bells, mixed powders and liquid in bowls, burned incense, and generally looked like he was having a great old time. Big fucking deal.

Then he picked up the silver-bladed knife.

That finally galvanized me into action. Or as much action as I was capable of, which turned out to be not much. I looked for the shotgun, but couldn't see where I'd dropped it, even in the glaringly bright light Sligo had brought to the pump house. I remembered the Beretta on my belt and fumbled for it, only to find the holster empty. Must have been knocked loose when I'd smashed into the wall. The pistol had to be on the floor close by, but every time I moved my head in search of it, the vertigo returned and my vision started acting funky again.

Sligo was holding the dagger reverently in both hands now, reading an incantation from the book in that incomprehensible language. Even in my fucked-up mental state, I figured it was only a matter of time before he'd stop chanting and start cutting – and the cutting was going to be on my little girl.

I fumbled my hands into my jacket pockets, an operation that seemed to take an hour. I was searching for my phone, with the vague notion of calling 911. I couldn't find the damn thing, and part me knew it didn't matter, really. There was nobody I could call who would possibly get here in–

The fingers of my right hand brushed metal. Not the phone – something smaller, and much thinner. Round and curved on one side, jagged on the other. It felt like... part of a coin.

Kulick's amulet.

The one I was supposed to hold while saying his full name five times, once I'd found Sligo.

The one that he promised would bring him to me.

Well, I'd located Sligo, at last. Guess it was time to make the call.

I wrapped my fingers around that slim little half-circle, and tried to remember. Four names. Okay, Kulick, I knew. First name was... George. That's two. The true name, his wizard name... it had sounded like something out of a science fiction novel. Trasis? No, Thraxis. George Thraxis Kulick. But there was another one, another name.

At the altar, Sligo had stopped chanting. Squinting, I could see that he had turned away from the book, and was facing Christine.

Herman? No, nothing so normal. Something a little weird, kind of like Herman, but...

Harmon.

George Harmon Thraxis Kulick

Say it out loud, dummy!

"George Harmon Thraxis Kulick."

Again.

"George Harmon Thraxis Kulick."

Three more. Hurry!

Sligo walked toward Christine, the dagger in his hands. "Georgeharmonthraxiskulickgeorgeharmon-thraxiskulickgeorgeharmonthraxiskulick!"

I couldn't see the altar anymore, because something was blocking my vision. A leg, a woman's leg in a skirt. It moved now, the woman stepping forward, away from me. I raised my head higher, fought the vertigo, made my fucking eyes focus.

It was Rachel. Or rather, it wasn't.

George Kulick had joined the party at last.

Rachel's head turned back, looked at me, and after a moment, nodded. Kulick's voice said, "A bargain made is a bargain kept. That's the law."

At the altar, Christine screamed.

Rachel Proctor collapsed bonelessly to the floor, like a puppet whose strings have been cut. The spirit of George Kulick had left her body, at long last, to go... where?

I made my eyes focus on Sligo, and almost wished I hadn't. He'd jabbed the silver blade into Christine's lower belly, bringing forth another scream, and now he was adjusting his grip, with the clear intention of pulling the knife upward toward Christine's breastbone, opening her up from groin to chest.

I closed my eyes. I couldn't watch, couldn't bear it. The only hope I had left was that she would die quickly, become truly dead, and go someplace where there was no more pain, and no more fear.

And for this I'd "saved" her from leukemia.

Christine, I couldn't protect you, and I'm sorry, baby, so sorry. But as long as I have breath in my body, I will dedicate myself to taking vengeance on this motherfucker, I swear it.

I guess I was crying, I don't know, but my head came up at the sound of another scream. Because this one was in a man's voice.

Sligo had withdrawn the knife from Christine's belly without cutting any further. He had dropped it on the altar, and was clutching both hands to the sides of his head, as he screeched "No! Get out! Leave me now – I command you!"

In my concussed state, it took me a few seconds to figure things out, but then I knew who Sligo was talking to: George Kulick.

And now I knew where Kulick had gone when he left Rachel – inside Sligo. He was taking possession of Sligo's body exactly as he had Rachel's – except that Kulick didn't hate Rachel when he'd assumed control of her. She'd been merely a tool. A tool for vengeance.

I don't know why Kulick was able to invade without any resistance, unless Sligo had used up all his psychic energy in destroying his father, and had none left to protect himself. But Kulick was in there now, and Sligo was clearly losing the battle for control over his own body. He dropped to his knees with the strain of trying to expel Kulick from inside him, then fell over on his face. But after, I don't know, a minute or two, Sligo's screaming and writhing stopped. He stood, slowly. I thought I could see something different in his face, but I was too far away and too fucked-up to say for sure.

I know for certain what happened next, though. Sligo's hand slowly reached out to the altar for the silver-bladed dagger. I had a moment's panic, thinking that he had somehow defeated Kulick, after all, and was planning to take the knife to Christine again.

I needn't have worried. He never even looked toward Christine.

That's not to say that the dagger didn't see a lot of use in the following few minutes – all of it upon the person of Richard Vollman, also known as Sligo.

I don't think I want to tell you all the things Kulick made Sligo do with that blade. In my job, I see a lot of blood and sadism, but this would have made Satan himself throw up.

Karl told me once about an article he'd read describing *Le Théâtre du Grand-Guignol* in Paris. I gather that back in the day those sickos used to put on performances that were the ancestors of our modern-day splatter films. What was going on at the front of the pump house was like that – except none of the blood was fake. And there was a *lot* of blood.

After a while, I couldn't look any more. You'd think I would be full of vengeful satisfaction over what was happening to that motherfucker, who'd tried to kill me, my partner, and my little girl. At first, yeah, that's pretty much how I felt. But the things Sligo was being made to do to himself with that knife – before I looked away, I actually started to feel some pity for him. Not a lot, but some.

I assumed this was all going to end by Sligo plunging the silver dagger into his own black heart, achieving true death, and by then glad to get it. But I'd underestimated George Kulick's appetite for revenge.

Kulick didn't make Sligo kill himself. Instead, when the last full measure of vengeance, short of death, had finally been extracted, he forced Sligo to fling the dagger out of reach – probably so that he *couldn't* use it for self-destruction.

Then Kulick just – left.

I happened to be looking at the precise moment when George Kulick's spirit left Sligo's body. I saw a brief ripple in the air just over where Sligo lay on the blood-soaked floor, and I thought that might be Kulick's departure. Then Sligo started screaming, and I was certain.

I call it "screaming," but what Sligo was doing sounded more like loud croaking, and it just went on and on. It's hard to scream when you don't have a tongue, or lips or... well, you get the idea.

I don't know where Kulick went, except that he never returned. He'd said something, back at the parking garage, about being intrigued by the afterlife. I guess he went off to see for himself.

Fuck both of them. I needed to reach Christine, who was still tied and hanging upside down from the ceiling, bleeding from the stomach puncture as well as the three symbols carved into her flesh. I had to get her loose, and find help for her. Hell, everybody left alive in that room needed help, including me. I tried to look for my cell phone, but every turn of my head brought the vertigo back. Fuck the phone, then.

Karl still lay in the position he'd landed in. It didn't look like he was still among the living , but I needed to know for sure. I tried to stand, and fell forward on my face. Tried again, with the same result. I'd decided to crawl, all the way to Karl and then to Christine, when I saw Rachel Proctor stir.

I hadn't even been sure she was alive.

Rachel moved her legs a little, then a little more. Then she gave the kind of groan you might hear from somebody waking up after a three-day bender. I managed to croak, "Rachel." Even that much made my head throb.

She started at my voice, then slowly rolled over until she was facing me, from maybe ten feet away.

Her eyes were open. They were Rachel's gray eyes, and they were open and they looked sane. I felt my heart lift a little, for the first time since I'd burst into this accursed place.

Rachel blinked a few times, then her gaze went vague, as if she was listening for something. "Kulick," she whispered, looking at me. "Is he really...?"

"Yeah, Rachel, he's gone... For good, I think."

"Thank the Goddess," she said, sounding like she meant it. She sat up slowly, and looked around the part of the pump house that was in her view. Fortunately, her back was to the altar area and the atrocities it contained, and she hadn't turned that way yet.

"Where are we, Stan?" she asked. "And why is it so damn *bright* in here?"

Sligo had stopped his inhuman bleating a little while ago. Maybe he'd passed out from blood loss. But now he gave another of those hoarse-sounding croaks that were his version of a scream.

"Aaah!" Rachel jumped, if you can jump sitting down, then started turning to look behind her. "What the fuck was–"

"Rachel! *Look at me!*"

She turned back quickly. "What is it Stan? What's wrong?"

"Don't look back there, yet. Please."

"Why? What's–" She started to turn again.

"*Rachel!*"

God, that made my head throb.

She looked at me again, eyes wide with concern.

"What, Stan? What's the–"

"Rachel, I'm not... tracking too well. I'm concussed, pretty bad. Maybe I can't... explain stuff as well as normal, okay?"

"Sure, but if you're concussed–"

"*Will you fucking listen to me?*" Bad idea, yelling. *Oh, God, my head...* "Sorry, I'm sorry, but there's something... behind you, that I don't... want you to see, yet. It's what's making that... sound. There's no danger, honest."

"All right, Stan. Whatever you say." Rachel spoke in the soothing tones you use with a lunatic. Who knows – maybe she was right.

"Short version: we're in the pump house, Lake Scranton Dam. Sligo... guy Kulick was after, was gonna do some big ritual, become a super-vampire."

"A what? A super... *what*?"

"Later. This is... short version, okay? When Kulick got here, he left your body... went into Sligo's. That's the guy... tortured Kulick, remember that?"

"Remember it? I *lived* it, through Kulick's memories."

"Right, sorry. Okay, so Kulick left you, then... possessed... Sligo. Took control. Then – payback time."

"You mean, he...? Oh, dear Goddess, no!"

"Yeah. He made Sligo... use a silver knife on himself. It's bad, Rachel – *real* bad. Then Kulick split... left Sligo still alive. That's him you hear. I think he's trying to scream."

"Stan, we've got to help the poor man–"

"Might not say... 'poor man,' if you knew... But we'll help him, in a minute. First, think you can help *me*... sit up?"

"Sure. Come on." Rachel got one arm around my shoulders and lifted. I assisted as much as I could, and then I was sitting up again. The vertigo came back, but then receded. Progress, I guess.

"Now, check on Karl," I said. "Please."

"Karl? Your partner?"

"Over there." I pointed. "Behind the pillar. I think maybe he's..." I couldn't finish the sentence.

Rachel said, "Can you stay upright by yourself?"

"Think so," I said. "If not, doesn't matter. Not far... to fall. Now go."

She hustled over to where Karl lay so still. I saw her press two fingers against his neck, frown, then try another spot.

No pulse. He's gone. Jeez, Karl, goddamn fucking–

"Stan? *He's alive.*"

With an effort, I pulled myself out of my wallow. "*What? You sure?*"

"I'm getting a pulse, but it's weak, and fast. He's hurt bad, Stan. I think his... back is broken, and he's been bleeding from the nose and mouth. Internal injuries. He needs a hospital, and quick!"

"See if you can find my phone," I said. "It's around here... someplace. Gotta be. Must've been jarred loose, when I hit the wall."

Rachel started casting about the floor, looking. At least, it wasn't hard to see in there, with all of Sligo's fucking lights.

"I don't see it, Stan. Are you sure you had it with you?"

"Yeah, I had it... oh, shit." I just remembered that I'd slipped the phone into my right hip pocket. It was so thin, and I already hurt all over anyway, I didn't even notice I'd been sitting on the damn thing. I reached back and pulled it out with clumsy fingers.

The phone had taken the full impact of my body against the wall. It was nothing more than cracked and broken junk. "Fuck!" I threw it aside, then looked at Rachel.

"Can't you do some... I dunno... healing magic, get him stabilized, until we get... paramedics here?"

She shook her head sadly. "I've got none of my gear with me, Stan, and no spells prepared in advance. For the moment, I'm all out of magic. I'm sorry."

"Shit." I tried to think, but my head hurt so much, and the vertigo kept coming and going, coming and going.

"Rachel."

"Yes?"

"My weapon's... here someplace. Two weapons, actually – pistol and shotgun. See if you can find the pistol, okay?"

"All right."

Rachel got slowly to her feet, tottered for a few steps, then began to walk around this part of the room, eyes on the floor. "Okay, found it."

"Bring it over here, will you?"

In a moment she was kneeling next to me. She handed me the Beretta, and I checked the loads. Silver. Good. That was what I'd thought, but I wasn't trusting my memory for anything, at the moment. I replaced the clip, then worked the action to bring a round into the chamber.

"Stan," Rachel said, "whatever you're thinking about doing, think some more. Please. We can do better for Karl than that."

"It's not for Karl."

I motioned toward the front of the room. "See the girl suspended from the ceiling? She's bleeding. Passed out, maybe."

Rachel turned and stared. "Oh my Goddess, Stan. Who is she? We've got to–"

"We will. Or, you will. She's a vampire, but... not one of... bad guys. Supposed to be... sacrifice number five."

"The poor girl, she looks like she's hurt pretty bad."

"Motherfucker cut her and stabbed her. Name's Christine. She's my... daughter."

Rachel nodded. "This must be so *awful* for you, Stan."

"Don't... seem surprised."

She shrugged. "I heard the rumor about Stan Markowski's vampire daughter more than a year ago. The way you were always going on about how you hated vamps, I figured it just might be true. But not my business."

"She is now," I said. "Knife, over there, on the floor. Cut her down, careful. Like you said, she's hurt bad."

"I will be – but why the gun? Surely you're not going to...?"

"Christine? No way," I said. I hefted the Beretta. "You know how to use one...?"

"Yes, I went to the range a few times, with an old boyfriend. Why?"

"When you've seen... Sligo, you'll know why. He's a vamp, but... bullets're silver. Get as close as you can stand to get, put two in his head. Make sure."

Rachel shook her head slowly. "Stan, that can't be the only way to help him."

"Only help he deserves, the worthless fuck... Look, even if we *could* keep him alive, or undead, whatever – he'd hate us for it. Christ, I'm almost tempted." I shook my head, which was a mistake. "You'll know, once you've seen what's left of him."

She was silent, but her face was distressed.

"Rachel?"

"What?"

"You got no idea, how fucking awful... Hate to ask you, but I'm too fucked-up. Guy's been *savaged*. Everything you could do to somebody, without... killing him, *everything* – Kulick did it. Major fucking nightmare material, okay? You'll puke, probably. Normal. Then, use the gun. Two rounds... finish him, then help Christine. Will you do that, Rachel?" I swallowed, or tried to. "For me? For... them?"

I held out the Beretta, with a hand that shook bad. After a brief hesitation that didn't seem to last longer than two hours, she took it.

"All right, Stan. You know what's been going on, and I don't. I'll rely on your judgment, fucked-up though it may be."

"Good. My judgment... my responsibility. Mine – not yours. Go on, get it done. Christine needs you."

I must have passed out again, because I suddenly realized I was on my back, squinting against the lights bouncing off the white stucco ceiling, with no memory of how I'd got there. I tried to turn my head toward the altar, but the pain and throbbing started, worse than before. Maybe I'd whacked my skull again when I fell over. Moving just hurt too fucking much, so I lay there, staring at the white – and listening.

I couldn't have been out for long, because the next thing I heard was Rachel's voice. "*Oh, dear fucking God... oh, fuck, noooo...*" Then came the sounds of vomiting. I can't say I blamed her.

After a while, the vomiting noises stopped, to be replaced by the sound of a woman crying. Didn't blame her for that, either. But it didn't last long.

I heard footsteps, moving fast, as if someone were in a hurry. Then they stopped abruptly.

Even though I'd been expecting it, the sound of the shots startled me. I guess that adrenaline rush overloaded my stressed circuits, because I found myself fading away again.

Three. She fired three times. Wanted to be absolutely sure, I guess.

"Stan? Can you hear me? Stan?"

Rachel's voice brought me up from the depths, like a diver heading for the light and air. I opened my eyes to find her face a few feet above mine.

"Stan?"

"Yeah, okay."

"It's done, Stan. I mean... Sligo. I..."

"I know. I heard."

"And I got Christine down and cut her loose. The rope had silver worked into it, and she had burns where she was tied up."

"Fucker. Maybe you shouldn't have..."

"She's still bleeding, Stan, from where he cut her. I thought vampires healed quickly, from non-mortal wounds."

"Not when it's silver... or wood. Sometimes they heal, sometimes don't. Can still die, later. All depends..."

"On what? Depends on what?"

I let air out in a long, loud sigh. "Check Karl again, will you, Rachel? Please?"

She stared down at me for a little, then said, "Sure. Be right back."

And she was, too. "Stan?"

Her face was sad, on top of everything else she'd gone through.

"Dead?" I asked her.

"No, but his pulse is even weaker. I... don't think he's got long, Stan. I'm so sorry."

I nodded, which made my head hurt more, but I didn't care. I had to push through the pain and dizziness and nausea. I had something important to do.

I asked Rachel, "Can you move Christine? Bring her over here?"

She bit her lip. "She's dead weight, Stan, or very nearly. I can't carry her, and no magic to help. And the bleeding... if I even *try* to lift her..."

"I understand." I commanded my brain to work, to think. "Okay, here's what you do. Get one... those big altar cloths. Put it on floor, next to her. Roll her on to it, careful. Then grab the cloth. Drag it. Drag her. Okay?"

"I understand what you mean. The travois principle. I can probably do it, but, Stan, is it worth it, just to bring her over here? I could hurt her more."

"Don't bring... over here. Next to Karl."

Like I said, I wasn't tracking too well. But Rachel's face was close to mine, and I thought I saw it register surprise, then doubt, then what I'm pretty sure what was determination. Then she was gone, without a word.

I faded away again, but came back when Rachel's voice, very close, said, "Stan? It's done. I've dragged her over to where Karl is. I don't think I hurt her."

"Good. Thank you." I opened my eyes and looked at her. "Rachel, how many steps you figure it is, from here to there?"

She looked up, then back. "Five, maybe six."

"Okay. Help me up."

Rachel got me to a sitting position again, then I said, "No, all the way. Wanna stand up."

"Stan, I'm not sure–"

"Gotta talk to Christine. Quickest way over is walking. Too weak to crawl, anyway."

"Stan, don't be stupid. If you can't crawl, what makes you think you can walk six steps, even with help?"

"Because I have to."

I dropped heavily to my knees next to Christine, the impact sending new jolts of pain through me, especially my head. I wanted to keep going downward – all the way to the floor and blessed unconsciousness, where I wouldn't have to think any more. But I stayed there, swaying a little, kneeling next to my vampire daughter.

Christine was still naked. Every inch of her that I could see was either filthy, or bloody, or burned, or some combination. Blood was seeping out of the three carved symbols, and there was a slow but steady flow from the stomach wound.

I leaned over as far as I could without falling on top of her. "Christine? Can you hear me? Christine?"

Her eyes were crusted over with dried tears, but she blinked a few times, then opened them. "Daddy?"

"Hi, baby. Don't try to move. You've been hurt pretty bad."

"I know. Hurts inside. Burns. Daddy, that man, where–"

"He's dead, baby. True dead. He won't hurt you anymore."

She smiled at me. I hadn't seen that smile in a long, long time.

"I know enough," I said, "about vamps – vampires to realize that you need blood, a lot of it, and soon. If you're gonna have a chance to heal. Otherwise..." I let my voice trail off.

"We're *s'pposed* to heal. It's... our nature."

"Not when it was done with silver – and that's what the sick fuck used, baby. He cut you and burned you with silver, and it won't heal by itself. Not unless you feed."

"Guess you'd know," she said, so soft I could barely hear her. "I musta skipped that part... of the vampire manual." The smile returned, just for a second.

I made myself not break down, or pass out, or change my mind. I made myself continue.

"Karl, my partner, remember him?"

"Yeah, sure."

"He's over there."

She moved her head slowly and looked. "Is he...?"

"No, he isn't, not yet."

She turned back, and stared at me, confused and afraid and in pain.

I turned to Rachel, who was kneeling close by. She looked at me, then at Christine, then Karl. Then back at me. Biting her lower lip, she nodded.

I didn't need her permission, I knew that. But I was still glad to see that nod.

I looked down again at my daughter.

"Christine, honey..." My throat was clogged, and I had to stop and clear it. "Christine, there's something I want you to do."

Time passed, as it has a way of doing. I gave depositions to half a dozen law enforcement agencies about certain events taking place at the Scranton Water Authority's pump house on a moonlit night in June.

I also gave a lengthy deposition to a Grand Jury that was considering whether to indict Rachel Proctor for the murder of two police officers. No indictment was handed down, since the "demonic possession" defense is widely recognized by the law in Pennsylvania, and most other states. Rachel is back at work as a consulting witch to the department. She keeps threatening to turn me into a toad, but she's just kidding around. I think.

A couple of witchfinders who had been making a nuisance of themselves around Scranton disappeared without a trace. McGuire's received a few phone calls from their boss, the Witchfinder General. Every time, he tells the WG that he's got no idea what happened to them. The last call, McGuire floated the theory that Ferris and Crane had decided to chuck the witchfinder business and open up a little antique shop in New Hampshire, someplace. Or maybe Delaware.

I spent four days in the hospital for treatment of severe concussion. I was released under strict doctor's orders to take it easy for a while. That worked out okay, since I spent the next three weeks on administrative leave while giving all those depositions.

Lacey Brennan came to visit me while I was in the hospital. Twice.

When the Powers That Be were as satisfied as they were likely to get that I hadn't broken any major laws, I went back to work with the Supe Squad. I've had to make some adjustments in my work schedule, though. Instead of a strict 9pm to 5am routine, McGuire lets me get my shift in between sunset and sunrise, no matter what times those may be. My partner needs to stay out of the sun, and he sleeps during the day, anyway. Despite the weird hours, we're still a pretty good team. We've cleared more than our share of cases, and busted a lot of bad supes.

I try to get home a little before sunrise every day, work permitting – so I can say "Goodnight" to my daughter before she heads down to the basement of our house for her day's rest.

Lots of changes, not all of them easy to make – but life is change, and adapting to it is one way of proving to yourself that you're still alive. And being alive feels pretty good.

My name's Markowski. I carry a badge.

ACKNOWLEDGMENTS

Betsy Brown, that most unlikely descendant of Cotton and Increase Mather, helped me avoid a fundamental error concerning these august gentlemen.

John Carroll, who has been my friend since dinosaurs walked the Earth, was very helpful concerning the details of life in the Wyoming Valley, where I no longer live but Stan Markowski does.

Karen Case sustained my soul.

Jean Cavelos, Director of the Odyssey Writing Workshop and sole proprietor of Jean Cavelos Editoral Services, Inc, has the best mind for story development of anyone I've ever met. She was of immense help to me in plotting this novel.

My agent, the lovely and talented Miriam Kriss of the Irene Goodman Agency, did her usual fine job of contract negotiations.

Terry Bear's job was providing snack suggestions, a responsibility he fulfilled admirably, as always.

ABOUT THE AUTHOR

Justin Gustainis was born in Northeast Pennsylvania in 1951. He attended college at the University of Scranton, a Jesuit university that figures prominently in several of his writings. After earning both Bachelor's and Master's degrees, he was commissioned a Lieutenant in the US Army. Following military service, he held a variety of jobs, including speechwriter and professional bodyguard, before earning a PhD at Bowling Green State University in Ohio.

Mr Gustainis currently lives in Plattsburgh, New York. He is a Professor of Communication at Plattsburgh State University, where he earned the SUNY Chancellor's Award for Excellence in Teaching in 2002. His academic publications include the book *American Rhetoric and the Vietnam War*, published in 1993, and a number of scholarly articles that hardly anybody has ever read. His popular series of urban fantasy novels featuring investigator Quincey Morris include *Evil Ways*, *Black Magic Woman* and the forthcoming *Sympathy for the Devil*.

www.justingustainis.com

Coming soon
EVIL DARK
**Here's an excerpt from the next
Occult Crimes Unit Investigation**

The red circle, which was maybe ten feet across, looked like it had been carefully painted on the concrete floor. The five-pointed star inside it had also been done with care, probably by someone who understood the consequences of getting it wrong. It was easy to see the detail under those bright lights, which would have done credit to any movie set.

Inside the circle squatted two heavy wooden chairs. One of them was stained and splattered all along its legs and sides with a brown substance. When it was fresh, the brown stuff might have been red – blood red.

A man sat in each chair. There was nothing remarkable about them – apart from the fact that they were both naked and bound firmly to the chairs with manacles at hands and feet.

Not far from the chairs stood a cheap-looking table, its wood scarred and pitted. Someone had laid out a number of instruments there, including a small hammer, a corkscrew, a pair of needle-nose pliers, a blowtorch, and several different sizes of knives.

A man's voice could be heard chanting, in a language that had been old when Christianity was young. This had been going on for several minutes. The men in the chairs sometimes looked outside the circle in the direction of the chanting, other times at each other. The one with dark hair looked confused. The other man was blond and clearly the more intelligent of the two, because he looked terrified.

Then came the moment when the air in the middle of the pentagram seemed to shiver and ripple. The ripple grew, but never crossed the boundary of the circle. After a while, some thin white smoke began to issue from that shimmering column. Over the next minute, the color of the smoke went from white to gray, then from gray to black. The chanting continued throughout all of this.

The dark-haired man went suddenly rigid in his chair. He threw his head back as if in great pain, the muscles and tendons in his skin standing out all over his body. This lasted for several seconds. Then, all at once, the man seemed to relax. He looked around the room, and the circle, as if seeing them for the first time. His facial expression was one he hadn't displayed before. It combined cunning and hatred in roughly equal proportions.

The chanting stopped. Then the voice said a couple of words in that same obscure language. It spoke sharply, as if giving a command.

The shackles holding the dark-haired man to the chair sprung open, as if by their own accord, and fell clattering to the floor.

The dark-haired man stood slowly, facing in the direction the voice had come from. He spoke in what sounded like the same language, his voice harsh and guttural. No human voice should sound like that. The voice from outside the circle replied, using the same commanding tone

343

as before. The dark-haired man bowed his head briefly, as if acknowledging the other's authority.

Then he walked slowly to the table and surveyed the instruments that had been lined up like a macabre smorgasbord. He turned and looked at the blond man, a terrible smile growing on his thin face. Then the dark-haired man picked up from the table the pair of pliers and the blowtorch. After taking a moment to make sure that the blowtorch was working, he walked over to the chair where the blond man sat chained, naked and helpless.

What happened next went from zero to unspeakable in a very few seconds. Soon afterward, it went beyond unspeakable, to a level of horror that there are no words to describe.

Twelve very long minutes later, the blond man gave one last, agonized scream and escaped into death. I sat there and watched him die.

Then somebody must've pressed "Stop," because the screen went mercifully dark. A few seconds later, the lights came on.

The nine people in the room sat in stunned silence, blinking in the sudden brightness. Then everybody started talking at once.

There had been eleven people in the room when the DVD started. But there'd been enough residual glow from the big monitor for me to see two tough, experienced police officers quietly leave over the last few minutes, one with a hand clasped tightly over his mouth.

I was glad nobody would know how close I came to being number three out the door.

My partner Karl leaned toward me and said softly,

"Sweet Jesus Christ on a pogo stick. And people say *vampires* are inhuman."

"Well, strictly speaking, you are," I told him, just to be saying something.

"You know what I mean, Stan."

"Yeah, I do. And I'm not arguing with you, either."

The two FBI agents walked to the front of the room and stood waiting for us to quiet down. They'd been introduced to us earlier, before the horror show started. Linda Thorwald was the senior agent, and she'd done most of the talking so far. She was of average height for a woman and slim, with the ice blue eyes you associate with Scandinavia. Her hair was jet black, and I wondered if she was a blonde who'd had it dyed to increase her chances of being taken seriously in the macho culture of the FBI. People have done stranger things, and for worse reasons.

Her partner was a guy named McCreery who had big shoulders, brown hair, and a wide mustache that probably had J. Edgar Hoover spinning in his grave. He moved like an athlete, and I thought he might be one of the many former college jocks who find their way into law enforcement once it sinks in that they're not quite good enough for the pros.

When the room was quiet, Thorwald said, "I regret that I had to subject all of you to that revolting exhibition of sadism and murder. If it's any consolation, I've seen more than one veteran FBI agent lose his lunch either during or immediately after a showing of this... supernatural snuff film."

Snuff films are an urban legend, probably started by the same kind of tight-ass public moralists who used to rant about comic books destroying the nation's moral fiber. But the myth made its way into popular culture, and stayed there. There's been plenty of counterfeit ones made over the years, with sleazeballs using special makeup effects to rip off the pervs who think torture and murder are fun. These days, you can see stuff like that at your local multiplex. It's all fake, but I still wouldn't want to know anybody who was a fan. If I'm going to hang out with ghouls, I prefer the real kind – they can't help what they are.

There have been some serial killers who took video of their victims to jerk off over between kills, but that was for their own private use. If by "snuff film" you mean a commercially available product depicting actual murder, then there's no such thing.

Or rather, there wasn't. Until now.

"I wanted you all to see that video," Thorwald said, "because it's important that you understand what we're up against, and what the stakes are. Copies of that DVD have surfaced within the last month in New York, Philadelphia, Pittsburgh, and, uh–" She turned to her partner.

"Baltimore," he said.

"–and Baltimore," she went on. "But the Bureau has been interested in this case for longer than a month. Quite a bit longer."

Thorwald took a step forward. "You know that expression, 'I've got good news and bad news?' Well, I'm afraid I don't have any good news to offer you today. Instead, I bring bad news, and worse news. Charlie?"

I could almost see the two of them rehearsing this act in their hotel room last night. The whole thing had a stagy quality that was getting on my nerves. Of course, after what I'd just witnessed, my nerves were pretty damn edgy already.

"The bad news," McCreery said, "is that what you just saw isn't the first video depicting this kind of torture-murder. I mean, one apparently carried out by a demon that's been conjured and then allowed to 'possess' an innocent party."

That must've been the dark-haired man we'd just seen. He hadn't done all those awful things to the blond guy – the demon who'd taken him over had done it, using his body as an instrument.

"In fact, it's the fourth one," McCreery said. "Or, at least, the fourth that we know of. Same M.O. every time, with the same ghastly result. All that varies is the technique, and the victim."

The technique varied. I guess that's why whoever was running the show had put out a selection of torture devices for the hellspawn to use. Nothing like variety.

Thorwald took over again. "The going price for one of these videos in the illicit-smut underground is one thousand dollars. To give you some perspective, you can buy one of a four year-old girl being raped for about three hundred." A look of disgust passed over her face, the first genuine expression I'd seen there. "Presumably, each one of the DVDs has sold well enough to keep those producing them in business. The economies of scale are pretty good, from their perspective. Once you've recorded the master, you can burn copies for less than a buck apiece. There's no way to know how many have been put into circulation. And no reason to think these people are going to stop doing it. That, as I said, is the bad news. But, as far as you officers are concerned, there is worse news." She paused for effect, and I wondered if she'd learned that at the FBI academy, or in some college speech class. Maybe she'd been on the debate team – she was the type.

"We have been unable to establish the location where these atrocities were made," Thorwald said. "As with the one you just saw, what's visible onscreen doesn't give us much to go on. However, based on information recently received, we now have reason to believe that at least one of these DVDs was shot right here in Scranton."

**Find out what happens next
in *Evil Dark* by Justin Gustainis
Coming soon from Angry Robot**

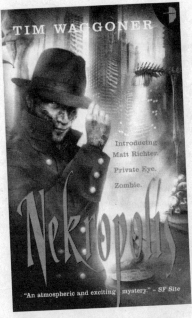